Pra

A LADY'S FOR

"Fizzy, engrossing romance . . . a wholehearted celebration of women who choose to live gleefully outside the bounds of patriarchy's limitations."
—*Entertainment Weekly*

"Explosive chemistry, a heroine who loves her science, and lines that made me laugh out loud—this witty debut delivered, and I'd like the next installment now, please."
—*USA Today* bestselling author Evie Dunmore

"A witty, dazzling debut with a science-minded heroine and her broody bodyguard. Fiercely feminist and intensely romantic, *A Lady's Formula for Love* is a fresh take on historical romance that's guaranteed to delight readers."
—Joanna Shupe, author of *The Devil of Downtown*

"A brilliant scientist and her brooding bodyguard discover that love can find you when you least expect it. *A Lady's Formula for Love* is full of wit, charm, and intrigue. You don't want to miss this exciting debut from Elizabeth Everett."
—Harper St. George, author of *The Heiress Gets a Duke*

"With its beguiling blend of danger, desire, and deliciously dry wit, the brilliantly conceived and smartly executed *A Lady's Formula for Love* is an exciting debut and a first-rate launch for Everett's Secret Scientists of London series. Fans of Evie Dunmore's A League of Extraordinary Women books or Olivia Waite's historical romances will savor this fiercely feminist, achingly romantic, and intensely sensual love story."
—*Booklist* (starred review)

ALSO BY ELIZABETH EVERETT

A Lady's Formula for Love

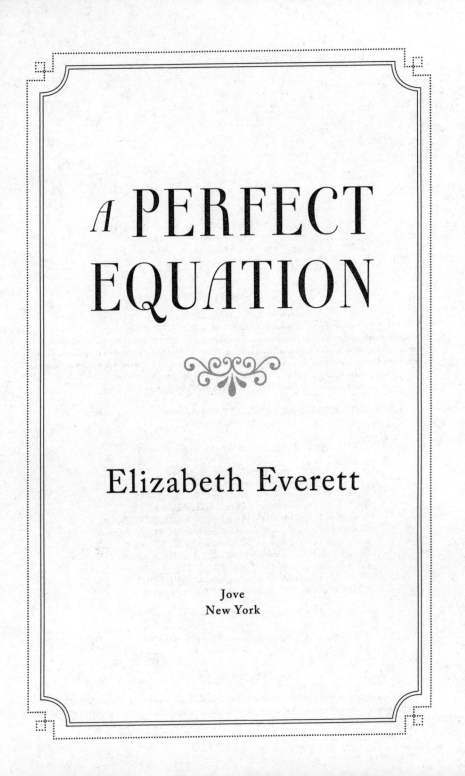

A PERFECT EQUATION

Elizabeth Everett

Jove
New York

A JOVE BOOK
Published by Berkley
An imprint of Penguin Random House LLC
penguinrandomhouse.com

Library of Congress Cataloging-in-Publication Data

Names: Everett, Elizabeth, author.
Title: A perfect equation / Elizabeth Everett.
Description: First Edition. | New York: Jove, 2022. |
Series: The secret scientists of London; 2
Identifiers: LCCN 2021021342 (print) | LCCN 2021021343 (ebook) |
ISBN 9780593200643 (trade paperback) | ISBN 9780593200650 (ebook)
Subjects: GSAFD: Love stories.
Classification: LCC PS3605.V435 P47 2022 (print) | LCC PS3605.V435
(ebook) | DDC 813/.6—dc23
LC record available at https://lccn.loc.gov/2021021342
LC ebook record available at https://lccn.loc.gov/2021021343

First Edition: February 2022

Printed in the United States of America
1st Printing

Book design by Alison Cnockaert

Dedicated to my husband, a real-life romantic hero.

A PERFECT
EQUATION

1

London, 1843

A WOMAN'S PLACE IS in the home!"

Miss Letitia Fenley stopped in her tracks at that declaration. What a choker! Everyone knew a woman's place was in charge, if you want something done right.

Another winter had come to London and stubbornly refused to be gone. These bleak weeks of March more resembled February, an in-between time when the sun sullenly peeked out from behind the clouds now and then, waiting for the world to be pretty enough to bother with.

Letty Fenley and her brother, Sam, traversed the streets of Clerkenwell. Strung out in a grim leer, buildings stained dark yellow and brown from decades of soot and humidity squeezed together like crooked teeth, the second and third stories leaning over to rub against the ones next door. The cobbles under their feet were greasy and half-submerged beneath a mix of mud, manure, and straw.

The two of them were headed for the grander environs of Bloomsbury, where, amid its walled gardens and wooden walkways, they'd be more likely to find a hack. Halting their progress was a crowd of angry men blocking the road, holding rudely painted signs and shouting ridiculous slogans in front of an unremarkable brick building. The shingle hanging over the door read MESSRS. JEWELL & HOYT, CANDLE-MAKERS. The store's owner had turned his sign to CLOSED and pulled the curtains tight against the ire of folks marching on the walk outside.

Letty stood on her toes at the edge of the crowd to better view the happenings. Another pea-souper of a fog had sprung up, and invisible motes of coal smut coated the back of her throat from breathing in the noxious air. She pulled the high collar of her mantle around her mouth and nose.

"Why are you stopping?" grumbled her brother, eyes fixed on the road as he tried to keep his boots clear of the worst of the ruts, his head no doubt filled with work. "Bad enough I have to take time away from the store to escort you to your club. Worse is when time is wasted by your..."

Glancing up, Sam took in the scene before them for the first time. "What nonsense is this?" He squinted through the fog at the commotion. "Who're these never-sweats blocking the street at midday when there is business to be conducted?"

With no time to read anything other than accounting ledgers, Sam had missed the latest news regarding the rise of the Guardians of Domesticity. Groveling at the feet of the aristocracy and blaming women for the ills of society, the Guardians hid behind a facade of respectability, with lectures and charity work that claimed to celebrate the traditional British family and women's role as keeper of the hearth. Their true colors came into view when they found a business contributing to the "downfall of civilization" by employing young women in their shops and factories.

"Ladies should be taking care of men's needs instead of taking men's wages," shouted one man, flushed with an angry joy. He'd found a captive audience for his complaints as he shook a meaty fist in the face of a slender young woman trying to sidle past him and make her way into the shop.

A shop's assistant, no doubt, hired for pennies per week, working dawn to dusk for a pittance of what a male assistant might make. Although the girl's poke bonnet hid her face, the set of her shoulders and bowed head signaled distress.

Letty clenched her fingers. Despite the dank mist freezing her toes, heat rose in her chest. "How dare those oafs frighten that poor girl. Why, I am going to—"

"You are going to do nothing but make your way to your ladies' club," Sam growled, pulling Letty by the sleeve away from the crowd.

Unlike the shopgirl's threadbare cloak, Letty's deep blue mantle was made of the finest wool, the discreet trim done in costly velvet.

"Da says I'm to get you there without incident, and that's what I intend to do." Scratching his head, Sam read a large banner near them. "What is this nonsense supposed to accomplish? 'Take care of men,' indeed."

His golden hair appeared dirty brown in the low light, but nothing could hide the sudden glint of humor in his piercing blue eyes. "Good luck getting you, or those secret scientists you keep company with, to have anything to do with men. Unless it's to blow them up."

Letty admonished her brother while keeping an eye on the clerk. "We haven't blown anyone up. Well, one time, by accident. Besides, the purpose of the club is to study all aspects of science, not just the ones that make noise."

Letty was accustomed to defending Athena's Retreat. Ostensibly a social club for ladies to gather for lectures on the natural sciences, behind closed doors it served as a haven for women to conduct experiments, do research, and simply take the time away from the pressures of their duties to reflect on theories and ideas. The Fenley family's wealth allowed Letty the freedom to study her passion—

mathematics—but that didn't mean her family understood why she and the other club members were driven to sacrifice their time and, in some cases, their opportunity to marry well or climb higher in society.

"Can't imagine what those scoundrels think shouting at ladies will accomplish," Sam continued, still clutching her sleeve. "If I shouted at you or our sisters, what would happen?"

"We'd tell you to shut up, and put toads in your bed," Letty said distractedly.

"You'd tell me to shut up, and put toads in my bed," Sam agreed with good-natured humor. He craned his neck to see over the thickening crowd.

"If I had a banner and waved it in your faces, would you listen to me?" he asked wistfully. "Big sign saying 'Stop Reading in Front of the Customers' or 'Stop Trying on the Bonnets You're Supposed to Sell' or 'Stop Putting Face Cream in the Icebox.'"

"Not likely," Letty told him. "If you want us to work for free at the emporium, you need to give us incentives."

Fenley's Fantastic Fripperies, the largest emporium in London, parted the city's ladies from their coin by offering a dazzling array of articles ranging from the utilitarian to the useless.

"It's a family business," he said. "Familial duty is your incentive. Not to mention free face cream, which does not belong in the icebox despite your incomprehensible blather about solids and temperature and matter-of-facts."

"Not matter-of-facts," Letty corrected him. "States of matter. You see, when the temperature increases, certain substances—"

"Twice now, I've put it on my toast." Sam pulled a face and shuddered. "Tastes like a scolding from Aunt Bess. Ugh."

Letty laughed, but when Sam checked his pocket watch, all traces of a smile vanished from his face. "I cannot be away from the emporium any longer. Let's slip away from this mess and—"

"Bring back the better days of Britain!"

Letty loosed herself from Sam's grip, the rest of his words muffled by the roaring of blood in her veins.

"Guardians of Stupidity is what you are." Letty raised her voice, glaring at the men around her. "Fools and bullies who think they know better than women. Back to the kitchen? As though running a household doesn't require as many skills as running a business."

Slipping through the crowd, Letty approached the building as a thin wail rose from the doorway. A beady-eyed man with a pinched mouth and spidery fingers had grabbed the shopgirl by the wrist, halting her escape.

"Don't bother trying to go to work. We're shutting this place down until they stop employing women in their factories and hire the men back," the man said.

A tinkling of broken glass punctuated his threat as someone launched a sign at the ground-floor window of the shop. The atmosphere turned in an instant from hectoring to predatory. With a foreshadowing of violence, the group of individuals molded into a single organism—a dragon ready to pounce on whatever threatened. This monster's hoard consisted of power rather than gold.

"Oh, no, you don't," Letty said through gritted teeth, clenching the straps of her heavy reticule in one hand.

"Letty!" Sam called after her. "Letty Fenley, you come back here this instant. I know you don't listen to me, but for goodness' sake, will you listen to me?"

Fear set her stomach to churning, but Letty allowed nothing to show on her face. Instead, she stuck her chin out and her shoulders back. Never again would she suffer a man intimidating her into submission, and she'd be damned if she watched this happen to any other woman. As Flavia Smythe-Harrows always said, sexual dimorphism does not excuse bad behavior.

What a pity Letty didn't have *that* printed on a banner.

Without benefit of a rival sign, she used what was available in the moment. Swinging her reticule around twice to achieve maximal momentum, Letty brought it down, hard, on the wrist of Beady Eyes.

"You let go of that girl, right now, you weasel-faced, onion-breathed..." Letty's stream of insults was drowned in the crowd's protest at the sight of their fellow man being assaulted by what someone deemed "half a pint-sized shrew."

"Half a pint indeed," Letty shouted back. "I'm less than an inch shorter than the median height for a woman of my weight, based on— Oy, stop waving that sign in my face."

Before Letty could take another swing at Beady Eyes, the sound of horses whinnying and men shouting from somewhere at the edge of the crowd broke the tension; a decrescendo from taunting voices to garbled protests heralded the arrival of authority. Jumping up for a better look, Letty spied two well-dressed men on horseback.

"On your way," a clipped, aristocratic voice shouted to the crowd. "Disperse at once."

The crowd buckled, its mood shifting from dangerous to frustrated. Letty protected the girl as best she could from the sudden shoving around them. Most of her attention, however, fixed on the familiarity of those crisp, clean syllables echoing in the air.

She would know that voice anywhere. Their rescue rode toward them in the form of Lord William Hughes, the Viscount Greycliff. A traitorous wave of relief that he would put an end to the danger was quickly followed by a cold dose of shame.

Six years ago, she'd believed him the epitome of nobility and elegance until that voice had delivered a verdict upon her head. The words he'd said and the pain they'd caused were etched into her memory forever.

"I don't care if you're Prince Albert himself. Move your arse, man!"

A deeper baritone, the voice of Greycliff's companion, now carried over the crowd. "Put down the signs, or I'll put them down for you."

"Are they here to rescue us?" the girl asked.

Visions of Greycliff riding up on a snow white steed flashed before Letty's eyes. A handful of years before, such an image would have set her heart to racing and put roses on her cheeks. She would have caught her ruffled skirts in one hand, ready to be swept away by a hero, lit from behind by a shaft of golden sunlight.

Not anymore. The dirty grey-brown reality of working-class London remained solid and smelly before her eyes. These days, romantic scenes remained between the pages of a well-thumbed book.

"Never wait for someone else to rescue you," Letty advised. "Especially a man. They'll ride away on those fine horses afterward, and where will you be? Still here, cleaning the mess, having to work for an owner who couldn't even be bothered to come out here after you. Rescue yourself, my dear."

"Shall we run for it?"

"We could, but I've a better idea." Letty turned to Beady Eyes and held up her reticule. The man flinched, but she had other plans.

"Want to get rid of two troublesome women?" she asked him. Pouring out a palmful of coins, Letty made an offer. "Here's your chance."

"LATE NIGHT OF drinking far too much, bracing ride on a cold morning through miles of mud and rain, and now we've the chance to knock heads together. Life is grand, isn't it, Grey?"

Greycliff sat unmoved by the same zeal for chaos that led his friend the Earl Grantham to whoop with glee and launch himself off his horse and into the angry crowd like a cormorant diving into the waves.

He was unaccustomed to being moved by any emotion approaching the strength and intensity of *zeal*. If zeal were at one end of a plank and numbness at the other, he would rest most comfortably at the fulcrum. As such, he allowed himself the slightest twinge of annoyance at this interruption in his journey to visit his former stepmother.

Placing a calming hand against his horse's neck, Grey repeated his threat to the crowd. "Break this up now, or I will have the Riot Act read."

Most of the demonstrators heeded his warning, though not without a show of reluctance. Still shouting their slogans, the men turned their attention away from the shop front and broke into smaller groups. Hoping for a brawl, Grantham chivvied them along.

As he scanned the thinning crowd, Grey caught sight of a man using his sign to force a clear path through the crowd for two feminine figures behind him. The women were too far away for him to pick out their individual features, but a tingling of recognition pricked the backs of his hands.

It couldn't be . . .

But of course it could. Here in the heart of chaos, why wouldn't he find a woman who excelled in stirring up trouble?

Before his mild irritation could grow into something approaching fear for her safety, Grey took a deep breath through his nose and blew the worry away. Setting his shoulders back, he took another breath and reached for equilibrium.

A handsome, square-jawed young man dressed in an elegant greatcoat stood out from the crowd. A head shorter than Grantham and slighter of build, nonetheless the man exuded an aura of determination.

"Letitia Fenley, where are you?" the man shouted with ill-concealed exasperation.

Suspicions confirmed, the tingling ran up Grey's arms and down his spine. Rationally, he knew she would be safe. This must be Miss Fenley's brother. If the resemblance hadn't proved it, the man's annoyance would have—a common reaction after a few minutes in Miss Fenley's presence.

The most logical course of action would be to continue his journey. Why should he care that a woman of questionable character had found herself in yet another predicament? Her brother would protect her. He was right now . . . walking in the opposite direction than his sister had gone.

Mindful of the men still milling about, Grey urged his horse forward toward a narrow alley running alongside the candlemaker's shop, where an abandoned sign leaned against the smutty bricks. Peering through the dimness, he spied Letty Fenley standing in consultation with another young woman, their escort having disappeared. Although they'd escaped the worst of the crowd, they weren't clear of danger yet. Yards away, a few stubborn protestors in front of the building held Grantham off, waving their handmade banners and wooden signs.

MAKE BABIES, NOT WAGES, read one. PROTECT THE SANCTITY OF THE HOME, read another.

Reflecting on the petite woman in the alleyway before him, Grey tried to think of any instance when she would do as he wanted simply because he was a man and told her so.

None.

No instance whatsoever.

In fact, Letty Fenley would do the opposite of anything he asked.

On a stoop next door to the candlemaker's, waiting for the crowd to quiet before he could go back to work, a bemused little street sweeper watched the proceedings. Grey tossed the boy a coin to mind his horse and made his way down the alley toward Letty Fenley.

It must have been the effects of the long ride to London that made his heart beat a tiny bit faster. Not the sight of this miniature termagant.

". . . let these idiots tell you otherwise. Women are as smart as men, if not more so," Letty was explaining to her companion.

She'd the same high cheekbones as her brother, only more pronounced, appearing almost gaunt in the low light. Beneath a sharp nose, her pale pink lips pursed in annoyance. The uncanny blue of her eyes, clear as the summer sky, shone with a passion visible even in the shadows.

"Not smart to hide in a dead end." Grey raised his voice, tipping his hat when the women started in surprise at the sight of him. The girl executed a passable curtsy, but all Letty Fenley offered by way of greeting was a brusque nod and a scowl.

"Smart enough to get us away from that crowd of beef-headed fools," Letty retorted.

She met his gaze, and everything that had passed between them thickened the air, putting a flush to her cheeks. Mutual admiration had been cut short when Letty had done the unforgivable, threatening those whom Grey held dear.

Thereafter followed six years of a frosty truce that had collapsed after no more than five minutes in each other's presence.

Shrinking from the silent confrontation in front of her, the shopgirl glanced between them, then at a door in the side of the building. "Pardon my saying, my lady . . ."

Letty broke her stare and gave the shopgirl her attention. "I'm the furthest from a noblewoman you'll find. Plain *miss* will do."

"Indeed. Don't want you lumped in with the oppressive aristocracy," Grey remarked with an exaggerated drawl.

Letty's eyes changed from turquoise to cobalt when challenged. Fascinating.

"Exactly, my lord," she said. "We have no need for your interference. You can go berate the masses out there without further concern." The smoky curl of her Clerkenwell dialect softened the vowels, smudging the edges of her words.

It sounded almost seductive.

"Um, I'm going to . . . er . . ." The girl stepped away.

"Perhaps they would grant me a more mannered welcome," he shot back. "Generally, when one is the object of someone's concern, they—"

"Lecture me on good manners, will you?" Letty interrupted his admonishment with her usual defiance. One time, he'd seen her tell a lord where to shove his quizzing glass when he'd used it to mock another woman. Grey had liked her back then.

Before she'd revealed her flaws.

Turning away from the young woman, Letty faced him full on, hands clenched and resting on her hips.

"I suppose you cannot help but school your social inferiors. This time, however, you are wasting your breath. Too bad." She walked toward him, stomping through the shadows as though kicking the dark away. "Oxygen is what you need high up there in the social strata."

"I'm not high up, Miss Fenley," he said, then paused to gauge the effect of his next words. "I only appear so to a person of your miniature stature."

His *brilliant* riposte went over her head.

Literally.

"Well, at least my head is proportional to my body, unlike some noblemen, whose ego renders their head nearly as large as their—"

"Where did she go?" Grey asked.

"Where did who go? Oh." Letty paused in her tirade and glanced behind her. The alley stood empty.

A rapping came from a window above them. There, the girl, joined by two others, waved and smiled her thanks.

Letty and Grey turned and waved back, smiling, then faced one another and dropped both hands and smiles.

"Well, now that is settled, I must be on my way," Letty said airily. "I'd like to say it was a pleasure to see you again, my lord, but lying is bad manners."

Brushing his arm, she sidled past Grey in the narrow alley. Sometime during her flight from the crowd, Letty's bonnet had come off. As she walked, she bent her head to examine the tangle of ribbons, exposing the fragile line of her neck above the collar of her mantle, a vulnerable column of smooth flesh and delicate bone.

Odd, how someone so fierce could at the same time seem . . . breakable.

"Just going to march back out there into the madness?" he asked.

"I am going to join my brother," she answered, not bothering to lift her head. Grey peered at the heavens and complimented himself on his saintly patience.

"Miss Fenley, if you will allow me to see you to safety?"

She waved him off. "Don't bother. I have this under—"

A knot of men spilled past the corner of the building, a few of them stumbling into the alleyway. Grey, reacting without hesitation, pulled Letty away from their flailing arms and into a recess between the side of the building and its facade. He blocked her from the men's path just as one fellow's punch went wild and hit Grey between his shoulders.

Grey didn't flinch. He kept his back to the tumult, leaning one arm against the wall, setting himself between her and danger.

"I suppose now you'll tell me how right you were," Letty complained. A few wisps of wheat blonde hair at her temples had escaped a tidy roll of braids.

This close, he could catch a faint scent of orange blossom and something tantalizingly familiar. Leaning in, he closed his eyes and inhaled, lungs filling with the sweet scent of vanilla.

How unexpected.

Letty Fenley smelled like cake.

"Are you smelling my hair?" she asked.

He opened his eyes, disconcerted. "No. I'm not . . . smelling your hair. What are you . . . ? You're simply so short that—"

"So short?" Letty stiffened and tipped her head up at the same time Grey leaned down to make his point. "I am less than an inch shorter than—"

"Are you standing on your toes to make yourself appear taller?" he accused.

"If I stood on my toes, like this, I would . . ."

Letty rose on her toes, and froze.

For an endless moment, everyone and everything else ceased to exist as their mouths came so close they drew each other's breath.

Expressions slid like quicksilver across her face before he could read them. Was she repulsed? Angry? Curious?

What might happen if he closed the distance between them another inch . . . ?

A rock hit the wall above his head and jerked him out of the moment of madness. For it must have been madness and not anything else.

"Letitia, where are you? Come here now, or I will remove the heels from your boots," a man shouted. "Then, when customers ask, I will tell them, yes, you *are* well-spoken for a ten-year-old."

"That is my brother. Let me go." Letty pushed at Grey's chest. Taking two steps back, he held his hands above his shoulders as though she'd threatened him at gunpoint, saying nothing as she bolted out of the passageway and into the street. Not even when he heard her mutter under her breath.

"I hate you," she'd whispered.

Before he could decide whether that had been issued as a complaint or a challenge, she'd disappeared.

2

TWO HOURS AFTER their encounter in Clerkenwell, Letty and Grey stood across the room from one another on the second floor of Beacon House, home for over a decade to Letty's closest friend, Violet Kneland. The town house stood on a quiet street off Knightsbridge, and during the past seven years, Violet had turned a series of outbuildings in the back of the structure into Athena's Retreat.

Bent over a tea table, Violet paused in the act of arranging plates while her husband, Arthur Kneland, sat on an overstuffed divan and watched his wife intently.

"I know what you're thinking," she said, a wicked grin lighting her face as she glanced between Letty and Grey.

"You do?" Letty's cheeks flooded with heat, and she shot a startled glance at Grey, who remained inscrutable.

"What are we thinking, Violet?" he asked. His demeanor softened as he took his cup and saucer from the woman who had been his father's third wife.

"You are wondering why I've asked you both to come here this afternoon," Violet answered, handing Letty her tea.

Letty bowed her head over the porcelain cup and said a silent prayer of thanks that Violet had not known what—or about *whom*—she was thinking, for her mind had been taken up with what had happened with Grey earlier today. His broad shoulders had blocked out the world, and instead of the familiar wave of prickly certainty that he held her in disregard, she'd felt . . . protected.

His troubled eyes, grey as the skies over the North Sea in winter, were ringed with thick black lashes and set deep beneath dark brows. Letty had never stood so close to him before, and she marveled at his smooth olive skin hinting at his mother's Italian blood, pulled tight over elegantly placed bones, and his cleft chin, peppered with stubble.

In the alleyway, he'd bent his head toward her and his breath had warmed her lips like the ghost of a kiss.

A dangerous path for her thoughts to travel.

Letty was a woman with a stain on her reputation. If anyone knew the direction of these thoughts, their low opinion of her would be confirmed.

Violet smiled a sad, wry smile. "One reason for the summons is to see you, Greycliff. I worry you do not come home enough."

Grey took Violet's hands in his while his gaze extended to include Arthur.

"I asked Arthur to protect you last year," Grey said, "because he is the most honorable man I know, and because you are dear to me. Though I may not have visited recently, the two of you are always in my thoughts."

What a sentimental speech from such a reserved man.

Violet colored prettily, and Kneland gave an abrupt nod, in the way men use a gesture to express anything from undying love to polite disinterest.

The parlor where Violet took tea with family and close friends was Letty's favorite. Faded periwinkle curtains kept most of the early-spring chill from the air. Two oil lamps were lit against the late-afternoon gloom; flames dancing behind clear glass etched with intricate patterns lent their light to the glow of a small fire in the grate. There were no portraits of judgmental ancestors or bland landscapes faded with age. A terrarium took pride of place on an oval end table; three prehistoric-looking plants with enormous needles grew out of a miniature mountain of geodes, housed beneath a glass dome and set atop a marble base. Beside it sat a small print of a tiny cottage amid the gorse-covered hills of the Scottish Highlands.

"Are you finished with your business in the North?" Violet asked Grey.

Greycliff released her hand and crossed the room to stand by the mantel, austere and aloof. Leaning against it, he examined Letty, perhaps considering what he could say aloud.

Had he forgotten she knew of his clandestine activities?

"You may feel free to speak of the Department in my presence," Letty assured him.

She had been given to understand that, unknown to the general populace, the Department was a quasi-governmental body funded by private individuals. It operated in conjunction with the prime minister yet held a degree of independence from the government. The loyalty of the office was to the men who provided the funding, as well as to the Crown, thus removing it from the vagaries of political whims.

Letty had been present a year ago when a fringe political group had created a lethal weapon. Grey had asked Violet to find an antidote and set Arthur to guard her while she worked.

"Violet was most forthcoming with information about your duties when we discussed her work on the aerosol delivery system," Letty explained.

Grey winced, and Violet's shoulders hitched. "You can trust Letty to be discreet," she said.

Letty lifted her chin a fraction when Grey glanced over at her, and hid her clenched fists in the folds of her navy wool skirts. A shaky breath left her lips when he nodded slightly.

It shouldn't matter that he trusted her enough to continue.

"The prime minister decided upon an unfortunate course of action to contain the unrest in the North and elsewhere," Grey said, pulling his navy brocade waistcoat straight against his flat stomach. "As usual, I oversaw an intelligence-gathering mission. This time, however, I inserted myself into a conflict." His head dropped a fraction of an inch. "Not my brightest moment."

"Don't punish yourself for not standing idly by when innocent people were caught in the riots, Greycliff," Arthur said. "You intervened in time and saved the youngest of them from hanging or transportation. That counts for something."

Letty inferred that they were speaking of the Plug Plot Riots. Although the beginnings of unrest among the millworkers in Stalybridge were over wage cuts, the protest spread to factories across the North as well as mines down south. The workers were inspired by the Chartists who spoke out for universal suffrage and other election reforms.

For men.

Women, of course, were not considered in the discussion of representation and fair wages.

The government had put the protests down quickly and violently. In Preston, eight men were shot and four of them died. Had Grey tried to prevent similar bloodshed?

"Perhaps." Grey flicked a piece of lint from the arm of his jacket, dismissing Arthur's reassurance. His appearance now impeccable, he smoothed his features as well, a vision of the ideal aristocrat. "Still, I acted without authority and compromised the mission. I assume I will be asked to tender my resignation. Now I am at your disposal, Violet."

"But, Grey . . ." Violet's hands fluttered, reaching out toward him. "You've given so much to the Department. Arthur and I were certain you were next in line—"

"The choice was made, and a summons sent. I see no need to waste my time on something as trivial as regrets."

Acknowledging the finality in his tone, Violet settled herself next to her husband and changed the subject. "You might remember, Letty, my aunt Rose runs a school for girls in Yorkshire."

With one last glance at Grey, Letty turned her attention to her friend. "Indeed, the Yorkshire Academy for the Education of Exceptional Young Women is famous among the younger members of Athena's Retreat."

Violet smiled. "Some of my fondest memories are of the academy. Aunt Rose wrote to me. It seems she's lost her chemistry teacher. I am enrolling my maid, Alice, at the academy this spring, and Arthur and I have decided to accompany her there. We've also agreed that I will take over the position until Aunt Rose finds a replacement."

A stack of papers had listed over the edge of a side table, and Grey, reaching over to rescue them before they fell, froze in midact.

"You mean to take employment as a chemistry teacher?"

The disbelief in his tone set Letty's teeth on edge. "Do you not approve, my lord?" she snipped. "Is Mrs. Kneland working for a living objectionable to you?"

Ignoring Letty's question, he slapped the pile into a tidy stack with one swift move and tilted his head a fraction, examining Violet with a penetrative stare.

"Why would you leave the club for so long?" he asked gently.

Arthur cleared his throat, and Violet placed her hand into his.

"Fresh air. Sun." Arthur's voice sounded rough and low from disuse. "Not too far from the moors. It will do us both good to be away from the dirt and the fog. Give us time to . . ."

He swallowed, and his large fingers curved over Violet's palm. The shadows beneath his eyes darkened, and Violet's chin dipped.

Six months ago, the entire household of Beacon House and every member of Athena's Retreat were giddy with excitement when Violet revealed she was with child. Winthram, the doorman, had consulted with the members to outfit a nursery at the club, filled with handmade chemistry primers, miniature pendulums, and blankets embroidered with Newton's laws. Lady Potts contributed a series of prints depicting every member of the family Theraphosidae—her beloved tarantulas— much to Violet's amusement and Arthur's dismay.

Violet's miscarriage had coincided with the early-winter fogs. Gloom and smoke had permeated the air, smothering the camaraderie and cheer. Ever since, Arthur walked the halls in a slight daze, as though something vital had leaked from him. Athena's Retreat went off-kilter as well, petty arguments turning into uproars, accidents lead- ing to some members going weeks without speaking to one another.

Violet was the heart of the club, and the heart was broken.

With the slightest nod, Grey signaled his understanding, offering calm reassurance without any excessive sympathy in his manner.

"A visit to see your family is an excellent idea. You will, no doubt, inspire a classful of girls to become great chemists like yourself." He paused. "Might you steer them toward the less, er, explosive areas of your field?"

"You and Arthur will be pleased to learn that combustible experi- ments are strictly forbidden," Violet said.

Grey let out a small sigh of relief, and Arthur's shoulders dropped.

"Until year three."

Letty remained silent, examining her friend's face. The pain from losing a pregnancy must be great indeed for Violet to contemplate leav- ing the club. Happily, Arthur could be relied upon to watch over her friend as she grieved.

It hurt a little to watch such love from the outside. Ashamed to be that small, Letty pushed her jealousy deep beneath her armor, where it rubbed against her in a constant ache.

In the past, she might have commiserated with Lady Phoebe, the third founding member of Athena's Retreat. Despite the gulf between them in social status, Letty and Phoebe had shared a propensity to mask their sensitivity with cynicism. Phoebe would have made a sharp but witty comment, distracting them all and enabling Letty to swallow the lump in her throat without anyone noticing. A master at ferreting out vulnerabilities, Phoebe could be just as skilled at compensating for them.

Phoebe had turned her back on them, however, betraying Violet and Letty both. The creator of the very weapon Violet had been tasked with disarming, Phoebe was now exiled to the American West.

With Violet's departure, Letty would be on her own.

Violet distracted Letty from her self-pity, returning to the subject at hand.

"The only setting more chaotic than a classroom full of aspiring chemists is Athena's Retreat. No one knows that better than you, Letty. That is why I've asked you here today."

Biting her lower lip, Violet cast a quick glance at Arthur's bland expression, then at her toes.

"I have given a great deal to Athena's Retreat," Violet continued. "I cannot conceive of leaving it for long unless it is in good hands."

Letty nodded in agreement. "It will take someone diplomatic; that is certain. You should begin the search now."

"Why, yes . . . diplomacy will be key," Violet agreed. "It also needs the steady hand of someone who knows the club members, understands their work, and can remain unflappable in the event of a crisis. Those Guardians of Domesticity have been sniffing around the club, and I fear they will take against us."

Letty frowned. "Did you wish for me to help you find someone?"

Arthur cleared his throat. "You see, we have a favor we'd like to ask of you."

A terrible premonition stopped Letty's breath.

Oh no. Surely Violet would never ask her to . . .

"Will you take over as president of Athena's Retreat while we are gone?" asked Violet.

Take over as president? Letty would rather be impaled on a spit and slow-roasted over a fire.

"I would rather be imp—" Her brain caught up with her mouth, and she left the sentence unfinished. "What I meant is that although I am flattered by the request, there are many other members with a temperament better suited to such a position."

While there were a handful of well-respected female scientists in Europe, they were still regarded as oddities and some were chastised as "unnatural." Others spent their entire lives fighting to be recognized by their male counterparts. At Athena's Retreat, the women's work was kept secret, but at least they could engage in it without censure. Letty would be the first to praise the creativity and ingenuity of the club members.

Letty would also be the first to complain about the nasty smells, loud noises, and small floods, explosions, infestations, and the general mayhem that occurred there every single day.

In fact, she *did* complain about them. Not always nicely. This had been a sore point with the members on occasion.

"You may specialize in mathematics," Violet told her now, "but you have a firm grasp on the basics of all the sciences. You already organize so much in your role as club secretary, it won't be that much more work."

Leaning forward, Violet's soft brown eyes held Letty's gaze. "Now that Phoebe is gone, you are the last person left who has been with me from the beginning of this dream, through thick and thin—and upside down. To whom else can I turn?"

"Oh, well played, Violet," Letty complained. How could Letty deny Violet when she called upon their friendship, evoking the late nights they'd spent drinking scandalous amounts of brandy and munching on forbidden tea cakes while envisioning a haven for women like them?

"I won't leave you without resources. A good friend of mine, Madame Margaret Gault, is due to arrive from France in a week's time. She is an engineer and has come to consult on a project in Southwark. She will assume your duties as club secretary and will be staying in the Retreat's guest rooms."

Wings of panic beat at the base of Letty's throat. "Even if I agree, it takes both you and Arthur to keep the club from imploding, exploding, and being overrun with creatures. How am I to do it alone, especially while getting ready for the Rosewood Prize for Mathematics?"

Unperturbed, Violet clapped her hands together, eyes wide with optimism. "You won't be alone. Why do you think we asked Greycliff to be here, too?"

NO, I WOULDN'T like *to stay here and fend off tarantulas and madwomen. Absolutely not,* Grey said.

In his head.

"Of course I do not mind staying at Beacon House and helping to oversee the club," Grey said.

Out loud.

A few hours after Letty had left and supper was over, Arthur had excused himself to go check on the Retreat's security. Violet had linked her arm into Grey's and invited him for an after-dinner drink.

They'd retired back to the cozy blue parlor, where Violet took a seat by the fire, glass of brandy in hand, and reiterated her request that he stay at Beacon House for a few months.

As usual, when Violet made a request of him, he'd acquiesced.

They'd been nearly the same age when Violet married his father. Although the marriage had not been a love match, in the beginning a certain level of respect lay between the young chemist and the older statesman. Grey had watched with sympathy as eighteen-year-old Violet tried to reconcile her aspirations with her wifely duties.

One of her first attempts was to try to repair the rift between Grey and his father.

She'd amassed dozens of periodicals and medical tomes to prove to the late viscount that the seizures Grey experienced throughout childhood were not caused by a lingering disease or a moral failing.

Despite her diligence, the viscount never quite believed her. Nonetheless, Grey was grateful.

"Thank you, Grey. I know you have never seen eye to eye with Letty . . . ," Violet said.

"She'd have to grow a few feet taller before that could happen," he muttered.

". . . but she is correct. She cannot manage the club by herself and at the same time prepare for the Rosewood Prize." Violet frowned into her glass. "Arthur and I both have concerns about the Guardians and their propensity to let their protests devolve into harassment. You will be able to protect the ladies if the worst were to happen."

Grey did not argue the logic in this. He was, if anything, an expert in managing conflicts.

"If the situation becomes untenable, you must write to us and say so," Violet continued. "Now, I will leave a detailed list of the locations of the fire exits. Also, a primer on how to discern whether something is flammable. You see . . ."

The situation became untenable the instant "exceedingly risky" and "explosive birth rates among small mammals" left Violet's mouth.

All in the same sentence.

Grey interrupted her. "What about the plan to sell you Beacon House?" He attempted to keep any complaint from his voice, but his expectation upon returning to London had been a quick visit to rid himself of the town house, then a retreat to his estate.

"This is temporary. We won't be gone forever. Don't forget, Madame Gault is arriving soon, and there is always Grantham," Violet said.

That caught his attention. His traveling companion earlier today, the Earl Grantham, had been friends with Violet since childhood. The earl was a big man who hid a soft heart beneath a booming voice, brash manners, and questionable impulses. A former soldier in the 24th Foot, he'd unexpectedly inherited a title six years earlier and had been alternately horrifying and enchanting the ton ever since.

"Giving Grantham entry to a building full of women with access to explosives is like giving a four-year-old boy command of an artillery battalion. When you put it like that, I am happy to help," Grey said.

As happy as he would be if someone dumped him in a bath of boiling lye and gave him a chimney brush with which to wash.

Grey's sole consolation at Violet's request that he live at Beacon House and help keep the club safe was the expression on Letty Fenley's face when Violet had asked them to work together.

With the scowl of a woman who'd bitten into something sour, Letty had told Violet that running Athena's Retreat required the skills of a diplomat, the endurance of an athlete, and the brilliance of a scientist.

As such, it was a job only a woman could do.

Violet and Arthur had chuckled as though Letty had made a joke. Grey knew that the words had been aimed at him. Once again, she'd asserted her disregard for his station and his sex.

He'd wanted to bite her petal pink lower lip, which pouted whenever she snapped at him. Crackling with ferocity, Letty had always appeared more vibrant than her surroundings. It might have been compensation for how little space her tiny body took up, but Grey had never walked into a room and been able to overlook her.

"Are you going to pour the brandy or massage it?" Violet asked.

Grey stared at the bottle in his hands, taken aback at where his thoughts had just led.

"Regardless," Violet continued, blissfully unaware of Grey's discomfort, "you'd rather be boiled in oil . . ."

Lye.

". . . than oversee the club. You said yes because you feel you owe me something."

Grey bowed his head. Violet had an unnerving way of cutting to the heart of a matter.

"You are feeling well?" she asked. "No seizures of any kind?"

A ghost of copper filled his mouth, and he swallowed, rubbing his palms against the smooth weave of his trousers.

"No," he replied. "I am still blessed free of them." He turned his back to her as he poured, making sure his hands were steady. He'd no desire to reminisce about how unexpected seizures had dominated his childhood and shaped his adolescence.

"I do owe you," he said, fitting the stopper into the bottle with exaggerated care, then joining her on the divan.

Violet lifted a shoulder as though she could slip sideways past his gratitude, but Grey wouldn't let her. Truth must always out.

"Father's disgust of my condition kept me bound to the estates and out of society until I came into my aunt's inheritance and left for good. I could never forgive him. When he fell ill, I simply . . ." He sipped at the drink. "I left everything for you to manage. I've never apologized. I'm sorry."

"Your seizures were out of his control and yours. It made him frightened for you," Violet said, her voice soft with pity.

For him or his father?

Finishing the drink, he left Violet's side and made his way back to the decanter but did not pour himself another.

One was his limit, and he always stayed within the limit.

Violet twisted in her seat and looked at him over the back of the divan. Grey refused to meet her eyes, loath to catch any additional hints of pity. Instead, he concentrated on lining up the glasses to fit on the drinks tray. After that, he centered the somewhat tarnished tray in the center of the table and wiped away a water mark with his thumb.

"If it helps, Grey, he truly seemed regretful in the end that he'd been so harsh. Seizures such as yours are still a mystery to most scientists."

He said nothing to this. The subject had taken enough of their time. Why speak of circumstances that could not be changed? Best to return the conversation to neutral subjects and leave the past alone.

"I suppose I owe it to Mrs. Sweet to remain and sort out the kitchens." Grey now adopted a teasing tone to lighten the mood. "It seems Arthur has corrupted Cook and let all manner of unhealthy foods into the house."

"I wouldn't ask you this favor if it weren't for Arthur," Violet confessed. She twisted around to stare at the fire once again and let out a profound sigh. "When he found out about the baby, an entirely new part of him emerged. Arthur would have been a wonderful father." Leaning forward, she put her elbows on her knees and rested her chin in her hands. "I suspected as much, watching him with Winthram. It devastated him when I lost the baby and he couldn't protect me from the pain."

Grey frowned. Should they be discussing her miscarriage in an open fashion? Such conversation with a woman regarding intimate matters was the height of impropriety.

"He needs to be away and under the open sky until he can find his way," she said, her voice soft with sympathy.

What could that mean?

"Find his way? It isn't as though he is lost," Grey said.

"Anyone who goes through a profound change, be it sorrow or love, can find themselves on a different path. It's . . . disorienting, to say the least."

Grey nodded as though he understood, but Violet's metaphor made no sense.

He would never make the mistake of succumbing to profound emotion of any kind if it led him somewhere different than the future he'd always planned.

3

A SINGLE CANDLE HELD back the worst of the gloom as Letty sat alone in her workroom at Athena's Retreat. Finding the smell of coal smoke a distraction, she had not set a fire in the tiny grate. Instead, she'd wrapped herself in a thick shawl woven from the beautiful wool of Kashmir, the tip of her nose sticking out from her improvised cocoon. With tufts of cotton stuffed in her ears, Letty closed her eyes and sank into what her brother called her math dreams.

As a girl, she had assumed everyone could do this: find a way to leave the outside skin of arithmetic behind and sink deeper into the truth of mathematics. Simply by closing her eyes, she traveled high mountain peaks, meandered through acres of heather, and sometimes leaned out the windows of high turrets until she found the space to think.

Today, she walked a familiar path to an empty beach where waves of numbers lapped at the shore. Wasting no time, she set her bare feet, one after the other, into the water. Swimming out to the center of her ocean, she then sank along the y axis, ribbons of theories tickling her bare calves, until she reached her current work.

Light as a feather, with as much patience as she could muster, she pulled ribbons from the sandy floor and tied them, one to the next and to the next after that. Unspooling a long swath of formulas, she let herself float along as symbols revealed themselves.

For months, she'd examined these same formulas until she was rewarded with a glimpse of a new revelation, a different method of arriving at her desired outcome. She reviewed her work for flaws. Had she left any questions unanswered? Were there any flashes of gold indicating something yet undiscovered?

The waters around her churned, disturbed by an outside force. Although she tried to focus for another moment, her work tore itself loose, following hidden currents. Pushing up from the depths, she opened her eyes in irritation at a persistent knock.

When she opened the door, Greycliff stood with his fist raised. "You answer quicker than Violet when she is in the throes of her research."

Letty raised her brows in surprise, and he smiled. Quick, that smile, like the rush of clouds high above on a windy day, sweeping light into his face one second and gone in the next. The beauty of it took her breath and left her with a restless resentment that he possessed an unconscious power to affect her.

Seeming unaware of her discomfort, he leaned against the doorframe in a casual pose.

"When Violet first formulated her proofs of Avogadro's law," he explained, "she'd disappear somewhere in her head—sometimes in the middle of a meal or conversation—and sit there, silent, for an amazing amount of time." He craned his neck to peer past her into the room. "Is that your defense for the Rosewood? It looks as though you still have work to do."

Letty glanced back at the morass of papers scattered over her worktable. The opening presentation of theories for the Rosewood Prize for Mathematics was to begin in six weeks.

The first textbook of advanced mathematics she'd ever studied had been authored by a Rosewood winner. Neither the most prestigious nor the most storied award, the Rosewood was known for the breadth of subject matter of its entrants and the eccentricities of some of the winners.

When Letty was at her lowest and nothing her family or Violet said could chivvy her from a certainty that her future would be forever circumscribed by her one great mistake, she'd found the book. The cloth cover had frayed, and some of the pages were glued together with what looked like strawberry preserves. Letty had interpreted it as a sign— despite not believing in omens. Picking up the work she'd abandoned years before, she'd begun to prepare for the Rosewood Prize.

It had saved her life.

"This mess is less an indication of my readiness than an example of my terrible housecleaning skills," Letty confessed.

Grey's arm brushed her shoulder when he walked past to examine her work. The infinitesimal amount of friction created had left tiny sparks behind, racing from Letty's shoulder to her belly. Bottle green wool stretched across his back, tight enough for her to see the outline of his muscles when he leaned over. The sparks burned brighter in response.

"Did a small animal dip its feet in ink and run across your pages while you were distracted?" he asked.

The sparks died a sudden death.

"Why does this say *'Ferry's Fast Teatime'*?" He pointed to the title page of her work.

Snatching the paper, Letty set it on the other side of the table, away from his gloved hands. "It says 'Fermat's Last Theorem.' That is the subject of my proof."

Grey peered around the room. "Tell me about this." With a wave of his arm, he included the handful of equations she had chalked out across her slate board, the piles of books on otherwise bare shelves, and her stacks of papers. "What was important about Mr. Fermat's last theorem?"

Suspicious now, Letty gathered the rest of her papers, careful to stay clear of him. Difficult, since his body was so large. The tug of his utter *maleness* on her attention unnerved her. Why did he have to be handsome? What purpose did it serve nature to disguise a man's arrogance with such beauty?

If only there were outward warnings for women that gave a clue to a man's character before he approached: a telltale angle of the brow signaling a lack of charity, the way their frown bent in the middle exposing a tendency to obfuscate, or a certain gait giving clues to whether they interfered with their servants or were unkind to children.

Imagine the disasters that could be averted.

Letty cleared her throat and pushed such dark thoughts to the side, choosing instead to fill her brain with the comfortable reliability of mathematics.

She took a piece of chalk and set it in a wooden holder so she might spare her gloves. Wiping an old equation from her slate board, she drew a right triangle.

"You are familiar with the Pythagorean theorem?" she asked.

Grey ceased his inspection, returning his attention to Letty. "I believe so." He frowned in thought. "The area of the square whose side is the hypotenuse is equal to the sum of the areas of the squares on the other two sides."

Letty drew the squares and nodded. "Indeed. $x^2 + y^2 = z^2$. There are an infinite number of *positive* integer solutions for x, y, and z. However, the more generic equation $x^n + y^n = z^n$ has no solutions in positive integers if n equals anything greater than two. The question is, how do you prove this?"

She set down the chalk and took a step back, regarding the diagram.

"Sometime in the 1630s, Pierre de Fermat left a conjecture in the margins of his copy of the *Arithmetica*," she said. "He wrote that he'd proof of a mathematical proposition, but not enough space remained on the page to complete it. His son published the claim after Fermat died."

Even after all her hours of toil, the story still thrilled her.

"Imagine, this two-hundred-year-old mystery has united mathematicians across the globe." Lowering her voice she leaned forward. "The search for the proof has led some of our greatest minds to discover new avenues of thought for other mathematical quandaries."

"It sounds like a plot from those ridiculous serial stories," he mused, peering at the chalked-out formulas on Letty's slate board. "A long-dead mathematician, the race to find his proof . . ."

Race?

He'd no idea how slow and methodical the process of working an elegant equation could be—how secure and comforting the world became while she swam into a problem. Letty held the papers tight against her chest.

Was his interest sincere, or was he somehow mocking her?

Insecurities tugged at her ankles, and she put a hand to the work-table to steady herself.

"Is there a reason for your interruption, my lord?" She flattened the words between her tongue and the roof of her mouth.

"Arthur and Violet are leaving now if you wish to say farewell," Grey told her. Tiny lines at the corners of his eyes appeared, his voice dropping low with amusement. "There's still time to tell them you've changed your mind about running the club with me."

For a moment, she fought the urge to do just that—close the door and hide away from this man and all he represented.

So he'd smiled at her. Asked her questions about her work. Softened those razor-sharp edges, albeit fleetingly.

Letty carefully stacked her papers on the table, tucked a stray lock of hair beneath a plain cap, and smoothed her hands down the front of her skirts, pulling at a few stubborn wrinkles.

Lord Greycliff might be pulling out his rarely used charm with her right now, but eventually he would revert to his customary hauteur. His beauty was a distraction.

In truth, he was just another dragon, and Letty had slain plenty in the past six years.

"Mrs. Kneland asked me to help her found Athena's Retreat at the lowest point in my life," Letty said, pushing the words through the sudden ache in her throat. "She believed in me when no one else in society would look at me, let alone be seen talking to me."

She raised her chin and locked gazes with him. "Including you."

Any hint of warmth he might have held toward her was frozen now by the chill that began in the depths of his ice grey eyes and traveled his body as he stiffened and drew his shoulders back.

Was there a hint of surprised hurt there as well?

No. It couldn't be.

Time to remember where she and Greycliff stood.

On opposite sides of Letty's greatest sorrow.

"I will do anything for Violet," Letty said. "No matter how distasteful."

She walked away from the glacial figure behind her, not looking back to see if her words had reached him.

VIOLET'S LAUGHTER RANG out, and Grey stopped in the hallway outside the kitchen to listen to the noise therein.

Cook alternated between scolding in her broad Geordie accent and crying, while the housekeeper, Mrs. Sweet, issued a stream of orders, which no one appeared to heed. He could also make out Arthur's deep voice as he gave last-minute instructions to the doorman, Winthram, and the young man's curt replies. If Letty was in there, she was staying silent. For once.

Earlier, she'd stalked past him before he could formulate a response to her words. Common sense told him to keep his distance, but something else—something best left unexamined—pushed him to search her out.

He shook his head, marveling at her self-possession in referencing the incident that removed her from eligibility in polite social circles. Grey had been prepared to ignore the controversy as a favor, but Letty had brought it up the first chance she could.

Her arrogant dismissal was the antithesis of her silent sobbing six years ago during the confrontation that had colored every interaction between them ever since.

At the time, he'd dismissed her weeping as a ploy—a crass mechanism to get his pity.

Except . . . over the years, he'd observed her many times in her function as the club secretary for Athena's Retreat as well as Violet's friend. Never had she evidenced the slightest propensity toward tears. In fact, her manner was frosty—not just with him, but with everyone.

Which was truth? Was Letty Fenley a conniving minx or—

Running footsteps sounded behind him then. Alice, the little maid Violet had taken an interest in, scurried along the hall, her thin face lit with excitement. A dull grey traveling cloak billowed out behind her, an overstuffed valise banging against her leg.

Grey bowed in greeting, and Alice dropped the valise in surprise, nearly falling on her bottom as she tried to curtsy despite her forward momentum.

He picked up the valise, then held out his palm when she tried to protest.

"Let me assist you, Miss Alice. As of today, you are no longer in the household's employ. You are a student at the Yorkshire Academy for the Education of Exceptional Young Women and should be treated with the deference accorded to an aspiring scholar."

A mottled flush spread over her neck, and she curtsied again, this time with more aplomb.

"Thank you, m'lord. A scholar—can you believe it?"

At the thrill of her voice, Grey made peace with his decision to stay and help at Beacon House. He might never allow himself to feel anything close to passion, but he recognized it in others. Best such passions find a suitable outlet. Given time, Alice would be taught the discipline of academics. Arthur and Violet would put aside their uncomfortable grief. Everything would settle into familiar patterns, and balance would be restored.

Glancing around to be sure they were unobserved, Grey pulled a handful of coins from his waistcoat pocket.

"This is for a cup of tea and a biscuit at the station and any other expenses you might have in the beginning," he told her, pressing the pin money into Alice's hand. When she shook her head in refusal, he spoke in a confiding tone. "Mrs. Kneland will forget to feed herself on the journey. I hope I can count on you to look after her?"

Later, he would send a note to his bank and arrange for a small sum to be set aside for Alice's use. Violet might be paying for her tuition, but there were other expenses the girl would encounter amid a student body of well-to-do young ladies.

Difficult at that age to be marked as different.

Gesturing for Alice to precede him, Grey entered the kitchen and beheld a scene of orderly chaos as servants and club members wandered in and out to say their goodbyes.

Madame Gault had arrived, and she stood in the center of the room speaking in low, mellow tones to Violet and Letty. She was tall for a woman, and her dark red hair was pulled back beneath a plain ivory bonnet. Wide hazel eyes peered over a spattering of freckles across her nose, and her full lips were set in an enigmatic smile.

Grey had met Madame Gault years before, while on a trip to Paris. She had left an impression of dogged determination and competency that couldn't entirely disguise an aura of hidden sorrow. An attractive widow, she might otherwise pique his interest if not for the scent of *complicated* lingering about her.

Besides, his tastes currently ran toward . . .

Grey wrenched his thoughts from dangerous directions and shook hands with Madame Gault.

Next, he turned his attention to consoling Cook, wary of engaging with Letty. She, on the other hand, evinced no discomfort with his presence, instead chatting amiably with Madame Gault.

At last, the bulk of Violet's staff and friends had departed, and Arthur held open the back door.

"Goodbye." Alice waved to Cook and Mrs. Sweet. She cocked her head and essayed a weak smile toward the club's doorman, Winthram, an attractive youth with a head of auburn hair that refused to be tamed no matter how much pomade he applied. "Goodbye, Winthram."

Slouching against the wall, Winthram lifted his shoulder a fraction of an inch. When he gave no other sign of farewell, Alice's face fell. Shoulders slumped and head bowed, she made her exit.

Arthur frowned at Winthram, and although the young man's ears pinked up, he held his ground, chin jutting forward in defiance.

Violet, meantime, issued a final flurry of embraces before she went to her husband's side.

"Goodbye and good luck," she said to them all. "I'm certain you will have no trouble whatsoever. And if you do, remember—fire needs oxygen. Your first step should be to smother the flames . . . Oh, are we going?"

Arthur threw one last enigmatic look over his shoulder, then escorted Violet, still waving and doling out fire safety advice, to the carriage.

A hollow silence settled then over the kitchen, like the moment after an orchestra ends the last waltz.

"Whatever am I going to do now?" asked Cook. Shaped like one of the dumplings for which she was famous, she slumped into a seat at the long kitchen table.

"We will miss Mrs. Kneland," Grey said with sympathy.

"Yes, I'm sure we will, but how will we go on without Mr. Kneland?" she countered.

Grey blinked.

How would they go on without *Arthur*? Violet was the heart and soul of this place. Grey's impression was that Arthur simply advised on security.

Mrs. Sweet sighed aloud and set her hand on Cook's shoulder, dark circles beneath her eyes marring the surface of her smooth brown skin. "I've had a few sleepless nights myself, Cook, wondering what will happen with the club now he's gone."

During Arthur's years as a counterassassin, he'd undertaken a mission or two with the Department. As such, Grey knew what his talents were. Arthur had made a career of blending into the background. How had such an unobtrusive man gained their adulation?

Grey cleared his throat, waiting for Mrs. Sweet to realize he was standing right there. And waited.

When she ignored him, he spoke up.

"I have much the same training as Kneland," he assured them. "You are in safe hands."

No one paid him any attention.

"The members have been bereft since Violet delivered the news," Letty contributed. "Lady Potts is simply beside herself at his departure."

"It appears Mr. Kneland has left behind large shoes to fill," Madame Gault remarked.

Cook and Mrs. Sweet agreed, both women extolling Arthur's virtues. Why, you'd have thought him a god among men. How and when had he managed to put these women under his spell?

Arthur knew exactly one joke and told it poorly. Grey had seen him laugh on only two occasions—both times after he'd been hit on the head. Arthur could kill a man ten different ways with a spoon and looked the part. How had he inveigled his way into these women's affections?

And why did Grey feel the sudden need to compete?

"Arthur and I worked closely together for many years," he said. Before he could explain how he might be helpful to the club members as well, Cook turned to him with pleading eyes.

"Then you know how he was, m'lord," she said. "Nothing ever upset him. He was solid as a rock, he was."

Mrs. Sweet nodded, one fist clenched and held to her stomach, as though sickened by Arthur's absence. "Never raised his voice, not even when Mrs. Hill's centipedes got loose in the cupboard."

Centipedes?

Madame Gault's gaze shifted nervously around the room.

"Remember when Lady Peckinpaugh tampered with Miss Makepeace's experiment with nitrous oxide?" Letty asked. She turned to Madame Gault and explained. "Miss Makepeace inhaled too much gas and thought Lady Potts's hair was a hornet's nest. She tried to bludgeon Lady Potts's head with her shoe."

Cook shook her head. "Mr. Kneland didn't say a word. Just scooped Miss Makepeace up in one arm and plonked Lady Potts's wig back on her head with his other hand."

Grey once again sought to reassure them. "As I have consented to Mrs. Kneland's request to reside once again at Beacon House, I'm certain everything will run just as smoothly after a few days."

An awkward pause followed. Cook frowned as though confused.

"Because I will lend myself to whatever Arthur did," he explained, with a vast deal of patience.

Silence followed—until Letty snorted.

In the warm light of the kitchen, her dark navy dress stood out like a bruise. Against the backdrop of the windows, pale lemon sunlight limned her modest linen cap and picked out her simple silhouette. Narrow sleeves reached past her wrists, and the neckline of her dress hid the hollow of her throat.

She dressed like a woman three times her age, but no matter how dull the colors she wore or how demure her costumes, they couldn't mask the vibrancy of her very person. Letty exuded an aura of barely leashed energy that shone in her eyes and glowed beneath her porcelain skin.

She had a way of attracting one's attention without seeming to try.

Was she aware of this power?

Did she know he was thinking about her even now?

"My lord, we are happy to have you back home." Mrs. Sweet adopted a tone one might use on children. "You mustn't worry yourself over the enormity of the task before you. No one is expecting miracles."

What?

Cook nodded. "Not many men can measure up to Mr. Kneland."

A long-dormant urge to compete rose in Grey's breast. It had nothing to do with the way a roomful of women had swooned over the taciturn Scot and was unrelated to Letty's scoffing.

Totally unrelated.

Meanwhile, the ladies went on to wax poetic with a litany of Arthur's attributes, which seemed to consist solely of the fact that he was *quiet*.

Well. Two could play that game. Grey decided he had pressing work to be done.

Somewhere else.

He excused himself and headed toward the corridor connecting Beacon House with the club.

Expecting miracles, indeed.

Winthram detached himself from the wall and followed.

"Left us without looking back, didn't he?" Winthram asked.

Was Grey about to be subjected to another monologue on the amazing accomplishments of Arthur Kneland? After all, the young doorman had been Arthur's constant shadow every time Grey visited.

"Just took her away with him. Who knows what those girls in the academy are like. Might be cruel to someone like her."

"I'm certain Mrs. Kneland can manage . . ." Grey paused when it occurred to him that Violet was not the object of Winthram's concern.

The young man's shoulders rose to his ears, his chin at his chest, misery twisting his smooth features into a mask of despair. An errant lock of hair fought free of his pomade and flopped over one eye.

They came to a passageway that branched into two corridors. One led to the public spaces; the other dead-ended in a door, behind which lay a maze of laboratories and workrooms hidden from the world. Grey waited as Winthram fumbled for his key.

"Four years." Winthram spoke to his feet. "You can turn into a whole 'nother person after four years."

Last year, Winthram's brother had been transported to Australia because of his role in an illegal workers' organization. Because he had been born female but lived as a man, Winthram was estranged from the rest of his family. Now, the young man's mentor had abandoned him, and taken away the object of his affection as well.

Grey sympathized with Winthram. He, too, had been abandoned by his family, left behind at his estate while his father, embarrassed by Grey's seizures, stayed in London. When a caring advisor had come into his life, it had left him stronger and forever changed.

Grey's godfather, the Earl Melton, had given him direction—a mission. He'd taught Grey the value of control: how to direct one's energies into deliberate action and not waste them on extraneous emotions.

Winthram would benefit from a mission of his own. The young man was experienced enough to graduate from the role of apprentice and move to the next step. Better to spend his time on something more important than indulging in fanciful notions of heartbreak and the like.

"Then it is incumbent on us to ensure that nothing here changes," Grey said.

Winthram lifted his head at the command in Grey's voice. "My lord?"

"Mrs. Kneland tasked us with the protection of Athena's Retreat. You have the knowledge of the personnel and the lay of the land. I shall rely on you as my second-in-command."

The young man paused in the act of opening the door and peered both ways, lowering his voice.

"My lord, Miss Fenley said *she* was in charge while Mrs. Kneland is away. I don't know as she will allow you to—"

Grey waved away Winthram's concerns. He'd planned and executed dozens of missions without ever losing a single operative.

How difficult would it be to ignore one tiny mathematician?

"Leave Miss Fenley to me," he told the young man. "Your mission is to bring me daily reports and inform me of any developments that might endanger the membership."

That should keep Winthram too busy to miss the little maid. If Alice returned after four years and still invited Winthram's attentions, that was one thing. If not, Grey had dozens of tricks he'd learned over the years, myriad ways to halt the flow of inconvenient passions. Later, he might offer Winthram further instruction.

Caution him that too much of any emotion—anger, sadness . . . love—can throw you off-balance and cause you to fall.

4

*S*OMEWHERE A CHILD *is crying while its mother sits listening to a stream of pseudoknowledge that she will never use. Somewhere a hem goes unmended or a dish uncooked because a woman leaves behind her family to sip tea with her gaggle of equally irresponsible sisters of science. What has science done for the common good? Why should—"* Mrs. Mala Hill stopped reading the broadsheet and frowned. "Don't throw things at me, Willy. The Guardians wrote this bosh, not me."

Miss Wilhelmina Smythe, better known as Willy, shrugged in apology while her erstwhile missile, one of Mrs. Sweet's inedible scones, rolled underneath a sofa.

"What has science done for the common good?" repeated Lady Potts. "Why, discovered inoculations for smallpox for one."

"Have they never heard of the steam engine?" added her cousin, Miss Althea Dertlinger.

"I can use science to blow up Victor Armitage, next time he spouts such drivel," muttered someone from the other side of the room.

"Remember, no explosions, please," Grey interjected.

Sweet Jesu, how many times since Violet left had he uttered those same words? *Good morning, and remember, no explosions, please. Pass the marmalade, and remember, no explosions, please.*

He'd been summoned to the common area on the second floor of the club, where a suspicious tang of saltpeter scented the air. On a far wall hung three large oil paintings, studies of light over the River Clyde, and gracing the mantel was an arrangement of silk flowers. Plush divans and comfortable armchairs were scattered about, and thick Persian carpets beneath their feet sported a few scorch marks.

Over the past week, Grey had introduced himself to the members of Athena's Retreat and tried to learn more about their work—more specifically, the levels of danger inherent in their work.

Lady Potts, a formidable dame with a wig the size of Kilimanjaro, had invited him to tea in her workrooms, poorly lit owing to the nocturnal nature of the creatures she studied. A series of chitterings and rustlings had accompanied the clink of teaspoons against bone china. On a scale of one to ten, she rated a six in danger—and a ten in unsettling.

Then there were members such as Miss Flavia Smythe-Harrows, who had waxed poetic for several hours about the controversy surrounding the classification of the red grouse as a willow ptarmigan rather than its own species. A zero on the danger scale, unless one nodded off while listening to her, then fell out of a chair and hit one's head on the way down.

When he'd visited Margaret Gault's rooms, she told him bluntly she was working and had no time to talk.

Grey appreciated Margaret Gault.

Mrs. Mala Hill—a woman who studied hedgehogs, for some incomprehensible reason—now shook the papers in her hand. She wore a day dress with the tight sleeves most of the club members favored— less material exposed to flammable or caustic substances. The bright yellow material lent her tawny skin a golden cast and contrasted with her dark black hair. "He's not an idiot. Victor Armitage is cunning enough to get people to pay attention. He says out loud what others might think but are too polite to say. This article does not bode well for any of us."

"What would Mr. Kneland have done?" Althea Dertlinger asked, and the room erupted in speculation over what the sainted Arthur Kneland might have advised.

On odd occasions, Grey's control slipped; a lurching sensation similar to misjudging the height of a step. He was tempted by the pleasure to be had in letting go and telling them exactly what he thought Arthur should have done.

Run away.

Instead, he counted to ten. Then he counted to ten again.

Winthram bristled on Grey's behalf. "Doesn't matter what Mr. Kneland would have done since he scarpered off to Yorkshire, of all places. Any road, m'lord has a plan."

The ribbons of a dozen ladies' caps rustled like leaves as heads turned his way. Althea Dertlinger pushed her glasses high on the bridge of her nose, and Lady Potts patted her mountain of brightly hennaed hair in anticipation.

"Ahem," he said, temporizing as he shot Winthram a nasty look. Plan? Right now, his plan was to hide from these women for the next three months until Violet returned and absolved him of any and all favors for her—*forever.*

"We don't need Lord Greycliff to tell us what to do. We did fine without a man before Mr. Kneland, and we'll do fine now." Letty spoke from the corner, where she'd no doubt been biding her time until a chance presented itself to cut Grey off at the knees. At her height, it was the only way she could look him in the eyes.

Margaret Gault did not appear convinced. "This leader of the Guardians is attacking the mere idea of a ladies' club. Imagine what might happen if he finds out what we do behind closed doors," she said.

"You are correct, madame," Grey said. "The public has become more disapproving of social progress for women since the passing of King George. Although it will reverse itself, we should curtail public activities until this domestic fervor dies out. Winthram has informed me of the upcoming lecture series you had planned. Given the subject matter—"

"'Fearless Findings in Familiar Frameworks: How Science Can Be Studied in Domestic Environs,'" Althea interjected. "It's a way to introduce ladies to the concepts of science in a less controversial manner."

"While I believe it is an admirable theme," Grey said, "it might be adding tinder to the fire. I suggest we cancel the lectures for the nonce."

Lady Potts nodded with approval. "Mr. Kneland would counsel this as well."

"Cancel the lectures because of one article in a broadsheet?" Letty countered. "As club president, I submit we should not back down. Bullies don't go away if you hide. Fear emboldens them."

Her eyes glittered. If you knew her history, you could hear the slightest tremor in her voice. A grace note of anguish.

There must have been plenty of people in society who had felt free to bully Letty Fenley after what had happened six years ago.

Or did she mean him?

"I agree," Mala Hill said, coming to stand at Letty's side. "The Guardians' influence is overestimated due to the volume of their attacks."

A tiny bundle of a woman clad in bright orange, grey hair tucked beneath a frothy lace cap, made her way to stand behind Lady Potts. "A lady's name does not belong in the broadsheets. This attention to our club is unseemly. I've always believed we should admit fewer members and keep our activities more circumscribed."

"Fewer members?" Althea cried, angling her body in line with Letty's. "We need more members, not fewer. The time of scientific advancement is upon us, and we cannot let women be left behind."

Arguments for and against the cancellation became heated. From what Grey could see, opposing sides were lined up by age and station. The atmosphere in the room roiled with emotions. No one paid any attention to him, and with a nod to Winthram, he made his escape from the sound of voices raised in passion.

He needed a few hours of respite from excitable women.

"Lord Greycliff, we must speak," came a voice from behind him.

Or not.

Whirling around, he used the element of surprise to halt Letty in her tracks, then leaned forward, counting on his height to intimidate her into retreat.

Stupid of him. Wild boars couldn't intimidate the woman. He contemplated the delicacy of her ear poking out from beneath her cap and the graceful curve from her chin to her chest; such fragility hid a character made of granite and steel.

"When Mrs. Kneland left, she made it clear I am in charge of Athena's Retreat," Letty said.

"With my help," he interjected.

Acknowledging that truth with a small frown, she continued. "Canceling the lecture series is not what I consider help. What you should be doing is going out and defending us with as much vigor as Mr. Armitage demeans us."

Letty trembled in outrage, and Grey resisted an urge to lay his palm against her cheek to calm her, assuring her that such raw emotion was unnecessary.

Unnecessary, yet compelling. Energy flowed from her through the floorboards, waking an answering thrum within him. It would, of course, be inappropriate for him to touch her in any manner. Especially a finger to the smooth skin of her cheek, no matter how soft it appeared.

He cleared his throat. Best to introduce a note of dispassion.

"It defeats our purpose to act in a similar manner to him," Grey told her. "I am offering a simple strategy, easily employed with little collateral damage. If you keep out of the public eye for a short period of time, this nonsense will quietly diminish."

"You don't understand," she said, shaking her head as hairpins threatened to dislodge themselves.

"I suppose I do not. Why are you agitated?" His question was genuine. "I saw your face when Violet asked you to step into her shoes. Serving as club president is the last thing you wanted to do before you present your work to the Rosewood judges. Why don't you save yourself the vexation and let me manage this?"

"*Manage* this?" Letty repeated. "This isn't a situation to be managed; it is a war to be fought." The rapidity at which she traveled from outrage to irritation to fear and back again astonished him.

Grey tucked his hand behind his back, fighting the temptation to push back a lock of her hair, which had finally slid free from the hairpins and brushed the delicate curve of her ear. The air around them hummed as if her emotions had caused the atmosphere to respond, and the scent of sugar and orange peel floated around them.

"A war? Such hyperbole, Miss Fenley," he teased, but his smile faded at the disappointment on her face.

"Do you not understand? Did Violet not explain when she asked for your help?" Letty shook her head again, frustrated. "Yes, it is a war when the stakes are so high."

The line of her mouth softened as she stared over his shoulder at the door behind him. "At any moment, another *me* might walk through those doors. A girl who wonders why the world won't let her learn about the one thing that makes sense to her."

Her delicate fingers, encased in ivory kidskin, pressed to her breastbone. "A handful of people in this country do work like mine, and they are all men. Their sex allows them the luxury of lectures and tutoring to help them in their progress. They get praise while I am treated as a curiosity. I have nothing but this club. A young woman is out there without even that much. Alone. Discouraged. Isolated. We have to be open for her."

Alone. Discouraged. Isolated.

She might as well have described his own childhood, separated from the rest of the world and subject to the displeasure of others for a condition he could not control.

Since then, every move he had made was an exercise in wresting back control. He'd rose to great heights in the Department, and his title was synonymous with judiciousness and sensibility in the polite world as a result of careful strategizing, a rejection of excess, and an ability to avoid the very emotions that shook her body even now.

She must trust him to manage this situation as he had so many others.

"I gave Violet my word that I would protect this club," he said. "I would never betray my promise to her. We share a common goal, Miss Fenley. I shall keep you safe."

Grey had hoped to calm her worries, but clouds of unhappiness rose around her as she slumped in discouragement.

"Lord save us from men who have all the answers. I fear, Lord Greycliff, your attempts to keep the club safe may lead to its undoing in the end."

NOT EVEN TWENTY-FOUR hours later, Letty was proven correct.

"I should have known you would run roughshod over me the first chance you got," Letty said.

Greycliff, with his usual arrogance, didn't bother to glance up from the papers on his desk when she strode, unannounced, into his office.

He'd chosen not to take over Violet's workroom on the third floor, instead ensconcing himself in a former bedroom at the front of the house. The bed and dressers were gone, replaced with a massive oak secretary. A set of armchairs covered with intricate Berlin wool work sat on either side of a small fireplace, reflected in a looking glass over the mantel. Its delicate wood frame was carved in the French Empire style, and the wallpaper sported tiny wildflowers on a mint background—a holdover from when the room had been used by visiting ladies.

Setting his pen down with infuriating deliberation, Grey deigned to meet her gaze. Outside, sunlight waged its battle with the omnipresent fog, and a chorus of birds sat in a tree next to the window, clamoring for its warmth and light. A few adventurous sunbeams made their way through the tall windows, picking out the lighter strands of chestnut in his dark hair.

"What do you mean?" he asked.

"You told Lady Potts not to post the announcement of this year's lecture series until further notice," Letty scolded. "Did you not heed a word I said yesterday about keeping the club open to any woman who needs us? Or is the problem that a *woman* spoke, and thus her words were inconsequential once the man made his decision?"

Grey steepled his long fingers, setting the tips to his mouth. This drew her attention to the cleft in his chin and, from there, downward, to where he'd loosened his cravat, revealing the column of his throat and a darkened hollow at the base.

The sight woke a subtle awareness in her of his body and the narrow distance between them in the snug chamber. He followed her with his eyes as she paced the length of the room. Like a touch, that stare—deliberate and calculated to make her feel unbalanced.

"Why do you insist on attributing the most negative of motives to any action a man takes?" Grey inquired.

"You oversimplify." Letty crossed her arms on the other side of the desk from him, while her gaze roamed the room for any signs of tea or biscuits.

She was hungry.

"It is not 'a man' in general I question. It is *your* motives that are suspect. Does Mrs. Sweet not bring a tea tray at eleven?"

Before she could back away, he'd left the chair and moved out from behind the desk. His speed belied the size of his body. Most everyone seemed large to her, but the way Grey was proportioned had made her forget how tall he was. Until he loomed over her.

"I can ring for a tray. You might need sustenance if this is going to be a lengthy tirade."

This close, she could feel the heat from his body at odds with the slight chill in the room. He smelled like bergamot soap and determination. If she could bottle that scent, her brother, Sam, would make a fortune from it.

"Why haven't you lit a fire?" she complained. "And it won't be a tirade. Must I again remind you that Violet left me in charge. Your role is *supportive*. I would prefer silent support, thank you."

"Have you never heard of chivalry, Miss Fenley?"

He'd moved closer now, and she resisted the urge to crane her neck to meet his gaze. The clouds behind his eyes roiled, at odds with the calm in his voice, and she shivered.

Grey's intimidation, unconscious though it might be, pushed her anger past the breaking point.

Would he speak to her of chivalry?

Their eyes clashed, and the air between them crackled. Six years of pain and resentment bubbled over, and Letty finally crossed their unspoken line.

"Chivalry is accorded to a lady, and the men of your family have made perfectly clear you do not consider me as such. Nothing you said to me six years ago would have been described as chivalrous."

Six years ago, her plan had been to go to the kitchens behind Melton's London town house and bribe a maid with a message for Nevin to meet her out back.

Fool that she was, Letty had believed Nevin Hughes loved her. He'd said as much, over and over again, and had sworn to her they would be man and wife—until his father found them together. Even days after her last letter to him had been returned unopened, she was convinced that with enough time and encouragement, Nevin would overcome his distress at his father's angry reaction to their love.

He had sworn they would be married, and he couldn't—wouldn't—have lied to her. He'd sent her poetry, pressed flowers, and long letters filled with myriad equations and his work on number theory. What else did that signify other than true love?

If she could simply get him to introduce her to his father, the Earl Melton, she'd thought, all would be made right.

Wearing a plain black bonnet and her sister Lucy's cloak, a shade of aubergine that melted against the night's sky, Letty had been certain no one would see her.

She hadn't counted on Lord Greycliff.

Dressed in a burgundy velvet dinner jacket and formal breeches, Nevin's cousin should have frozen in the chill December air. Instead, it was Letty who shivered uncontrollably the entire length of their conversation, the carriage ride home afterward, and the rest of her sleepless night.

"How dare you come skulking around in the dark, ready to disturb our family's peace," he'd said. "Whatever sordid business you have here is finished. Have you no respect for Nevin's parents? For yourself? No one wants you here. You don't belong."

Grey had condemned her with words so cold and biting that Letty bore the scars of them still. This was why she lost herself to mathematics and filled her head with numbers—words *hurt*.

The chamber shrank, and sunlight fled in the wake of his frosted voice.

"What you did to Nevin—"

"What *I* did to Nevin?" Red-hot rage burned her throat as Letty drew in a breath. As always when she encountered Grey, she walked a tightrope between humiliation and fury. His icy retort served to turn up the heat.

Plus, she was *hungry*.

"Do you mean giving Nevin my heart? My trust? My maidenhood?" Her voice rose to nearly a shout, but Grey's sole reaction was the slight elevation of one sleek brow. Damn him.

What had Grey called her that night as she shivered beneath his cold gaze? A conniving baggage? She'd been devastated; bending her head, she'd let the accusations fall over her like hailstones, unable to summon a single word in her own defense.

Now, she had the words—and then some.

Letty spat them as though they were daggers, hoping to find a soft spot in Grey's hide.

"Of course. *I* ruined Nevin. A girl raised in Farringdon until her father moved her to the rarefied environs of Clerkenwell—we practiced entrapping aristocrats all the time there. Why, I had the most polished, sophisticated man I'd ever encountered in the palm of my working-class, unmannered seventeen-year-old hand." She snorted. "For goodness' sake, at first I was so flattered by his attention. I couldn't even speak in complete sentences around him."

A slight depression formed between Grey's brows as she spoke.

"I am indeed cold and calculating, my lord. Behold the alluring gowns I am always wearing." Letty gestured to the bodice of her high-necked dress. "Remember how I flirted with the gentlemen at the balls my father bought my way into? Somehow, I overcame their disgust of my common roots and they overlooked the small matter of my interest in mathematics, and I left them swooning in my wake."

They both knew she had done none of this. An awkward girl, she'd been thrust into society and served as an example of how a merchant's fortune might buy a new gown but could never purchase the approval of the aristocracy.

"You are . . ." He stopped and frowned, cocking his head and burrowing beneath her skin with his gaze. "Melton said . . ."

Despite his skill at remaining enigmatic, she could see wheels spinning inside Grey's head.

He doubted.

Too late. Too late for her, at least.

"Didn't you once name me a seductress, my lord? Do you still think me so?" Letty had meant the question to be rhetorical.

Advancing on him as he leaned with one hip perched on the side of the desk, Letty's skirts brushed the insides of his thighs when she came to a stop. A scant inch of space between them, and the tension shifted from quarrelsome to anticipatory. The slightest intake of his breath snapped loose an invisible tether holding back her common sense.

"Are you?" he asked in a bored drawl.

As ever, his expression hinted at intelligence and command, but nothing else. A desperate urge to force this man to acknowledge her—to be as affected by her presence as Letty was by his—kept her from turning tail.

"Shall we test it?" she asked. The husky tremble in her voice betrayed the delayed onset of reason.

With his arms spread out on either side of him, only the whites of his knuckles as he gripped the sides of the desk gave her any hint to his feelings. Did he want this?

Did she?

Catching hold of his shoulders, she raised herself on tiptoe. If he believed her to be a temptress, then that is what he would get.

She waited for him to stop her. Her gaze dropped from the storms in his eyes and fell to his lips.

"Go ahead," he whispered. "Ruin me."

Though stern and unyielding when glimpsed across a ballroom floor, they were soft, those lips. She brushed her own against them, relishing the sensation. A foreign, utterly wicked urge to taste him snuck up on her. Would it be out of bounds if she touched the tip of her tongue to his mouth? Instead, she pressed her closed mouth harder against his, dismissing the thought as ludicrous.

His arms remained stubbornly fixed at his sides. How lovely it would be if he held her in an embrace. Still, Letty supposed she'd made her point. She broke the kiss, stepped away from his hard body, and tossed her head.

"I have proven myself wicked in your eyes, haven't I?" she asked. She put her hands on her hips, steeling herself for whatever insults he might hurl her way.

Instead, he examined her with a mystified air.

"What was that?"

Letty blinked, taken aback.

Where was his outrage? Shouldn't he be outraged at her seductive ways?

"What was what?" she asked.

Grey did not have the expression of a man accosted by a wily siren. He had the expression of a man with questions. Many questions.

"Was it a joke?"

His words punched her in the stomach, and she held her middle, preventing a collapse.

"A joke?" Letty gasped with the last of her breath. All the daring it had taken to set her mouth to his, and he thought it a joke?

Straightening, he took one step toward her and clasped her face in both of his large, warm palms before she could protest.

Rallying her pride, Letty jerked her chin. "Are you so jaded that a kiss from a fallen woman would count as farce?" she asked.

"You call that a kiss?" His voice held no scorn or ridicule, only a hint of amusement.

Like the slow slide of a raindrop down the hollow of a leaf, his thumb traced the line of her cheekbone until it stopped at the corner of her mouth.

"I . . . What would you call it?" she stammered.

"Do you want to try again?" he whispered, lowering his head toward hers, his breath warming the tip of her nose.

Tiny tremors began low in her belly as he settled his hand on the small of her back, nudging her to step forward. Even through the many layers of cloth, a jolt ran through her at the contact. Beneath his tan trousers, his legs might have been carved of stone, muscled from years of riding and fencing.

"Yes," she said faintly. "I mean, no. I mean . . ."

"Open," he said.

Letty shook her head, confused, while his thumb brushed along the edge of her bottom lip. How could a gentle touch to the smallest part of her affect her entire body? The question fluttered through her mind. Perhaps a reaction of the nervous system to various stimuli . . . But the rest of the theory left her brain along with any other rational thought.

Because now, he'd taken away his thumb and set his beautiful mouth nearly against hers. Not touching, but nearly so. And for the second time, he repeated his demand.

"Open to me, Letty."

She had lied. She was not a siren, not a seductress, not even much of a woman, and she didn't understand what he wanted.

So he demonstrated.

Tilting his head, he brushed his lips against hers in a motion both sweet and devilish at the same time. The tip of his tongue against the seam of her lips scorched her, liquified her barricades, leaving her vulnerable to him.

This was nothing like her idea of a kiss.

This was . . . bliss.

Her body took control from her fevered brain as it dawned on her what he wanted. He swallowed her sigh of capitulation as she opened her lips, gasping when he forced her mouth wider, slipping his tongue inside. With swift, gentle strokes he licked the contours of her mouth, stoking an unaccustomed fire in her belly and her blood.

Pressing against him to soak in more of his heat, Letty dared to match his motions with her own. He tightened his embrace and deepened the kiss, eating at her mouth as though to sate a hunger.

Every single barrier Letty had labored to construct melted beneath the warmth of him. How could she ever have thought him made of ice?

Ramparts down, guards fleeing left and right, she was a castle begging to be pillaged.

At the notion of becoming another man's conquest, panic tore through her and she broke the kiss.

"What have you done?" she whispered, her hands clenching at her sides, clutching at the tattered remains of her anger and resolve.

Grey stared at her as though she were a stranger.

After a moment, he answered.

"Ruined us both."

5

THE NEXT MORNING, Grey welcomed the Earl Melton into a formal parlor on the first floor of Beacon House. Violet had never used the chamber, complaining of the stiffness in the cushions and the haughty disapproval in the family portraits along one wall.

"Greycliff, my boy," Melton said, hailing him with a warm smile.

His father's cousin, Melton was not just Grey's godfather; he was the director of the Department and one of the most powerful men in England.

The earl had always loomed large in Grey's memories, but now Grey could see the top of Melton's greying head, and when they shook hands, the strength of the earl's grip no longer matched his own.

As Melton took a seat by the fire, Grey noticed a slight stoop to his shoulders and a new flap of skin beneath his chin.

The vulnerabilities took Grey aback; a hero wasn't supposed to show his susceptibility to the passage of time.

Crossing the parlor to a small tantalus, he rummaged through the bottles to see if Violet had left anything drinkable in them. Unbidden, Letty Fenley's heated words from yesterday rang in Grey's head.

In six years, Grey had never once questioned Melton's assertions that a shameless girl from Clerkenwell had tried to trap Nevin into marriage.

Yet yesterday, Letty had been utterly believable.

Disloyalty flooded his mouth with the taste of ashes.

Instead of asking to whom he felt disloyal, Grey distracted himself by bringing up a great-aunt who had been feuding with Melton for years.

"Is Aunt Marigold still opening an asylum for turtles on her estate?"

Melton sighed. "We will be the laughingstock of Cumbria. Did I tell you the latest?"

Handing Melton a small glass of brandy, Grey relaxed as his godfather's stentorian voice recited the family news. When learning his Bible passages as a child, it had always been Melton's authoritative baritone in Grey's head in place of the angel's exhortations.

Grey had been eight years old when Melton changed his life. His mother was long dead, and his father's second wife, a stern, unhappy woman, wanted little to do with her husband's flawed offspring. Like many of the time, she believed his seizures to be a fault of his character. She kept him confined to the dark, stultifying nursery suite in the west wing of the manor and pretended he was not there when she visited the estate—a pretension he reciprocated.

He closed his eyes and could still see the late-summer sun piercing the milky windows of his bedroom.

The day was unseasonably hot, and a passel of older cousins had decided to hold races on the broad sweep of the east lawn. Longing to join in the fun, Grey snuck out of the nursery and made his way downstairs. He'd been steps away from escaping when his tutor grabbed him by the collar.

"Back upstairs with you. With your infirmities, you cannot be jostling in this heat."

If there had been even a hint of regret in Master Jackson's voice, Grey might have heeded him. Instead, he'd heard pity alongside a dose of scorn.

"I can!" Grey shouted. Anger had bubbled up, and sweat rolled down his forehead. Fists clenched, he punched the air between himself and the tutor. "I can run, I can ride, I can climb a tree. If you would—"

In the presage to a seizure, the light changed, bending to trace the objects around him with a sickening halo. Grey was powerless to stop it as his tongue lost the shape of words and lightning slid into his head and blinded him for a fraction of a second. To him at least.

"—leave me alone," Grey finished, only to find himself lying on his back, staring at the ceiling. As he recovered his senses, Melton appeared, standing over him.

Grey waited for a hand, but his godfather did nothing. After an internal check to see if he'd broken anything, Grey rolled to his side and sat slowly.

"You want to be like those other boys?" the earl asked.

Grey didn't want to be like those boys; he wanted to be more than them. He wanted to be bigger and faster—he wanted to take up more space than them.

"Yes, sir," Grey answered.

"Will shouting like this is a corroboree help you?"

"No, sir," Grey responded, twisting with shame at his loss of temper.

He wanted to be what his father expected of him: well-behaved, righteous, and courteous. Pleasant. Perfect.

Grey hadn't the vocabulary to express these desires. Instead, he hung his head, expecting a scolding no matter what his answer. "I was angry."

Melton knelt and locked eyes with him. "If you want to stay off the floor and get out of this house, you must be strong, William."

"How?"

"If you control your feelings, you can control your body," Melton promised.

The words rang like church bells in Grey's eight-year-old head. Another way of living had presented itself. A path to freedom.

Melton reached out his hand and helped Grey to his feet. "Let's go outside and see what you can do."

It hadn't been easy. The fits had returned without rhyme or reason during his childhood, no matter how hard Grey tried to rein in his emotions. Melton had never stopped believing in him, and Grey had spent his summers at Wayside, Melton's snug country house in the Lake District. Each time a seizure left Grey despairing that he would never be allowed a normal life, Melton was at his side with words of encouragement.

"Do not let this give you cause to doubt yourself, William," Melton would say. "Think of yourself as made of ice. Nothing can harm you if you do not let yourself feel the pain."

Slowly, Grey learned control. His destiny was not to join those cousins in their mad rush across the lawn and the overexcited celebrations afterward. He'd found his place on the sidelines, apart from the ruckus, as an observer. Then, over the years, as an advisor.

He'd gained the trust of men with grander titles and far more riches than himself, with a well-placed word here or a suggestion there. Power, he'd come to understand, was a thin blade wielded with discretion and detachment.

"Shall we speak of what happened?" Melton asked.

Lost in his memories, Grey jerked in surprise, brandy sloshing over the side of his glass at Melton's words.

"Has she said something to you?" Grey blurted out, shocked that Melton would broach the subject of Letty Fenley.

"She?" Melton cocked his head. "Was there a woman involved in the riots?"

Grey pressed his forefingers to his brow and blew out a breath. This was what happened when stronger emotions were engaged. Distraction could be deadly in his line of work. He ruthlessly pushed Letty from his brain and concentrated on the man standing before him. Grey owed him his full attention.

"No. I misspoke," Grey said. They stared at one another, and the years fell away. The yearning to please his godfather filled his chest, and it took great force of will to keep any note of pleading from his voice. "I have prepared for you my letter of resignation in the aftermath of my actions. You must know I did not intervene in the prime minister's orders without considering first how it might reflect on you."

He paused, and a distant thump from the club punctuated the silence as he drew another breath to finish. "The only thing more important to me than you and the Department are the tenets by which I was raised. Those you taught me yourself. The strong are beholden to protect the weak, and it is not enough to hold power, one must wield it justly. The Queen's soldiers' reactions to the rioters were excessive and based on fear and ignorance. I could not let them stand."

Settling back against the stiff brocade, the earl regarded Grey with a wry tilt to his mouth. Despite the signs of age, his moss green eyes sparkled with intelligence. Grey submitted himself to a thorough examination.

"I reject your offer of resignation," Melton informed him. "Now is not the time to back away from your duty, Greycliff."

Mild as Melton's tone was, the rebuke stung.

"I am not backing away from duty," Grey said. "I am accepting responsibility for my actions that were in contradiction to the directives of Her Majesty's government and the Department."

Melton waved away Grey's words with a wrinkled hand. "You stepped out of your role as an observer and became a participant. This weighs as heavily on you as the actions themselves, doesn't it? You must learn to stay above the fray. If you do not remain apart from the lives of those you control, you will lose your perspective. Decisions based on fleeting emotions can have far-reaching consequences."

Grey sucked at his lower lip while considering his response. Melton wouldn't be swayed by arguments based on anything but hard, cold logic. Impressions of the workers' living conditions, "feelings" about fairness or justice—these were of no importance when deciding matters of state.

"Those men in the riots," Grey said finally. "Many of them have no malice toward Parliament or the Queen. They are losing their livelihoods and, like any man, want control over their destiny. Rather than hang or transport them, we should be helping them."

"Would you have illiterate workers decide our fate?" Melton countered, setting his untouched drink on the end table at his elbow and leaning forward.

"I would have the Department look forward instead of to the past," Grey said calmly.

Melton sat back and pulled at his pant leg so that the material fell straight.

"I am stepping down from the directorship next month."

The words, spoken without inflection, rattled around him like hail. Melton had been the director of the Department for a quarter of a century. Sinking into a chair, Grey once again catalogued the changes in Melton's appearance, and a sharp needle of sorrow pierced his heart.

"You would tell me if there were . . ." Dozens of scenarios raced through Grey's head, and he braced himself.

Melton shook his head. "Do not get ahead of me, boy. I'm retiring, not dying."

Grey huffed in disbelief. "What else but death would have you loosening your grip on the Department? You were one of its founders."

"I don't know if Lady Melton would be insulted or flattered by the comparison to the grim reaper." Melton chuckled, and Grey joined him at the thought of the diminutive, soft-spoken woman being cast in such a light.

"For as long as I've been director," Melton said, "she's been a devotee of the arts and has begged me to accompany her to the Continent for a tour. Each summer, I put her off with the promise of a trip the next year. This winter, she suffered a bout of pneumonia and it made us think . . ." Melton shrugged. "For everything, there is a season."

A heady burst of pure, unadulterated *desire* surged through Grey's body, and he clenched his jaw to keep from speaking. The directorship would be vacant for the first time in a quarter of a century.

"I have spoken with the Funders. A meeting will be held tomorrow to decide my successor. Yours is the name I have put forth as my replacement. Will you be there?"

"I suppose I can find time to attend such a meeting," Grey allowed, his tongue thick with something close to lust.

He'd left the army and come to learn at Melton's knee in anticipation of this moment. For years, Grey had subsumed his passions, along with his displeasure, to fashion himself into the kind of man who could be trusted with such a position.

With a dry chuckle, Melton sipped at the brandy. "I have waited a long time to see you take your place. These times cry out for the leadership of men like you, who value reason and syllogism." He winked. "Even if I do not agree with such nonsense as universal suffrage for all and sundry."

Over time, Melton's political views had become more conservative. To stand in the way of progress was to shout into the wind. Was this the fate of men as they aged?

Would Grey want to turn back time once its cold grasp came for him?

"You cannot fight change," he reminded his godfather.

"I am not fighting change," Melton objected. "I simply wish to control the direction of the change."

Clapping his hands on his thighs, Melton signaled a new subject. "Come to dinner tonight and pay your respects to Lady Melton. Nevin is here for the season."

At the mention of Nevin, Grey's euphoria dimmed. He'd managed to banish Letty from his thoughts while discussing the directorship, but now his doubts came roaring back. He would speak with Melton about her circumstances.

After the meeting tomorrow.

Grey cleared his throat as the taste of ashes intensified, then made an approving noise as he took Melton's glass and set it on a sideboard.

"It's a celebration," Melton continued. "Nevin is competing this year for the Rosewood Prize. Lady Melton and I have great hopes for his success."

All Melton's objectiveness and judgment flew out the door when it came to his son. While many believed Nevin to be like his father in intelligence and rectitude, Grey saw him more clearly. A fault line of weakness ran through Nevin's character. Unlike his father, he'd never been tempted by the lure of power and had no interest in the machinations of politics. Even as he sought to differentiate himself by studying mathematics, Nevin still craved his father's approval.

Why would Letty have chosen Nevin to conduct an affair with and subsequently try to entrap into marriage? It made no sense. Although the Department was a secret to everyone except for a select few in the government—and now, apparently, anyone within a six-foot radius of Violet Kneland—the Earl Melton was a politically powerful and intimidating man. Letty must have known Melton would never let his son be used in such a manner.

It took a moment before Grey made another connection.

"The Rosewood Prize?" he asked. "In mathematics?"

"Indeed." Melton's voice rang with pride. "Finally, there is a Council this year who recognize Nevin's talents. I will allow some disappointment that the boy has never shown any interest in the soldierly arts like you, Greycliff. However, winning the Rosewood will be a feather in his cap. Won't be long before he's a Fellow and sitting on the Royal Society's Council."

Grey kept his doubts to himself. "Nevin must be delighted at your support."

"He's my son. I would do anything for him."

Grey kept his expression blank, but he could not squelch a sudden wave of pride when Melton continued.

"If your father were alive, he would be proud of you, too, William. You will make an excellent director."

WIGS.

Letty contemplated both the existence and limitations of them as she bustled through the hallway at Beacon House. Lady Potts's wig was famous among the members of Athena's Retreat, both for its towering height and its indestructability. Letty needed a wig that shouted "nondescript" not "flaming-red mountain range" if she were to pass herself off as a man for the Rosewood presentation.

For reasons still unfathomable, Violet had mentioned in her last letter that she possessed such a wig, which was currently mounted on a bust of Theophrastus von Hohenheim in her library.

Letty was on her way there when she spied an older man emerging from the more formal downstairs parlor. He looked unfamiliar at first. It wasn't until he turned and said goodbye to someone therein that Letty's knees buckled.

She'd seen him up close once—six years ago. Even then, there had been blinding light from a hallway behind him, obscuring his features.

But it couldn't obscure his voice: a sonorous baritone steeped in pride and certainty. The man standing in the doorway that night knew right from wrong. Nothing would shake his faith. Nothing could mitigate his disgust.

The Earl Melton walked toward her now, and his unnerving eyes, the color of algae, swept her from toe to cap, discounting her worth by the lack of adornment on her plain wool skirts, adding some back at the expert of its tailoring and the quality of leather in the belt at her waist.

A foot or two away, he touched one finger to the brim of his hat—no more. If she were someone worth stopping to speak with, he would have known her. For he knew all the best people. *Only* the best people.

A million and one times, she'd imagined what she might say to him if their paths crossed once more: She'd give an impassioned speech about integrity, how he'd dismissed hers and inflated his own. Or a tirade on the hypocrisy of men.

In her mind, she'd been a few inches taller and hovered over him, and he'd been captive to her lessons on what it was like to be a woman in their time.

How every article in the women's periodicals instructed her to make herself attractive to a man. How every ladies' shop sold items to aid in this attraction. How mothers primped their daughters for social events in pursuit of a man's attentions. How men criticized women who were not engaged in such pursuits.

Not a day went by when she was younger that Letty did not regard herself in the mirror and wonder if a man might find the vision appealing. Her father's entire fortune was founded on women asking this question. All the books on her shelf told the same story with the same endings. A goose girl gave in to the wishes of the hero and she was rewarded with a crown.

Yet once Letty did become irresistible, like everyone had told her to, she was punished for it.

Be pretty, but not prettier than the others. Look like you want their attention, but turn away from it when offered. Act as though you wish to kiss him, but do not do it. Spend your time and money to get them to want you, but then you must deny them.

Make him love you, but do not act upon it.

A cunning trap for girls who listened to their hearts instead of the messages not so subtly communicated by society.

In the pages of a book, love is its own reward.

In the real world, it was a transaction.

"You." He'd come to a halt right before he passed her, recognition in his eyes. He threw the word at her as though it were filth, his voice making sure she was aware he thought of her as such.

Little did he know, Letty wore her armor every minute of every day because of encounters like this. She stepped back as his voice hit her barriers and slid right off again. Leaning against the invisible supports, she tried to keep her breath from speeding ahead.

"It's not surprising I didn't recognize you at first. You're clothed," he sneered.

The last time Letty had seen him, she had indeed been naked. Holding a sheet to cover her chest while Melton insulted her. Groping for Nevin's hand, waiting for him to protect her from his father's invectives. Waiting in vain as the man she loved moved as far away from her as he could get, bleating out apologies and lies.

Now, here in the hallway, heart pounding hard enough that it pained her, she bent her numb lips into a curve of defiance. Sweat soaked her gloves, and she turned her hands palms inward to hide the stains. She made an exaggerated curtsy, holding his gaze.

Never again would she appear humble in front of him.

"What is a woman like you doing in this house?" he asked.

A woman like her?

A woman torn apart by this man and his son.

A woman left to carry the burden of his disapproval by herself.

A woman who'd rebuilt her life from shambles after he'd broken it.

"A woman like me is thriving, despite your best efforts," Letty answered without slurring, although her mouth was dry as cotton and her tongue swollen. Rage pushed against the wall of her chest, and she stumbled sideways, desperate to leave his company before her armor failed her.

"I suppose it is no surprise you lack the shame to keep away from decent folk."

Before Nevin had entreated her to come to his bed and fulfill the earthly promise of their heaven-sent love, Letty had been considered "decent folk."

Once Melton had discovered the two of them, Letty's decency had been revoked.

Nevin's was not, even though he'd been a full partner in the act.

Ashes filled her nose, detritus from the girlish dreams this man had set fire to, and Letty walked past him, no longer able to speak. For the length of the hallway, she kept herself at a steady pace until Grey emerged from the parlor just as she passed.

"Melton? Who are you . . . ?"

Grey locked eyes with Letty for what seemed like an eternity, and the ice there melted as he took in the sight of her. Was it sympathy in his gaze? Guilt?

Pity?

He broke the stare and peered down the hallway, where his godfather had disappeared, and her cheeks burned like fire. The shame she'd been holding back flooded through her, and Letty grabbed her skirts and ran.

"Miss Fenley . . . ," Grey called after her.

It only made her run faster. She slammed her hip into a corner as she made for the servants' back staircase and nearly fell on the stairs but righted herself in time. The pain served as a deserved reminder of what happened when you let down your guard. Through the twisting halls she ran until reaching the sanctuary of her darkened workroom.

Pushing deep into the corner of her sagging couch, she stared at her unlit fireplace and pulled the Kashmiri shawl tight around her shoulders, concentrating on the slide of the wool over her skin. Such pieces were sold in her father's emporium at prices too dear for anyone but the most discerning customers.

She'd long coveted the lengths of delicate, soft wool and nearly wept when her brother presented her with one. Only after she'd unrolled the cloth had she seen the enormous flaw in the weave. Her disappointment lasted mere seconds before she made a discovery.

The blemish amid perfection made the piece more precious.

Rummaging beneath the cushions, she pulled out a slim volume, the gilt letters long since dulled by repeated handling. Knees to her chin, Letty opened the book at random and read the familiar story of a naive but courageous young woman who encountered an enigmatic nobleman who harbored a dark secret.

Nowhere other than in the pages of her formulas did Letty find such comfort. In her novels, the righteous were triumphant over the evildoers and there was always a way out of even the worst of situations.

She clasped those happy endings tight to her chest as if they were charms.

As if, someday, she could use them to call forth a happy ending of her own.

6

EARL GRANTHAM'S BOOMING laugh rolled along the dinner table, rattling the saltcellar and setting the wine to swaying in the glasses. From the opposite end of the table, Grey observed while his friend held court, whispering naughty imprecations in a dowager countess's ear and causing another old dame to slap his hand with pleasure. Seated to Grey's right, Miss Elizabeth Wainwright watched the earl as well, mouth slightly parted with ill-concealed longing.

Lady Melton had not been subtle in her seating arrangements. Grey's end of the table was awash with unmarried misses while Grantham entertained their mamas. Made no difference. The charismatic blond earl still attracted the attention of any female in a hundred-yard radius.

Meanwhile, Grey achieved the reverse effect.

By the time he had joined the army, Grey's experience with women his own age was nonexistent. His tongue-tied confusion was perceived as standoffishness, and not until he left the army for the Department did he discover the delightful companionship of widows. Lonely enough not to mind having to tutor him, independent enough that he needn't fear any emotions stronger than affection. Conversation—other than about matters pertaining to their pleasure—had been limited but instructive enough that he could now hold his own in mixed company. Somewhat.

Lord Melton and his wife believed that now that he was a few years into his thirties, Grey ought to expand his circle of female acquaintances into a younger and more marriageable pool.

The stalwart Miss Wainwright did her duty. Turning to Grey, she plastered an expression of interest on her face.

"Nevin tells me your seat is in Herefordshire, my lord. The countryside there is charming."

Grey redirected his attention from his soup to her blandly pretty face. "It is, indeed, Miss Wainwright."

"Are you acquainted with Baron Fetch and his family?" she asked. "Their property, Standing Stones, is outside Leominster. I toured it last summer and found the grounds to be impressive."

"No," Grey replied. He tried to think of what else to say. "Not that I know of."

Brilliant.

Nearly two dozen guests sat in Melton's formal dining room. Glasses sparkled in the light of the chandelier, and cunning little bud vases had been set at even intervals, sporting the tiny pink rosebuds found on the Melton family crest. No expense had been spared tonight, and it showed.

The man Grey had avoided speaking with all night leaned over from his side of the table, intent on drawing Grey's attention.

"Lizzie is trying to figure out the size of your estate and whether it's worth pursuing your acquaintance."

The words carried despite a slight slur, and a few heads turned.

Miss Wainwright stilled, and a heretofore hidden intelligence gleamed in her eyes. "How like a man to be consumed with the size of another man's . . . *estate*. I don't doubt Lord Greycliff's . . . *holdings* . . . are bigger than yours, Nevin."

Grey blinked at the young lady. How unexpected.

"Simply trying to look out for my kinsman," Nevin drawled, oblivious to the insult. "Ladies can be devious when they want to secure their future."

Miss Wainwright rolled her eyes. "Or they can be obvious and ignore the men who would be detrimental to it."

With that, she turned her shoulders toward the gentleman on her right, the third son of a baronet from somewhere in Shropshire.

Pity. Miss Wainwright had just shot up tenfold in Grey's estimation.

Nevin acknowledged her cut with pursed lips. A slight sheen of perspiration dampened the dark chestnut curls of his hair, which had been carefully styled with a perfumed oil. His thin lips pursed with disdain beneath the drooping sides of his mustache, making his long face appear still narrower.

Even if Nevin had not been four years his junior, he and Grey were too different to truly be friends.

Grey had joined the army against his father's express wishes as soon as he came of age and could tap the funds from his late aunt's trust.

Nevin, on the other hand, would have never defied Melton by brazenly enlisting without permission, content for his parents to chart his future. Nevin found the life of the mind far preferable to any occupation or pastime requiring physical exertion.

Over the years, Grey had tried to find common ground, but Nevin had put a quick end to it. One summer afternoon, Grey had gone out of his way to invite Nevin along on a shoot with himself and Melton.

"I know what you're trying to do, William." Nevin had waved him off. "Believe me, tromping through the woods with dirty, smelly men who lie in wait to fill hapless animals with buckshot is the last thing I want. You distract my father, and I will sneak off for a rendezvous with the works of Gottfried Leibniz."

Nevin had assumed Grey did not have an interest in Herr Leibniz's works. To be fair, Grey hadn't tried to convince Nevin of the joys of walking through the woods for an afternoon.

They were joined by their mutual love for Melton, and not much else.

"You would never let a woman get under your skin, would you, Greycliff?" Nevin said now, frowning at Miss Wainwright as he finished the last drops of wine in his glass and signaled the footman for a refill. "Not like the rest of us romantic fools. Why, I wager you know as much about romance and sentimentality as you do 'bout knitting, eh?"

Grey examined Nevin, trying to hide his disdain at the man's inability to handle his drink. "Charming the ladies has never been my forte. I leave that to men like Grantham."

Just then, roars of hilarity erupted around the earl. Nevin's brows drew together as though he were puzzled over the allure of a man such as Grantham. He grabbed at the refilled wineglass. "I prefer attention from females who can see past the superficial to a man's true character," he said with a hint of wistfulness. "A woman with a mind as sparkling as her eyes."

When Nevin drummed on the tablecloth with his fingers, Grey had the unwelcome thought that those hands had been on Letty Fenley's naked body.

Even more unwelcome was the question of how Nevin could have taken Letty to bed without teaching her to kiss. The widows had taught Grey the importance of a slow, tender buildup to the act itself.

In need of distraction, Grey busied himself with procuring another glass of wine as well, although he wouldn't take more than a sip or two.

All things in moderation. Nothing in excess. As such, he should not be thinking about kissing.

Kisses.

A kiss.

That kiss.

Like a bee exploring the tender folds inside a blossom, he'd tasted Letty's mouth. There'd been no hiding her inexperience, nor the unfeigned excitement of her reaction. That kiss niggled at him like a loose thread, but if he were to pull at it, a dangerous tangle of too many other questions would unravel and present themselves to him.

Not simply how Letty could have been to bed with Nevin and not known how to kiss.

Why had a woman who almost entrapped Nevin into an unwanted marriage not tried to do the same to Grey? Letty could have arranged for them to be discovered and made a scene. After a kiss like that, she could have demanded anything from Grey and, for a few moments there, he would have capitulated.

For years, Grey had had no cause to question Melton's version of the scandal. In fact, he'd thought his godfather generous to have kept the incident secret, but rumors had swirled the instant Melton struck her from his guest list and pressured others to do the same. Nevin had never spoken Letty's name aloud, as far as Grey knew, and her father's store survived—thrived, even—but the woman herself was no longer considered polite company.

Grey and Violet had once quarreled over her friendship with Letty.

"Your love for Melton blinds you to his faults," Violet had countered. "Letty made a mistake. Plain and simple. Everyone deserves a second chance."

As the evening dragged on, Grey planted himself next to Grantham, knowing he'd little chance of having to engage in conversation when the earl told his stories.

"I know they are incapable of any gentler emotions, but the baby elephant was bleating for its mama. How could I resist the plea of a child for the bosom of its mother?" Grantham asked. The ladies around him sighed, and an enthusiastic young miss set her palm above her heart in such a way that it drew Grantham's eyes to her lace-framed bosom.

Grey bit down on a smile. No doubt this was a version of Grantham's picked-an-enormous-weight-up-with-one-hand-then-rescued-the-baby-elephant story. (Or bird or puppy or kitten.) Somehow the women of the ton never seemed to recognize his stories always revolved around these variables.

". . . picked up the baby elephant in one hand, while keeping an eye on the baby bird . . ."

As soon as he could politely take his leave, Grey stepped out into the night, accompanied by the soft clapping of the women now circling Grantham with hearts in their eyes.

Grey breathed in the damp, sooty London air as he continued to ruminate on what Melton had told him six years ago and Letty's reaction when he'd confronted her. Ambivalence tugged at his thoughts. Was Letty a scheming temptress or an innocent who'd let her passion overcome her better judgment? Was Nevin a seducer or a young man easily swayed by his father's perceived disapproval?

A terrible, chilling thought entered Grey's mind: What if the coupling had not been consensual?

For the first time in days, the fog had cleared, and stars cut through the purple velvet of the night sky. Deciding to walk home unhindered by the distraction of others, he returned to the question of his behavior with Letty earlier. Grey had meant to call her bluff—daring her to ruin him. Convinced she was putting on an act, he'd tried to force her hand by kissing her with all the skill and experience he could muster.

He'd been wrong.

What have you done? the stranger had whispered.

For the Letty Fenley he knew had disappeared after that kiss. Left behind was a shaken young woman staring at him, her rose pink lips, swollen from the force of their kiss, open in an O of surprise and wonder. He'd set his bare hands to her face, and she'd burned him with the sparks living beneath her skin.

Letty Fenley was pretty enough, with her fine bones and flashing eyes, but the woman he'd encountered after that kiss was a revelation.

Was *beautiful.*

What had she said about Nevin?

Do you mean giving Nevin my heart? My trust? My maidenhood?

It hadn't been a hardened temptress kissing him. She'd smooshed her mouth against his, for goodness' sake. If Grey didn't know she'd been to bed with Nevin, he would have sworn Letty Fenley was a virgin.

Letty made a mistake. Plain and simple. Everyone deserves a second chance.

LETTY'S EYES FLEW open at the dull thud of a fist banging on her workroom door. After three days and nights of alternating between working in the club and pacing the tiny room she shared with her sisters, her body had gone and betrayed her.

Having fallen asleep atop a pile of her equations, she dried a tiny puddle of drool with her stained pen wipe and called for the person at her door to enter.

Winthram took in her appearance with a quick glance from top to bottom. "I'd send for a tea tray, but Lord Greycliff wished to see you before he has to leave for his next meeting."

Her objection was forestalled when Winthram shook his head,

mouth in a firm line. "Please, miss. Otherwise, he will come here. If Mrs. Hill sees him, she's bound to turn sneak on Milly and Willy's experiments with phosphorus. Then we'll get a speech about explosions and Milly will hatch some mad plan for revenge."

The doorman had the right of it. Letty cursed those rivals soundly, much to Winthram's amusement and possible edification. Waving him away, she tried to brush the worst of the wrinkles from her dress as she traveled through the connecting corridor to Beacon House and, from there, upstairs.

Grey was waiting behind his desk when she entered, much as he had been the day of their kiss.

Rattled by the direction of her thoughts, she plopped into a chair opposite him without much aplomb.

"Nothing has blown up in the past two days, I promise," she blurted.

Coals hissed in the grate as scattered raindrops made their way down the chimney. Grey had chosen his office well; no sounds from the kitchens below reached them here. The house could be empty, for all they knew.

"The fire may not be any use against this weather, but I had it made for you," he said by way of greeting, gesturing to the grate. "A tea tray will be along shortly as well."

What was this? Peace offerings?

Grey cleared his throat, then frowned and squinted. "There is a . . ." Grey gestured to her face.

"A what?" she asked. What was he doing? Pointing at her mouth? Why would he do that?

"A piece of something on your . . ." Blushing, he gestured again.

Gentlemen did not point to young ladies' body parts, but before Letty could take umbrage, she set her hand to her face. A scrap of paper was stuck to her cheek.

"Oh, I fell asleep on a pile of my work, and . . . oh." Letty rubbed her cheek furiously and checked her glove to see if ink came off. How humiliating.

"You have been working on your Rosewood presentation, I assume."

Something in his tone caused her to forget her unkempt appearance and try once more to decipher his expression, yet she could discern nothing from his features, which were immobile as stone.

"I have," she allowed.

"I attended a celebratory dinner last night for my cousin's anticipated presentation at the Rosewood."

A mixture of pain and shame shot through her fast enough to leave her dizzy.

"Nevin spoke a great deal about his competitors." Grey paused. "He did not mention you."

Something that might have been a laugh left her dry mouth. "Letty Fenley is not presenting."

Grey frowned, confused.

Letty bowed at the waist, pitching her voice as low as it would go. "Rupert Finchley-Buttonwood, at your service."

Now she could read him.

Disdain traced tiny semicircles around the corners of Grey's mouth. "How amusing it will be when they find out how you've tricked them."

"No, it isn't a trick." Letty struggled to explain, the cobwebs of her interrupted sleep still fogging her brain. "They cannot find out. All will be lost."

She clasped her hands together convulsively. "I never meant it to go so far, but they kept sending back my application, unopened, until I addressed it as a man. Once they accepted and I made the list of finalists"—Letty raised her hands in supplication—"I didn't know what else to do."

Grey's pupils darkened for a second before he shook his head. "I am sorry the judges of the Rosewood are shortsighted and cannot allow for the acceptance of women."

Genuine regret laced his words. His next question, however, reminded her that while Lord Greycliff might find the judges shortsighted, he had full confidence in his own judgment.

"Do the rules expressly *forbid* women to enter?"

He phrased it as a question.

Letty heard an accusation.

After three days with no sleep, Letty threw her hands in the air and dispensed with caution.

"Not expressly, but then again, I am . . . Oh, how did you describe me once?" she spat. "Conniving?"

Thunderclouds gathered in the depths of his eyes, the barest hint that her words had had any impact. He leaned forward in his chair, then back again. She swayed in tandem, an invisible wire strung between them.

Enough.

She had no desire to proffer any more explanations for her choices, past or present. Their business was done for the moment. Why stay and subject herself to his interrogation simply so he could comfortably categorize her?

"What would you do?" Letty asked in parting as she rose from her chair. "How would you fight for what is rightfully yours if the rules were made to keep you out?"

Before she could reach for the door handle, he spoke.

"Don't go." Rising from his chair, his fingertips stroked the polished surface of his desk.

Although the fog had receded, the murk outside was unrelenting, pushing itself against the glass, intimidating the cheery little fire into a heap of sullen coals. The world outside was cold and damp but infinitely safer than if she stayed here with him.

"I must beg your pardon," he said. "I could have phrased my question more delicately." The corner of his mouth lifted in a rueful expression. "I could have phrased many of our exchanges differently. Sit, please."

Grey walked to the window and pushed aside the curtain. During the seconds it took her to decide, he said nothing, simply stared out into the fog.

Wary, Letty settled herself in a dainty chair next to the grate, hands in her lap but toes pressed against the floor, in case she needed to push herself out of the room. He set one muscled forearm against the window ledge and faced the street below.

"Somehow, we never manage to conduct a friendly conversation."

"That is an understatement," she agreed.

"We will never be right until I address what I said to you that night outside of Melton's house."

Tremors of apprehension forced her to lace her fingers together.

"I must apologize, Miss Fenley."

Apologize?

Letty hadn't known how tightly she'd held her shoulders in until they rolled down, her elbows hitting the chair's arms.

Apologize.

"I said things . . ." Grey paused and rubbed a spot on the window-pane.

Conniving. Seductress. Liar.

"In hindsight, my assumptions and my language were unduly harsh."

Shifting, he put his back to the wall, arms crossed at his chest, and regarded her. In the low light, his eyes appeared almost black.

"I don't wish to be your enemy, Miss Fenley."

Unduly harsh. Was that apology enough?

Letty accepted the words and examined them carefully. They were solid, but slippery in their own way. He didn't wish to be her enemy. Did he want to be her friend? One did not follow from the other.

The space between them rearranged itself as they shifted their present and examined the past.

Letty had met Nevin at a series of lectures given by Rosewood alumni, ironically. One of the handful of women present, she would walk home afterward with her maid, making a habit of stopping in the park to write ideas that occurred to her while they were still fresh in her head.

Nevin had followed her after the second lecture. Diffident at first, he'd flattered her by asking her opinion of the lectures. He'd been different than any man of her acquaintance.

Letty tried to explain. "I didn't know enough to be embarrassed by my manners or my accent. A handsome, beautifully spoken, and well-mannered man had taken notice of me. He didn't roll his eyes or laugh at me when I spoke of Bernoulli numbers. He understood—he encouraged me. Can you imagine?"

"I can," Grey replied in a low voice.

Strangely enough, Letty believed him. Twisting in her seat, she held his gaze as the coals cracked and popped, the wind scraping its nails against the walls outside in a wistful counterpoint.

"Nevin always spoke of his father with respect, but they seemed to have little in common," she said, remembering the ambivalence in Nevin's voice when he spoke of his father. "He said he was free to follow his passion in mathematics because his father had a godson to mold in his own image."

When the corners of Grey's eyes tightened, Letty shook her head. "Nevin wasn't jealous. He was relieved and grateful and . . . impressed, I suppose. I worked hard to be introduced to you at the Simpson ball."

When Grey cocked his head in question, Letty explained. "I had heard so much about you, I needed to put a face to the name. Everyone spoke of your integrity and self-discipline. When you condemned me that night, the impact was almost as terrible as Nevin's original lies."

"His lies." Grey didn't bother to phrase the words in a question, the resignation in his voice revealing that he finally believed her.

He *believed* her.

Far too late, of course.

"He told his father I'd tricked him. Spun a web to entrap him." A dry crack of laughter burned her throat.

"Was it . . . ?" Grey pushed away from the wall and came to stand behind the chair opposite her, setting his hands on the chairback. He'd left off his gloves while writing, and he rubbed his calloused thumb against the length of satiny wood as though examining the grain.

"Letty," he whispered gently.

Her heart beat double-time at the sound of her name coming from his lips.

"Did Nevin force you?" he asked.

She flew from the chair, hands raised as though to ward off the thought. "No. Do not ascribe him any wrongs other than cowardice and selfishness. I went willingly to what I believed to be my wedding bower."

A whoosh of relief blew back a lock of hair as Grey bowed his head, and Letty's eyes prickled with the threat of tears at his reaction. For the first time in so long, the tightrope she walked was broadening. With his question, he'd communicated concern for her regard. Knowing she now could count on his protection broke a piece of her armor in a way even his kisses hadn't.

"I thought it was love, plain and simple." Letty tried to explain, but even as she spoke, she knew she never could. "In my mind, whatever

Nevin offered would be different than what passed for love in Farringdon. Stupid to think simply because he was Quality, everything we did would be clean and pure."

Then, to her everlasting horror, Letty lost her hard-won control and began to cry.

Before she could fumble for her reticule, Grey scrambled through his pockets and pulled out a handkerchief.

"There, now." He proffered the white linen square, speaking words of comfort as though they were a death sentence, his face screwed into a rictus of dread.

As well he should be dismayed. How childish of her. Once she stopped crying, she would apologize. If she could only stop. Years of shame and humiliation couldn't be plugged like a hole in a dam, however.

"I can stop," she said out loud, drawing in huge breaths of air.

Grey nodded in relief.

The tears continued to fall.

"I can stop. I know I can," she assured him, pointing to her wet cheeks. "Look, it's stopping."

The line of his jaw softened, and he nodded again, less certainly this time. As she strained to hold in her sobs, the most remarkable thing happened.

Grey stepped closer until they stood toe to toe. For a terrible moment, she thought he would kiss her again. Instead, he reached one arm out at an awkward angle and gingerly settled it around her shoulders.

Shock dried her tears within seconds of whatever . . . whatever was he . . . ?

Grey reached around with his other arm and rested his large, warm palm on her back.

Pat, pat, pat.

His hand thumped against her back in a jarring rhythm.

"There, now," Grey said in the same tone as one would use to tell a dog to sit or a horse to stand still.

Confused, Letty endured the patting and thumping, drying her eyes and blowing her nose into the handkerchief as her mind wrestled with a few facts.

One, Grey was embracing her.

Two, Grey had most likely never embraced anyone before in order to comfort them.

Three, Grey did not seem to be enjoying this at all, but was persevering for her sake.

Letty didn't care. The circle of his arms sheltered her as she peeled back the covering on wounds that hadn't healed, and she leaned into the comfort he offered.

"Nevin promised me we would be wed," she explained to Grey's waistcoat. "He told me a nobleman's vow is sacred; the contracts and codicils were to come later. Such concerns had no place in our consummation."

Letty kept her head resting against his chest, embarrassed. It truly sounded ridiculous when she said it aloud.

Grey must have agreed. The patting stopped, thankfully, and he pulled her closer into a more natural embrace.

"You believed this nonsense?" he asked, his chin resting gently on her head.

"I was seventeen," she protested weakly, "steeped in romance from head to toe, not understanding that a noble knight did not hover around every corner waiting to whisk a goose-girl away on his steed."

Grey moved his body back a few steps but kept his arms on her shoulders. He shook his head at her, then rolled his eyes.

"Knights. Romance," he chided, but his mouth quirked in a sympathetic grin.

Let him scoff. How could he ever know the feeling of being swept off your feet by a man seemingly straight from the pages of a fairy tale?

"Like any young girl, I indulged in a belief in true love and that other nonsense you disdain, my lord." Her sarcastic tone lost its edge when she sniffled and had to blow her nose again.

Grey tilted his head, and the last of the storms departed his eyes. "Then you were punished for your beliefs," he said softly.

Indeed.

"I am punished for them still," she pointed out.

The time for comfort was finished. There were truths to be acknowledged. Letty broke away from the luxury of his embrace and went to stand behind her chair.

Later, she would retreat to her workroom and stare at a page of scribbling and smears. Reliving his embrace in her head while pretending to work, refitting squared pieces into previously rounded holes, there would be time enough to make sense of how the world had forever changed in an instant.

Greycliff may have admitted to his mistake, but the rest of society would never be as humble. Dragons remained guarding the gates of respectability and independence, and Letty still had little in the way of weaponry.

It would be nice to have an ally, however.

"I don't want to be enemies, either," she told him. "Instead, perhaps we can be . . ."

Caught between the words Grey had called her that night long ago and his awkward comfort just now, Letty could not quite describe the two of them.

"Whatever we are, it's unique," Grey offered, teeth flashing in a wry grin.

Good thing it disappeared quickly. Those smiles turned him from handsome enough to staggeringly beautiful.

The sun made an appearance, abruptly lifting the mood. Pale spears of light defied the fog, piercing the glass behind him. As the room brightened and the clouds drew away, Letty allowed herself a wish.

That the task of running Athena's Retreat in peace and comfort wouldn't be hopeless after all.

GREYCLIFF SAT AT one end of a long, well-polished table. Down its length, two rows of men sat opposite one another, hands clasped and heads nodding in unison. Unless one looked closely, one might be fooled into thinking they were identical: thin, fussy men with hair almost the exact color of their scalps, watery brown eyes, and narrow, colorless lips. Outside the Department, they faded into the background of whatever room they occupied, unnoticed and far too often underestimated.

Grey, however, was not one of those fools who equated quiet with stupid.

A veil of stubborn early-spring fog pressed against the only two windows in the room. Despite having pulled back the curtains, the staff had been forced to light extra candles and the room was overheated, smelling of cracked leather and old men. Wood paneling, blackened with age, wrapped around them, contributing to the sense that they sat deep within a cave, divorced from the populace promenading in the streets below.

This was the domain of the Funders, a group of eight men who paid enormous amounts of money for the running of the Department in exchange for access to the information the Department collected.

"I'm sorry, my boy," Melton had said to Grey when he'd arrived at the meeting twenty minutes earlier. "I'd been assured the nomination was a formality. Instead, it seems we are in for a surprise."

Surprise indeed.

Victor Armitage, leader of the Guardians, stood at the opposite end of the table from Grey, addressing the men assembled.

"Gentlemen. My lords," Armitage said, nodding deferentially to the Earl Melton. "Our country is in peril."

Armitage had been a fixture in Tory circles for many years. Walking a fine line between brash and charismatic, he'd made a reputation for himself as a "fixer"—a man who would help cover a gambling debt or clean up a scandal in exchange for a future favor. He'd grown out his hair on the left side of his head, then pasted it over the top of his balding pate with a generous dollop of pomade. The smoothed locks contrasted with his wiry sideburns, which grew over half his cheeks, as though he wished to prove he was capable of sprouting hair on some part of his head.

Polite society regarded him as somewhat crass—until they found his help necessary.

There were rumors that the Guardians were Armitage's stepping-stone to something bigger. Grey wondered what sorts of favors Armitage had called in to be addressing the Funders in person. Considering the Department did not officially exist, it must have been a scandal that was quieted.

"There are madmen on our streets shooting at the Queen. The prime minister's personal secretary was assassinated in broad daylight. The backbone of our country, the hardworking families from our great estates and farms, are leaving the honest, upright life of the country for the false promises of the cities. Our factories and mills may bring new wealth, but they are also responsible for the social upheaval and loose morals of today, by employing women and children rather than their menfolk. While reformers cry about the Corn Laws and the Chartists radicalize the people, *chaos*, gentlemen, chaos, is just around the corner."

A few wattled chins shook in agreement.

Part of what Armitage said was true. Whole villages were emptying themselves as families who once made a living from agriculture moved to the cities in search of factory jobs. A recent series of poor harvests had plagued Scotland and the Outer Hebrides. The Chartists were still popular, although not as popular as they had been five years before, with their calls for electoral reform and suffrage for all men, not just landowners.

"'Chaos' is a strong word," Grey said, interrupting.

Armitage pursed his full lips and, tilting his head, issued an indulgent sigh, as one might when a child wished to make a point.

"Ah, yes. I have heard you do not agree with the government's handling of the Chartists and their ilk, Lord Greycliff," he said. "Is it true you stepped out of your role as commander of an operation to personally intervene in the punishment of rioters on your last mission outside of Staffordshire?"

Grey and Melton exchanged a sharp look. How had Victor Armitage found out about Grey's mission? The Department's activities were strictly sub-rosa.

Instead of acknowledging Armitage, Grey pointed his chin at one of the Funders, Sir Gerald Ramsey, adopting a familiar tone, as though it were the two of them simply conversing, peer to peer. "The prime minister may send as many soldiers as he wishes to put down these riots, but the ideas have taken root. It won't just be the weavers and potters the next time. Discussions of election reforms are happening in middle-class parlors and even the country houses of the gentry. Soon, there won't be demonstrations; soon, there will be legislation."

Grey nodded to the man nearest him, as though they were already in agreement, careful to keep his voice level and without a hint of sentiment. "Why punish those men for something that will happen eventually?"

Armitage spoke up. "Universal suffrage may come, but it will come when men such as you and I decide, not because the British government bows to the wishes of the common masses." He was pressing what he saw as his advantage. "I understand what is best for them. We must return this country to the ways that made us great."

Why was a return to the past always so appealing when times were difficult?

"Gentlemen," Armitage continued, speaking to the group with one hand placed above his heart. "I love this country and its Queen. I will do anything to help usher it back to its greatest glory. I humbly ask that you appoint me as the new director of the Department."

Melton placed both of his hands on the table, and the eight men leaned in slightly toward him. Grey marveled at his godfather's effortless aura of power as he made them wait for a long second while his gaze traveled from Grey to Armitage, then back again.

"I thank you for your offer of help, Mr. Armitage," Melton intoned. "I will also commend you on your ability to ferret out even the most confidential of information."

A chill permeated the room.

"However, the position of director has already been—"

"I understand I am come late to the game." Armitage interrupted Melton with a confidence Grey found misplaced. "I'd like the chance to make a case for myself before you decide."

Enough.

Resisting the urge to check the hidden pocket in his jacket where he kept a knife, Grey cleared his throat. The directorship was his. He'd sacrificed far too much to let a lizard like Victor Armitage slither his way to power.

"Mr. Armitage," Grey said, "you have no background in the military and no experience in intelligence gathering. You court notoriety by leading a group of ruffians who harass shopkeepers and write incendiary letters in the broadsheets." Grey kept any hint of his disgust for the man from his voice, picturing instead an empty tundra, cold white snow as far as the eye could see.

"I may not have as much experience as you, my lord." Armitage smoothed a hand over his greasy hair and wiped his palms together. "Neither do I harbor any sympathy for radicals who would bring the country down."

Grey raised one brow, keeping his face expressionless. "Are you implying I am a radical, sir?"

"I would never. I merely question whether you can remain detached from politics, given your associations."

"My associations?" Grey repeated.

"Why, yes. Are you not a champion of the women at Athena's Retreat?" Armitage asked. "A perfect example of how society is being corrupted. A social club for women? Why, the very existence is an anathema."

This was unexpected. What had the club to do with Armitage's power reach?

"You are speaking of the club formed by my late father's wife," Grey said, his tone carrying a dry warning for Armitage to watch his step when it came to Violet. "What does it matter if ladies gather to drink tea and discuss botany and the like?" asked Grey.

Armitage cut him off with a raised finger. "I speak of the work the members do behind closed doors. We can't have a building full of women conducting scientific research, independent of any oversight."

How did Armitage know about the real work of Retreat? Which of the Funders had given him the information?

"That work saved countless lives last year when the Omnis introduced their chemical weapon," Grey argued. "From what I understand, many of them are ahead of their male counterparts. Perhaps the Department should aid them in their endeavors."

Armitage shook his head, eyes widening and mouth drooping in a parody of concern.

"My lord, this is the type of situation you will be called upon to evaluate should you take over the directorship. Ask yourself, what will happen if we let these women have their success? An entire social order rests on the shoulders of the women who keep house for the men who fuel our economy. If women decide to go off and follow their passions the same way as men, who will tend the children? Who will keep house? Should men be forced to work all day, then come home and make their own meals? Clean their own homes? Imagine, what if these women should succeed in their endeavors?"

It struck Grey that this wasn't about science.

This was about power.

"You are concerned that equity in the sciences will lead women to demand equity in other areas of life," Grey said.

Armitage nodded with smug approval. "You are championing the means by which our illustrious society is being decimated." He looked out over the men in the room, then narrowed his gaze and commenced his own study of Grey.

Aha.

This was not about Armitage's fear of women's autonomy. He'd cleverly constructed a criticism of Grey himself. It wasn't enough to question Grey's decision to intervene in the North. That could be explained as an outlier. No, Armitage had created a way to sow doubt in the Funders' minds about whether Grey could stay removed from any attachments should he be called upon to act.

"I assure you, Mr. Armitage, in the many years I have worked for the Department, I have never, ever let emotions or affections play any role in my decisions. I have also . . ." Grey now leaned forward, elbows resting on the table and letting an edge of steel underline his next words. "I have also kept every secret ever given into my keeping. Including the existence of this Department and the operations we have undertaken. Can you explain to me how exactly you came to find out about the confidential work going on at Athena's Retreat?"

The slight fluttering of Armitage's hand, falling from his chest to touch a stack of papers before him on the table and then returning to stroke his lapel betrayed his wariness.

"Why, the depredations of the women at Athena's Retreat are common knowledge," he said, hedging.

Too late.

None of the Funders would meet Armitage's roving gaze. The tide having shifted, Melton nodded brusquely at Sir Gerald Ramsey.

"I hereby appoint . . . ," Sir Gerald said. Dots of perspiration flecked his upper lip, and his voice shook. "In light of Mr. Armitage's . . . erm, interest in the position of director, I . . ."

A frisson of unease rippled through the other seven Funders at this breach in etiquette. At least the mystery of who had given Armitage the information was clear.

"We should postpone our approval until the next meeting," Sir Gerald blurted. A nervous silence followed, broken only by his audible gulp.

Melton's uncanny eyes glowed jade in the gloom, and Sir Gerald swallowed once more.

Another man, Lord Helmsley, broke the tension by quickly second-ing the motion.

A pleased smile stretched across Armitage's face, and Grey's fists clenched and unclenched beneath the table.

"There has been a request we postpone the vote to fill the director-ship for four weeks hence. All agreed?" Melton asked, the honey drip-ping from his words lending them a sinister air.

All were agreed.

As the old men stood to the chorus of popping joints and creaking bones, Melton pulled Grey to the side.

"Why did you not put the directorship to a vote here and now?" Grey asked. "We had the numbers."

"Obviously, Armitage has found some way to compromise Ramsey. I need some time to figure out why and how. In the meantime, simply give the Funders a show of good faith, and the directorship is yours," said Melton.

The muscles in Grey's jaw quivered as he tamped his frustration. To have come so close!

"What the devil am I supposed to do?" he whispered to Melton through gritted teeth.

"Seems obvious to me," Melton said. "Simply close Athena's Re-treat."

"WHY SHOULD WE limit ourselves? The bigger the better. An explo-sion of sorts."

Letty halted, midstride, on her way to the third-floor laboratories. Every hair that could stand on end did. A workroom door stood half-way open along the corridor, and she tiptoed closer. The hallway was redolent with the familiar odor of lemon and beeswax wood polish. Muted conversation came from one of the smaller parlors farther along, and an arrangement of slightly wilting hothouse lilies stood on a small table at the end of the corridor.

"No explosions, if you please, ladies," said a woman in clipped tones.

Letty smiled. That was Mala Hill doing an excellent imitation of Lord Greycliff to a chorus of appreciative laughter.

"You might consider leaving the walls intact for Mrs. Kneland's return, ladies." That was Althea Dertlinger trying her hand. She'd gotten the intonation right, but it lacked the comedic punch of Mala's performance. Letty leaned against the wall, enjoying herself.

"We don't need a man telling us not to blow things up. Why, a woman can blow up a building in half the time as a man."

Letty straightened in indignation. Was that an imitation of *her*? Why, that wasn't funny at all. Althea's voice had been harsh and abrupt—altogether devoid of humor.

Did she truly sound like that? Turning away from the laughter, Letty walked briskly down the hallway. Althea's tone had been one of a woman commanding obedience.

In truth, Letty wasn't in command of anything. She felt unmoored. Exposed. Her ever-present armor had cracked since her conversation with Greycliff yesterday.

He believed her.

Letty now had a protector. A bulwark against the nasty looks and barely concealed scorn she encountered whenever she left the club. It had changed everything between the two of them, even more than their kiss.

Abruptly coming to a halt, Letty pressed her back against the uneven walnut paneling and thumped the back of her head against the wall.

For days now, she'd carried that kiss like a locket strung around her neck. It bumped against her collarbone with a heavy, smooth unfamiliarity, knocking at her thoughts day and night, wanting to be pulled out and examined.

If it even was a kiss.

It might have been something else, something sweet and secret just the two of them could create. What she'd done with Nevin, the pressing of lips, the rough groping, the shame, and the pain was vastly different than the thrilling loops and dips the floor had made beneath her when she'd opened herself to Grey.

He hadn't been unaffected, either. He'd stared at her afterward, eyes darkened and fixed on her lips, breathing labored, and hands clenched as though to keep himself from reaching for her.

Could a single perfectly executed kiss have the power to break her open? How else to describe the strange sensation of living in her skin that she'd had ever since?

"Miss Fenley?" Margaret Gault approached, dressed in a beautifully tailored day dress of soft creamy wool, the shawl collar stitched with tiny umber starflowers. Her smile faltered when Letty failed to greet her.

"Ah," she said. "I saw you in the hall. Did you overhear Althea and Mala earlier? They meant no harm."

Letty shook the thoughts from her head. "Oh, I took no offense." She reddened. "Sometimes I can be . . ."

"Intimidating?" Margaret offered.

Uncertain. Anxious. Alone.

"Outspoken," Letty said.

"A fine character trait," Margaret said, one corner of her mouth pulling to the side. "One not generally appreciated by most men."

"Indeed." Letty returned her grin, feeling a modicum of solidarity with the other woman.

Margaret had taken over the position of club secretary with impressive speed. Having spent thirteen years as a member of her father-in-law's engineering firm, she exuded an air of detached competence tempered by her willingness to listen to any member's complaint with admirable patience.

"I do not hold any grudge against them, I assure you," Letty said, pulling down the hem of her smart grey jacket. "If you'll excuse me, I must take my leave. My father no longer allows me to spend my days at the club if I do not return home each evening for supper. His Wednesday roast waits for no one."

"Mmm. An English roast." Margaret's eyes closed with pleasure. "I can't remember the last time I had a roast. How delightful."

"Have you not been given meals from the Beacon House kitchens?" Letty asked. Other women scientists from the Continent had visited Athena's Retreat in the past year. When they stayed in the guest rooms, Violet had always ensured they were fed the same meals she was served at Beacon House.

"Oh, indeed," Margaret assured her. "Only . . ." Her gaze flicked to the side as she tried to find a polite explanation, and she leaned in to deliver a confidence. "Mrs. Sweet and Lord Greycliff believe a healthful diet is essential. He does not enjoy cream or butter in his sauces, fills himself with greens, never calls for dessert, and is fond of fish. Very fond."

Margaret's shoulders sagged, and a hint of rebellion appeared in her eyes. "I am tempted to take my meals at a chophouse on Knightsbridge, did I not fear Mrs. Sweet would find out and be hurt."

"I don't suppose . . ."

After Nevin ruined her life, most of Letty's friends had abandoned her. The only women who'd stood by her were Lady Phoebe and Violet. Then last year, Lady Phoebe had betrayed their friendship, and now Violet had left her.

She should turn around right now and go home to her noisy family and their humble set of rooms, cozy and unpretentious, despite their fortune and fine clothes.

She and Margaret wouldn't become friends. Friends were far too much trouble. They went and held you at gunpoint or left you in charge of a club full of hedgehog orgies and cockroaches.

For no reason should Letty open her mouth and—

"There is always room at the table on Wednesday nights, Madame Gault," Letty said. "Why don't you join us?"

She could not help but laugh as Margaret's sangfroid slipped and she clasped her hands and looked toward the heavens with a huge sigh of relief.

"Oh, yes, please," Margaret exclaimed. "I know it is gauche for me to accept on the spot, but I have no countenance left to me after five straight days without butter."

"You may not be as enthused after a meal spent in the Fenley family's company," Letty warned her as they headed over to Beacon House to tell Mrs. Sweet not to make extra for supper. "We are a rowdy bunch."

"I can't imagine any family who indulges in a roast each week would be poor company," Margaret said. "It sounds delightful."

As Letty pulled the keys from her belt, the door between Beacon House and Athena's Retreat swung open. Greycliff stood in the doorway, eyes the color of rain clouds in the low light.

"My lord." Margaret gave a slight curtsy and made small talk with him before excusing herself to speak with Mrs. Sweet.

How did Margaret walk past him without stammering or blushing even the tiniest bit?

Did he not have the same effect on every woman?

Was it only Letty whose heart sped enough to cause an uncomfortable heat to rise in her chest, whose mouth dried, and whose brain promptly dissolved in a fog thicker than the one creeping along the walkway outside?

Unfair.

"... tomorrow, Miss Fenley?"

What? What had he said while her womanly bits were sabotaging her well-developed common sense?

"Um . . ." Letty hedged. "What do *you* think, my lord?"

Grey squinted, lips thinning into a slight frown.

Oh dear God, what had he said?

"Calling a meeting of the executive committee for Athena's Retreat is of the utmost importance in light of the Guardians' recent activity. However, it is not for me to say if two or three o'clock is better suited for everyone."

Ah. A meeting. Letty knew her smile must look idiotic, but she could not hide her relief that her ridiculous reaction had not been noticed.

"Two o'clock will be perfect, my lord. I shall send notes around first thing in the morning," she said.

Grey nodded. "Excellent."

A thick lock of hair by his right ear curled just enough to come around the back of his ear to the front of his lobe like an ebony earring. That tiny rebellion on his person sent Letty's thoughts scattering. If you replaced Grey's simple black jacket with a scarlet coat and convinced the rest of his hair to run riot, he would look like a pirate—the most exquisite pirate imaginable.

"Is there something . . . Is there something on *my* face this time, Miss Fenley?" he asked.

Letty's head went back in surprise. "No, why do you ask, my lord?"

"You seem to be staring..." Grey reached to touch his ear, brushing the curl back into his tidy coiffure, dousing the rebellion before it had had time to truly begin.

Margaret returned then, linking her arm with Letty's. "All is in order," she said, nodding her farewell to Grey as she pulled Letty away.

Letty peeked over her shoulder to where Grey still stood. What had she been thinking?

Ramrod straight, his posture impeccable, and his clothing in perfect order, he appeared every inch the respectable aristocrat she'd known for years.

Not a hint of pirate lingered about him.

8

GREY FINGERED THE secret pocket in his jacket where he concealed a blade and considered abandoning ship.

Across the room from him, a bevy of enemy combatants had come armed. Not with knives (Grey was expert at sussing out whether someone carried a knife—his weapon of choice as well). Nor with guns.

Instead, they'd brought weapons against which he had no defense. *Tears.*

Big, fat, accusatory teardrops, all aquiver on their lashes.

No one had ever cried at him before. Thank goodness, or his missions would have been disasters.

Not all of them were ruthless. To be honest, only Lady Potts and Althea Dertlinger stared at him with round, wet eyes.

Letty Fenley's darkening blue eyes were dry as a bone, and her tongue was as sharp as a razor's edge.

"I don't care if you own the earth beneath our feet," Letty said, practically spitting at him. "Violet signed a contract transferring ownership of this building—"

"She is a saint," declared Lady Potts.

"Indeed. So generous," whispered Althea, pushing her spectacles on her forehead to wipe the tears away with her handkerchief.

Both stared at Grey with matching expressions of woe.

He'd been under the impression that Lady Potts and her cousin were barely on speaking terms. Here in their capacity as co-treasurers of Athena's Retreat, their sole function had seemed to be bickering over who last purchased tea and how bad a bargain they'd made. Apparently, the one thing that could unite them was their shared disillusionment with him. Margaret, the temporary club secretary, methodically took notes without saying a word.

Grey really did appreciate Margaret.

"Ownership of the building is contingent upon the sale of Beacon House to Violet," he explained for a third time. "The sale has not yet gone through. I have the right to close Athena's Retreat."

The smell of Darjeeling tea and raspberry jam overlay a homey scent of beeswax in a cozy sitting room on the first floor of Athena's Retreat. Another day of grey skies and relentless damp awaited outside, but the pretty gold curtains were drawn against the gloom, and glass bowls filled with arrangements of dried lavender and hydrangea dotted the room.

Grey had thought long and hard about Melton's suggestion to close Athena's Retreat, keeping in mind that all sentiment must be excised from the decision-making process and his reasoning based solely on logic.

Having run missions where the information obtained was tainted by the operatives' competing agendas, he had resolved that quick action was the best policy and had called an immediate meeting of the club's officers, as well as Winthram, who now took a post at the back of the room. Calmly and quietly, Grey told them of his desire to close the club at once.

Calm and *quiet* were not words with which Letty Fenley seemed familiar.

Instead, she vibrated with fury, her tidy braids curled like serpents beneath the lacy brim of her cap. Grey frowned at the most obstinate woman in England—nay, the entire British Empire. The frown deepened to an outright scowl when he realized that he liked it when she was stubborn. She gave off a particular heat that crept into his bones and lit the room better than the sullen heap of coals in the grate.

"If you would let me speak, Miss Fenley," he said. "I have the right to close the club, but what I suggest"—he held up a finger to ward off her interjections—"is that we discontinue the club's public-facing activities for a year. No lecture series, no gatherings, and no new members. Once you fade from the notice of the Guardians and we see no more opinion pieces in the broadsheets, everything can go back to the way it was before. If you adhere to this plan, your secret laboratories may remain open. Even those will be shut, however, if even the slightest hint of your activities therein reaches the Guardians' notice."

This was the compromise he'd devised after thinking long and hard.

Compromise.

Also a word with which Letty seemed unfamiliar.

"Run and hide?" Letty erupted from her chair like a petite blonde volcano. "That is tantamount to giving the Guardians their victory. It is a denial—"

Margaret wiped her pen with a blue felted pen wipe and blew on her notes. "According to the bylaws, we should take this to the membership for consultation," she said, putting the pen away in a clever little writing box.

"I am afraid the time for consultation has come to an end," Grey said. "Either you take the compromise, or I close the club."

Lady Potts turned to her cousin, lips pursed in thought. Something must have been communicated in that glance, for Althea nodded in agreement.

"We shall put it to a vote in three weeks," Lady Potts announced, "giving us enough time to write to the members who are not in London, so that their voices can be heard."

Grey pinched the bridge of his nose. "There is nothing to vote upon. Either you—"

"I will send out the invitations in tomorrow's post," Margaret assured the ladies. "No, you do not need to help, Miss Fenley. You must devote your time—and your abominable penmanship—to your Rosewood preparations."

Twice more, Grey attempted to explain that there was nothing to vote on, but the ladies gathered their shawls and cleared away the teacups without acknowledging him. Listening to them bicker over the strength of the tea, he spared a moment to admire the saintly patience of Arthur Kneland and to heap a mountain of curses on his wife.

Letty remained behind, rummaging through her reticule. He'd hoped after his apology yesterday they could finally call a truce. Instead, he was back to being a villain in her eyes.

"Miss Fenley, I am trying to find a way to save this club," he said as she buttoned her gloves. "You are a mathematician. You understand the concept of risk."

The stare Letty gave him was a mixture of disbelief and regret and sent his heart sinking to his toes. The fact that his promotion to the directorship was tied to the decision sat like a stone in the pit of his belly.

Letty was wearing another one of her plain gowns today. An unappealing shade of sparrow's wing brown, it more resembled a habit than a dress.

On Henrietta Place stood the shop of the famous dressmaker Madame Mensonge, whose dressing rooms were hung with velvet curtains and smelled of attar of roses and watered silk. Some men of the ton would bring their mistresses there and remain to observe the fittings, sipping bootleg brandy in plush chairs while the seamstresses danced in attendance.

Of course, Grey kept no mistress. Even if he did, he would never engage in such pretentious displays of affection. Why anyone would sit through such a farce had been beyond him—until now.

Now, confronted by the suit of India cotton armor that shrouded Letty Fenley from toe to nearly below her ear, he knew a sudden urge to recline before her as she stripped herself of the camouflage and stood naked before a mirror. He wanted to see her draped in the sheerest muslin, the brightest silks, and the most vibrant cottons: reds and golds and the green of a spring long delayed.

"I understand the concept of risk better than most," Letty said, in answer to his question. "I also believe that for every problem there are multiple solutions. The equations may not always be elegant, but if you put in the effort, you can find your way to the answer."

"What if there is no solution?" How could Letty insist on risking public censure after all she'd been through? "Why do you even need the club?" he asked. "Surely you can do your calculations anywhere."

"Do you understand the first thing about what we do here?" she asked.

"I interviewed a few members when this began—"

"I challenge you," she said, voice trembling. "I challenge you to stop standing to the side and observing us as if we are another species. If by the end of the week you can tell me why I don't need this club, I will not stand in the way if the vote is to close the Retreat."

"It's not up for a vote . . ."

Too late. He was now speaking to the set of her shoulders as she turned her back on him and walked out.

"No one is voting," he said to Winthram.

Winthram nodded, face diplomatically blank. "If you say so, my lord."

"I didn't say anything about a vote," he told the empty room once Winthram had gone.

The leftover tarts glinted in the light like tiny jewels, beckoning to him.

"Damn this place," he whispered to himself, then left the room in a hurry, making his way to Violet's office.

Despite the windows looking out into a narrow alley at the side of the building, it was a cheerful room. The walls were painted bright yellow, and someone had set a vase of cut pussy willows on a side table. A Violet-like clutter covered the tops of the cabinets and chairs: motheaten crazy quilts, stacks of well-thumbed periodicals, and bowls of oddly shaped pebbles and seashells. Shelves full of brass and rosewood scientific instruments ran along one wall above his head, and as he searched through the drawers for more paper, he found six balls of string, empty husks of some insect, and two bags full of lemon drops.

While penning a letter to Violet, complaining about this idea of a vote, dueling loyalties warred in his breast. His time in the army and the Department did not lend itself to moral quandaries. Undeterred by trifles such as sentiment, Grey had made his decisions based on facts. Nuance made him uneasy.

Either he shut the club, took the directorship, and pleased Melton, or he left it open, lost the directorship, and pleased Violet.

And Letty.

Letty.

Grey had hoped putting an end to their animosity might put an end to his attraction.

It hadn't.

"This is hopeless."

Grey lifted his head in surprise to hear his thoughts spoken out loud in the corridor next to the office.

"Nothing is ever hopeless, my love. We simply break a problem down into its basic elements and begin from there," replied a comforting voice.

"Your eternal optimism is beginning to wear thin, dear. I should think after thirty years . . . Oh, Lord Greycliff. How do you do?"

Standing in the doorway were Mildred Thornton and her partner in science, and in life, Wilhelmina Smythe.

"What is hopeless?" Grey asked, swiveling in his seat and stretching his long legs out to the side, eager for a distraction from his own unsolvable problem.

Milly bustled into the office and took a seat in front of his desk. Silver hair spiraled out from under the confinement of a beribboned cap, despite her attempts to tuck the wayward curls back into place, and her grey eyes shone with good humor.

Willy took the seat next to her. Although the hair beneath her cap held only a few strands of steel grey, her years could be read on the lines of her face in contrast to Milly's soft white cheeks, glowing with health.

"Reasoning with anyone under the age of thirty," said Willy glumly. "Lady Potts has informed us of this vote we are to take. From what I understand, you have offered an ultimatum disguised as a choice."

"It isn't up for a vote," he explained with a superhuman amount of patience.

Milly cocked her head. "Do you truly believe these Guardians are so dangerous?"

As he regarded the women, Armitage's words echoed in his head.

Women like Milly and Willy did not constitute threats to society. On the other hand, people in England were hurting. Armitage knew that complex solutions were not easily conveyed to the public. Scapegoats and slogans were the preferred methods of men like him.

Grey agreed with Plato: Ignorance was not the greatest evil. No, a far greater evil was a preponderance of misinformation and the inability to discern fact from fabrication.

"I cannot see another way to keep you safe from exposure," he said, picturing Armitage's smug grin. "You must sacrifice a part to save the whole."

"You see, dear." Milly turned to Willy. "I told you Mr. Kneland would not have left if he weren't certain of his replacement."

Grey forced his scowl to flatten into something resembling a smile, but it took effort. He supposed this was a lesson in humility, hearing odes to Arthur's sainthood day after day.

They were an odd pair. Milly wore a bright blue gown speckled with a pattern of upside-down green and yellow birds, her manner open and cheerful. Willy was clad in navy and brown, her rawboned features softening when she smiled at her companion.

Willy sniffed. "I tried to explain to Althea Dertlinger the inconvenience we put the members through to hold a general meeting. Many of them must parcel out their time away from home carefully, and their schedules are not their own. Of course, she dismissed my concerns out of hand. Althea and her fellow students of the academy have a bias against those of us who were self-taught."

"Truly?" Grey tried to imagine why that might be. "Violet told me you and Miss Thornton have made outstanding contributions in your field, albeit under pseudonyms. She had nothing but respect for your work."

"Mrs. Kneland was being kind," said Willy, "but even she regarded our work with skepticism at first. Her aunt founded the academy, and she had the benefit of coming from a scientifically inclined family. My father, on the other hand, wasn't convinced gently bred girls should even be taught to read."

Willy nodded at Grey's noise of surprise. "Housekeepers did our marketing, maids did the cleaning, and estate agents managed our properties. This left women free to appear decorative and provide heirs, for what more might we want in life? I had to steal books from my older brothers and teach myself."

Grey winced with sympathy. "Was the same true for you, Miss Thornton?"

"Oh, no." Milly shook her head cheerfully. "My parents were part of a group with William Godwin and his wife, Mary Wollstonecraft. They educated their daughters the same as their boys. We had an eclectic education and studied everything from Latin to animal husbandry."

She regarded the woman next to her with affection. "I didn't know much about science, but my family was poor—never a penny between us when I was younger. At the time I met Wilhelmina, I was so hungry I would attend every single lecture open to young ladies simply for the refreshments."

Willy's stern mouth curved as she returned Milly's regard. "I thought to myself, 'Who is this silly woman appearing everywhere and slipping tea cakes into her reticule?'"

"You mentioned the law of conservation of energy and how I would be better off limiting my attendance at lectures to the ones with more food and fewer attendees." Milly reached out a hand toward Willy, then recalled herself and placed it in her lap, turning her attention to Grey.

"Did you know, the Marquise du Châtelet first proposed the law of conservation of energy? Not much is made of her contributions to science because of the notoriety of her love affair with Voltaire. Wilhelmina told me her story the first day we met."

"I am amazed you remember, considering how devoted your attention was to the spread of sandwiches," Willy said with a smile.

A volley of gentle teasing followed, with the easy cadence of long familiarity. They were so different in appearance yet so similar in purpose that even if they'd been on opposite sides of a room, Grey would have sensed the link between them. A stab of longing flared in his gut. Many times during his youth, he'd wanted a companion, someone he could trust not to flee when a seizure came.

Milly sniffed. "I am of a more forgiving nature than Wilhelmina. However"—she fussed with the wooden buttons at the side of her sleeves—"those ladies have all the hubris of youth and none of the deference owed their elders."

Grey raised his brow, and Milly rushed to defend herself. "Althea Dertlinger is awfully condescending, what with her complaints about the smells coming from our workrooms. Not to mention Mala Hill's disgusting little animals and the great fuss she made over the tiniest hole in the wall that one time."

Willy grumbled. "I'm not an *elder*."

"You are sixty-eight years of age. Elder is what you are," Milly said. "The problem is they have not been taught to fail."

"Taught to fail?" Grey rubbed his forehead at the change in direction of the conversation. Had he misunderstood? "I should hope not."

Willy disagreed. "Failure is part of the scientific process. They won't be good scientists—or good people, for that matter—if they won't allow for mistakes."

"Or be prepared to look the fool and charge ahead despite that. Lord knows *we* do—over and over again. Pity our errors are flammable." Milly winced. "And smelly."

This made no sense. Grey leaned forward, elbows on the desk, his posture forgotten as he tried to pin down the elusive concept. "If your experiments fail, doesn't that mean you should try something else? How does following the wrong path and risking ridicule make you a better scientist?"

"Science is the act of constant discovery," Willy explained gently. "There is no certainty in what we do. A true scientist always accepts the possibility of change; everything we believe today may be proven false tomorrow."

"Because we do not traffic in absolutes," Milly continued, without pause, "the risk of failure is one hundred percent. The first time. What happens next is the making of you. If you've too much care for what others think, there is no room for errors—and no space for transformation."

What an unsettling philosophy. Grey squirmed in his chair as he digested their words. How could one live by a set of principles that extol uncertainty and see error as beneficial?

Willy screwed her thin lips into a tight ball as though she'd sucked on something sour. "We've been working with Ascanio Sobrero at the University of Turin, but he has become increasingly paranoid and proprietary regarding the formula. I fear the partnership is near an end. If that is the case, our contributions will never be recognized, let alone move forward."

She turned to Milly. "All this talk of failure leads me to think it might be time to try something new, dear."

"How can you let go of something you've worked so hard for?" Grey asked, astonished that Willy would walk away from years of labor. Once again, he stood on the other side of what motivated these women. "What of the risks?"

Milly shrugged. "If you don't let go of something that doesn't bring you pleasure, you can't grab hold of something that does."

"MY GOD, LETTY. Is this a social club or an asylum?" Sam whispered in shock.

Letty's brother had been begging to accompany her inside the club since she'd delivered news of Caro Pettigrew.

Caro had invented an aerosol delivery system for Violet as part of their government mission last year. She'd planned to modify it for home use—and give Fenley's Fripperies the exclusive rights to sell it—when she'd been told to take to her bed for the last five months of an uncomfortable pregnancy.

Although her twins were delivered safely, the aftereffects of the difficult birth left her weak and she'd fallen ill with pneumonia of the lungs. Her husband had taken her and the babies to stay with his parents in Shropshire while the promised invention languished in a workroom upstairs.

Denied his prize for the time being, Sam had hit upon the idea of visiting the club and learning more about the current experiments, in case any of the ladies had something else worth selling.

"It doesn't take much, Letts," he'd confided in her as she led him into the common area under Winthram's watchful gaze. "They may not be able to see the potential for profit, but with the right product and the Fenley flair, I can sell anything," he bragged.

"What about earplugs?" she asked now.

In Athena's Retreat's public lecture room, a knot of women stood arguing with one another, two wearing aprons stained in a multitude of hues never seen before in nature, in varying states of untidiness. Milly was on her hands and knees on the carpet by the tea tray, scolding Mala while daubing at a large dark stain. When Milly shifted, Letty spotted a hole that went through her apron and dress, revealing scorched petticoats beneath. Althea Dertlinger's eyeglasses were hung askew, and Flavia Smythe-Harrows appeared to be sleeping upright in a low-slung armchair, feathers sticking out from her hair at odd angles.

From somewhere upstairs came a heavy, rhythmic *thud*, and occasionally a low shudder vibrated from the floorboards. The entire club smelled like burnt orange peels and cheese.

Upon the announcement that the club would close, the atmosphere at Athena's Retreat had turned from endearing and collegial to . . .

"A hellscape is what it is," her brother announced, peering around the room with horror. "Why is that woman over there weeping? And what is on that woman's head—is that wig made of chiseled stone? And why does it smell like a dairy on fire?" Sam shook his head and backed up. "Forget what I said before. I am going back to work, where I belong, and . . . Oh my, would you look? Have you ever seen the like?"

Mouth open with an *ooh* of longing, Sam bounded over to where Mala Hill sat with a blanket in her lap. Two tiny eyes and a miniature nose peeked out from beneath the blue and gold flannel.

Making the introductions while Sam cooed with delight over the hedgehog, Letty sighed at the chaos.

There were two camps now at Athena's Retreat. Firmly behind Greycliff's decision to close the club except for the work currently ongoing in the laboratories were the older guard and those women who did not have powerful families or means at their disposal. They were working day and night at their experiments in case the club were to close.

The second group, spearheaded by Mala and Althea, was hatching plans to use the meeting in a week and a half hence to advocate for a full-scale rebellion against the Guardians. They refused to consider closing any portion of the club, and a flurry of correspondence had been launched between them and Violet. In the meantime, they were also rushing their experiments forward, determined to prove their work so vital and important the club could not close, lest their findings be lost forever.

Letty stood somewhere in the middle, if she could even stand upright. Despite her loyalty to Violet and her anxiety about the club, her mind was more and more focused on her work for the Rosewood.

She hadn't seen Grey. After having ushered in the apocalypse, he now seemed to be hiding away from the resulting petulance and plague.

The man confounded her.

First, he'd kissed her and upended every notion she'd had about a man touching his lips to hers.

Then, he'd apologized.

She'd never in a million years imagined such tenderness from the same person whose words had cut her to her bone. Letty felt lighter now that she no longer carried years' worth of animosity toward him. Still, not wanting to hit him over the head with a brick each time hadn't erased the frustration at his decision to close the social activities of the club.

"What type of invention are you looking for?" asked Flavia Smythe-Harrows. A tall, angular young woman with a sweet smile and kind brown eyes, she had an apologetic air about her most of the time. As the oldest of five daughters in a fabulously wealthy family, she was the only one of her siblings who cared more about jackdaws than jewels.

"I am searching for a novelty, my dear lady," Sam explained. "Something the public has never seen before. There's a reason Fenley's Fantastic Fripperies is the premier emporium in London. Why, we have the greatest—"

Letty wagged her finger, mouthing the words *Not now.*

Sam caught her glance and shot her a glimpse of his white teeth, a product of rigorous brushing with Dr. Aloysius Youngville's Terrifically Trustworthy Tooth Powder.

"I would put forward to any of the members the same generous offer I made to Mrs. Pettigrew. A split down the middle of profits and, if needs be, total anonymity on your part."

Milly scuttled over, asking questions about cosmetics, while Mala and Althea tried to pretend they weren't eavesdropping.

"What is going on here, Miss Fenley?"

A man-sized storm cloud rumbled at her back, his breath on her neck sending thrills down her spine. Too much to ask, she supposed, that he amble into a room like everyone else. No, he must *hover*.

Letty turned and regarded Grey as he took in the scene around them. "Things are getting out of hand, Lord Greycliff," she said. "This idea of a vote—"

"Numerous times I have tried to explain they do not get a vote," Grey said, wincing. "I even tried it in Latin. They simply . . . talk through me."

Try as she might, Letty had difficulty maintaining her animosity toward him as he puzzled over exactly how the ladies had managed to make him superfluous.

"I understand wanting to sell something novel, Mr. Fenley," Margaret was saying to Sam. "My question was about the utility of the object."

"Utility is in the eye of the beholder, Madame Gault," Sam explained. "You would be amazed at what I can convince a lady she needs. Why, there are those who don't believe a dab of eau de parfum is useful for anything but vanity."

Flavia shook her head, confused. "That is because it isn't useful. Not like a net or a piece of rope. Unless one needs a lure for something."

Without reservation, Sam turned the power of his grin on poor Flavia. Letty sighed as the young woman swayed—like a mouse caught in a cobra's gaze.

"A lure," Sam repeated. "Exactly. Imagine you wanted to attract a certain gentleman's attention and have dabbed a few drops of perfume on your wrists. That night, you dance across a crowded ballroom, and the gentleman in question drifts past. He catches the scent of . . ."

Sam raised his eyes, searching the air for a clue. "Is it lilacs he smells? Why, lilacs grew beneath his window as a child and recall his happiest memories." The other ladies quieted as Sam fell under his own spell.

Pounding a fist in his hand, he lowered his brows in determination. "He must find that elusive scent and the woman who is wearing it. He races through the room in search of the lady, determined to hold her in his arms."

"What on earth is he talking about?" Grey asked in disbelief.

Letty held up a hand. "Wait for it," she whispered.

"What is the utility of a bottle of scented liquid?" Sam asked. "Why, miss, to some it has none. To others . . ." He stared into Flavia's eyes as though they held the answer to life's questions.

"To others, it is the key to a lifetime of love."

For a moment, the scene Sam had painted unfolded before every woman in the room. Even Letty—who'd been subjected to this drivel every day of her life—heard the faint draw of a violin's bow across the strings, felt the cool slick silk of a ball gown beneath her fingertips, and caught the elusive scent of lilacs in the air. A vestige of the life before, when she, too, twirled around the dance floor, willing to believe herself beautiful for the space of a waltz.

Sam took a bow as the women around him burst into spontaneous applause. While they thronged her brother with questions regarding exactly what he would buy and whether Fenley's carried lilac-scented eau de parfum, Letty watched nervously as Althea scowled, whispering in Mala's ear, and Willy glared at them from the other side of the room, with her arms crossed over her chest.

"Your brother might make everything worse," Grey remarked.

"How can it get worse?" Letty glanced over her shoulder at the group of exhausted women. "Athena's Retreat is about to melt down around us, and not because we've set anything on fire. You've given us a death sentence."

"A *death* sentence?" Grey sighed. "I can see where your brother learned his powers of description. Come with me."

"Oh, for the love of . . ." Letty tried not to ogle anything hard and firm about his person as Grey walked down the corridor outside the lecture hall. Ogling him would diminish her irritation with his high-handedness.

"Here." Grey ushered her into one of the community workrooms. There were three such spaces in Athena's Retreat. Street-facing, the windows caught natural light during the day and the eerie orange glow of the streetlights at dusk. Three of the walls were covered with large slabs of slate. Beneath the blackboards were low shelves filled with periodicals from across the globe, alongside classic books in a variety of disciplines. Two settees and myriad mismatched chairs were scattered across the room, and a long worktable stood near the windows, littered with paper, inkwells, and a few battered candelabras.

Grey leaned one hip against the table, assessing Letty with an inscrutable expression.

Except he wasn't inscrutable. Not anymore.

They were not friends, but they weren't enemies, either, despite his wish to close the club. They had finally managed to speak with one another on small matters without listening for hidden meanings. The more time they'd spent in one another's company, the more Letty had learned to read his face.

Right now, although he'd assumed a position of irritation, his eyes were clear of any storm clouds and his mouth remained relaxed. Resisting the urge to pull at her cap ribbons, Letty clasped her hands at her waist, mimicking the pose of a biddable woman.

It wasn't easy.

"Could the members invent a folding stool for you to carry?" Grey said. "This way I do not have to argue with the top of your cap."

Biddable went out the door.

Letty rested her fists on her hips. "Why not issue pronouncements seated in a chair while I stand?" she countered. "This way I do not have permanent pain in my neck, as your head is so swollen it floats to the treetops like a hot-air balloon."

Preparing herself for a riposte, she had no warning for the shocking thrill launching into her chest when Greycliff laughed.

Laughed!

His smile banished the shadows; a tiny sun punching through the clouds, warming her to her toes.

Letty rarely attempted to entertain others. Her manner was too prickly, and she'd no talent for humorous anecdotes or devastating bons mots. For a glimpse of that smile, however, she'd consider riding on horseback at Astley's.

Then the smile disappeared, and surprise flashed across Grey's face—as though bending his lips had triggered a shock.

"We are a pair, are we not?" he asked. "Might we someday have a discussion without you exaggerating my head size?"

She couldn't help it. A grin of her own burst forth. "Not unless you run out of moronic jokes about my perfectly normal height."

"What did you want to speak with me about?" she asked.

"Ah." He grimaced. "I hadn't anticipated the consequences of my announcement. If I am honest, I will admit you have a certain amount of . . . foresight that I am lacking."

Right now, the heavens prepared space for their newest saint when Letty did not roll her eyes at him and say, *I could have told you so.* Angels were measuring her for a robe. Rather than gloat and point out that a large head did not necessarily equate to the possession of intelligence with which to fill it, she took the high road.

Sort of.

"Encountered a mission you cannot run on your own, have you?" Letty chuckled and reached to pat his arm in mock sympathy just as he leaned toward her, and her palm landed on his chest. Like a spark to tinder, a thick, heady awareness of how close they stood saturated the air.

This wasn't like the other day, when he took her into his arms and delivered comfort—it was charged and insistent. Her fingertips brushed the top button of his cream-colored shirt, but she couldn't seem to draw her hand back to where it belonged. It belonged at her side and not right above his heart, rising and falling with each breath.

"I have considered what you said yesterday," he said, brows slightly raised as her regarded her hand. Neither of them moved. "You were right. I do not have a full grasp of the entirety of what you do here, and I have resolved to investigate more deeply. Did . . ." He hesitated. "Did Arthur get involved in the ladies' experiments?"

"Oh, never," Letty assured him. "Arthur's near godhood among the members owes less to what he *did* do than what he *didn't* do—or say— when an experiment turned into a dog's dinner."

"I knew it," he said, punching the air slightly.

"Because," she continued, "they are so used to condemnation or ridicule that when someone simply listens, the act of listening is a form of validation."

Grey sobered and placed his own warm palm over the back of her hand. "I understand."

Letty knew him well enough by now to accept that he did understand.

"When will you begin?" she asked.

"I thought I might begin with you," he said, his eyes pinning her with an intensity that took her breath. One might have thought her skirts had been set alight when a wave of heat rushed through her body.

"I would . . ." Letty stumbled when she took a step back, and Grey clasped her elbow to steady her. Dizzy from the contact, she wobbled away like a colt and walked over to one of the slate boards, well away from him. If he had even an inkling of what her overheated brain and traitorous body wanted to do with him, she would ruin everything.

Here was her chance to impress upon him the necessity of Athena's Retreat—or simply to impress him.

"This is a common workroom," she explained, picking a shard of soft chalk from a basket. "Sometimes when a member is struggling with a particular problem, they will leave it on one of the boards as an invitation for comment."

Grey nodded. "I see. If Violet had a question about Avogadro's law, for example, another chemist—"

"Not necessarily." Letty pointed to a diagram someone else had already chalked. "You asked why I could not do my calculations from home."

Recognizing Miss Adelaide Timms's beautiful hand, Letty had a moment of regret before she despoiled the slate with markings of her own.

"First off, it is impossible to think when you share a house with four sisters and a brother," she said as she wrote.

The equation dealt with Miss Timms's work following on John Scott Russell's theory of a wave of translation.

"Second, Miss Timms is a physicist, with an interest in hydrodynamics. What she is positing here has mathematical implications, too. She is inviting another viewpoint, hoping it might reveal a different path by which to find a solution."

Tapping her teeth, Letty regarded the diagram and the equations chalked beneath. Her toes tingled in anticipation of sinking into the problem before her. "You see, Russell observed a phenomenon in a canal where a solitary wave traveled for miles without changing speed or height. He transferred his observations to the laboratory and is in the process of writing his findings. In the meantime, Miss Timms has developed theories to explain his subsequent discoveries about these waves."

Letty chalked the expression for the velocity of propagation of the wave.

$$v = \sqrt{g(h + k)}$$

"Now, k is the height of the crest of the wave above the plane of repose . . ."

The walls melted away, and a quiet canal stood before her. A perfectly rounded wave rolled past her in the serene water. It traveled at an unchanging speed, keeping its shape within the confines of the grassy banks. Superimposed upon the wave was the expression Letty had just written on the board, shifting in real time as the phenomenon played out before her eyes.

". . . another piece of chalk, Miss Fenley?"

A voice from farther down the canal interrupted her concentration, and the variables tumbled over themselves and sank to the bottom of the waterway.

". . . think? Miss Fenley?"

Letty blinked at the wall of navy wool now standing before her. With a shake of her head, she came back to herself and tipped her head to meet Grey's worried gaze.

"I beg your pardon, my lord. What was your question?"

Slowly, Grey took her hand in his. Whatever was he . . . ?

Clenched in her fingers was the tiniest sliver of chalk.

"Oh," she said.

With equal care, he put his hands on her shoulders and turned her around to face the slate board. Her shaky hand covered the entire surface in an inelegant series of equations and diagrams based on Russell's expression for the velocity of propagation of the wave.

"Oh," she said. Again.

A tingle of pleasure spread over her when he leaned down and spoke into her ear. "I don't know that I've ever seen such concentration, Miss Fenley. I count myself lucky you do not bring the same effort to conjuring insults."

It took a moment for the tingling to subside and his words to sink in. "What do you mean?" She whirled around to face him, scowling. "I'll have you know my insults are crafted with the same amount of..."

He hadn't removed his hands when she turned, and when his thumbs glided over her collarbone, the sensation robbed her of speech. She shivered with awareness.

"Are you cold?"

Without waiting for an answer, Grey ran his palms down her arms and back up again. The friction made her the tiniest bit delirious, and Letty took a step closer to him, skirts swirling around his legs, breasts barely brushing against the soft wool of his jacket. Beneath her own layers of cotton and lawn, her nipples furled, aching for similar friction.

"I am..." Letty tried to think of the word, but her brain was useless, sabotaged by every other part of her body clamoring for more touch.

Darkening eyes, the color of a coming storm, held her gaze as he slowly lowered his mouth toward hers.

"Miss Fenley. Just the person I wished to speak with." Flavia popped her head through the doorway. "Oh, hello, Lord Greycliff."

Like tearing a plaster from a wound, Letty ripped herself from Grey's embrace—goodness, when had he embraced her?—and crossed her arms over her chest.

"Hello, Flavia," Letty said in a strangled voice. She hazarded a peek at Grey's face. He appeared completely unperturbed, other than a slight flush delineating the arc of his cheekbones. A faint scent of bergamot hovered in the air.

"How can I help you?" she asked, clearing her throat.

Flavia's head swiveled between Grey and Letty, and a speculative expression crossed her face.

"I didn't mean to interrupt, but . . ." A single feather dropped from Flavia's hair and wafted to the floor. Grey stared at the feather, then at Flavia's head.

Flavia swooped it up. "I am determined to show my family the value of my studies. After having spoken with Mr. Fenley, I have found a way. I need your expertise as my creativity and inspiration are running into an insurmountable obstacle."

"Whatever could that be?" Grey asked, appearing intrigued.

"Math," Flavia whimpered. "It hurts my head."

Letty wanted to point out that the biggest obstacle Flavia faced was a refusal to learn long division, but she refrained, in keeping with her resolution to be more patient with the members.

"Of course I would be happy to help." She turned back to Grey. "If you will excuse me?"

Grey bowed to them both, and Letty hustled Flavia off without peeking back. In the future, she would try to avoid being alone with him until she saw him as just another obdurate acquaintance.

Anything more would be a disaster.

Letty could bring no further ruin upon herself and, by extension, everyone else around her.

She must fight to keep her armor intact.

9

D O YOU HAVE an opinion on suffrage, Madame Gault?" asked Lucy, the oldest of Letty's sisters as she leaned over her plate, elbow dragging a stream of gravy over the tablecloth when she gestured at their supper guest.

"Why should she be forced to have an opinion, Lucy?" Sam interjected. "They're a load of trouble if you ask me. Especially if they're like yours. Obnoxious and—"

"Is it true the Frenchwomen favor passementerie trims over lace this season, madame?" Da inquired. "Seems to me we've had enough of these dark-colored braids and cording."

"Are the Frenchmen truly as ferocious as we've heard?" someone else piped up over Da's question. "Do they guillotine each other on sight, or must there be an insult first?"

"I like your dress."

This last was Sadie, the baby of the family, who had been much taken with Margaret earlier when she'd graciously allowed Sadie to hold her thick, soft ermine muff.

Truth be told, the entire Fenley clan had been taken with Margaret when Letty brought her home for a roast last week. Mam and Da had issued another invitation for today, and Margaret had accepted with alacrity.

At first, Letty had been frightened that one of her many voluble siblings would say something about her past, and she would be forced to watch any respect or admiration die in Margaret's gaze when the truth came out.

She should have known better.

Instead, as the six Fenley children argued and teased each other, Margaret made her way steadily through two servings of roast and gravy, roasted potatoes, braised leeks, stewed carrots and cress without having to say a word.

After dinner, they retired to the cramped parlor, where Margaret sat at the chessboard opposite Da, and Letty entertained her younger sisters. Anyone joining their revelry would have had no clue about the Fenley family's great wealth.

After Letty's society debut met with such spectacular failure, the family had retrenched. They'd remained in their tiny house in Clerkenwell and kept to themselves. Letty's fateful choice to believe Nevin hadn't just affected her life—it had changed the lives of everyone around her, and she carried that knowledge with her every time she left the safety of her family's embrace.

Letty organized a game of pass the slipper while Sam read aloud from the broadsheets and tried to make witty asides to catch Margaret's attention.

"You're cheating, Lucy," Sadie complained. "I can see your eye through the space between your fingers."

"Oh ho, you sneak-a-muffin." Letty grabbed a scarf draped over the side of an armchair and wrapped it around Lucy's eyes while the girls clapped their approval.

"There now, Sadie. You can't complain, though, when Mam asks Lucy to keep an *eye* on you and she lets you wander off," Letty teased.

"Well, *eye've* had enough of your whinging," said Lucy, patting the scarf to keep it from slipping down her nose. "Don't lose *sight* of how kind I am to you most times."

Sam chuckled. "We've turned a blind eye to your cheating ways for too long, Lucy."

Letty spun her sister around once more and gave her a little squeeze on her shoulder. Poor Lucy was almost marriageable age. She'd a large enough dowry to attract a gentleman of good standing, but because of Letty's reputation, she'd be relegated to the fringes of society.

Regrets wove themselves between her ankles as she played with her sisters and mocked her brother. They sat atop her shoulder, whispering in her ear the next day when Margaret stopped by to thank Letty again for the invitation.

"The meal was delicious, and your family have been wonderful." Margaret tapped the pile of papers that buried the scarred oak table beneath. "I would love to repay your kindness. Mala, Althea, and I are going to visit a delightful tearoom in Mayfair if you—"

"I cannot," Letty said quickly. "I have already eaten and have far too much work." The refusal had come out too fast, like a slap, and she flushed. Better, though, for these women to think poorly of her. Better for them to keep their distance, no matter how marvelous it might be to sit with a group of women and laugh about nothing.

Letty wouldn't be responsible for anyone else's pain and embarrassment because of her stupid choices.

A few hours later, however, she regretted her haste, if only because she was starving. Donning her pelisse, she crept down the back stairway of the club, hoping to avoid encountering Margaret and the embarrassment of refusing a second invitation, and careful to hold her breath while passing Milly and Willy's workrooms. It smelled awfully strange in there.

"Can I touch this?" a man asked.

"Oh, *yes*. Please do," a woman answered.

Letty slapped her hand to her forehead and pulled it down her face, as though to wash away the incongruity of the words she'd just heard and the tone in which they were said.

"What about this? Can I touch this part?"

"Yes, you can touch everywhere. Just be gentle. It won't be any fun if it goes off half-cocked."

The occupants of the darkened workroom either did not hear Letty's knock or did not care who stood outside and begged entrance. Pushing open the door, Letty peered into the enormous chamber.

A long, low table stood almost directly in front of her. Against the wall, behind the table, was a bank of waist-high cabinets littered with jars and canisters of varying heights. The windows in this room let out onto a side yard where nothing grew, and were framed with black canvas curtains, thick enough to block out any sunlight. In the front half of the room, some of the curtains had been tied back and the windows thrown open, leaving the other half semidarkened.

There, at the far end of the room, a bucket of water sat on a piece of slate. Next to it were three figures, garbed in heavy canvas aprons with cloths tied around their faces. Two of the figures had tucked their hair away beneath plain white caps and wore tight-sleeved day dresses without any ruffles or extra petticoats to fill them out.

The third figure wore trousers and had left his hair dangerously exposed.

Greycliff stood between Milly and Willy, holding a pair of tongs over the bucket. A silvery substance sat in the grip of the iron pincers.

"Sodium is an alkali metal," Willy explained. "Sir Humphry

Davy—a complicated man, but a genius, nonetheless—discovered pure sodium around forty years ago. He used the process of electrolysis to separate it from caustic soda. When you mix sodium with water you get an exothermic—"

Whatever lesson Willy had hoped to impart was abandoned when Grey lost his grip on the tongs and dropped the lump of sodium into the bucket of water. Within seconds, steam rose from the bucket as the water bubbled.

"Run for cover!" Milly shouted. She grabbed Grey's elbow and pulled him behind an overturned table, its provenance unknowable, due to the blackened, scarred surface. She and Willy ducked their heads, and Letty bolted behind a low cabinet a few feet away.

Grey, on the other hand, barely made it behind the barrier before the reaction of the sodium metal with the water created sodium hydroxide, releasing hydrogen gas.

As Milly and Willy had seen the outcome of this experiment many times, they didn't bother to watch, but Letty peered out from her hiding place to witness the resulting explosion. An eruption of sparks lit the dim room and revealed Grey's expression in startling clarity. The cloth had slipped from his face, and a look of marvel had transformed his stern countenance into that of a young man.

Oh, he was beautiful even in his iciest of moods. No one could ever find fault with the precise slope of his cheekbones, the hauteur of his perfectly shaped nose, and his piercing eyes. In the brilliance of the flames before him, however, the expression of sheer delight increased his beauty tenfold. Something akin to awe forced the breath from Letty's chest.

Who might this man be, newly revealed in the white fire of an elemental reaction? What reasons would Grey have to hide this part of himself from the world?

"Did you *see* that? Did you see?" Grey leaped to his feet when the last spark had died and ran over to the bucket, heedless of the puddles.

"As I was saying"—Milly bustled over, lifting the hem of her dress while trying to step around the mess and recapture Grey's attention—"the explosion is an exothermic reaction. 'Exothermic' means—"

"What if we were to dump a load of this in a lake," he enthused. "That would be amazing, wouldn't it?"

Milly blinked, and a considering glimmer entered her eyes. Willy cleared her throat. "The purpose of this experiment is not simply to create an explosion. You see, an exothermic reaction—"

"Or what if we made tiny balls of the stuff and tossed them into puddles or fountains for a lark?" Grey spotted Letty and waved her over. "Miss Fenley. I say, did you ever see the like?"

Like a magnet, his unfettered excitement drew Letty closer despite the warning bell in the back of her head.

When two volatile substances combined, the reaction resulted in an excess of light and heat.

If she let herself forget, someone was going to get burned.

GREY HELPED MILLY open the rest of the laboratory windows. He couldn't remember the last time he'd enjoyed himself this much.

Who knew sciencing could be fun? Why, he'd have paid much more attention to his tutor when he'd droned on about substances and Newton and what all if he'd known about *blowing things up*.

"Lord Greycliff, what are you doing?"

Letty Fenley advanced upon them, skirting the water on the floor and waving away the last of the smoke. Grey grinned, then pointed to the half-empty barrel.

"Blowing things up."

Milly heaved a sigh. "Observing an experiment illustrating the principles of ..."

Blowing things up, he mouthed at Letty.

He'd stopped in here an hour ago after having been accosted earlier in the day by Althea Dertlinger. She'd complained about the noise coming from the workrooms and Grey decided he would kill two birds with one stone. He would keep his promise to Letty and, at the same time, take the opportunity to instill more discipline overall. He would institute a schedule for the entire club, listing when certain experiments could be run as well as a new set of safety rules. Each of the experiments would have to fall beneath the new set of guidelines, and any exceptions would require permission from him.

He'd spoken to Winthram about it, but his plan had fallen on unreceptive ears.

"More *discipline*? Guidelines?" Winthram had pushed back a thick lock of hair that had fallen over one eye. "Mrs. Kneland would go visit with every intention of quieting them, and next thing you know they're doubling their experiments. Mr. Kneland read them the riot act about once a fortnight only to turn 'round and run errands for them. Have you heard the term 'force of nature'?"

Many a time Grey had undertaken missions where he'd had to extricate information from a recalcitrant source. There were techniques he preferred not to speak about that haunted him to this day. While he wouldn't go to such extremes here, he knew he could certainly handle two elderly chemists with a minimum of fuss.

"I won't be too hard on the old dears," he'd said, "but I cannot allow them to disrupt the equanimity of the other club members."

Shaking his head, Winthram hadn't bothered to hide his disbelief. "Watch and see."

Of course, that was before Willy tried explaining the difference between exothermic and endo-whatever-ithic and he *blew things up*!

Some of the smoke must have gotten in her throat, for Willy sounded strangled when she spoke now. "We weren't blowing things up. We were giving a demonstration of an exothermic reaction."

"A demonstration of why half the club is in arms over the flashing lights and loud noises coming from your workroom," Letty said. Setting her hands on her hips, she gave Milly and Willy the talking-to Grey had come here for in the first place. "If the two of you . . ."

My God. There *had* been flashing lights and loud noises, and he'd not even flinched.

How could he have let down his guard?

The first few months in the army, Grey had existed in a fog of sheer panic that the discharge of muzzles and cannons would set off a seizure. He'd maintained an endless vigilance in case an eruption caused a relapse—an innate watchfulness that never left him. Over the years in the Department, such caution had saved his life and the lives of his operatives.

Vigilance hadn't even occurred to him in the laboratory a few minutes ago. The realization froze him in his tracks.

Letty continued. "Some of the ladies don't have the constitutions for sudden explosions."

Neither had he. Excitement had raced through his veins like the headiest of wines, and he'd forgotten to be cautious. To be discerning. To be removed. The weeks here had lulled him into a false sense of safety.

"Well, this has been illustrative. I can understand why Miss Dertlinger has lodged complaints about the noise and the smell." Grey delivered the pronouncement in the same tone with which he chastised his operatives. "I've seen enough here to satisfy my curiosity. Keep the noise and the smell confined to the workroom, ladies."

Willy paused in the act of setting up a second experiment, and Milly's sweet face crumpled at the icy inflection in his voice.

Good.

Excellent.

Grey did not want these women to labor under any misapprehensions. He brushed past Letty Fenley as he kept talking. "While I appreciate your passion, it would be for the best if you spent less time setting fires and more time planning for the eventuality they will be put out permanently."

By the time he reached the door, his own enthusiasm had been safely doused.

"Why are you angry with them?"

Letty had left the workroom and was trotting behind him, her little legs working twice as hard to match his stride. Sighing, he slowed his pace.

"I am not angry. I have no strong feelings about them whatsoever," he said, glancing at the woman next to him, her linen cap slowly slipping down the back of her head, revealing a sliver of white scalp. It struck him as intimate and far too vulnerable. He looked away.

"I am doing what you asked, Miss Fenley. Trying to ascertain what it is about their work that necessitates that Athena's Retreat remain open."

"And have you come to any conclusions?" she asked.

Grey murmured something noncommittal and increased his pace. Yesterday when they had been alone in the community workroom, he had come far too close to crossing a line. The kiss they had shared in his office needed to be a singular occurrence.

"I have concluded the threat to Athena's Retreat remains unchanged. No matter how brilliant the club's members or how fascinating their experiments—"

"If you ask me, starting with Milly and Willy's work was a mistake," Letty interrupted. "Now, if you wish to speak of fascinating, take an afternoon to visit with Mrs. Abernathy, who is investigating Gauss's claim of the possibility of non-Euclidean geometries. It simply boggles the mind."

Grey rubbed his hand over his forehead. He should have sent Winthram to speak with Willy and Milly after all.

"Miss Fenley. My mind has no need of boggling . . ."

Her brows arched. "That's not a word."

". . . because the threat is still out there."

Grey had heard nothing from Melton yet on why Sir Ramsey would be backing Armitage's bid for the directorship. He'd discreetly set one of his own men to sniffing about, but they were more suited to gathering information on the general populace than on the aristocracy, and the next meeting was only two weeks away.

Time was running out.

For all of them.

10

G O BACK TO YOUR CHILDREN, WHERE YOU BELONG!
SCIENCE IS A SHAM!

LISTEN TO THE LORD INSTEAD OF LECTURES!

"Do they get points for alliteration?" asked Milly. A group of club members stood at the windows of the second-floor lecture hall and gazed into the street.

"I always appreciate alliterating," said Mala Hill. "The art of alliteration is actually—"

"Don't," Althea warned, pointing a finger at her friend. "Don't start. It isn't funny."

Mala muttered a few more creative slogans under her breath as they examined the crowd of men on the walkway below, who were holding their handmade signs and shouting at them.

From this distance, Letty could not be sure if they were the same men who had terrorized the shopgirl a few weeks before. They seemed to have changed their focus of attack from women stealing men's wages to women having large brains.

"'Stop Wasting Women's Wits on Wicked Work,'" Mala said.

Althea rolled her eyes, but a few of the other women laughed.

"'Down with Thinking, Up with Drinking,'" Flavia offered.

"That's not alliterative," Margaret objected.

"It's funny, though," Mala replied. "What about 'Stop with Science and Start with Service'?"

"What a load of rot," Althea declared. "A handful of signs and a few ruffians aren't going to throw us off course. They can't even be bothered to think of slogans as clever as ours!"

Winthram appeared in the entrance and gestured to Letty.

"Can you not get them to leave?" she asked.

Winthram shook his head. "I told them to pike off, and one said they're going nowhere till the reporters show up."

"Reporters?"

This had the hallmarks of a disaster.

"Lord Greycliff?" she asked hopefully.

Winthram shook his head. "Lord Greycliff is at his club. I've sent a footman, but it will take an hour at least."

They could cower indoors and let Grey come rescue them. But what if the men were not content to stay outside? The roomful of women relied on Letty. She, in turn, had no one to rely on.

"We are not going to cower behind these walls, Winthram."

Letty started down the stairs, Winthram at her heels.

"Beg your pardon, miss, but Lord Greycliff is teaching me to fence. A lot of the fighting happens here," Winthram said earnestly, tapping his forehead. "You might not want to go for a direct attack. If you let your temper guide your thrust, you—oh, wait. Miss? Miss?"

Winthram's summons echoed in the hallway as Letty marched toward the crowd of men without even pausing for her bonnet or coat. Winthram was only partly wrong. If you let emotion guide you, you would expose yourself to pain.

But if you stoked your rage, if you shrouded yourself in an anger deep and pure, you encased yourself and could never be hurt again. She stalked outside, furious that these men would belittle the women upstairs by characterizing them with slogans, by diminishing their intelligence and their gifts as distractions from their physical functions.

Standing on the top step, she cupped her hands around her lips. "You will disperse at once," she shouted, her voice carrying over the crowd, "or I will personally take each and every one of your signs and shove them up your—"

"Something's wrong with Davey!"

A commotion among the men drowned out Letty's scolding. One of their numbers fell to the ground, his hands to his throat. The crowd around him pitched and heaved like a wave as members on the outside of the group tried to see what had happened, while those closest to the man who had collapsed pushed back against the others.

"What is happening?" she called.

Receiving no reply, Letty hesitated. There were a good thirty men in the crowd, all of them larger than she was. She should turn around and go inside for help.

Instead, taking a deep breath, she plunged into the crowd.

"Move aside," she ordered the morass of elbows and backs. By the time she had made her way to the fallen man, some of the demonstrators had quit the scene, leaving behind their painted signs. A few of them had stopped on the street corner and said a word or two to a thin, stoop-shouldered man, who had then pressed something in their hands.

A shout pulled Letty's attention back to the prone body before her. A fellow protestor had unbuttoned Davey's shirt, revealing a thatch of ginger hair, and slapped him about his face. His skin had an awful bluish tint to it. Letty knelt and grabbed the man's clammy hand.

"Is he breathing?" she asked the nearest man.

"No, milady," the man replied. "He was shouting somethin' fierce, then fell like someone hit him from behind."

"Are you wanting me to fetch the bellows from the fireplace in the parlor?" Winthram said. He had pushed through the crowd and now crouched beside her. "I remember in one lecture, the gent from Aberdeen said to use it for when there's no breathing in a body."

"You'll do no such thing. Those bellows would be filthy. Step aside and let me treat this man." Mrs. Sweet now joined them, along with her carpetbag. The men who'd said nothing to Letty and Winthram objected at her presence.

"Here, leave him be," said an older man, his unkempt beard strewn with grey hairs and what might have been the leavings from this morning's breakfast. "He's overwrought, like. Give him time to rest."

A man in a brown felted hat hawked loudly, then spat perilously close to where Mrs. Sweet was kneeling. She propped Davey's head at a slight angle, then rolled a cloth and set it beneath his neck so it remained stationary.

"'E's not resting. 'E's dead," the man in the brown hat said. "Lookit his face. Why don't you leave the man be? Ain't proper one such as you should be touchin' him."

"One such as me?" said Mrs. Sweet, never looking away from her work. "Do you mean the one person here who can save this man's life?"

Without waiting for an answer, Mrs. Sweet ordered Winthram to follow her directions as she took a small set of medical bellows from her bag. Despite mutterings about where Black women belonged and how Davey would be better served being carted over to the nearest pub, Mrs. Sweet kept her eyes forward and her touch gentle.

A combination of her leftover irritation at the demonstration and her fear for Mrs. Sweet propelled Letty to her feet. She picked up Brown Hat's discarded sign and pushed it against his chest.

"Shame on you," she said. "Trying to terrify a woman who wants to save your friend's life."

Winthram had pulled Davey into his lap and held the man's chest in a reverse embrace, his arms beneath the breastbone. Davey's own arms were limply draped over Winthram's shoulders in a listless pose of surrender while Mrs. Sweet pumped the small bellows into the man's mouth.

"What are you doing? What's she doing with Davey?" Brown Hat cried. The murmurs in the crowd grew louder, and Letty's heart pounded.

"She is saving his life," Letty exclaimed.

"Better off if you call a doctor," the man with the grey beard countered. "Not proper a woman be touchin' him like this."

His friends in the crowd repeated the call for a doctor, some castigating Mrs. Sweet for trying to take a man's place as a healer.

As Mrs. Sweet and Winthram worked furiously behind her, Letty searched about desperately for some means of escape. Within moments, however, the insults turned to shouts of surprise. In the back of the crowd, someone grabbed the men by the scruffs of their necks and tossed them into the unswept street.

"'Ere now, leggo," Brown Hat shouted as a fist emerged and caught hold of his topcoat. Before he could draw breath for a second complaint, he flew through the air, revealing Greycliff, who brushed his hands together with an air of satisfaction.

Grey Beard held his hands up and backed away. "Don't want no trouble, milord."

"Really?"

Letty trembled at the fury in Grey's voice as the other man turned tail and hurried away.

"Stop," Grey commanded.

The man stopped and peered over his shoulder with trepidation. "My lord?"

"You forgot this." Grey hurled a sign reading FILL BELLIES, NOT BRAINS at Grey Beard's chest. "If I ever see you again anywhere near these women, I will take that sign . . ."

"And shove it right up your . . . ," Letty said, under her breath.

"And knock you over the head with it," Grey finished, shooting Letty a quelling frown. He came to stand at her side, one hand resting slightly inside his topcoat. She leaned closer and squinted, making out the flash of a blade.

"It won't do us any good if the resident nobleman beheads the peasantry," she whispered.

In a fraction of a second, the blade disappeared and he held out an empty hand.

"Clever trick," she said with approval. She'd forgotten for a moment that his work with the Department likely meant he'd acquired a few dangerous skills along the way. "Is it up your sleeve?"

Expressionless, he set a finger to the side of his nose and winked. Despite the acid burn of fear still in her belly, Letty had to laugh. The moments Grey exposed his other self, the man not encased in a suit of ice, he became irresistible.

Damn him.

The bulk of the men had dispersed by the time Mrs. Sweet had packed her bag and Winthram had helped Davey to his feet. Brown Hat had ventured back, and now he looped one arm under Davey's armpit, steering him toward the street.

A slight wash of color still high on his cheeks, Grey stood in front of Brown Hat and raised a hand.

"Do you not have something to say to the woman who saved your life?" Grey asked Davey.

Davey's unfocused eyes rolled around. As he squinted at Mrs. Sweet, he swayed forward. "Was an angel come and breathed the life into me," Davey whispered. "Thought I were in heaven."

Brown Hat was having none of that from his friend. "Wouldn't've been sick in the first place if not for women like these." He gestured at Beacon House with his chin. "Wife went and left him. Got herself a job, she did, and now he's taken to drink."

Grey's mouth thinned with distaste. "How is it these women's fault that this man makes himself sick?"

"An angel, I tell you," Davey whispered.

"Beggin' your pardon, milord," Brown Hat said, "but Mr. Armitage explains it in his speeches. There are noblemen there, too, like you. Mr. Armitage will tell you how these ladies upset the social order. Make them think they're too good to clean and cook for us. Ask for more than is their due."

As repulsive as she found his views, Letty could not deny that Brown Hat believed what he said. He had the conviction of the zealot.

"That man will be weak for a long time." Mrs. Sweet stood and brushed her skirts. "I'd like you to send him home in your carriage and spare him the walk."

Grey and Letty stared at her, incredulous.

"Are you saying you wish to send this man—who didn't even thank you—home in my carriage?" Grey asked.

Mrs. Sweet wiped her hands on her skirt. "Whether he possesses any gratitude is beside the point. I worked hard to keep him alive. What will it do for my reputation if he dies five minutes later? It will go even worse for me."

Grey exchanged a look with Winthram, who shook his head, indicating surrender. "All right. Winthram, see the man arrives home alive."

Winthram's brow rose. "How'm I to do that?"

"I don't know. Just do it," Grey growled. Then he took Letty by the elbow. "And as for you—"

"See here . . . ," Letty objected.

Turning away from the club, he steered her through the kitchen door into Beacon House.

"Were you aware of how much danger—" He broke off when a frazzled footman came into the kitchen.

"See to Mrs. Sweet," Grey ordered the boy. "Tell her she has the rest of the day free, and be sure to tell Cook as well. Otherwise, Mrs. Sweet will protest."

The boy took off running, and Grey gentled his grip.

"How much danger," he continued, pulling Letty through the back hallway, past Mrs. Sweet's office, and into a stillroom, "you put yourself in just now? Rushing into a crowd of men who meant you no good, without anyone at your back?"

Letty could say nothing to this stranger beside her. Where had the enigmatic ice prince disappeared to, and who was this fevered brute? Goodness, she'd found him attractive when he'd barely blinked an eye, but now that his hair was out of place and his face clouded with thunder, he was . . .

"You are insufferable," she told him. "Everything was under control."

"By sheer chance, I came home early from my club and heard those men's voices," he said. Letting go of his hold on her, he lit a candle and placed it on a clean wooden table.

Bunches of salvia, lavender, and lemon verbena hung from a drying rack. On either side of the cozy little room were shelves stocked with baskets of more herbs; rosemary and fenugreek, rose hip and valerian. Small jars of ointments and salves stood next to stacks of folded linen strips beneath the baskets. At the end of the space, a built-in cupboard reached from floor to ceiling, housing Mrs. Sweet's more potent ingredients for her cures.

"After we see to your hand, I will speak with Winthram about securing the perimeter of the club. And there will be no more talk of a vote. Do you hear me?"

"My hand?" Letty stared at the trickle of blood on her palm in shock. She'd taken off her gloves in her workroom and forgotten to put them back on when Mala had come to warn her earlier. The injury must have happened when she grabbed the rough wood of Brown Hat's sign. She hadn't noticed, but now that Grey had drawn her attention to it, she shivered.

"Here." Grey grabbed one of the folded strips of linen and held one end against her palm with his thumb.

At his touch, a tiny flower of awareness bloomed in her belly. This close, she could see the individual threads of the gold embroidery on his garnet waistcoat. His breath ghosted across her brow as he slowly wound the cloth around her hand and tucked the end in neatly.

"Let go of me, Greycliff. I am not a child," she said, forcing the words from deep within her, hoping they sounded confident.

Still holding her hand, he took a step forward as she moved backward until she hit a cupboard door.

"No, not a child, but you have been just as careless of your own safety. You are not allowed back in the club until you promise never to do such a foolhardy thing again," Grey said.

"You cannot make such demands," she protested. "You have no claim over me."

"This is my claim," he told her right before he took her mouth in a searing kiss.

She'd known this would happen.

They had been rushing toward each other's touch ever since their first kiss, no matter how hard they tried to stay away.

The touch of his lips lit a fire in her veins, and his thick, heady scent filled her nose, mouth, and skin. Lust slammed into her, sending her reeling, as an echo of her heartbeat pounded between her legs. On impulse, she tilted her hips forward, straining against his hard thigh. Bright white sparks of pleasure coursed through her, burning a path behind her half-closed eyelids. Pieces of the world around them vanished as her focus narrowed to the demands of her foolish body.

Slowly, he caressed her arms from wrists to shoulders, then followed the curve of her waist, pulling her closer. Afraid her knees might give out, Letty clutched at his lapels. A low rumble of approval in his chest vibrated against her breasts, and he smoothed his palm along the crease where her bottom met her leg. The sensible part of her brain, the part that had navigated the torturous path of the past six years, sent out an alarm.

The rest of her burned with reckless joy.

Grey softened his grip and nuzzled her cheek, the velvety warmth of his mouth waking tiny flutters in her chest. Light as promises spoken against her skin, he made a trail of kisses to the curve of her neck, where her collar began. Her lips brushed his temple, and she tasted the salt of his skin with the tip of her tongue.

He rewarded her daring with the swift return of his mouth to hers, giving her deep, hungry, intoxicating kisses that flipped the sky over to rest at her feet. At the same time, the evidence of his desire came between them, hard against her belly.

"I want...," she whispered into his ear, pressing herself even tighter against him. A delightful, steady burn at the juncture of her thighs spread throughout her. She'd been intimate with Nevin, but nothing about that uncomfortable coupling had prepared her for the clamoring need that now had her wanting to writhe against Grey in search of unnameable relief.

Grey captured Letty's chin and forced her gaze to his.

"Tell me what you want, Letty," he said, his voice low and guttural. The clouds in his eyes roiled as his chest rose and fell. "I won't do anything unless you give me leave."

"I ache," she confided.

"Yes." He bent his head and set his lips a hairsbreadth away from hers. "You want me to take that away for you."

"Please."

As he ate at her mouth, his kisses were slick and rough at the same time, and she thrilled to his intrusion. Heedless of propriety, she wrapped her arms around his neck and let her fingers rest in the thick waves of his hair.

The force of his kisses left her lips throbbing, but instead of pulling away, she met his need with more of her own. Craving the taste of him, she lapped against his tongue like a cat licking cream, and he kneaded her bottom with his hands, then lifted her off the floor, pinning her shoulders to the cabinet. Seeking purchase, her legs came around his waist, and she whimpered as the invisible string tied to the center of her pleasure tightened.

Dressed for the spring chill, Letty now resented the protection of her many layers. The fine lawn of her chemise, the corseting of canvas and bone, and the thick bodice of wool stood between her and the friction she needed.

Clever man, he understood. Grey pulled her thighs farther apart as she tipped her hips to meet him. An unfilled need hammered at her, and even through the cage of her voluminous skirts, she could feel his erection pulse.

Letty lost her bearings. All she knew was the heat of his mouth, all she could feel was his cock between her legs, all she could hear was the rustle of cloth when she tightened her legs around him, and all she could taste was bergamot and heat as his tongue twined with hers. He slipped his hand between them and cupped her breast, causing her to cry out in frustration.

Pulling his mouth from hers, he gasped as though they'd been running for miles. "Let me touch you?" he begged, one hand already pulling her skirts up to reveal her stockinged calf.

Every cell in her body cried out for relief: If he touched her, he could give her what she wanted. It would be so easy.

Somewhere in the kitchen, a few yards away, a footman called out to a passing parlor maid, and the world returned with a blow.

One of Grey's hands was at her breast, the other held her petticoats. If someone saw them . . .

"Stop." Letty lurched sideways and nearly tumbled to the floor. When Grey tried to break her fall, she panicked and slapped his chest.

He didn't flinch, just set her carefully on her feet. Pulling her skirts straight, she tried to hide how her hands shook with the aftereffects of the delirium that had overtaken her.

"You must think I am everything you once accused me of," Letty said. As she spoke, a burning behind her eyes meant that tears threatened.

Grey paled, shaking his head as though to remove her words from his ears. "No, it is I who am at fault. I lost control."

He repeated himself in a tone of disbelief. "I lost control."

A blanket of shame smothered any residual pleasure from their encounter. This was why Letty could only be trusted with a man between the pages of a book. She would let herself be ruined again—and for what?

"I am not . . ." Letty pressed her fingertips to the corners of her eyes. "I do not want . . . this." She flung her hands out to encompass the two of them. "Us . . . A man. What I did before was not . . ."

She had no words for her shame. She'd lost important pieces of her armor that could have protected her from the inevitable pain of giving in to her desires.

"You are not the woman I accused you of being six years ago, Letty. I *know* that." His voice lowered to a whisper as he bent his head toward her and placed a warm hand on her shoulder. "I know you."

Those last words sounded like a question.

What was the answer?

11

"WHY DOES THIS say powders do not collide?"

Letty stood in the center of her workroom, talking to herself while staring at the sheaf of papers in her hand, knee-deep in the process of scattering her wits beyond retrieval.

Could Grey's assertion that her handwriting was less than legible have some merit?

Firmly confident in her proof . . . fairly confident . . . somewhat confident . . . Letty now needed to practice the actual presentation of her work. More than any other participant, Letty needed to be certain no one would question her theory—or her appearance.

She lowered her voice.

"Ahem. Let p be an odd prime if there exists . . ." Letty coughed. Too low. She took a sip of cold tea and tried again.

"Let p be an—"

"Why don't you try letting c be the speed of you putting on your bonnet, or we will miss our coach. Unless you have forgotten your promise to accompany me today?"

Margaret stood in the doorway, clad in a fine rose-colored paletot, holding Letty's cloak and bonnet in her hand.

While dining with the Fenleys the other night, Margaret had invited Letty to visit the site of a proposed railway project. If her current project went smoothly, Margaret and her father-in-law back in Paris hoped their firm would be given a contract to design the bridge carrying a private railway over the Thames and linking Richmond with Saint Margarets.

Letty had demurred at first, but the more she'd considered it, the more she'd thought a trip to the river might be the trick to getting her mind clear of extraneous things.

Kisses, for example.

Da had given his approval only if Sam accompanied them, one of the many consequences of Nevin's seduction. Other than the club and her home, Letty could not be left alone, lest she fall into another nobleman's bed. As though they were covered with leaves and hiding in wait along the walkways for stupid girls to stumble into.

Of course, she hadn't stumbled the first time, had she? Given time and distance, was it fair to blame her entire fate upon Nevin and his father? Nevin hadn't thrown Letty over his shoulder and dragged her to his bed, had he?

Now, another nobleman had found his way beneath—halfway beneath—her skirts. Letty could have told him no at any point between his lips hitting hers and her thighs clinging to his, but she hadn't.

You are not the woman I accused you of being six years ago, Letty. I know *that.*

She should be ashamed of her behavior.

Shouldn't she?

The glorious thrum of pleasure between her legs was sinful.

Wasn't it?

Letty communicated none of this distress to Margaret. Instead, she, Margaret, and Sam took a coach to Richmond. As the brown skies and blackened walls of the city fell away, they were reminded that in the rest of England, it was springtime.

Upon alighting in Richmond, they took a delightful walk to where the crossing would be constructed. Margaret pulled a small book from her reticule and made notes. She explained that because of the slope of the land to the river, the height of the water at this site, and the projected path of the railway, there was more than one way to design a crossing.

"Do you have a chance of getting the commission, Margaret?" Letty asked.

Margaret drew in a deep breath and bit her lip as she gazed to the shoreline opposite them.

"When I was first married, my husband and I would represent my father-in-law's firm together, so that the heads of the railway companies would become familiar with me. Only once the Gault firm won a commission would Marcel reveal that I was the engineer, and he an accountant."

Letty chuckled, and Sam scratched his head. "Surely it didn't matter to them that you were a woman," Sam said, "once they'd approved of the plans."

Margaret smiled at him with such pleasure that he turned the color of beet soup. The curse of having fair hair. "You would think, wouldn't you? It took many years, and after Marcel's death, it became more difficult. Still . . ."

Squaring her shoulders, Margaret again gazed over the landscape. "I'm close to mastering the art of being an unwomanly woman who is just womanly enough."

Sam mouthed the phrase to himself, but Letty knew exactly what Margaret meant. Not so feminine that men did not trust her to do the work, but not too competent that they were threatened.

"I wish you luck," Letty told her. "You might call upon Lord Grey-cliff for support. He has a superlative reputation among the ton."

Even as the words left her mouth, Letty considered whether Grey's stature might diminish if he were to be caught kissing her like he did yesterday. Given his standing, it wouldn't destroy him, but it would set tongues to wagging. The assumption would be that he simply dallied with her. No one in their right mind would assume a peer in his position was courting her.

Letty Fenley was not the kind of girl an aristocrat would marry.

"Are you coming, Letty?" Sam called.

Her uncomfortable thoughts lodged like tiny pebbles beneath her skin as she hurried forward to the safety of her brother's company. While no one said it aloud, they assumed Letty would not marry. She was twenty-three and, with no prospects in sight, could be discounted by most of society as "firmly on the shelf."

Letty smiled, then laughed outright, at the image of herself sitting high on a shelf in the Fenley's parlor and shouting down accusations of cheating while the rest of the family played parlor games.

"What's funny, Letts?" Sam asked.

Letty shook her head. "Oh, don't mind me. Bit addled in my old age is all."

The rest of the morning passed by uneventfully except when Sam, trying to show off, nearly fell into the Thames.

Twice.

Afterward, he took each of them by the arm and squinted at the sun. "I'd forgotten how big it is. Surely it isn't natural, all this golden sunlight and beautiful blue sky?"

Margaret and Letty laughed, and he preened as they walked down a hill.

Letty untied her bonnet strings and pushed the hat back, exposing as much skin as she dared to the buttery sun.

"I forget a world exists outside the club," she remarked.

She glanced over at her brother. Dark circles sat beneath his eyes, and his skin had an unhealthy pallor. Despite his cheerful demeanor, the long days in the emporium and longer nights poring over ledgers were beginning to take a toll. Hard to remember the little boy with the generous heart who'd hidden half his dinner to give to his friends who had none, and who'd cried when Mam went after mice with her broom.

Why did they lose so much of their better selves as they grew older?

Later, they took tea in a charming inn on the Old King's Walk. Much to their dismay, when they emerged, the sun had hidden its fickle face and a bank of clouds had made their surly way across the sky.

Still, the air was fresh and clean, and they decided to stroll along the riverbank toward the center of Richmond, tramping on green grass and speedwell. In a small copse, a bank of wild hyacinths scented the air, and Letty's heart lifted, despite her worries about the club. Even with the darkening skies and the strengthening wind, the myriad greens and rich scent of grass were a balm after the dirt and smoke of London this spring.

"Well, is this worth missing an afternoon of work at the emporium?" Margaret teased Sam, knowing full well he'd come with them under duress.

Sam cheerfully took her lure. "With such a view?" he asked, letting his gaze sweep her face. "Without doubt."

Margaret's laugh unrolled like velvet beneath the silver notes of birdsong, and Letty admired Margaret's easy manner. She had never—could never—be at ease with an attentive gentleman.

Changing course, in case they needed shelter, they headed toward the green. The haute monde had long claimed this pretty town for their own, but this new rail line would be the fastest connection yet to London, which would bring even greater building opportunities.

"I told Da we could expand and open a Fenley's Fripperies here." Sam gestured toward the high street at the other end of the green.

"Mayfair isn't the only place ladies with too much coin and too little sense do their shopping. Open a separate establishment with comestibles, perhaps even a tearoom for the ladies. Lots of scope for expanding into something bigger."

Margaret squinted. "Speaking of gentry, isn't that Lord Greycliff?"

It was indeed. He stood in conversation with a slope-shouldered man with the features of a shrunken hound. While they did not appear to be arguing, Greycliff exuded an irritated restlessness at odds with his usual stoicism. A few feet away, an older woman stood next to an elegantly dressed young lady, both twirling their parasols in thinly veiled impatience as the lightest sprinkle of raindrops began.

"He is conducting business," Letty said. "We should leave him alone and not—"

Too late. Margaret had waved in Grey's direction and attracted his notice. The thin man scowled and took his leave, along with the two ladies. Letty angled her face away from them and hid behind Sam's broad shoulders.

As Grey walked toward them, Letty could not help but admire the lean lines of his body when the wind sent the skirts of his dark navy overcoat billowing out around his legs.

No. Never mind his legs.

Look away from the legs, she chastised herself.

"Well met, my lord," said Margaret. "Have you come to view the rare sight of sunlight in London's environs?"

They glanced at the bank of thick grey clouds and laughed.

"I am here on business," he said easily. "And, yes, I was as delighted by the appearance of the sun as you. Richmond has the added benefit of being free from any looming catastrophes," Grey added. "It is restful to spend an hour or so without worrying if the walls will fall down around us or the Guardians will show up again."

As he spoke, a low rumble of thunder filled the air around them.

Margaret wiped a raindrop from her nose with a handkerchief. "When is the coach back to London due to arrive, Letty?"

"Any minute now," she said.

"I brought my carriage," Grey remarked. "You are welcome to ride back to London with me."

"No. No, thank you," Letty blurted even as the rain plonked on her bonnet. "I see the coach coming now."

A carriage? Toe to toe with the man who had his hand on her breast yesterday? Absolutely not.

Sam, oblivious to Letty's distress, shook his head. "You're mistaken, Letts. It isn't due for another hour. We should accept his lordship's offer and—"

"No, no," Letty insisted. "In fact, the clouds seem to be clearing away."

A bolt of lightning lit the far side of the Thames, putting an end to her arguments.

Greycliff's well-trained coachman appeared at their side seconds later. Letty clambered aboard, careful to take a seat next to Margaret and opposite Sam. Inside, the carriage was well-appointed: The leather of the seat cushions was supple and without cracks; the windows were covered with brown cotton curtains, matching the color of the carriage blanket Grey had provided the ladies.

Whether the reason was a return to the gloom or her unsettled reaction to their encounter yesterday, she couldn't say, but a melancholy of sorts descended on Letty. Grey's gaze turned inward, and he stared at the stitching of his gloves. Margaret watched the landscape outside the window.

Sam, incapable of remaining still for long, jiggled his leg like a puppy with fleas, dislodging his hat, which fell at Letty's feet.

Being a woman of the advanced age of three and twenty, she refrained from teasing her younger brother.

For three seconds.

"Look at the state of your topper, Sam," she said while she examined it. "Whatever has been chewing on the brim? Have you been rescuing mice again?"

Sam leaned over and yanked the hat from her hands, turning it around and tsking over it. "Don't know how that happened," he said, a touch of pink coloring his cheeks. "Rescuing mice. What nonsense is that?"

He shifted in his seat and glanced sideways at Margaret.

"Oh, rescuing mice? How sweet, Mr. Fenley," she said.

Sam obviously did not want Margaret using the word *sweet* about him. "My sister is joking, of course," he said as he glared at Letty. "If you are intent on entertaining us, why don't you read one of your *stories*, Letty."

Drat.

Letty scrambled for the handles of her reticule, but Sam was too fast. Quick as an eel, he grabbed the cloth bag from the seat next to her and, with a flourish, pulled out a book.

Heat suffused her cheeks. She shouldn't have teased her brother in an enclosed space with no exit.

"What do you have there, Miss Fenley? Something uplifting and pious I presume?" Grey drawled.

"Oh ho. None of that," Sam said. "What I hold in my hand is the ultimate in foolishness. It is a *novel*." He squinted in the low light. "*The Perils of Miss Cordelia Braveheart and the Castle of Doom*."

Margaret blinked. "The Castle of Doom?" She turned to Letty with a slight frown. "Cordelia Braveheart? Do you truly read such drivel?"

All her life, Letty had been teased about her devotion to novels.

Titles ranging from *Julia de Saint Pierre* and *Emma* to a bound copy of the *Oliver Twist* installments sat on a shelf in her bedroom. Funny how those books were constantly disappearing and reappearing in a household that professed to disdain such stories.

"They aren't drivel," Letty protested. "Love stories are the oldest and best stories we have."

Sam scoffed as he flipped through the pages. "Oldest story is the Bible. That isn't a love story."

"The New Testament is," Letty said. She folded her hands in her lap, however, and let Sam keep the book. "Not a story of romantic love, but a tale of a great love all the same."

Margaret sniffed, but Letty had thought long and hard about why she found such solace in these books.

"Greek mythology, fairy tales, epic poems—the stories we remember and repeat are about love," Letty insisted. "Think of Romeo and Juliet. Or Pyramus and Thisbe. Even the worst tragedies hold out a possibility of redemption in the end."

Redemption.

For Letty, the hope of redemption rested squarely on the promise that love could be had without artifice, without shame. Perhaps she wasn't irrevocably sullied by an act she'd always meant to be partaken of out of love—or, if the act itself wasn't a sin, by the absence of love that made it so—and one day she could begin afresh.

"I'd *love* for you to quit this gabbing so I can read," teased Sam.

"Indeed," Grey said. "Entertain us if you please, Mr. Fenley." The more intense Grey's stare, the more heated Letty's blush.

Was self-immolation an actual phenomenon?

"Ahem," Sam cleared his throat.

An hour later, he was still reading, pitching his voice to match the characters:

"*Cordelia gasped as Count Blacksoul grasped her elbow. 'Heed my* words, Miss Braveheart. If you venture out into the forest, you will surely find yourself in great peril not even I can save you from.'

"'No greater peril exists in those woods than the one standing before me,' she cried. With a . . ."

Sam put his face to the page as they finally cleared an enormous snarl in London traffic.

"It's too dark. I can't see what this says."

"Let me try," Grey held out a hand for the book, then brought the pages close to his face. "With a . . ." He returned the book with a disappointed sigh. "I can't read it, either."

"Well, we don't need you to read it," Margaret said. "Cordelia is smart enough not to trust the count. She will return to her village and go back to her virtuous life caring for her papa."

"What are you saying?" Grey objected. "Blacksoul went into a snowstorm without a coat to rescue her from the maddened horses. I'm certain he's to be redeemed."

"You're both wrong," Sam said. "The hero is Sir Goldenhawk."

"How is that?" Grey asked, voice raised in incredulity. "The man is utterly useless. Where was he when Cordelia almost drowned in the swamp?"

"He has *golden* hair." Sam ran a hand through his own blond locks, preening. "Golden hair is a sure sign of the hero. Ask Letty."

Three pairs of eyes swiveled in her direction. Mrs. Foster, author of *The Perils of Miss Cordelia Braveheart*, was Letty's favorite author. She did, however, tend to rely overmuch on certain tropes.

"You will have to buy the book to find out," Letty said. Seeing an opportunity, she snatched the book from Sam's hands and stuffed it back into her bag.

Outrage all around met her statement, but Letty refused to back down.

"You mocked me before beginning the book, and now look at you," she pointed out. "I shan't spoil the ending, and the author deserves your shillings for her hard work."

Knowing full well he never could win an argument with her, Sam crossed his arms over his chest and leaned back, tipping his hat over his eyes and pretending not to care.

Grey, on the other hand, would not be put off. He and Margaret dissected the evidence pointing to Blacksoul as the lost heir to an eccentric marquessate who had left a hidden fortune, and whether such a claim would hold in the courts.

Running a hand over his chin, Grey examined Letty with curiosity. "How is a mathematician fond of something as fantastical as a novel?"

"What do you mean?" Letty asked. "What does mathematics have to do with it?"

"Isn't your discipline steeped in the rational?"

Letty could detect no censure in his question.

"I can't imagine anything more irrational than this story," Grey continued. "All the falling off cliffs into wagons full of reeds, or being able to conjure vials of an antidote minutes after one is bit by spiders."

Considering his question, Letty chewed her bottom lip while she gathered her thoughts.

"What do you think the probability is of landing in a passing wagon if you fell off a cliff?" she asked him.

"One in one thousand?" he guessed.

"Don't throw numbers out at Letty," Sam cautioned from beneath his hat. "She'll throw them right back at you. Learned that the hard way." He pushed the brim of his hat up and squinted at her. "You have to ask about vegetables."

"Variables," Letty corrected.

"First, you would have to calculate how many wagons passed on that road," Margaret said.

"Exactly. Also, the speed at which the wagon is traveling, the population of the surrounding countryside, the relative wind strength . . ." Letty ticked the variables off with her fingers. "Then you must consider the constants. The height of the cliff, the weight of the jumper." A tiny stream of satisfaction loosened her shoulders as the numbers started soothing her.

"Doesn't it take away from the drama when Cordelia falls into the mine shaft if you are wondering about the speed of her descent?" Grey asked.

Letty watched shadows play over Grey's face, smoothing out the hard planes, taking away some years, adding in some gentleness.

"Consider Cordelia and the count," she said. "How many random occurrences must have taken place for them to meet at the country assembly? The lame horse, the rainstorm, the sick musicians—if you calculate the odds of their finding each other, you understand why love, when it happens, is rare and precious."

"Or a fluke," Grey said.

"I don't believe in flukes." Letty was speaking to them all now, but she'd told herself this message many times. "I believe in mathematics. I believe in the scientific laws governing our universe, and the infinite equations that allow humans to find a way together. I believe mistakes can be mended, grudges can be reconciled, mysteries solved, and happy endings can come to each of us."

If love couldn't happen to Letty, she wouldn't despair. She had earned her isolation. That didn't mean love wasn't waiting for others.

Margaret spoke up. "When I design a bridge, I must always allow for gravity trying its best to pull it down, balancing the weight of materials against the forces of nature." A note of reverence entered her voice. "We cannot fight gravity, but for thousands of years we have still found a way to span our divides. It is human nature for a person to stand on one side of a chasm and face any challenge to reach the person on the other side. Communion and balance—esoteric concepts indeed for an engineer to contemplate." She tilted her head as though examining something new for the first time. "My discipline has made me a believer in the power of human contact to change our world. I suppose one might say a bridge is its own form of love story."

"What a beautiful thought." Letty smiled at her friend. "Finding and remaining in love requires the same set of circumstances. Communion and balance."

She examined Greycliff, hoping to see comprehension in his eyes.

Instead, the shadows parted to reveal a disapproving curve to his stern mouth. "What you say proves the opposite."

Appearing almost angry, Grey crossed his arms over his chest. "Romantic love is a product of chance—or, more likely, a figment of imagination designed to explain away lust."

"All *I* know," declared her brother, breaking the mood, "is that Sir Goldenhawk needs to escape from the runaway carriage pretty quick if he means to find the hidden cache of emeralds before midnight. I don't need to be a mathematician to figure his chances are slim."

Introspection abandoned, the company remained silent until they turned into the mews of Beacon House and came to a halt.

As Grey handed her down, Letty remembered the heat of his touch on her thigh, and she swallowed a sigh.

Sam hopped out and took her arm, eyeing her reticule with a speculative gaze. "How can I fall asleep tonight without knowing what became of Miss Cordelia Braveheart?"

The others laughed, but as Letty watched Grey walk away, she knew Sam wouldn't be the only one lying awake tonight.

"WHAT IS THIS?"

Barely restraining himself from leaping across the room and pushing his godfather to the floor, Grey snatched the copy of *The Perils of*

Miss Cordelia Braveheart and the Castle of Doom out from under Melton's prying eyes and shoved it into his desk drawer.

"A treatise regarding the phenomena of probabilities." Grey ushered Melton to a chair before a small fire. "I would have received you in the parlor, but we are having it painted. Shall I ring for cakes?"

"Cakes?" Melton peered at Grey. "Are you well, my boy?"

Cakes.

What was he saying? He hadn't had a slice of cake in almost fifteen years.

Grey's carefully ordered world had come apart at its seams. Days after assuring Letty he did not think her a temptress, he'd nearly debauched her against a wall. He'd lain awake all night, partly from the discomfort of an unresolvable cock-stand, and partly the result of a guilty conscience.

No wonder he was craving cake.

As Melton sat, a square patch of sunlight fell on his lap, revealing a spray of liver spots across the backs of his hands. The reminders of his godfather's mortality struck a chord of foreboding.

"Will you take a cup of tea instead?" Grey asked. "There is still a chill in the air, despite the better turn of weather." Wanting the fire built up, he rang the bell to summon a servant and left the door partway open so the maid could slip in without interrupting them.

Three vertical lines between Melton's brow deepened as he frowned. "Never mind the tea. I thought you were going to close this ill-conceived club next door, but when I arrived, there were women going in and out of the place. One of them had a bird on her head."

He paused, then reiterated. "A bird. On her head."

Grey had no idea why anyone would wear a bird on their head, but, given time, someone would provide him an explanation that would make his eyes cross with confusion.

"Is there a reason for the delay?" Melton asked.

"It will be done soon," Grey assured him. "In the meantime, the women have harmed no one with their work."

Yet.

Melton's head moved back and forth as he examined Grey, seeming to measure his commitment.

"As to that," Melton said, "you might consider the reputation of the women who frequent this social club."

Grey straightened. Here was the subject he'd been loath to broach with Melton.

Yesterday's carriage ride had led to a startling revelation.

Letty Fenley was a *romantic.*

Six years ago, a young woman with a head full of mathematics and a heart full of dashing knights had been ill-done by three wellborn and powerful men. After Grey had kissed her in the stillroom—although he should *not* have kissed her in the stillroom—her face had reflected shame and terror, void of her usual bright spark of defiance.

"You are referring to Miss Fenley?"

"If that is the name of the grocer's daughter, then yes," Melton answered. "Among others. Last year, Lady Phoebe Hunt was responsible for creating a deadly weapon that killed a constable. Lady Agatha Potts has been advocating for a change in the divorce laws for twenty years now. Why, they might have just as easily painted the outside of the club red for all they wave a flag in Armitage's direction."

Despite his intention to have a rational discussion, Grey's temper flared. How he wished he could reconcile his competing allegiances. When Melton spoke, he heard the voice of a man with total integrity, the man who had saved his life as a child. In his next breath, he thought of how the spark of life that defined Letty Fenley had dimmed when she spoke of Nevin's betrayal.

Melton stood. "Your concentration must be aimed at the ultimate target. This is not about some roundheel trickster. This is about your future."

The unfamiliar sensation of anger toward his godfather had Grey setting his fingers to his pulse.

"She is not a roundheel," Grey said, objecting to the euphemism, "and she has a name."

"Her name is not the point." Wrinkles at the sides of Melton's green eyes deepened with concern. "You cannot let Armitage take over the directorship. A man so in love with the sound of his own voice would be a disaster. With your character and steady hand, the Department can continue its mission as a neutral arbiter in the country's internal struggles, a voice independent of politics."

And here was the rub. Even discounting Grey's genuine hunger to control the world around him, he knew Melton was correct. His was the ideal character for such a position.

The rational part of him pointed out that Letty Fenley could take care of herself. Grey had witnessed this firsthand. There were masses of people out there who were without a champion, who did not have her courage or a family upon whom they could rely.

Yet why did the closure of a social club weighed against the chance to change government policy for the better feel like such a betrayal?

"This is simply a token show of your loyalty," Melton continued. "Close the club and—"

At a noise behind him, Grey glanced over, expecting to see the maid come to tend the fire. Instead, he caught a glimpse of Letty's panicked face in the slit between the partly opened door and the hallway.

Damn it. What had she heard?

"Grey?" Melton turned his head, but Letty had already ducked out of sight.

Grey scraped his chair back with as much noise as he could on the plush carpets. He could not continue arguing with Melton with Letty right outside the door.

"I have another appointment this afternoon, my lord," he told Melton. "We will speak on this further. In the meantime, I'll see you at the Rosewood presentation."

The surprise on Melton's face gave Grey a start of guilt.

"Will you come after all?" Melton asked. "Nevin will be pleased, although lately he's come down with a case of nerves."

"He seemed confident the other night," said Grey. He glanced at the space between the floor and the bottom of the door, where Letty's dark blue skirts twitched.

"In many ways, Nevin is still the young boy you taught to play cricket one summer."

Grey hadn't thought about that summer in years. He couldn't remember whose idea it had been to teach Nevin cricket. Not Nevin's. All knobby knees and awkward limbs, Nevin had calculated to the nearest degree the arc in which a cricket ball should fly to hit a wicket, but the translation from theory to practice had eluded him.

"I don't remember being a good tutor," he confessed. "I didn't have much patience back then, and the lessons didn't run long."

"No, you were afraid you would have a fit while the two of you were playing," said Melton. He continued, as though he had not spoken Grey's terrible shame out loud. "To avoid any danger, you constructed a plan the night before and taught him one position at a time."

Acutely aware of the woman on the other side of the doorway, Grey swallowed and bent his head, silently begging Melton not to say anything else.

"Nevin would try the patience of a saint when he was young," Melton reminisced. "Everything was a question with him. 'Why do you do this? Why not this?'" He shook his head, but a warm smile graced his countenance. "Every question he asked, you took the time to answer. If you didn't know the answer, you promised to find it. You put him first, despite your seizures."

A handful of memories came to Grey of Nevin following behind as he saddled a horse or went fishing in the brook.

Where do fish sleep? Do horses have bad dreams? Why did the water look dark when still and turn white when it bubbled over the rocks?

"Nevin still asks questions." Melton went to the door and laid his hand on Grey's shoulder. "Your presence will mean a great deal to him. Despite our difference of opinion concerning this club and the women in it, you might see your way to spending time with him again."

Melton squeezed Grey's shoulder briefly, then dropped his hand as though he'd touched something hot, and Grey felt the ache as if he'd already lost his godfather's presence in his life.

Everything was about to change. Melton would retire, and Grey would assume the directorship. The power would shift between the two of them irrevocably.

A whisper of air brushed his ankles, and Grey caught the shadow of a dark wool skirt out of the corner of his eye.

Everything would change for him, but if he didn't act, Letty Fenley's life would go on much as it did before, with her reputation stained and her prospects limited.

"But I will see you sooner than then," Melton said. "You received the invitation to the Ackleys' ball, didn't you?" he asked, his voice now gruff.

Taking the cue, Grey stepped away and tugged at his jacket, as though the gesture of affection had never taken place.

"A ball?" Grey said. "Whyever would I want to attend a ball? I don't play cards, and I do not dance."

Melton chuckled. "You do not dance *well* is the problem. Pushing your partner around at arm's length, as though she held a weapon." He shook his head in mock disapproval.

Grey supposed the analogy fit. He'd warded off most marriageable misses over the years. Marriage was another of those circumstances where it would become difficult to remain removed. He thought of Violet, whose first marriage to his father had brought her such disappointment. Her marriage to Arthur Kneland might have brought her love, but there was sorrow now as well.

Love was as dangerous as sorrow and impossible to control.

"It's time you thought of getting an heir, Greycliff. As well, you should go because Armitage will be there," Melton said. "It is important to present a contrast with the man."

Grey coughed and pushed the door open slowly to give Letty time to hide herself.

No one was in sight as they left the office, but the curtains on the window at the far end of the hall rippled suspiciously. Making sure to block the view, Grey ushered Melton to the front foyer.

Waving off the footman, Grey handed his godfather his hat and overcoat. They stood in silence in the small space while Melton's carriage was brought around. Gleaming red paint on the front door contrasted sharply with the black-and-white tiles beneath their feet.

"I want to see you happy, my boy." Melton examined his hat, turning the brim around in his fingers. "I worry . . ."

Grey's breath caught as he waited for Melton to finish, but the older man left his worries unsaid as the carriage arrived out front.

Watching his godfather walk slowly down the stairs, Grey imagined the rest of the sentence.

I worry you have forgotten to be vigilant against your weaknesses— anger, disappointment, sorrow . . . love. Remember to always remain in control.

"My lord?"

Grey tore his gaze from the checkered squares at his feet to behold Mrs. Sweet standing in the front hallway, hands clasped primly at her waist. How long had he been lost in thought?

"Yes, Mrs. Sweet?"

"I wanted to check with you about the menu this week. Perhaps you would like to change—"

"No," he said, walking past her to climb the stairs. "I'd like the same menu as the week before. Keep everything the same. I don't want any surprises."

12

LETTY WAITED IN Grey's office, her eyes downcast in what she hoped was a penitent pose. She'd heard bits and pieces of the conversation, and the shock of hearing Melton's voice was making it difficult to think straight.

Ten minutes after Grey escorted Melton out, he returned. His eyes were unreadable as he watched her straighten her skirts, the luminous beauty of his immobile features giving the impression he'd been carved from marble. Coldly perfect.

"I never meant to eavesdrop," Letty said.

One black eyebrow rose as he scrutinized her from his infuriating height.

"I had a good reason for coming to your office," she continued. "When I saw that you had company, I planned on leaving right away, except . . . I heard the Earl Melton's voice."

She hung her head and confessed her sin to the worn carpet beneath her feet. "I wanted to hear if he mentioned me. What he might say. If it would change your mind back to before."

Letty wanted Grey to treat her like he did in the carriage yesterday.

As though her company pleased him. As though she weren't a disappointment.

Grey said nothing, then crossed the room and closed the door. Her breath caught, but he made no move toward her. Instead, he walked in the opposite direction and sorted through stacks of invitations and cards, clearing the desk so all one could see was its polished surface.

"He was kind," Letty said.

He glanced at her with a question in his eyes. "To you?" he asked with disbelief.

"No. Never." She laughed without humor. "He was kind to you." She shook her head. "I don't know why I expected him to be angry and cruel. I suppose in my head he is such a terrifying figure. It never occurred to me he could do anything as benign as take tea with someone."

Grey cocked his head. "If the two of you were to meet . . ."

The breath left Letty in an instant. She put a hand on the chair beside her as the room seemed to spin.

"Oh, no. Please don't. I couldn't bear it." Letty shuddered at the thought of having to listen to Melton's invectives. All those defenses she'd spent years building would be submerged in the humiliation.

A tiny ember of anger burned in her belly at Grey's look of mild surprise. A petty desire to see him on the back foot sent her words flying out before common sense caught up with her.

"Melton said you were worried you would have a fit," Letty said. "Are you well?"

That marble mouth of his flattened into a sharpened blade, and Grey's eyes lightened with icy rage until nearly colorless. Letty had to clench her jaw to stop from chattering at the glacial silence that fell between them, the careful goodwill they'd assembled these past few weeks undone in one stupid moment of spite.

"I don't owe an explanation to someone who eavesdropped on a conversation not meant for them." Grey had withdrawn into the untouchable aristocrat, and she was once again the blundering upstart, trespassing where she didn't belong.

Letty forced herself to meet Grey's stare. "I never thought you might have—"

"Weaknesses?" he spat. He gripped the side of the desk as though to keep himself from wringing her neck.

Letty fumbled for the right words, shaken by his anger. "I simply never pictured your life as anything less than perfect."

The word *perfect* bounced from her mouth and hit him between the eyes. He jerked his head back in disbelief.

"*Perfect*? Is that what you think?"

Shock seemed to supplant Grey's anger, which shocked her in turn.

"I must have thrown that epithet at you once before," she said. "What with having a passable intellect, a title, money, all your teeth and hair, no wens or scars." Letty paused to take stock. "Lovely eyes and a strong chin, a healthy body . . ."

A canny light came into his eye, and she shut her mouth.

"Am I not in possession of the largest head in Christendom, so enormous a family of four could stand next to me in a rainstorm and never get wet?" Grey mocked.

Letty winced at her words thrown back at her.

"Am I not standoffish? Do I not speak as though delivering pronouncements from on high . . . ?"

Head slowly sinking into her shoulders, Letty essayed a weak smile. "Was it me who said those things?"

"And more." Grey loosened his grip and rested his hip against the desk in a casual pose. Dropping his head back, he surveyed the cracked ceiling overhead. Letty followed his stare but could see nothing, except that the maids had not dusted in a while.

Grey's anger now banked; she could breathe freely again. While his attention was diverted, she took the opportunity to study the line of his nose and the arcs of his cheeks. His long legs were crossed, and she remembered writhing against his hard thigh. How he held her firmly against him, but with a grip tender enough that it left no mark.

"I only said those things out of disgust with your perfection." She raised one shoulder at the admission. "I assumed you were egotistical, because what man as perfect as you wouldn't be?"

His head swiveled, and his gaze came to rest on her. "So, I *don't* have a big head?"

Chagrined, Letty shook her own tiny head back and forth. "Not really."

"I still find you needlessly short."

A hint of bergamot rose when he wandered over to the drinks table. Rather than pouring a drink, he put the bottles into a circle, then back into line.

"Violet knows," he said.

"That I am short?"

Grey might as well have pushed her to the floor when he sent her a sideways grin. How did he do that? Knock the breath from her even as he terrified her?

"She knows I suffered fits during my childhood."

It had cost him to say this.

The more nonchalant he acted, the whiter the skin at his knuckles as he held on to the glass bottle stop.

He sniffed the air. "Have you been eating cake?"

"No."

Carefully, Letty crossed the narrow bridge between the two of them, mindful of the rapids eager to pull her under and end his confessions. "Violet never said anything. How did you . . . ? It must have been terrifying to be a soldier with such a condition."

Studying the etched roses and thorns on the set of sherry glasses as though they held the answers to the world's questions, he answered.

"I haven't had one since I turned seventeen. My father kept me away from society. No one knew except for Violet. Once I was certain the fits were under control, I joined the army."

Letty cocked her head. "I've heard many children outgrow them."

Grey stared at her as though she'd insulted him. "I didn't outgrow them. I *conquered* them."

Here was another of those moments when the world shifted. For so long, Grey had been a simple equation. One plus one equaled two. Straightforward. Inflexible.

Now, with each revelation, the equation was expanding. Different factors were added. Unknown variables became known and changed the product entirely.

"We had a member of Athena's Retreat who studied epilepsy," she ventured.

Try as she might, she couldn't decipher his expression. When he said nothing, Letty continued.

"Miss Tabitha Westford. She had a cousin with the condition."

Still, Grey didn't move, not even the twitch of a muscle.

"I remember she wanted to medically prevent the seizures. The other treatments on offer were . . ."

Her mouth dried as the storms in his eyes intensified.

"Cold-water baths," he said, supplying the words. "Bloodletting."

Had they cut into his beautiful body with their torturous instruments? Submerged him in freezing water until he cried out? She didn't ask. Such knowledge was unbearably intimate. More intimate than his hands on her bare skin.

"They tried any number of cures," Grey said, answering her unspoken question.

"I'm sorry." A stupid handful of words for what must have been agony for a little boy.

"Some doctors say the fits are caused by an excess of emotions," he continued, as though he weren't recounting the history of his own pain, leaving the drinks table, and walking toward her. "One man has gone so far as to surgically remove the wombs of some women to limit what he believes is their unhealthy exuberance. At least I did not have to suffer that indignity."

How many times had she and others assumed this man impervious to any pain? And yet he'd suffered incalculable harm at the hands of people trying to make him better. Hesitantly, Letty closed the space between them, raised a hand, and rested the backs of her trembling fingers against his cheek.

Grey caught hold of her in an implacable grip. "It was long ago."

Letty left her hand imprisoned in his grasp.

Any touch could be comfort.

"You say you conquered them. How did you do it?" she asked.

Turning her hand over, he examined her palm, a pale pink shell in his dark grip. With his other hand, he touched his fingertip to hers as he ticked off a litany of denial as though it were a prayer. "Cold baths did not stop my seizures, but they do increase one's tolerance for pain. I start every day with a cold bath."

"Oh." What was she to say? A strange dichotomy of sympathy and arousal rose in her while he stroked the length of her thumb.

Deliberately, he caressed her index finger next. "I ride for an hour and fence for an hour, once in the morning and again in the afternoon."

Letty blinked, envisioning a sweat-soaked linen shirt stretched across his powerful muscles. She tried to formulate her question while transfixed by the sight and the sensation of his touch. "That seems somewhat excessive. Why do you do it?"

"It helps me to sleep." His thumb rubbed the delicate skin between her second and third fingers, sending shivers straight to the center of her. "My diet is both simple and healthful."

"Greens and fish," she blurted.

"Exactly." His fingers stilled, and she tore her gaze from their hands. Nothing in his expression hinted at whether he was similarly affected by this game. She knew what he was doing. Caught out in his weakness, he was punishing her with a touch of seduction.

"Drink, only in moderation."

When Letty nodded, he resumed his touches.

"Socializing, also in moderation." The velvet in his voice stiffened, and he let go of her hand. "Any excess, be it food, drink, or sentiment, is to be avoided."

Bereft of his touch, Letty curled her palm into a ball and cradled it against her chest. A warning lurked behind his last few words, but she pressed ahead, marking the boundaries of his fortress.

"I don't understand how going without company is beneficial."

"Polite company is allowed, of course. All other associations are kept strictly *physical*, Miss Fenley." His eyes darkened to the hungry gaze she recognized from their kisses. Nevertheless, Grey's mouth was set in a dismissive frown.

Associations. Did he mean liaisons with women? Was he speaking of her?

"You allow yourself to care for others," she told him. "I have seen for myself your affection for Violet."

"Affection, yes," he allowed. "Anything more is superfluous. A man in my position, any man who would assume great responsibilities, should guard against base sentiment, Miss Fenley."

He switched the subject. "There is a ball tomorrow night."

"I know." Letty swallowed and scrunched her nose, embarrassed. "Melton mentioned it when I was *overhearing* things."

"Hmm." He left the word *overhearing* alone. "Armitage will be there."

She fisted her hands. "Pompous goat."

"What if you came with me?"

"Go to a ball?" She stepped back, setting a hand to her chest.

He scoffed at her horrified expression. "Yes, a ball. It is an event where one dances and drinks ratafia. Isn't it time you went back out among the ton?"

Letty shook her head. What rubbish was this? "Why? What would it accomplish?"

The sympathy in his gaze made her turn away. "Violet is gone, and I can only do so much. If Athena's Retreat is under threat, it needs all the defenders it can get."

Unable to find the words to explain, she shook her head again, feeling like a stubborn child.

"Don't be scared," he cajoled. "It isn't as though I asked you to jump off a bridge into a moat filled with man-eating sharks to save a—"

Realizing his mistake, Grey clamped his lips shut.

Too late.

Letty gasped. Although she covered her gaping mouth with her hand, a stream of giggles bubbled up at the chagrin on his face.

"That is exactly what the count had to do to save Cordelia in chapter fourteen," Letty said. "We never made it past chapter ten the other day in the carriage. Have you been reading *romantic rubbish*, my lord?"

"Your hair is come undone," he told her.

It hadn't.

"What are . . . ?"

Letty stood still in shock as he circled her with his arms. Pulling at the ribbons of her cap, he let it fall to the ground. The breath left her as he deliberately unraveled her braids and settled her hair like a shawl of silk over her shoulders and back.

"You don't have to keep . . . distracting me," she whispered. "I won't ever tell anyone our secret."

A laugh as small as a sigh brushed against her cheek.

"I know," Grey told her. "But to make certain, I am going to kiss you again, Letty. I want more than that, but I will not take anything you cannot give. I will do nothing without your permission."

"When you say more . . . ?"

To her shock, he gently caught her bottom lip between his teeth, then sucked it. Gasping with pleasure, she pushed her hips against him.

Reaching to hold her head steady for his kisses, she sensed that he was touching her with restraint, chuckling when she wrapped her arm around his neck and pulled him to her so she wouldn't have to bend her neck.

When Letty lifted her leg, though, and rubbed the outside of his thigh with hers, the restraint fell away. Picking her up, he sat her on the desk behind them and crowded between her legs. Breaking the kiss, Grey fingered the collar of her high-necked dress.

"I want to see you, Letty," he told her. "I am going to take off your dress, if you will allow it."

Without hesitation, she nodded her consent.

"And then . . . ," he whispered as he undid her outer defenses. "And then I am going to give you as much pleasure as you desire. If you feel even the slightest hesitation at any time, you must tell me to stop."

Stop?

She couldn't stop.

All of the reasons this was stupid and dangerous marched through Letty's head with the precision of the Queen's Guards. It didn't matter.

What mattered was the unnameable hunger for Grey gnawing at her night after night since their first kiss. Nothing had ever felt like this: terrifying and empowering at the same time.

"Yes," she whispered.

Too soft. It could have been either a question or a declaration.

"Yes, I want you to touch me," she declared. The choice made, a heady wave of both lust and tenderness rose up, making the room spin, so Letty had to lean forward and set her head on Grey's shoulder.

His powerful body had shuddered when she'd granted permission, and he now set to unbuttoning the back of her dress.

"I want to touch you as well," she told him.

Letty took stock of the colors swirling in his eyes, the dark skies of passion without any evidence of anger or judgment.

"We will do this together, Grey. It will be for ourselves alone, and I won't be ashamed."

"No," he said. Barely grazing her skin, he traced a line from her forehead, down the bridge of her nose, and over her lips to rest at the base of her throat, where her heart sent out a message.

"We won't allow for any shame here."

With great deliberation, Grey pulled her dress from her shoulders, revealing her plain cotton chemise. For an instant, Letty wanted to cover her shoulders, embarrassed by the simple cut of her lingerie, unadorned and functional.

The next second, the embarrassment was gone. His kisses were tender as he pulled her sleeves down and bared her to the room. Cool air made her skin pebble, but he rubbed her arms and she warmed from his touch.

Once Letty had acknowledged her desire, she'd been in control of her body as she hadn't that night with Nevin. Now, she was unafraid that her urges—to touch, to lick, to press or pull—might be ridiculed or scorned.

Outside the door to this room, a network of unwritten rules and edicts piled higher than the hedgerows, and she would have to make her way in the world without breaking them down. In here, with this man, those rules would not stand.

Letty pulled her mouth away from his and tested her newfound freedom. "I want to see you. I want to touch you."

Grey nodded and turned to the side.

"Help me, then."

Letty laughed at his imperious tone, so at odds with the haste with which they were yanking at his jacket and unbuttoning his waistcoat.

Facing her again, he pulled his shirttails from his trousers, and a spurt of joy kicked through her, quickly boiling over to awe as he dragged the shirt over his head.

"How beautiful," she said, struck by the symmetry on display before her. Grey's chest was a study in quadrates: the rounded squares of his pectorals, an equilateral quilt of stomach muscles bisected by a trail of curly black hair that ended somewhere beneath the unbuttoned waistband of his trousers.

Leaning forward, she examined the expanse of taut skin with the tip of her tongue.

"Mother of God," he exclaimed in a thick whisper. As she tasted the rough skin of his nipple, he reached behind her and undid her corset cover, then unlaced her corset. He groaned in disappointment when she left off her exploration of his chest. He groaned again, this time with pleasure, when she peeled off the corset.

A *thunk* of boning and canvas hitting the floorboards echoed in the room, setting Letty's nerves afire. Although she affected a certain matter-of-factness about the size of her breasts, Letty still had to resist the urge to cross her arms over them and apologize.

Grey's face lit like a boy staring at a plate of sweets.

"How pretty you are," he crooned, brushing his thumbs across her nipples. A tight fist of pleasure clenched and unclenched between her legs.

Watching Grey's face for clues while following her own instincts, Letty arched her back, then grasped her skirts and petticoats, pulling them to her waist.

"Yesss," he hissed as he pushed down his waistband and slipped one hand into his smalls. The knuckles of his first two fingers were visible in the slit at the front as he grasped his cock in his hand. "So pretty. More beautiful than I'd imagined."

"You imagined me naked?" she asked.

He'd imagined this?

Easy peals of mellow brass laughter fell like a shower of coins as he traced the outline of her areola. "So many times."

Letty squirmed, transfixed by the sight of Grey touching himself with such ease. A liquid plea for friction between her thighs warred with her ignorance. Could she do the same to herself, or was that unnatural?

"Show me. Show me how you touch yourself," she demanded. The storms in his eyes darkened as the pupils overtook the irises and his face turned hard, and he brushed aside his trousers and smalls until they barely clung to his hips.

Letty stared at the thick column of flesh as Grey's hand grasped the skin and pulled it down, exposing the dark plum head of his cock. It glistened invitingly in the palm of his hand.

She had no idea what he would do if she told him of her strange urge to set her mouth on him. In marked contrast to her eager entreaties, he picked at the knots of her garters with maddening deliberation, removing her stockings with one hand, still grasping himself with the other.

Unwilling to wait any longer, Letty fumbled blindly for the tapes at her drawers, her eyes never leaving his body.

While he watched her conundrum, nostrils flaring, lips thinning even more, he left off his self-pleasure. Warm, heavy palms rested on her knees, then smoothed their way up her thighs, over the translucent lawn of her drawers, to rest at her hips while his lips brushed the curve of her neck with maddening lightness.

"What is the name of the scent you wear?" he asked, taking tiny bites of her as though she were made of sugar.

"Scent?" she asked, bewildered. How was she to formulate an answer as he trailed his tongue along her collarbone, then took her breast in his hand?

"Vanilla," he whispered, running his finger around her areola. "Plums," he said as he pinched her nipple gently, and she gasped in delighted surprise.

"Sugar," he growled, then bent his head and set his mouth to her and suckled.

Warm and wet, the suction drove her mad. Her heels pressed against the side of the desk as sparks lit behind her eyelids.

She shivered and cried out with a mixture of disappointment and relief when he lifted his head from her breast and pulled her hips against his. The base of his penis brushed against the slit in her drawers, teasing her. Leaning her back in his arms, his eyes heavy-lidded with lust, Grey caught her gaze.

"We cannot lose control," he warned.

He was wasting his breath with his caution.

Complex expressions of how light travels solidified into the shadow thrown by the arc of his lashes. Esoteric theories of sound were made simple at the shush of her clothing falling to the floor, the slick glide of his tongue over her nipple, and the unabashed pleasure of her cries.

Grey's touch tethered her to this world so firmly she might have vanished into her head and swum the ocean of discovery and never lost sight of the shore.

He returned his attention to her breasts, biting her nipple, as her hands explored his body in return. All the while, he held back, brushing himself lightly against her core. It was not enough, and yet the sensations overwhelmed her.

"It aches again," she complained, frustrated with his restraint.

Grey took her mouth in response, sliding her closer. His wicked, clever hands had reached the center of her, and he cupped her with a warm palm. Letty pushed back, and he hissed, then pressed the heel of his hand against her, making slow, torturous circles.

Time fell apart as her brain finally fell silent, her attention focusing itself on the pressure of his hand at her core. Despite the easement of her ache, she became aware of an emptiness within her. Fumbling, she reached out and grasped hold of him. Beneath her hand, the column of his erection was steel encased in silk, hot and hard.

Here was a call for communion she hadn't felt with Nevin. She swallowed the words of invitation hammering at her chest.

Be in me. Be with me. Fill me.

They suffocated in the coming tide of pleasure when Grey searched through the soft curls between her thighs and found the pearl at the center of her. His finger brushed the tip of her clit as his palm eased against her, and everything disappeared except for white-hot need.

Letty's body shook with tiny tremors as he set his mouth to her ear.

"I am going to make you come now, Letty."

What did that mean? From the satisfaction in his voice, she knew it boded well. Unable to form the words, she nodded her consent. His hot mouth sucked at the lobe of her ear, and he increased the pressure and pace of his ministrations.

He thrust his hips in time with his fingers, and she arched her back. Her breasts pressed against his chest as she reveled in the drag of his skin beneath her grasp. Pressure built too hard and too tight—until, with a shout of joy, everything she'd held back burst free with the unfamiliar taste of freedom.

13

GREY BROUGHT DOWN his arm and slashed at his opponent's unguarded shoulder. When the man stumbled, he pressed his advantage.

"M'lord?" The other man scrambled backward, but Grey kept moving, cutting patterns in the air, reveling in the unfettered honesty of a blade.

"*Arrêtez!*" a third figure cried. "Blades up, man!"

The note of fear in Grantham's voice wrenched Grey out of his head and back to the world. Winthram stood drenched in sweat, his sword arm shaking with fatigue, holding his hands out in a gesture of surrender. Grantham, having finished his practice bout, stood partly in front of Winthram, brows drawn.

Feck.

"I am sorry, Winthram," Grey said as he pulled the mask from his head. "Forgive me."

Removing his face mask as well, the young man's wary expression made Grey sick with guilt.

"That's no matter, my lord," Winthram assured him. "It was good training."

"A soldier must know when practice ends and the battle is engaged. You pushed too far, Greycliff," Grantham chastised.

"You're right, of course," Grey agreed. "I should have stopped earlier. I am . . ."

How to describe the state he occupied these days? A litany of uncomfortable and unfamiliar words marched through his head.

Something more than tenderness? Something deeper than lust?

There was fear as well.

Fear he'd told Letty too much. Grown too close. Stood at the precipice of something too foreign to contemplate.

Words he would not acknowledge added to an ever-growing list of feelings he'd never had before and did not want now. Or ever. Tossing Winthram a towel, Grey grabbed one for himself and sat in a rectangle of sunlight falling to the floor from the high windows in the fencing salon while Grantham gave Winthram his critique.

Since yesterday, memories of the impossibly soft skin of Letty's thighs had ghosted beneath his fingertips; ringing in his ears were the quick, urgent mewls she'd made upon reaching her climax. His plan had been to distract Letty so thoroughly with pleasure that it would blunt the memory of Grey's confessions. The plan had partly worked. After he'd helped her tidy herself, he'd left off his shirt. While he buttoned her dress, he'd made a glib joke about her needing a ladder to look him in the eye. There had been no sparkling reply to his witticism, just the dazed expression of sexual satisfaction and the strange awkwardness that accompanied the aftermath of mutual pleasure. Letty had left the office on unsteady feet.

Grey couldn't pretend he wasn't similarly affected. That tiny woman had burst open beneath him like a shower of sparks atop a bonfire. She'd held her own. No, more than that. She'd taken control of her

body and voiced her desires, and it had been glorious—intoxicating—
to answer her commands and watch her glow.

Years of discipline had kept Grey from going any further with her.
He could be complicit in Letty's pleasure only so far. There were lines
they could not—*he* could not—cross. No matter her station or her
reputation in society, if they made love, he would be bound by honor to
offer for her.

Grey slashed the air with his épée, whittling away his ambivalence.

Winthram eyed the slashing blade with alarm. "Did you want to
practice more, my lord?"

Grey shook his head. What he wanted to do was walk away—from
this club, from his responsibilities, and, most of all, from the woman
who had turned his world upside down.

Marriage was not a state to which he aspired. Marriage meant intimacy of another order altogether. A woman like Letty would never let
herself be controlled or made to fit a particular shape or mold.

"I have to agree with you, Grey," Grantham said.

Grey stared at the two men, who had already put away their blades.

"Won't be long before Winthram will be better than the both of us
combined."

Despite his common upbringing and massive size, Grantham was
an excellent fencer and knew whereof he spoke.

Accepting Grey's weapon, Winthram packed it away next to his after wiping it off one more time. His eyes were downcast, but a telling
blush of pride stained his cheeks.

Before he left, Winthram made sure to give them the latest updates.
Apparently, Flavia had decided to make hats in the shape of birds, complete with feathers and claws, and wished to sell them at Fenley's Fripperies.

"They can be worn by ladies to keep off the sun, and also used by
farmers to put in their crops and scare away the crows," Winthram ex-

plained. "At first, she thought to put a real bird in a cage on a hat, but the mess was something awful."

That is what Melton must have seen yesterday. Flavia *had* been wearing an actual bird on her head. No wonder Arthur was beloved by the ladies of Athena's Retreat. When faced with such outrageous ideas, his natural reticence to speak must have been interpreted as support.

Grey sighed, and the men shared a moment in charity at the burdens they must carry, being such sensible creatures surrounded by such whimsical scientists.

"You can be certain Violet would have ordered three already and made Kneland wear one, too," Grantham said once Winthram had left the room. He chuckled. "Poor besotted bastard. Lucky for Violet I let him marry her. She has him wrapped around her little finger. Myself, I'd never turn fool for a woman."

"You *let* him have her, did you?" Grey asked.

Rather, Arthur and Violet had been so in love that not even the threat of scandal nor the loss of the club had come between them in the end.

"Of course. What woman in her right mind would take a brooding little Scot who has to be tortured to say more than five words at a time over *me*?" With a bright grin, Grantham stretched his arms so that his shirt pulled across his massive biceps, and he ran a hand through his thick blond hair. "Look at these locks," he said. "And I've all my teeth as well. What does Arthur have?"

"The adoration of every woman in this club, including his wife," Grey pointed out.

"True," Grantham acknowledged good-naturedly. They sat in silence, Grantham slumped against the wall and staring at the window, lower lip pushing out in thought. "Kneland lived for his assignments for twenty years yet doesn't seem to miss his work now that he's married," he said. "You have your missions with the Department to occupy you when you're not taking your seat in the House of Lords, and we both know Melton has been grooming you for something bigger."

Grey hesitated, wanting to tell Grantham about the directorship, but he needed to hold back until the confirmation was certain.

His friend continued. "Violet might be correct. I've been working on an act to protect child laborers, but once it is passed, I ought to search 'round for a bride to keep myself busy."

Grey peered over at the big man, surprised at the note of melancholy. Grantham and Violet had been friends since childhood. The earl had proposed to Violet while Arthur was guarding her, but mostly out of convenience. He needed a wife to help with his estate and a younger sister who was soon to debut. It had also partly been out of love for Violet. Grantham had been worried that Violet was substituting the club for the love of a family and wanted to ensure she would never be alone.

"Well," Grey said, "I don't suppose it inconceivable that you might fall in love."

"Love?" Grantham shook his head. "Not for me, my friend. Do you know, the worst part of Violet losing her child was the few weeks when I thought she might lose Arthur as well."

Gone was Grantham's pretend preening and silly grin. Grey reached over and picked a clean towel off a shelf, tossing it to his friend.

"What do you mean?"

Grantham rubbed his curls dry and slung the towel around his neck. "Arthur is the kind of man who loves so deeply; that love is what feeds him. Losing a child he'd come to love even before it was born was like starvation."

Grey sat on the hard bench, motionless despite the cooling sweat setting chills down his back.

Love is what feeds him.

He'd always considered love to be an explosive emotion, synonymous with intensity and pathos.

What had Letty said in the carriage the other day?

If you calculate the odds of their finding each other, you understand why love, when it happens, is rare and precious.

Rare and precious, and powerful indeed. Love was a force that could topple even the strongest of men.

And for a man who could not afford to fall, something best avoided.

LETTY LEANED FORWARD, fingers pressed to her mouth in anticipation.

"Why do you ascribe to me the qualities of a beast, sweet lady? Is it my scarred visage which causes you to malign me?"

Cordelia turned her face from the window, where a silver moon looked on her with what she fancied was a frown of sympathy.

"No, your injuries are of no consequence to me, my lord," she insisted. Taking in the sight of the tall, dark, and handsome man before her—despite the scars which marred the skin beneath his eyes—Cordelia knew a moment of hesitation.

Should she tell him the truth? Her protestations against his tyrannical decree that she must remained locked away in this tower were not as genuine as they sounded. She had begun to feel a tenderness toward the arrogant count.

He lifted his hand and . . .

Having long ago learned Newton's laws governing Earth's gravity, Letty knew she did not truly jump four feet into the air when a knock on her workroom door scared the breath from her. Nevertheless, it took several seconds for her to rearrange her limbs and pick up the novel she had dropped in her fright.

Letty's final touches on the Rosewood presentation were leading her in circles. With only a week and a half left, she'd begun to doubt herself, working and reworking the same equations endlessly. After a fruitless morning of questioning herself to the point of tears, she'd succumbed to the comfort of *The Perils of Miss Cordelia Braveheart and the Castle of Doom*. Unwilling to be discovered procrastinating from her work with such frivolous activity as reading a novel, she slipped the book into her reticule before opening the door.

"I am in love."

Letty stepped back as Margaret marched into her workroom, holding a basket in either hand, followed by Mala and Althea.

"You mustn't tell a soul," Margaret continued, making her way to the other side of the room, where two sagging armchairs and a decrepit settee puddled before an unlit grate. Setting the baskets carefully on the low table next to a chair, Margaret knelt gracefully before the coal scuttle.

"Why do you never give yourself a fire, Letty?" she asked.

Letty shook her head, trying to sort out Margaret's declaration from the anxious knot in her stomach as Mala poked her head into a rickety cabinet and Althea plumped a threadbare cushion, then curled atop it.

"Who are you in love with? And why is it a secret?" Letty asked Margaret. "What are you looking for?" she asked Mala. "What is going on?" she said to no one in particular.

Before she had finished the sentence, a small blaze had sprung to life. Margaret sat back on her heels and brushed her hands off with a gesture that somehow conveyed both pride and indifference at the chore. Mala stood and held a set of dusty jars. "Perfect."

"The identity of my love is a secret because if Mrs. Sweet finds out, she will give me a look." Margaret lifted her chin and peered down her nose in an admirable impression of Mrs. Sweet at her sternest. "And Cook will sigh and make those cow's eyes."

Even Letty had to laugh aloud at the expression on Margaret's face as she widened her eyes and pursed her lips, as Cook did when overwrought.

"You have a marvelous talent as a mimic," Letty said to Margaret as she handed Mala a cloth with which to wipe the jars. "If you run out of work as an engineer, you can always find employment in the theater."

"I know the identity of your secret lover, Margaret," Althea confided, sniffing at the basket closest to her.

"If it weren't for Lord Greycliff and Mrs. Sweet's unconscionable insistence on a healthy diet of fish and lukewarm green things"— Margaret's face scrunched as she emphasized *healthy*—"I wouldn't be driven to making a public display of my affections for the whole of London to witness."

With great deliberation, Althea peeled back the linen covering and revealed a heap of flaky pastries, their fillings of raspberry jam glistening like rubies.

"Monsieur Robeson is rumored to be a genius," Mala said, licking her lips with anticipation.

"Don't be taken in, Mala," Margaret admonished. "He's no more a Frenchman than I am a Dane."

"I don't care if the man is from the steppes of Russia; he's a dab hand with tarts," Althea said.

Well, if they were bearing tarts, Letty supposed she could let them stay. From a low cupboard, she took out four plates and set them in front of Althea, who nodded her thanks.

Carefully setting a pastry on each plate, Althea hesitated, then, with a show of generosity, handed out the larger tarts, keeping the smallest for herself.

"We decided to bring you a treat," said Mala. "Once your presenta-

tion is finished, you will have much more free time to come and social-
ize with the rest of the club members. We miss you at our teas."

Easier to let the comment go unchallenged and pretend along with
the others that she was avoiding socializing because of her work.

Letty would be the first to admit she used her words like spikes on
the breastplate of a suit of armor, keeping the world at bay from her soft
and tender parts. If she weren't sharp-tongued and standoffish, if she
let down her guard, someone could get hurt.

She could get hurt.

"I do not take tea with the ladies out of . . ."

Out of fear.

"Out of habit," Letty said, losing her nerve.

"Perhaps it is time you broke that habit," Margaret said with gentle
sternness.

"Mala and I believe you miss Mrs. Kneland and even Lady Phoebe,"
said Althea as Mala pulled back the cover on the second basket, revealing a bottle of port.

"Oh ho, that is what the jars are for." Letty chuckled.

Raising a brow in acknowledgment, Mala poured four glasses of the
fortified wine and handed them around.

Sometimes certain scents, like the combination of alcohol and
sugar, conjured a web of colors behind Letty's closed eyelids, each
strand a happy memory. If she closed her eyes now, red and gold strands
crossed and recrossed in a complex pattern of warmth and friendship.

"The three of us snuck pastries past Mrs. Sweet as well," Letty told
them. "Lady Phoebe, Violet, and I."

"We call you the founding mothers," said Althea.

"The founding mothers?" Letty considered the moniker. "The
three of us were more like soldiers in arms." She took a sip and let the
liquid warm her insides before she continued. "I miss my friends," she
confessed. "Without them, I feel lost at the club."

"How can you say that? We are such admirers of your work," exclaimed Althea.

"The truth is . . ." Letty stopped.

Margaret put down her empty plate, and Althea leaned her head on her hand, the heel of her palm pushing her bottom lip out, and examined Letty with something close to sympathy in her expression. Close, but not quite, prompting Letty to continue.

"I do not take tea with the members because there is a world outside of Athena's Retreat," she said, running a finger around the edge of the glass. "Other than Caro Pettigrew and me, most of the ladies are . . . ladies. I am not, and it sits there, invisible but present nonetheless."

"Hmm," Margaret hummed in agreement. "As much as we try to convince ourselves otherwise behind these walls, we are not equal on the outside and it carries over into the club."

No one even tried to argue the opposite. They had been born into a class that would define them for the rest of their lives. This was an irrefutable fact of British society.

Mala took a sip of port and shuddered at the taste. "You may not be a gentlewoman by birth, but you are well educated and your family is rich."

Margaret blinked, but Letty and the other club members were used to Mala's direct way of speaking.

She continued. "Mr. Hill and I meet with occasional resistance; however, we are accepted in most places, despite my race. I don't see anything in your manner preventing you from sharing our company."

The glass felt good against her palms. Letty rolled it back and forth, watching the port slop from one side to the other. For an instant, her mind caught on the shape of the wave in the tiny pond. Her thoughts traveled back to the slate board, and formulas unfurled like petals in her brain, floating to the surface and offering distraction.

Letty pushed them out and took a leap of faith.

"My acceptance in society hasn't solely to do with my origins," Letty explained. "It has also to do with rumors surrounding my actions."

Mala and Althea exchanged knowing glances, but Margaret regarded her with surprise.

"No one here has ever mentioned it to me," she objected.

"They should have." Letty kept the bitterness from her voice. It wasn't Margaret's fault. The other members had taken to her despite her lack of title or social connections, impressed by her equanimity and work ethic. Why would they burden her with the rumors surrounding Letty?

No, that was unfair.

"If I were to befriend the ladies outside of the club, I could do them damage," Letty said. "Many of them are already in precarious straits. Willy's family provides Milly and Willy's living, and they must be careful not to cause a stir. Althea, you are starting your third season. It won't help you to secure invitations to the right parties if it is known you associate with me."

"Ugh. I don't care about the season more than I care about my fellow club members," Althea objected.

"Well, you should," Letty said. "Your cousin does."

The young woman rolled her eyes. "She is living in the past."

Letty shook her head. "She is not the only one. Without Violet acting as the public face of the club, and Lady Phoebe causing scandals enough to distract society, I will bring you down." She turned the plate around but left the tart untouched.

A woman's reputation functioned as currency in the "polite world" of London. Damaged reputations denied one access to anything resembling a normal life.

"Why don't you give *us* the choice," said Mala. "Instead of making the choice for us."

"I, for one, won't be swayed by a bunch of baseless rumors," Althea declared.

Dread unfurled and took up residence in Letty's stomach, spoiling her enjoyment of the tarts and port. "They aren't entirely baseless."

The three other women remained silent, and Letty waited to see if any of them would leave now.

"I should have told you, Margaret, before I invited you home," Letty confessed. "I should have told you the truth."

Margaret spoke up. "You do not have to relate anything you do not wish to, Letty. I will continue our acquaintance, no matter what."

Setting aside their plates, Althea and Mala spoke over one another to endorse Margaret's sentiments. A twinge in Letty's chest might have been indigestion from the combination of strong port and sweet tarts. It might also have been the slow split at the seams of another piece of her armor failing to keep her protected from the outside elements: the steady pulse of friendship beating against its weakening defense.

The words stuck to her tongue. If Greycliff could confess to Letty his darkest secret and let her see his greatest vulnerability, wasn't it time she made a similar show of trust?

"The truth is . . . there was a man," Letty said.

Margaret sighed, the weary exhalation of a woman who had heard such a preface too many times to count.

"A man," she repeated while leaning over to refill Letty's empty jar. Althea pushed off her slippers, then lifted her legs and tucked them under her skirts, curling like a cat in the threadbare chair.

The women settled in as, for the second time, Letty told the story of how she had met Nevin. Strange how some of the guilt and shame faded in the retelling. Was it true that time healed all wounds? Would she someday be able to tell the story without the sting of remembered humiliation biting at her belly?

Mala and Althea gasped and growled in all the right places, and

Margaret threatened Melton's person in such a terrifying and creative manner that Mala copied it in a little notebook for posterity and possible reuse.

By the end of the tale, they'd drunk the port, and Letty felt . . . lighter somehow.

Althea rummaged through an empty basket, sighing in disappointment when all she could unearth were crumbs.

"They have never said anything outright, but Melton made certain my family and I are no longer welcome except in the most obscure circles of society," Letty explained.

Margaret shook her head. "And you've let this go unchallenged for six years? No dances? No assemblies or parties?"

"It doesn't matter," Letty insisted. "My family are all the company I need."

"Hmm." Mala squinted into the opening of the empty port bottle with disappointment. "I remember Mrs. Kneland practically forcing you to attend the lectures. I thought it was because you would rather be working the entire time."

She set the bottle back in the basket. "If they never named you, could it be folks will have forgotten? You should attend a small rout or a crowded ball."

Letty shook her head. "No. Lord Greycliff made the same suggestion, wanting me to attend the Ackley ball, and—"

"The Ackley ball? My cousin and I are going as well," Althea said. "You can come with us."

"Oh, no." Letty stood and braced herself. The delightful camaraderie of the past few days would have to end at some point. Her past would never stay fully buried. "You and your cousin cannot acknowledge me at a social function. It is one thing to be seen in the company of Lord Greycliff. His reputation is unassailable, and besides, he is a man and does not have to abide by the same standards. You, however, are on the marriage mart, Althea. I cannot let my reputation stain yours by association."

"Stain?" Althea snorted. "I could attend a ball wearing scarlet petticoats and a turban made of live snakes, and no one would care. I am too tall, too intelligent, and too plain."

Unperturbed, Althea waved away her friends' vehement protestations, slumping as much as a corset would allow, her back curved into a misshapen C.

"If only my cousin weren't so wedded to the past," she complained. "She was the most daring member of our family, and now all I hear from her is about caution and preservation. I've told her a hundred times anything worth living for is worth fighting for."

Mala's brows dipped. "Not everyone is comfortable standing out. It took a long time for my mother-in-law to accept that her son married an Indian woman." She fingered a coral ribbon flounce on her dress. "Lady Potts caused quite a stir twenty years ago when she set up a household apart from her husband. The thought of going through similar scrutiny once again might be painful."

"Pfft." Althea flipped her palm out in a gesture of impatience. "If they can't stand up for us, they should step aside."

Letty's sympathies lay in both directions.

"None of this changes the fact that Letty is going out in society. She will need protection," Margaret observed.

"No, I didn't say—"

"She'll need a gown as well. If she hasn't been out in six years, anything she has will be out of date," Mala said.

Letty tried again. "I'm not going."

Bouncing on her cushion, Althea clapped with glee. "I have a fitting appointment with Madame Mensonge. You can take my place. Madame always has unfinished gowns that ladies are unable to pay for and can quickly be made over."

Unbidden sympathy for Grey rose in Letty's chest when she tried once more to get the ladies to listen to her. "I never said—"

"And I shall lend you my new wrap, which just arrived from Paris," Margaret exclaimed. "It is made of the finest material and looks like a night sky sprinkled with stars. You will be the prettiest woman there."

Letty opened her mouth to shoo them away so she could work on her presentation, yet somehow, twenty minutes later, she found herself buttoning her pelisse and asking directions to the dressmaker.

She could only hope that following the advice of her new friends didn't meant they were leading her in a merry dance right off the side of a cliff.

14

THE FIRST BALL of the season was always a narrow path across a canyon. Grey had avoided as many balls as he could through the years, accepting the alternative: being thought a cold fish, and thus placed lower on London hostesses' lists than men with less wealth and lower station.

He paced the edge of the room with measured steps, observing the swirling skirts and flashing jewels, flickering candles, and glittering cravat pins. Occasionally, his memories rose to the surface, from the grave in which he'd hoped to bury them forever. How sunlight peeking through diamond-shaped holes in the overlapping leaves would leave him with migraines or the strange auras that heralded a seizure.

As soon as he could, he would leave for the garden, where he could stare steadily out into the safety of the cold and darkness while at his back, the voices from a crowd spoke a secret language of reckless abandon.

"Why do you scowl at those poor dancers? Are they not executing the steps to your liking, my lord? Do they dance with an excess of pleasure?"

Grey turned his head at the familiar voice. His retort died on his lips.

It was her.

The woman he'd kissed. The Letty Fenley who appeared after he'd somehow stumbled upon the key to melting the sheath of combativeness she always wore. The beautiful one, with the soft mouth and shining eyes, who had bared herself before him, turning his ordered existence upside down.

What was *she* doing here? Where was the other Letty?

"Miss Fenley"—he bowed—"you are . . ."

He faltered.

Low light gave a pearly sheen to her skin. Even lower was the neckline of her dress, exposing the curved, white mounds of her shoulders. The contrast of the bright golden daffodil shade of her overdress with the deeper gold of her washed silk skirts called to mind spring in Herefordshire.

The latest fashion in ball gowns had narrowed pointed waists and belled skirts. They pushed a man to the side, the better for him to admire the woman's figure, Grey assumed. Some miracle of needlework and boning had given Letty more curves than she'd ever before displayed.

The ensemble was eminently stylish, right down to the understated coral combs holding back her fine blonde hair. Even with the unaccustomed expanse of skin she presented, the overall effect was demure yet stylish, as though a debutant's dress had been altered to fit a woman.

He hated it.

Just yesterday, he'd been panting with anticipation at seeing her exposed. Now he wanted nothing more than to cover her up.

Where were her sensible caps and severe lines, her long sleeves? How could she let herself be displayed so? Anyone could see the elegant arc of her clavicle and the secret rhythm of her pulse, at the base of her throat, unprotected by her high collar and ribbons. What if they guessed at the creamy softness of her breasts, the tender sweetness in her hidden places?

Worse, her expression was a mixture of nerves and hope. He didn't want to see her like this. Young. Trusting. Like any other woman, anticipating the warm touch of a man's gloved hand on the small of her back.

Vulnerable.

"I thought Lady Ackley might strangle on her words of welcome," Letty said. "I hope you didn't expend too much goodwill on wrangling the invitation."

"Lady Ackley did not need much convincing," he lied.

"Well." Were her fingers trembling as she shook out her skirts? Grey longed to take her hand in his and give her comfort. He could never, of course. He would remain an observer. If he was to convince the Funders of his fitness for the directorship, he could not be seen squiring around the president of Athena's Retreat.

Lady Potts swooped down upon them, Althea loping along in her cousin's wake, the tension between the two of them evident as they made stilted conversation about the music. Letty shifted awkwardly from one foot to another, watching the dance floor with trepidation and a trace of longing.

This would not do. Grey needed her to stay armed and armored. For both their sakes.

"You are kind to lend us your presence," said Lady Potts. "Society is not tolerant of the club members these days. It seems the Guardians have expanded their influence into the heart of the ton."

"As if the ton has ever shown any evidence of a heart," said Letty. "I thought the Guardians were committed to the betterment of the poor. They should try to lower the cost of bread instead of currying favor with a bunch of useless aristocrats."

As the secret softness of Letty's mouth disappeared, Grey released a sigh of relief. Angry, unreasonable, dynamic Letty. She was the woman he wanted to see tonight. The one who held her own.

"Hullo. Looks as though all the pretty ladies are in this corner." Grantham shouldered his way through the crowd and now presented the women with his most elaborate bow, soaking up the resulting giggles and blushes like a sponge. Grey's ears itched at the sound, especially when an all-too-familiar look of delight crossed Letty's face at Grantham's ridiculous compliments.

"Miss Fenley, you look like a daffodil in that gown. Why, you put me in mind of spring in Sussex," Grantham exclaimed.

"Oh, please," Grey muttered, irritated at the earl's presumption. "Puts you in mind of spring. How trite."

A devilish grin split Grantham's face, and he spun on one heel, coming face-to-face with Grey. "Trite, is it? And how would you describe Miss Fenley tonight?"

"Ahem," Grey said, temporizing. He grasped for words as Letty's smile sank in on itself. What was he to say? She looked . . .

"You stand out like a piece of sunlight made flesh," he said, then promptly considered fleeing the ballroom—nay, the country—when Grantham's mouth dropped open and Lady Potts fanned herself.

The only thing keeping him from turning tail was Letty's rounded eyes as she set her gloved hand over her mouth.

Well. For the first time since he'd known her, Grey had rendered Letty speechless.

"Why, darling, look who is here. The reclusive Lord Greycliff in the flesh. How delightful."

At those words, the five of them turned to confront the sight of Victor Armitage and his wife.

Armitage's bland features were fixed into a patently false expression of delight, the smile too wide and the eyes dead still.

Tonight, he was dressed in the first state of fashion, with a bright yellow velvet waistcoat peeping out from under a dark green coat, and a tight pair of breeches the color of moldy bread.

Attached to his arm was his wife, Fanny, a thoroughly unpleasant woman lacking any desire to mimic amiability. Younger than her husband, she had pursued Grey's late father, Daniel, the same year he had met and married Violet.

She, too, had opted for a fashionable ensemble, but her spindly arms were lost amid the waterfalls of lace spilling from the tops of her sleeves. Pink ribbon roses adorned her braids to match the pink of her skirts, reminding Grey of a porcelain shepherdess, if shepherdesses wore a nasty sneer and smelled of too much ambergris.

Grey bowed and engaged in the empty pleasantries that had been drummed into all gentlemen since birth.

"A pleasure to see you again, Mrs. Armitage. You are in excellent looks tonight."

At this last compliment, Letty's eyes darkened ten shades, to nearly indigo.

Grey cleared his throat in warning. "Are you acquainted with the estimable Lady Potts and her delightful cousin, Miss Althea Dertlinger?"

The women exchanged thin-lipped nods.

Grey continued. "No one could overlook the Earl Grantham, of course, and I'm pleased to introduce the former Lady Greycliff's *close* friend Miss Fenley." Grey laid a subtle emphasis on his words.

Armitage glanced in surprise at Grey, perhaps wondering if this was part of some larger plan. His wife recalled him to the social niceties by squeezing his upper arm with clawed fingers.

"Hooowww do you do?" Armitage chuckled, but he sounded pained.

Fanny disengaged her claws to flutter her fan beneath her nose as though she smelled something disagreeable.

Rather than glaring at Fanny, however, Letty's eyes were fixed on something else entirely. Grey followed her gaze across the ballroom. On the other side of the dance floor, next to Lady Ackley, stood Melton. Beside him, and staring right back at Letty, was Nevin.

Fanny leered, her nostrils quivering with the scent of wounded prey. Tendrils of unease wrapped themselves around Grey. He'd been confident Letty would hold her own at this event and that if tonight went well, she might make her way back into society.

Oddly enough, none of the guilt he felt at closing Athena's Retreat was mitigated by this thought.

An older woman sporting a limp purple turban joined their company. Lady Olivia, a particular friend of Fanny's with a sour disposition and a voice that carried. Behind her trailed three or four more ladies of their set, all with narrow minds and deep pockets.

"Ahem. As you are no doubt aware, Lord Greycliff"—Armitage, unhappy with having lost the center of attention, raised his voice— "many people say Mrs. Kneland ought to have bent her philanthropic endeavors toward activities that benefited our great nation, rather than wasted them on distractions like her club."

"That *club*," echoed Lady Olivia, "gives the ladies of London a bad name. Why, what will the lower orders think if their betters take to aping men by gathering in a club and avoiding their home and family?"

"It is unseemly is what it is," hissed Fanny, ignoring her husband's attempt to polish his words of condemnation.

"Athena's Retreat provides a great service to society," Lady Potts protested. "There are many young matrons who benefit from learning how science can help the household."

Althea did not seem as enthused as her cousin about the myriad ways science could be applied to daily chores. Nevertheless, she dutifully listed some of the properties of vinegar and the small experiments they'd done in their last lecture series.

Meanwhile, Letty stood stock-still, seemingly oblivious to what was happening around her.

Grey considered making a joke about her being so short he could rest his elbow on her topknot. Or goading her into a temper with an observation about how her tied tongue was more attractive than her new gown. Something, anything to calm the tiny signals of distress, the almost imperceptible shaking of the curls at her temple, the clenching and unclenching of her clasped fingers, the deepening blush across her delicate cheekbones.

The sounds of the ballroom overwhelmed him. The violas' strings were scratchy, and the harpsichord was out of tune. What seemed like a crowd of dozens now surrounded them, mouths agape with malevolent glee as Armitage held forth on the selfishness of women who spent their time away from hearth and home.

Althea, beringed by Fanny's friends and allies, tried valiantly to counter his arguments. However, Armitage's smug assertions and Fanny's needle-sharp jabs tore holes in Althea's gentle rebuttals. A red-faced Lady Potts stood arguing with a portly gentleman, his jowls quivering with outrage, spittle flying from his lips, as he repeated nonsensical arguments linking female education to mental deficiencies and increased criminal behavior.

On the periphery of the crowd, Nevin watched Letty with hungry eyes. Fanny stood a few feet away, earrings rattling, whispering behind her fan with emotion. Disdain? Or was it envy?

Althea tried again. "The ladies of Athena's Retreat do not contribute to the moral decline of England by taking a dish of tea with one another and learning proper methods of orchid cultivation."

"That isn't all that happens at your club, is it?" Fanny countered.

Her sharp teeth glinted as she advanced on the younger woman. "What of the strange explosions in the middle of the night? The sudden disappearance of Lady Phoebe? What of the *character* of your membership?"

Appearing pained at Fanny's tone, Armitage patted her shoulder, keeping his eyes on Grey even as he addressed his wife.

"The larger point, my dear, is the poor and hungry who sit out on our streets, no dignity, no respectability left to them because of the self-indulgence and profligacy of the last generation." Armitage's voice, still silvery and genteel, contained a firmer tone, as though he were speaking to naughty children. "Families have gone astray, leaving the clean and wholesome life of the countryside, along with their faith and their morals. We must show them the proper way to live. If women are absent from the home, who is to raise the children to know right from wrong?"

As though the words had turned a key, they unlocked Letty from her frozen state, and she turned her head toward Armitage.

"What exactly would you have us teach our children?" she asked.

A hush fell on the crowd. Those surrounding Fanny and her husband smiled, with anticipation of engaging in a debate about morals with a woman who had no claim to them. The bottom fell out of Grey's stomach, but it was too late to intervene.

"Or, shall I say, what will you have us teach half of our children?" Letty asked.

There are some wars that are unwinnable. Some opinions will never change, not because the people holding them are stupid or bad, but because their stories are narrow. To widen their horizons meant toppling their world—they were scared.

Fear is a powerful force.

Of all the women in attendance tonight, Grey assumed Letty knew this better than any of them. Nerves thinned her voice, but she spoke steadily.

"Fully half of our children will grow up in the dark, watching the other half walk out into the light, simply because some were born girls and some were born boys. Fully half our children will spend their lives without recourse to safety when they are brutalized, because marriage turns them into chattel, not people. Half of them will be free to travel the world and bring the ideals of our culture to another place, and the other half will never travel more than four streets over from where they were born."

She looked over at Grey briefly, and he willed his approval to show in his eyes, dipping his chin slightly in a sign meant just for her. Letty took a deep breath and continued.

"If women who gather to improve themselves are a harmful influence on the poor, it is because you believe the poor should remain poor," Letty continued. "If learning reason and logic is harmful, it is because you want women to remain confused and ignorant."

No longer a protest, her words became a plea.

"You have a choice, however."

Grey had meant for her to take her place in society. Had she ruined that tonight? Would any of her speech fall on fertile ground, or had these people already taken a side?

"You can choose to meet us where we are," she continued, "to welcome women who wish to educate themselves, to respect the desire to learn and encourage those who want to explore the world. Or"—Letty drew a breath, knowing she might suffer for her words—"or your methods of bullying and intimidation will eventually grow more repressive and more violent, because you cannot push us backward. We will not be denied."

"What nonsense." Fanny Armitage, dripping with disdain, spat the words.

A hiss traveled through the crowd of Armitage's supporters, and Letty recoiled at the sound.

"What does someone like her know of *denial*?" The speaker was farther back in the crowd, but his question was audible, and someone else laughed in response. The power of Letty's words dissolved in the acid of manufactured indignation.

"What does she know about desire is what *I'm* asking." The portly gentleman had left off his harangue of Lady Potts and now waggled his eyebrows.

Enough. Letty had spoken for the rights of women to gather at the club. Not for her own benefit, but for the benefit of a stranger—a girl who might someday need the haven of Athena's Retreat.

Time for Grey to step in.

THE MORE THE crowd convulsed around her, the sicker Letty felt. The orchestra finished a reel, pulling aside the buffer of musical distraction. Whatever pretense of bravery she'd donned at the beginning of the evening had disappeared in the face of Fanny Armitage's knowing sneer.

Each glance at her from one of the beautifully dressed ladies was like a pin stuck into her skin with terrible deliberation. No matter where Letty's eyes rested, she saw heads bent together and mouths forming familiar words.

She didn't need to hear them to know what they were saying. Two of the young bucks who'd been flanking Armitage whispered and laughed as they looked in her direction. One of them, once he caught her eyes, winked with exaggeration, a nasty leer pulling at the side of his wet lips.

At any moment, someone could point a finger at her and call her out. The words people whispered behind their hands might be said aloud.

Fallen woman. Sinner. No longer a virgin. No longer considered respectable.

Those words were not the whole of her. Even if they were true, they didn't make the rest of her concerns any less valid. That wouldn't matter, though. Redemption did not exist in the ton. A woman must adhere to their rules—rules written in black and white—or risk ostracism forever. No matter that life was unwieldy and complex. No matter that the choices she'd made at seventeen were far different than the ones she might make at twenty-three.

This had been a terrible idea.

Letty was peering around the figures closest to her, searching for an exit, when Grey cupped her elbow and leaned to whisper in her ear.

"Will you do me the honor of a dance?"

A dance? They stood at the shore of a parquet ocean teeming with silk-clad sharks, teeth glinting like gemstones in polished gold settings. A dance would put them in the center of those dazzling predators, and her reputation was just the blood they thirsted for.

"I must decline your offer, my lord," she replied, glancing at his fingers wrapped around her arm. So frightened was she that she could barely feel the heat of them even through the tissue-thin silk of her ball gown. "It cannot improve your countenance to be any more in my company."

Grey's hand slid down her arm, and he grasped her hand gently. Raising it to his mouth, he bowed, holding her gaze, and brushed the back of her silk glove with his lips.

Now *that* she could feel.

It burned.

"I do believe I am coming to understand Arthur's sway over your sisterhood of scientists," he murmured. "The reason he never spoke is that if he asked any of you a question, you would give him the opposite answer from that which he required. I am not asking, Letty." Grey smiled and caressed her hand with his thumb. "Dance with me."

Letty should take him to task for his high-handedness. A wealth of retorts that correlated his arrogance with the size of his head ran through her brain, but none of them sprang to her lips.

For the truth was that she wanted to dance with him. In his company was the one place she felt safe tonight.

"Good evening, Greycliff. Miss Fenley," a familiar voice said from over Grey's shoulder.

Damn.

She'd hesitated too long, and now her past had finally caught her.

Before Grey acknowledged Nevin standing behind him, he squeezed her trembling fingers. Letty swallowed and nodded quickly. Keeping her hand in his as he turned around, Grey gave his cousin the slightest of bows in greeting.

"That was a moving defense of your sex, Miss Fenley," Nevin said, his limpid brown eyes gazing at her. "You have always"—his voice rose when he caught sight of the icy hauteur on Grey's face—"erm, always made a sound and reasoned argument for the scientific education of women," he finished in a burst, the words mashing together.

After craning his neck to look around—checking to see if his father was nearby—Nevin cleared his throat.

"If you would allow me the honor . . ."

Grey blinked at the force with which Letty gripped his hand.

"I'm afraid Miss Fenley has already promised me this dance," he said, interrupting Nevin's invitation.

Fingers entwined with Letty's, he strode past Nevin, then stopped abruptly and turned toward her.

"Unless . . ." He regarded her solemnly. "Did you want to dance with Mr. Hughes instead, Miss Fenley? I would give you the choice of where to bestow your attention. You are a person who has shown the grace and fortitude to make your beliefs known in even the most harrowing of circumstances."

Letty gaped. Had he lost his mind? Out of the corner of her eye, she glimpsed the Earl Melton in conversation with a sour-faced man. The earl was staring right back at her.

Nevin waited, a penitent droop to his shoulders, hands rubbing the sides of his evening coat. He'd adopted the popular trend of the mustache, and it looked as though one of Lady Pott's tarantulas had climbed into his nose and gotten stuck halfway.

He resembled a nervous, untested young man who lived in his head most days unless prodded forth by an outside force—the same as the day she'd met him six years earlier. Nothing in his life had happened to give him wrinkles at the corners of his eyes. No sorrow had marked him; no great joy had transformed his mouth from petulant to determined.

"I am certain of my choice, Lord Greycliff," she replied. "I will have no regrets."

Twirling skirts of watered silk and diaphanous netting beckoned to her. Without looking back, she set her hand in the crook of Grey's elbow and let him lead her to the dance floor. Like tiny flames, the stares from the crowd licked at her neck and the backs of her arms as they waltzed. As it was impossible to keep herself from flushing, Letty kept her head up and her eyes on a point somewhere above Grey's thick black brows as he drew breath to speak.

"You have been extraordinarily brave tonight," he told her.

A dazzling rush of candlelight reflecting off the myriad crystals in the Ackley chandeliers spun across his face. If she closed her eyes halfway, the crowd melted into a hazy rainbow of blacks and blues, pinks, yellows, and whites. She should feel triumphant. All she wanted to do was crawl beneath her covers and never think of tonight again.

"Bravery is much less exciting than the novels make it out to be," she confessed.

Grey shook his head. "You read too many novels."

"I want nothing more than to run away," she said. The thought of her narrow little bed at home with the pile of worn blankets and the sound of her sisters snoring nearly brought tears to her eyes. The man spinning his partner next to them glanced over at her, and she felt every inch of exposed skin bared to his gaze.

"Most young ladies of my acquaintance enjoy the waltz," Grey mused. He turned her away from the man with greedy eyes, pulling her closer.

"Do you have no ear for music?" he asked. But Letty did not want to be teased. Too many truths had been uncovered between them for lighthearted conversations, even in the midst of a ball.

"I have no wish to be a spectacle." A piece of her heart tore off and winged its way up with the smoke from the candles. "I wish I *could* just dance. I wish I could be any other girl in the arms of a beautiful man. They're looking at me."

She wouldn't give the ton the satisfaction of her tears.

"Who?"

"Everyone. Everyone is talking about me or looking at me, and it isn't because of what I said to Victor Armitage. It's because of Nevin and what I did."

"You did nothing."

Letty tried to pull away, but he would not release his hold. "For six years, I've carried this weight, and I hate it. I hate the way they look at me."

The tundra of his eyes blazed with an unfamiliar heat, and Grey deliberately turned them toward the center of the dance floor.

"Yet you found the fortitude to stand up and stand out, even after the pain those people have caused you."

Whatever fortitude she might have exhibited was gone now. Her mouth was bone-dry, and her palms were sweaty.

Like upside-down peonies, ladies floated past them, the lace of their petticoats peeping out when their partners twirled them.

"What I said tonight was born of necessity and pained me," Letty said. "When I was younger, before Nevin, that's when I was brave."

"Then I shall return some bravery to you," Grey declared. "Look at me." They passed directly beneath the Ackleys' ridiculous chandelier, festooned with paper flowers that drifted in the breeze of the whirling couples. "Look at me looking at you."

Slowly, she straightened her back and held his gaze.

"Nothing anyone here thinks about you has any bearing on who you are or what you can do," he said.

A low snicker drifted past, and Letty clenched her jaw, but she kept her eyes on Grey's.

"Look at me looking at you," he repeated. "I am looking at a beautiful woman. A woman who inspires others, who is fiercely loyal, and who has a brilliant, stunning mind. Even though most of what people say goes over her head." He paused. "Because she is ridiculously short."

She swallowed a lump in her throat and blinked.

"You have no reason to hide from them," Grey declared. "You are brave, and you are good. Shine, Letty."

Brighter than every single candle in all the ballrooms of London, Grey's smile burned away the fog of guilt and shame.

"Let them see you shine."

So for the rest of the dance, Letty shone.

Her heartbeat settled into the joyous rhythm of a woman waltzing with a handsome man, and her head tipped back a little as she smiled her assent.

Grey nodded once, then plunged them both in wide sweeping arcs across the floor again and again, skimming by the other couples, who seemed lugubrious and muted in comparison. A breathy laugh escaped her when he pulled her toward him to avoid a collision, and her belly clenched at the look on his face at the sound.

Awareness of his heat and the flush high on his cheeks overwhelmed her senses when he bowed low at the end of the dance.

"I . . . I believe I've had enough attention for one night," she said. "I will find a retiring room and wait until Lady Potts is ready to leave."

"No," he said, the word clipped short and his gaze lingering on her mouth. "Get your wrap and meet me at the side entrance. I will take you home myself."

She supposed she wasn't done following his lead, for, after a whispered word with Althea, she stole through the crowd, threading herself this way and that so that no one noticed her departure. Draping her shawl over her coiffure, she hid her face when she slipped out the side and into Grey's carriage.

With a jerk, the horses pulled forward, and Letty fell back against the soft cushions and shook her head.

"I hope no one saw me leave with you. I would hate to ruin myself all over again, simply because I turned coward at the last minute."

"Coward?" he asked. "I would call you anything but."

The wrap did nothing to protect her from the chilled night air, and her skin pebbled. She rubbed her arms, and Grey switched sides to sit next to her, helping her pull a clean, soft carriage blanket around her shoulders.

"Still," Letty said, "I believe I shall wait a while before attending another ball."

Even now, her nerves still clamored, although that had more to do with Grey's large, hard body taking up most of the seat. The blanket had slipped, and if she leaned back from the window, her bare shoulders would rub against the fine wool of his jacket. He'd been the most beautiful man in the ballroom tonight. Steady. Unruffled.

Grey moved closer and whispered in her ear, his lips brushing her earlobe.

"You were inspiring."

He said nothing more, but neither did he move away, leaving the choice to her, his mouth less than an inch from her neck, his firm thigh pressed against the thin silk of her ball gown. When the carriage hit a rut, the comb in her hair slipped, and he sucked in his breath. A noise of pleasure—and anticipation.

Every time they came together, her skin tightened and her senses exploded. She peeled the elbow-length gloves from her arms, the indescribably sensuous scent of citrus and spice sending her back in memory to their first kiss.

She put the gloves to the side, then turned so she and Grey were eye to eye.

Courage. Grace.

No inane compliments for this man. Instead, he saw into the heart of her and repeated back her aspirations.

Shine, he'd told her.

She traced the lines of his lips with her fingertip. Too dark to gauge his mood by the color of his eyes. Instead, the hitch in his breath served as a guide.

"I would like to kiss you," she told him. "I want to feel the heat of you between my thighs again."

She put her lips to his and asked the question.

"Do you want me to touch you, Grey?"

He opened his mouth to answer, and they fell into one another, restraint snapping free, as he pulled her onto his lap, heedless of the yards of silk crushed between the two of them.

Hunger spilled over and scorched her bones, stole her reason, while his hands roamed her body. Within seconds, her bodice sagged at her waist and he'd removed her corset, exposing her to the night air.

Pulling away from his ravenous kisses, Letty set a hand on his chest.

"Wait."

He'd taken her breast in his palm, but at her command he froze, holding her nipple between his forefinger and thumb, exerting the barest amount of pressure.

While he waited, Letty reached between them and opened the fall of his trousers. His thick length pushed against the linen of his drawers, and she licked her lips in satisfaction when she freed the whole of him. One hand clenched the edge of the seat cushion when she circled the plum-shaped tip of him with her fingertip, but his other hand never moved, not even when she fondled his heavy sac and his head dropped back in pleasure.

"Letty." His voice rumbled and vibrated through his bones into the center of her. "Stop torturing me. Tell me I can move again."

She paused in her ministrations and relished the feeling of tamped potential between her legs. It would be easy to pretend, to repeat everything they'd done in Violet's office.

Tonight was not about easy. Tonight was about truth.

"The truth is, I do not know what to do next," she told him.

His head came up, and he snared her with his black stare.

"What we did together before," she said, "I hadn't even known it was possible."

Grey said nothing to her confession, but his thumb made small circles around her areola.

"I know at the end, I felt empty. I want to be closer."

Yards away, the rest of London went about its business and its pleasure in the dim cobbled alleyways and brightly lit taprooms. Amid it all, Letty and Grey tossed possibilities back and forth to one another with a speaking glance, a slow caress, the languid stroke of wet flesh against wet flesh.

"I want you inside me," she confessed.

No, not a confession.

A declaration.

Weightlessness buoyed Letty up, up—her arms raised over her head to grasp hold of the looped leather of the carriage strap. The tiny coral combs fell to the ground, and her hair spilled down her back as he shifted them so the head of his cock sat at her wet entrance.

"You are in control," he assured her. "I will not spill my seed inside you. Stop. Go. Fast. Slow. Your every wish is my command. Tonight, I am here for your pleasure."

True to his word, Grey murmured his praise while she slowly allowed him in. Whatever ghosts had remained of that night with Nevin were exorcised in the confines of Lord Greycliff's carriage. There was no sharp pain or confusion. Instead, he stretched her tender tissues with his thick shaft, remaining perfectly still while she let herself sink inch by inch until the whole of him filled her and her clit tightened into a knot of need.

"My God, so perfect," he said, wrapping her hair around his fist, his lips to her forehead, eyes half-closed. "So slick and sweet."

The curtains fluttered in the spring night air as Letty swayed back and forth, grinding herself against Grey's hips in search of relief. He detailed his delight in the softness of her skin, the slope of her breasts, the sound she made when he met her strokes with deep thrusts of his own.

The taste of his tongue, the caress of his hands, they grounded her, reattaching her body to her mind. Move like *this*, and stars appeared behind her eyelids, move like *that*, and he growled naughty words that made her laugh. Into the night, they came against each other again and again, removed from reality, firmly in place, skin to skin.

Making love to Grey revealed the world in the same way turning a page or beginning an equation opened endless doors. All this and more went through her head, then disappeared as his hips lost their rhythm and she clenched her legs to keep from falling. Her focus narrowed to the pulse between her thighs that was making her lose her mind.

"Are you with me, sweetheart?" he asked.

Startled by the endearment, her eyes flew to his. Even in the dark, she could see his jaw clenched with the effort it took to let her have charge of their pace.

No doubt a slip of the tongue. A careless piece of nonsense, like his praise of her breasts and her sheath.

No doubt.

Holding Letty close, her breasts rubbing against the damask of his waistcoat, Grey urged her to her peak, his compliments growing shorter, his voice more guttural, until all he could do was rasp against her mouth.

"Come with me, Letty."

"Oh, yes," she said. "Always."

Faster and faster she rode him—until the tethers broke and joy engulfed her. The world disappeared, then reappeared, utterly new and even more dangerous, as wave after wave of release shuddered through her.

Before she was completely sensible, Grey pulled her by her hips and thrust himself against her belly—once, twice, and then a third time with a deep groan. The hot rush of seed across her stomach pulled Letty out of her dreamlike state. Still, she could not bring herself to move away.

For the longest time, they remained pressed together. Grey covered her neck and shoulders with kisses that burned like little sparks. The creak of the carriage wheels and clopping of horse's hooves blended into a soothing, syncopated background while Letty came back to herself.

"Don't move just yet," he whispered, and rummaged beneath her skirts. "Let me . . ."

He wiped away his seed as best he could with his handkerchief. Letty buried her face in his shoulder in embarrassment, but Grey continued to put her to rights with his customary efficiency.

There were no more endearments or odes to her breasts, but neither was there any stiffness or hint of censure as he helped her pull up her bodice and smooth her skirts while she settled herself at his side.

"If you would bring me back to the club, I can have Winthram order me a hack," she said, rubbing at the wrinkles in her overdress.

Grey sniffed. "You cannot travel abroad at night alone in a hired cab. I will bring you home myself."

Shine, he'd told her. But only in his arms and only for that moment. The instant they'd left the ballroom, she'd turned back into Letty Fenley, the girl who'd said yes. Grey was not the perfect being she'd once thought him. Still, he occupied an entirely different stratum than she. Why else would he be so obtuse?

"You cannot set me down in front of my home," she said. "What will my family and my neighbors say if they see you hand me out of a carriage alone, with my hair undone and dress wrinkled?"

Staring at her lap, she fumbled with her elbow-length gloves while the silence smothered the last of her pleasure.

"Let me," he said. With deft fingers, he turned her glove right side out and slid the satin casing over her hand. When he was finished, he held her palm in his and rubbed his thumb across her knuckles.

She looked over when he cleared his throat.

"Thank you, for sharing yourself with me," he said.

Oh. That was a surprising way to think of their intimacy. Letty supposed she had shared herself with him. The thought made her giddy and a little frightened.

"If there should be any consequences . . ." The corner of Grey's eye twitched, and a lump formed in the middle of her throat. "That is to say . . . What I mean is . . ."

The carriage turned the corner into the mews behind Beacon House. Letty pulled her hand from Grey's grasp and set her forefinger against his lips.

The ball was over. They'd had their waltz. Everything they'd said and felt must remain within the confines of the dark interior of the viscount's conveyance. Once she stepped foot outside this cocoon, she was back to being the daughter of a shopkeeper with a questionable reputation.

Still, she had her pride.

"Do not say anything you do not mean," she told him. "I have no expectations beyond those accorded a woman of my station."

"Letty," he admonished gently, pushing her hand away and fixing one of the coral combs that kept slipping in her hair. "I meant . . ."

But the carriage had stopped.

She pushed open the door before the footman had finished pulling out the folding stair.

"Any consequences will be mine to bear," she told him over her shoulder. "Do not trouble yourself about me, my lord. I have always been able to take care of myself."

15

When Grey Returned home to Beacon House after a lengthy ride that morning, he'd been told Letty had paid a call. Hoping to catch her, he'd taken the stairs to his office two at a time, without bothering to change out of his riding boots, senses still reeling from their lovemaking in the carriage the evening before. His conscience had eaten at him all night, and he'd resolved to speak with her. It wasn't right for him to conduct an affair with her—especially after what Nevin had done.

The realization that he must break it off with her was contributing to a dull headache, which intensified when he found a scribbled note on his desk.

"'*I'm sorry I couldn't mate with you*'? No, '*wait for you.*'" Squinting at Letty's illegible scrawl, he tried to read the message aloud. What did that say? "'*Emergency*'? '*Explosions*'?"

Either gigantic pants were coming to get them, or something had happened regarding Milly and Willy's latest experiment. What did it mean that neither option was causing him much concern?

Falling into his chair, Grey noticed a splash of color on the floor by the side of his desk. A thickly woven shawl lay in a heap next to a fraying cloth bag. Letty must have set them to the side when she wrote the note, then forgotten them. Grey picked up the shawl and held it to his nose. His mouth watered at the scent of vanilla and raspberry tarts, and he fantasized about licking Letty's plump pink nipples until she cried out.

Astounding how that prickly bundle of fury had handed him her trust last night without hesitation.

He'd thought to stay removed.

Instead, Grey had come undone.

Deftly, Letty had turned the tables with a single whisper.

Always.

Crumpling the shawl into a ball, he was trying to thrust it into the cloth bag when the bag's contents spilled out. Pages and pages of Letty's terrible handwriting littered the floor. Looking from the papers to the note on his desk, he had an idea.

Exiting from the back of a stationer two hours later, Grey adjusted his topper and squinted at the sky. Noise from the front of the store, which faced out onto the heavy traffic of Piccadilly, filtered between the cramped spaces between the buildings. Here on Jermyn Street, only a few small carriages stood waiting for shoppers. A handful of hearty trees that could survive the London air had decided to trust in the warming weather and send forth their tiny green buds into the world. The sight put a spring in his step, and Grey decided against a hack. Instead, he walked toward St. James's Street.

Despite the fresh air, his headache had intensified. The pain was settling into his bones, and he felt the lack of sleep the night before. This must account for why it had taken him so long to recognize that the small black carriage a few feet behind him had been outside the stationer. With a flip of his wrist, he adjusted the grip of his gold-topped walking stick. In a matter of seconds, the knob would twist off and a blade would emerge—sharp enough to be fatal.

Grey turned to confront the vehicle just as the carriage curtain was pulled back and a familiar face peered out from its confines.

"White's, is it?" Armitage asked as the carriage came to a halt.

What was this about? Grey nodded his thanks and let the footman open the door.

The carriage smelled of old tobacco and parchment. It wasn't an unpleasant scent, but neither did it carry any comfort.

"I understand Athena's Retreat is still in operation," Armitage said as Grey settled back against the cushions.

"I see no reason for urgency," he countered without inflection. "What does it matter when it closes?"

Armitage appeared slightly pained, as though he'd bitten into an apple only to find it tasted of pear. "I gave you several reasons last night at the ball."

Grey would not give the appearance of kowtowing to a man like Victor Armitage. "The state of England's moral fiber does not rest on whether or not I close a club for female scientists."

Armitage folded and unfolded his hands while he peered out the carriage window with apparent disinterest. "You think much of yourself if you imagine the directorship will fall into your lap without a test of loyalty."

"A loyalty test? To whom do I owe my allegiance?" Grey asked. "Not to you. To the Funders? Perhaps. To my country? Always."

"This country needs a strong hand to guide it." Armitage dropped his pretense of ambivalence and leaned forward. "Power must remain with men who look and think like us. The more we allow others to share in it, the less control we can wield when things go wrong."

A terrible realization that Armitage's naked lust for power was just that—naked, unadorned with the wrappings of responsibility or duty—made Grey sick to his stomach. Were his own desires as base and selfish?

"You may set me here," Grey said. He'd lost his taste for company and wished to return home. "I will walk the rest of the way."

Instead, Armitage called out the directions for Beacon House to his driver and sat back, his Adam's apple jerking in the loose skin at his neck as he swallowed. He glanced out the window and shook his head once quickly, as if dislodging something unpleasant, then continued as though Grey had not spoken.

"This is about our country. This is about what we will lose—what you will lose—if political reforms go forward. Upheaval is dangerous. These women are to serve as an example to others. I do not believe women should be shut up at home and kept ignorant, but it must be impressed upon them that neither can they participate in radical acts. Everyone has a place in society, *Lord* Greycliff."

Armitage's emphasis was an unsubtle reminder of where Grey's own place in society lay. For all his high-minded beliefs about the rights of men to control their own destiny and the unerring conviction that the men of Stalybridge were the voice of the future, Grey could not lie to himself. He was a member of the nobility and enjoyed authority and influence simply by virtue of his birth. It would be a radical act indeed for him to give even a portion of this away.

Power was its own addictive pleasure, and a small, unattractive part of him wanted it more than anything. More than his love for Violet, his sympathy for Milly and Willy, and his unnameable feelings for Letty Fenley.

"It is our duty to protect the divisions in our society," Armitage continued. "Upon them rest the fortunes of our queen and our country."

What if the opposite were true? What if fortunes of the empire were hampered by the divisions?

"I'm told the women in the club experiment with flammable materials." Armitage's voice had turned sugary with false concern. "It would be a pity if one of the experiments went too far." He sighed. "Athena's Retreat is attached to Beacon House, is it not? Why, the entire structure could go up in flames. You must be careful, my lord."

Grey squeezed his walking stick. "How dare you threaten—"

"It's not a threat." Armitage waved away the concept with a hand. "It's an illustration. Of power. Of control. Of how close chaos lurks beneath the surface."

A sickening foreboding punched Grey in the chest as they turned the corner. Sure enough, thin wisps of smoke rose from behind Beacon House.

"What have you done?" he asked, knowing the answer already and reaching for the door handle before he'd finished his question.

Armitage widened his eyes, attempting to appear guileless. "You've been sitting on a tinderbox, Greycliff."

As Grey flung himself from the carriage, the rest of Armitage's answer reached his ears.

"How long did you think it would take before someone lit a match?"

AS THE LAST of the fire brigade wagons rolled away, straggling bystanders huddled outside, amid the dirty puddles and the foul scent of burnt timber and wet sand. Inside, the smell was worse, and the sound of dripping water punctuated the murmured conversations.

"How many dead?" asked Letty.

Winthram paused in the act of wiping his soot-stained face on a piece of toweling. He and Letty stood huddled in a corner of the small lecture room, away from everyone else.

Squinting in thought, he answered her question haltingly. "We were lucky the fire started over the public rooms. In the end, it was the cockroaches . . ."

Poor Lady Potts sat weeping quietly into Lady Peckinpaugh's arms a few feet away.

". . . and one of the older hedgehogs. Flavia Smythe-Harrow's cockatoo is not expected to survive, but she was sickly even before the fire."

Letty sighed, and Winthram nodded in commiseration. A handful of members were gathered in small groups, consoling one another, almost six hours after the first cries of warning had gone out. There had been a few in the club when the fire began, well away from the workrooms.

Most had heeded Greycliff's plea that they return to their homes. Only stragglers remained drinking Mrs. Sweet's terrible tea while she listened to their chests for any smoke damage.

Aside from the fatalities Winthram had listed, there were no serious injuries among the rest of them, other than a few scrapes and bruises when they'd tried to hide their experiments and close off the secret part of the club before the men of the fire brigade entered the building.

"Yes, Violet paid for fire insurance," Grey was saying as he came striding into the room from the back entrance, Grantham at his side. Bareheaded, he bore similar soot marks as Winthram.

"Lucky I came to the club early for fencing practice with Winthram," the earl said.

Having arrived at the club at the same time as the fire brigade, Grantham had been instrumental in keeping the club from being discovered. He'd hectored the brigade workers to mind their feet on the carpets and shooed them away from the door to the laboratories by telling them the ladies' retiring rooms were back there.

Letty had been coming out of the front door to the club, hoping to convince the brigade to move their conveyance, when a black carriage had pulled in front and Grey had leaped out. She'd caught a glimpse of his companion as the door swung open, but the carriage never stopped.

Fear had etched itself on his features, his dark skin blanched to a pale grey.

Letty had never seen him so unguarded, except when making love. He'd run up to her and, without checking to see who was looking, cupped her chin in his hand.

"Are you all right?" he'd asked.

The middle of a catastrophe was the worst time to swoon, but Letty was sorely tempted by the concern in Grey's voice and the tenderness in his eyes. Thankfully, she was made of sterner stuff, and she backed away from his touch before anyone had noticed. He'd stared at her for another second, then at his hand, as though it belonged to someone else.

"A fire . . . ," she'd said.

"I know." Taking the stairs two at a time, he disappeared inside the club without looking back again.

"There's a fire mark on the side of the building," Grey said now. "They've never been called before today."

Although the various fire insurance brigades were now consolidated into the London Fire Engine Establishment, each individual company still gave out fire marks when a policy was purchased—metal signs to alert the brigade if the owners had insurance.

"Violet bought the insurance on the advice of her lawyers when she built the Retreat," Letty said. "Athena's Retreat has its own fire safety system."

Coming to stand at her side, Grantham rubbed his chin in thought as he leaned against the wall. "Arthur told me he'd instituted something like that. What went wrong?"

At the implied criticism, Winthram bristled. "Nothing went wrong."

When Grantham cocked a brow in surprise at the tone, the doorman remembered himself. "Nothing went wrong, my lord." His glance flicked over to Grey, who was watching Lady Potts with an enigmatic expression.

"We're meant to fight fires from the *inside* of the club," the doorman explained. "There are warning bells and different buckets, depending on what is on fire and where."

Nodding, Grey turned his attention back to them. "It is an excellent system. We think the blaze was caused by a bird's nest on top of one of the chimneys."

"We have them swept on the regular," Winthram objected.

"By machines, not by sweepers," Grey countered.

This was true. None of the women could stomach the practice of sending children into the flues to clean them.

Exhaustion and worry sharpened Letty's tongue. "I suppose you'd rather we shove orphaned boys up."

The finest of lines appeared at the corners of Grey's mouth. Tiny cracks in his facade. Letty fought the urge to set a finger to them and wipe them away.

"Of course not," he said. "I am in full support of Lord Ashley's reforms. I merely point out that a sweep might have seen the nesting birds, though there is no guarantee."

She couldn't believe this was accidental.

"The Guardians did this," Letty said. "The fire was too large and spread too fast for one nest to be the cause."

Grantham shook his head. "That doesn't make sense. Armitage is an arse on each end, but he wouldn't stoop to this. More than likely, he thinks he came out the winner in his exchange with you last night. Why would he threaten the club if he believes he has the upper hand?"

When Grey said nothing, Grantham's eyes narrowed, and Letty shivered with foreboding.

"What aren't you saying, Greycliff?" Grantham asked.

"It doesn't matter what caused it," Grey said, raising his voice. "The story will be in the broadsheets tomorrow. Half a dozen insurance men were tramping through the public rooms. You tried your best, but they might have seen something. Your reprieve is at an end."

"Oh no," Letty said, grasping hold of his sleeve. "Don't do this. Not now."

Her words fell on deaf ears. Storms over the North Sea had returned to Grey's eyes, and Letty knew there would be no more pretend bemusement at the talk of a vote and no way anyone could change this man's mind.

This couldn't be the end of everything. They'd come so far and fought so hard.

"You promised us, Greycliff," she pleaded, uncaring of who watched them as she gripped his arm. Hating the thread of fear in her voice, nonetheless she tried to reason with him.

"You promised Violet to take care of the club. We can come up with a plan. There has to be . . ." Nothing sprang to mind.

Mala's head popped up from a settee where she was bundled in a quilt while Althea and Flavia consoled her.

"What do you mean, we 'tried our best'?" she said, loud enough that everyone else in the room fell silent. "We are having a vote in four days. That is when we will decide about the club."

Her protests were a waste of breath.

Grey strode to the center of the room. Despite his filthy attire and his dirty face, he was every inch the nobleman, an ice prince at his most impenetrable.

"You have forty-eight hours to collect your belongings and clear out your workrooms," he announced. "Anything you cannot take home, we will store for you in the eventuality the club reopens."

"No. You cannot do this," Flavia wailed. Lady Peckinpaugh leveled a ferocious stare at Grey, and Lady Potts's quiet weeping turned to a feral growl.

Loss sucked the color from the room as Letty's gaze settled on each member. Weeks ago, she would have sworn these women were eccentric, irritating, and bent on driving her mad. This hadn't changed.

What had changed was Letty's acknowledgment of how much they meant to her.

On the other side of the room, Althea Dertlinger rose from the settee. Letty braced herself for a fight. Instead, Althea's words were faint but measured.

"He's right. This could have been much worse." She held out her shaking hands. Beneath a dirty strip of linen, one palm was red and blistered.

"In the end, we have to take care of one another." Glancing over at her cousin, Althea's eyes filled with tears, but she spoke without a note of regret. "We have to admit defeat before anyone else is hurt. Athena's Retreat must close."

16

"YOU DID THE right thing, Greycliff."

Uncertain how much faith to put in Grantham's assurances, Grey said nothing and turned his attention back to the glass of whiskey he held.

Drink, only in moderation.

Setting the tumbler on his desk, he regarded his friend, who was lounging in a great chair as though it were a bed.

"Are you certain you don't want a whiskey?" he asked Grantham.

"Nay. Mrs. Sweet managed to get past my guard, and I drank a cup of her tea." Shaking his head like a dog with something in its ear, Grantham scraped the top of his tongue with his teeth. "Can't taste a damn thing."

Leaning back, he crossed one ankle over the other and stretched his massive arms above his head, then cradled his skull in his hands.

"Did you write to Violet?" Grantham asked.

"I did," Grey replied. "Pity the postmasters of North Yorkshire this month. There must have been fifty letters on their way before I filled my pen."

If anything had happened . . . A shiver racked him, and Grey downed the rest of the whiskey. How many more glasses would it take to douse the leftover fear?

He'd taken time to bathe and change into fresh clothing while Grantham prowled the hallways of the club, gathering those ladies who would have kept working even if the fire hadn't been put out, and sending them on their way home.

Now, the two of them tossed inanities back and forth as night fell, and the shock of seeing Letty standing in the doorway of a building on fire finally wore off.

"Did the Guardians do this?" Grantham asked.

Grey turned the glass around to catch the light.

"No, but it doesn't matter." This was true. It didn't matter if it were an accident or if Armitage had thought to force his hand. "I cannot allow for the possibility of more harm to come to these women. They are my responsibility, and I do not take that lightly."

Grantham groaned as he straightened in his seat and leaned forward, elbows resting on his thighs.

The earl's easy bonhomie was nowhere in evidence while shadows deepened the brackets around his mouth. "Caring for these women doesn't mean swaddling them like babies. They are not infants, and you cannot play nursemaid to them, Greycliff. Would you keep them safe by keeping them away from the one thing they love? Mark my words, the greater peril is that they stop courting danger and taking risks. You would kill their dream to keep them safe."

For a moment, Grey was tempted to put words to his suspicions about Armitage and the conflict he felt over closing the club. In the early days after receiving his title, Grantham had performed some discreet services for Prince Albert. He knew about the Department and, despite his affable demeanor, had a cunning mind and a ruthless streak when someone he cared for was threatened.

Before Grey could say anything, however, a voice interrupted them. "William?"

Melton stood in the doorway, and Grey leaped to his feet at the sight of his godfather's distress. Eyes rheumy and bloodshot, cravat askew, and mouth trembling, he looked close to collapse.

"Come sit, my lord." Grantham gestured to a chair by the fire as Grey led Melton into the room.

"I'll take my leave now. I shall see you in the morning." Grantham nodded to Grey on his way out the door. "I'll have Mrs. Sweet send tea. Good night, Lord Melton. Greycliff."

Melton watched Grantham leave with a faint frown on his face.

Grey took hold of the bellows and fed the fire. "Did you want a drink?"

Melton's chin trembled when he shook his head.

Setting down the bellows, Grey took a seat in the chair next to the older man.

"I came as soon as I heard. I was . . ." Melton reached over and grasped Grey's hand. "When I heard about a fire, I was afraid for you."

Grey looked at their clasped hands, both weathered, both strong, where they had once been so different, a child and a protector. A terrible rush of love pushed him back against the seat cushion, and he pulled the breath into his lungs as though preparing to take a wound.

"You didn't have to worry, sir," he said.

"This damned club." Melton clasped his hand even tighter as he shook his head. "I never liked Violet much, you know. I thought she was too smart for your father."

Grey froze in surprise at the change in subject.

"Daniel thought because she was young and intelligent, she would prop him up. Instead, she was like a shooting star and left him behind."

"Why . . . ?"

Melton shifted in his seat. "Why am I telling you this?" He sighed. "That girl . . . Miss Fenley. She is like Violet. She would have made Nevin miserable, forever chasing after her brilliance. Over time, he would have turned cold and bitter."

"You ruined her—"

"She was in bed with him," Melton snapped, snatching back his hand and rubbing his balding pate. "I did what I needed to do to protect my child."

The throbbing pain behind his eyes intensified, and Grey pushed his fingers into his forehead. Grantham's words uttered moments ago echoed in his head.

You would kill their dream to keep them safe.

He loved Melton more than almost anyone, but right now they stood across a divide, watching one another as the fire sent shadows racing across their faces.

What had Margaret Gault said that day in the carriage? A bridge was a love story.

Communion and balance.

Grey swallowed, wishing desperately he knew how to navigate this situation. Each of them must take a step forward if they were to meet in the middle. Otherwise, they would be lost to one another.

"Nevin told Miss Fenley he would marry her," Grey said. Melton examined the toes of his shoes while Grey memorized the cut of Melton's lapel, picking his way through a mountain of words. "Whether or not she should have gone to his bed is not for you or me to judge. That judgment is hers alone, and it is one she wrestles with every single day."

"A woman's purity is—"

"No." Grey's voice rang out as he confronted his godfather. "We do not have the right to discount a woman's worth—her intelligence, her bravery, her heart—simply because of the state of her hymen. Nevin lied to her, and you compounded the injury by shunning her. You lied to me, Melton."

"I was protecting my son," Melton said, the words sounding like a whisper in the wake of Grey's accusation.

"You weren't protecting him," Grey shot back. "You were damaging him more, by taking responsibility for his actions away from him. He cannot be the man you want him to be if he faces no consequences for his actions."

Melton's eyes searched Grey's face. "What would you have me do, Greycliff? I cannot turn back the clock."

Nevin should be made to offer for Letty. He was the one who had wronged her. The honorable solution was marriage, yet Grey revolted at the thought of Letty in Nevin's arms.

"Rectify the damage as much as possible," Grey said. "Between you and Lady Melton, it should be easy enough. An invitation here. A good word there. You've been cleaning up after Nevin's messes for far too long. Let this be the last one."

With a solid *thud*, Melton banged his walking stick against the floor and heaved himself from his seat. For a charged moment, they held each other's stare in a silent push and pull.

Compression and tension.

Rebalancing.

"It will be done," Melton said.

Grey nodded.

"And this place?" Melton asked. "You will close it?"

He and his godfather were finished speaking of Letty for now. Grey fought to order his thoughts beneath the pounding beat of pain.

"What will that do to stop Armitage's power grab? Have you figured out how he pressured Ramsey?"

The earl's voice changed back to its familiar trumpetlike authority.

"Sir Gerald has fathered two bastards with a woman he keeps in the North. There is some question of whether marriage lines exist predating his marriage to Lady Ramsey."

This, then, was what Armitage was holding over Ramsey's head.

Melton shook his head, hands clenched. "Armitage has managed to compromise two more. Once you take over the directorship, there will have to be a purge. Your first step will be to find replacements, men with deep purses and a loyalty to England that goes beyond any loyalty to who lives at Downing Street."

"If we hold the vote next week, can we be certain of the other five?"

Melton pulled his hand over his face and stared at the fire. "Yes. Even if Armitage has been whispering in their ears, closing the club is a demonstration of your resolve, although the fire made the decision for you."

"I cannot believe he would put lives in danger simply to force my hand," Grey said.

"Unless he thought it would have the opposite effect. Men have done worse for power such as that the Department wields," Melton said. "I won't feel safe until you have won the vote. Finish the job and take your rightful place."

"TELL ME THAT is not a tarantula you have in your hand."

At Grey's horrified demand, Letty whipped around, closing her hands around her precious cargo and clasping it gently to her chest. If he thought she was holding a spider, that must mean Lady Potts had once again lost track of her "dear friends."

"Tell me there are no tarantulas on the loose again," Letty cried.

The last time Lady Potts's tarantulas had escaped, it took two weeks to find them and the staff at Beacon House had to be given a hefty rise in pay.

Grey's shoulders dropped, and he pinched the bridge of his nose. "I beg your pardon. I have not slept well. I must have been seeing things. As far as I know, no tarantulas are on the loose."

He'd found her in the cozy little chamber used to entertain visiting lecturers when they came to the club. The walls were covered with a scarlet flocked paper, and gold damask curtains bracketed the window. Hung across one wall were a series of etchings, each showing a site in England where notable fossils had been found. A brass clock centered on the dark oak mantelpiece told time with a cheerful *tock*.

Every inch the unflappable aristocrat, from his forest green cravat perfectly creased and secured with a silver stick pin to his gleaming boots, Grey entered the room. The pale yellow daffodils in a vase by his side appeared faded next to his navy blue fitted jacket.

"You are not supposed to be here," he said.

Not even the tiniest suggestion that a smile had once crossed his lips was evident in his demeanor.

Letty sighed. The frost in Grey's voice had doused the warmth in her chest from the sight of him. "Good day to you, too, Lord Greycliff."

"Winthram told me you'd finished collecting your belongings." He scowled at the fire and the china cup at her side. "There is no point to staying. Members can pack up, but no socializing permitted."

Thick black brows rose at her laughter.

"I cannot help it, Greycliff," she said. "'No socializing permitted.' You sound like those Methodists who were always chivvying the folks of Farringdon to leave off our sinfulness, like dancing and drinking."

His demeanor gave no hint of their intimacy. Instead, he stood a respectable distance away from her, hands clasped behind his back.

Despite the cheerful fire in the grate, the room turned damp and cold.

She hadn't time to prepare her arguments, and the set of his shoulders gave her little hope anything she said today would convince him.

"Winthram is doing a fine job with the cleanup," she told him, hoping to delay while she marshaled her thoughts. "We were lucky Earl Grantham came when he did and kept the fire brigade at bay."

Letty wanted him to say something—anything—about last night in the carriage. With the clouds outside and the curtains closed, the outlines of the end tables and the settees softened in the low light and Grey's eyes were unreadable.

Had the fire somehow changed his feelings? Why did he frown in that way? She racked her brain for some reason other than he'd taken a disgust of her.

What if he truly did not care that the end of the club was the end of their dreams?

Showing no recognition of her turmoil, he gestured to the closed curtains. "Why is it dark in here?"

"She is nocturnal."

"She?" Grey surveyed the room.

"Her name is Fermat." Letty opened her palms to reveal a little brown bundle.

Grey recoiled. "What the . . . ? It looks like a giant burr."

"No, she doesn't." Letty clucked her tongue, offended on Fermat's behalf. "She is sweet. I am taking her home with me, as a gift for Sam's birthday."

Fermat ignored them, curling tight into a ball, her sides quivering. Mala had told Letty that hedgehogs rolled themselves up when they found themselves in danger. Letty drew the creature back to her chest and murmured words of comfort.

"Fermat, as in Fermat's last theorem? The subject of your Rosewood defense?" Grey asked.

"Yes."

His frown deepened into a scowl, and her stomach plunged even more.

This man had kissed her as though she were precious to him. He'd handed her control, despite how uncomfortable this had made him, and praised her bravery. Nothing of what they experienced had felt the least bit false.

Why was he pulling away now?

Letty's distress communicated itself to the animal, and she stroked Fermat's back, soothing the poor thing.

"Can you leave off petting that animal and pay attention?" he complained. "It isn't safe here anymore. You must leave."

"She has wound herself into a knot and will stay this way, unable to eat or drink, until her fear goes away. I can't let her suffer," Letty explained.

"Is it not better to let it stay protected?" Grey asked. "See how small it is—how easily it could be trod upon. Those spines look prickly enough. Given time, people will let it be and it can come out on its own."

His gaze rested on the hedgehog, but his brows were furrowed as though he were wrestling with a difficult problem.

"If she stays hidden, she won't ever be able to explore the world." Were they even pretending to speak about the hedgehog anymore? "Her existence will be limited to dark and lonely spaces," Letty said. "She has to take the risk."

Grey drew near and examined the tiny ball as Letty held her breath. Every bit of this man's beautiful body lay covered beneath layers of linen and silk, but she knew what he looked like, the sounds he made when he was pleased, the taste of his skin: How were they to go on with this secret knowledge of one another?

She held the little creature out toward Grey. "Hold on to her for a moment."

Letty might have asked him to stick his hand in a viper pit, at his expression of horror.

"What?" Grey stepped back, aghast.

"She won't bite. Even if she did, she's a pygmy hedgehog. Her teeth are smaller than the head of a pin. Or are you scared?"

Carefully, she placed Fermat in his outstretched hands, then rummaged through a basket of supplies that Mala had provided.

Holding out a tiny branch of parsley, she wiggled it where she thought Fermat's nose might be.

Grey regarded Letty without blinking. She could almost hear him thinking, constructing analysis and arguments one brick at a time. Solid. Considering.

Unemotional.

How Letty wanted inside that fortress.

Her skin tightened beneath his stare as he drew close enough that she could smell the lemon verbena water used to scent his handkerchiefs. Underlying every word they had exchanged, every sentiment they had tried to restrain, was this undertow of *want*. Each step they had taken brought them closer to the point at which they could no longer resist the temptation to shed their clothes and revel in each other's skin.

He was in her blood.

"Friday is the Rosewood," he said.

Letty looked up. "Yes, I know."

"I shall send Grantham to watch over you," he said. "If you feel you are in the slightest bit of danger of being found out, you will leave the stage and—"

"You cannot control everything," she said. "Someday you will face a problem that cannot be conquered with strength or logic alone."

Stepping closer, he answered in his most aristocratic fashion. "I can control this," he said. "I can be certain no one in this club will come to harm."

Desire rose thick and heady between them. Neither of them could control that—it made her drunk with sensation and uncaring of the myriad boundaries between them.

"Mmm." Letty was humming with anticipation, moving so close that the edge of her skirts brushed his polished boots.

Wait.

That sound hadn't come from her.

The moan came again, and she and Grey jerked apart.

"I'd forgotten about the beast," he exclaimed.

Letty had forgotten about the hedgehog as well. Grey held out his hands to reveal Fermat, who, having unrolled herself, was now holding the parsley delicately in her paws.

"Put this back in its basket," he said, thrusting Fermat toward Letty. "I don't know what you see in its little black eyes, and . . ." Grey paused as he peered at the creature. "Oh, how sweet," he said. "Its nose is the shape of a heart."

Fermat's nose was indeed heart-shaped. The hedgehog munched her snack with relish, making a happy grunting noise.

"Look at its white, fuzzy stomach," he cooed.

When Letty reached for the animal, Grey pulled his arms back and examined the hedgehog, a lightness in his face reminding her of the day he'd blown things up with Milly and Willy.

"I think she likes me."

It only took five words.

They weren't even directed toward Letty, but the happy wonder in Grey's voice broke the last of her defenses.

Letty loved him.

She *loved* him.

"Do you have anything else to feed her?" Grey stroked the hedgehog's belly carefully. "One stalk of parsley isn't enough. She seems hungry."

Unable to comply, Letty stood there like a gudgeon.

She'd thought the ties between them were about sex, about reclaiming her body and her courage.

All this time, there had been more—there had been love.

Yet how could she give her heart to a man who wouldn't ever acknowledge his own? She might be able to remove her armor, but Grey would never live outside his halls of ice. He'd barred the women of the club from the one place they could truly call home.

The gulf between them remained as wide as ever.

"I should take her now," Letty said, managing to keep her voice even. "I told Sam I would be back before three. Da worries if I am late."

Rearranging her features, she tried to summon the resentment of her old self: the woman who had built her life into something approaching contentment after Grey's family had ruined it. That woman could cut Grey down to size, match his frigid stares with her own, and stay blissfully apart from any threat of entanglement.

But Letty didn't want to be the woman she was before she'd fallen in love.

She didn't want to be burdened by the stupid prejudices of people she didn't know and didn't care for. She didn't want to throw the first punch, expect the worst and hide from jabs that hadn't happened yet.

Taking a deep breath, she turned to face Grey. He was cradling Fermat as though she were made of glass, rather than a lumpy little hedgehog who was munching contentedly on a stalk of parsley. Despite angling his chin to the precise degree that allowed him to stare down his nose at her, two lines scored the skin between his brows, hinting at his ambivalence.

She was going to do it.

She was going to tell him she loved him.

She was going to open her mouth and—

"What the blazes are the two of you doing in here with the door closed and the curtains shut?"

The Earl Grantham stood in the doorway, his enormous shoulders nearly larger than the doorframe. Swinging his top hat loosely in one hand, a great scowl on his face, he made a huge show of opening the door wide, then stomped in the room.

For the love of . . .

Seldom had Letty wanted to do violence to others, but Grantham's ill-timed entrance had her eyeing the fireplace poker.

Grantham marched over to the windows and tugged at one of the curtains. "First, it's Violet. Now it's you, Miss Fenley. The women of this club may be geniuses at sciencing things, but they're no good at following the basic rules of society." He folded his arms and glared at Letty.

"When they made me an earl, I had to listen to hours of can-dos and can't-dos, and I tell you, unmarried misses *can't* be in closed rooms with men without a chaperone. Lucky for you I happened by."

"What are *you* doing here, Grantham?" Grey asked with ill-concealed irritation.

"I've just come from my club, and Armitage was there," Grantham replied. "He's boasting that he is responsible for the closing of Athena's Retreat, and hinting that he holds something over you. You need to put a stop to this."

Grey bit out a curse. "Can't it wait until later?"

"Coupled with the fact that the Earl Melton is apparently readying to leave for a tour of the Continent with his wife? I'm not daft. Armitage is angling to be the next director of the Department, isn't he? How did this happen?"

Grey clutched Fermat to his chest. "You are speaking of confidential matters within the government. Don't—"

"As if Miss Fenley doesn't know about the Department. Violet couldn't keep a secret for all the shillings in England. It's not me you should be shutting up. It's Armitage. His mouth is bigger than an elephant's . . . er . . . trunk. He isn't concerned with confidentiality."

Grantham grimaced in distaste, pausing in the act of opening a window. "I thought Melton was handing the whole thing over to you when he retires. What changed?"

. . . responsible for the closing of Athena's Retreat, and hinting that he holds something over you.

Grey's stumbling attempts to divert Grantham took Letty back to the scene outside his office when she'd overheard him and Melton discussing his childhood seizures. Before he'd done his best to distract her, they had been discussing something else.

This is simply a token show of your loyalty. Close the club and—

The heart is a muscle. It can weaken over time, but it does not break. It continues to pound, second after second, minute after minute, no matter what tumult or tragedy might occur.

For Letty, the inevitability of her next heartbeat was both a promise and a punishment.

17

"*H*OLY HELL! WHAT in the devil is in your hand?"

Letty stared at the earl, astonishment at his language distracting her from her pain.

"Good God, Grantham. There is a lady present," Grey admonished.

Grantham had leaped atop a spindly chair and was now pointing at Fermat as though he'd seen a ghost. "There is a *creature* writhing in your hands. Of all the unfathomable . . . That thing is disgusting."

The hedgehog, meanwhile, kept chewing, unconcerned by the trials and tribulations of the giant figures around her.

"You are the human version of a locomotive," Grey scolded while cupping Fermat possessively. "You have the *worst* timing, you produce an excess of noise and botheration, you—"

"Insult me all you want," Grantham retorted. "Curse my name to the moon and back, but for the love of Christ, put that away."

The two men continued to argue about Fermat, heedless of the fact that Letty's heart had just been broken.

"I had completely forgotten." Letty raised her voice and spoke over

Grantham as though he weren't there. "You were speaking with Melton about taking on a directorship. He said something about the club . . ."

Still holding Fermat close to his chest, Grey opened and closed his mouth, unable for once to appear unruffled.

"Give the Funders what they want. Close the club," Letty said, eyes blinking unshed tears. "I was so distracted by what came after that I didn't remember the words until now. Is this why the fire was set?" she asked. "So you would have a reason to close the club?"

"No, of course not." Grey's head reared back in a show of shock. "How could you think I would put you in danger?"

What was the truth?

Letty pointed at him. "Look at what you've done."

Grey squinted at her in confusion until he realized Letty was pointing at his chest. Fermat had rolled into a ball again, the stalk of parsley forgotten on the floor.

"Give her to me. Obviously, you cannot protect her." With remarkably steady hands, she took the hedgehog from him.

"You must understand . . ."

"My lord?" Johnson, the footman from Beacon House, stood in the doorway. "There are representatives from the fire insurance consortium here to see you. They claim they have an appointment with you," the man announced.

Grey stared at Letty, then rubbed a hand across his forehead. "Yes, of course. I'll be right there."

"What do they want?" she asked, belly suddenly cold with unease.

"I invited them," he said. "I wanted to ensure none of the brigade workers had reported any suspicions about the secret rooms of the club."

Letty waited, hoping for some word from him that she'd misunderstood, but as Grey glanced from the footman to Grantham, then back at her, his enigmatic eyes revealed not even a hint of regret.

"It's not safe," he said finally, gesturing for the footman to precede him. "You need to leave, Miss Fenley. It's time for you to go home."

With that said, he left. Spine straight and shoulders back, every inch the unflappable Lord Greycliff.

Letty carefully pulled the piece of linen back over Fermat's basket as the creature squeaked with delight upon finding more stalks of parsley within. The sound comforted Letty.

Grantham remained standing on the chair, frowning at her, hands on hips. "You cannot believe Grey had something to do with the fire."

Letty declined to answer.

What *did* she believe? How could she ever trust him again? How could she trust herself? Walls were much easier to reconstruct than to tear down for good.

"I've tucked Fermat away, my lord. You can come down from your perch. She won't hurt you."

Grantham peered at the chair in surprise. "Ye gods. How did I get here?"

A twinkle in his eye hinted that Grantham was back to playing a version of himself. Everyone fashioned their own set of armor of different stuff. Suits of polished humor could deflect as well as suits of sharpness or disdain.

Too bad Letty had little patience for such games right now.

"Are you certain you wouldn't like to hold Fermat?" she asked. "Sometimes you can get over a fear by spending time with what scares you the most."

Grantham recoiled in real horror. "Not on your life, Miss Fenley. Not on my life. Not on the life of the Queen herself. I am not getting off this . . . Hellooooo."

Margaret stood in the shadows by the doorway, looking bemused.

"I beg your pardon, Miss Fenley. I did not realize you were entertaining a visitor," she said. "I'm sorry I wasn't here yesterday to help. I'd made a trip to Canterbury and stayed the night."

Grantham interrupted, two feet now on solid ground. "I don't believe I've had the pleasure." He bowed and stepped forward, eager for an introduction.

"Earl Grantham, may I present . . . ," Letty said.

As Margaret stepped fully into the room, the clouds parted and a fingertip of sunlight made its way through the half-opened curtain, illuminating her black lashes and hazel eyes.

"*Maggie?*"

Margaret's milk-white skin paled to grey at Grantham's utterance of surprise, and she gasped.

Not even a mote of dust moved in the next instant as the past rode into the room on a cascade of sudden sunlight. Before Letty's eyes, years fell away from Margaret's sophisticated countenance. All the clever tailoring no longer hid how tall and broad Margaret stood for a woman. She held her arms crossed, shoulders rounded, as though to hide herself.

Staring as though the ground had split open, Grantham also underwent a change. One foot behind the other, hands fisted, good-humored bravado left his flushed face. An awed, uncomfortable younger man stood in his place.

"My lord," Letty said, speaking into the lull, "I did not know you were already acquainted with Madame Gault." She was deeply disturbed with standing witness to whatever was happening between these two.

Grantham ignored her. "Madame . . . I . . . Of course, Violet told me. You are married."

Drawing in a short breath, Margaret returned to herself on a long, slow exhale. Her shoulders melted back into place, the placid smile reappearing.

"Indeed. And you are an earl," Margaret said. With a show of indifference, she switched her attention to Letty. "What is this nonsense I hear about Lord Greycliff closing the club?"

"Nonsense?" Grantham frowned. "If you had been here, you could have . . . someone could have been hurt."

Margaret's mouth pursed, and two spots of red sat high on her cheeks, the spray of freckles across her nose emerging from beneath her face powder. She pointed a shaking finger at him. "This is not for you to wade into, Georgie."

Grantham's gaze darted between the basket and Margaret, clearly unsure which presented the greater threat. "It is now that you are involved."

"I'm not your concern," she spat at him. Spinning on her heel, she faced Letty, cheeks crimson and lips drawn tight. "Whether Lord Greycliff tries to close the club or not, the members won't abandon you when you need us most."

"He hasn't abandoned you," Grantham insisted. "Believe me—"

"Believe you?" Margaret laughed. "Why, of course. You would never lie to a girl, would you, Georgie?"

Letty shrank into herself as another story played itself out in the waning light. The characters might be different, but the outcome was still the same.

A heart broken.

A woman left to pick up the pieces.

The sudden lash of rain against the windowpanes startled them as the skies thundered and the world around them wept.

"If you will both excuse me . . ." Letty held Fermat's basket tight to her chest and hurried out of the room, ignoring Margaret, who called something after her.

The rain continued to fall as she clambered into a hack, holding the basket in her lap. The cobbles beneath them were slick with rain, and dirty rivers ran down the sides of the streets as the conveyance swayed back and forth. Letty fed Fermat the last of the parsley and tried to quiet her thoughts.

Her sisters were still at the emporium when she returned home, and Letty was grateful for the respite. She hung her cloak to dry and brought Fermat with her into the empty parlor. The ordinary tasks of laying a fire and closing the curtains against the angry skies had a soothing effect, and her heartbeat slowed.

Setting Fermat's basket close to the fire, Letty lit the lamp on a low table next to a chair. Something rustled in her reticule, and she fished out the latest missive from Violet.

Weekly now, Letty received a letter marked from the Yorkshire Academy for the Education of Exceptional Young Women. The letters were never long but served as a reminder of the brilliant mind and generous heart of the founder of Athena's Retreat. What would Violet think of Letty's failure to protect her beloved club?

Despite her guilt, longing to hear her friend's voice, even if only in her head, had Letty pulling up the sealing wax and reading the letter aloud.

Dearest Letty,

I have had many thoughts recently on the nature of snow. While I appreciate the atmospheric wonders leading to the creation of an infinite number of complex crystals, my reflections are mostly taken up with how cold and uncomfortable it is when it gets into my shoes and down my collar. It is spring, for goodness' sake. Why is there snow? Well, of course I know why . . .

Thereafter followed a Violet-like digression, on some of the weather notation coding of Francis Beaufort, until she came to the point.

> *... new student admitted to the school. Her parents are in trade, and she's had some difficulty settling in with the other girls. I've managed to discover that Amy has an interest in geometry and wondered if you might recommend a lesson plan. Aunt Rose is currently teaching mathematics, since she's lost yet another teacher to that dreaded disease of matrimony, and would appreciate the help. Perhaps something to do with the Pythagorean theorem?*

Letty crossed over to a chipped and battered old secretary they used for correspondence. Taking a seat, she opened a drawer and pulled out a sheaf of parchment.

Her world was turning upside down over and over with a frightening speed. In one week, she would stand on a stage and hide behind a man's name to do what she loved most.

With great care, Letty dipped a pen into ink and drew three straight lines to create a right triangle. The hypotenuse, the adjacent side, and the opposite side.

So perfectly simple, so simply perfect.

That night, after practicing her entry, Letty would write up a lesson plan for Amy. She would lay out the elegance of the proof, the joy to be found in the beauty of an uncomplicated equation, and the clean lines of squares and triangles.

And, perhaps, she would tease Amy with the hint that the world would offer more someday. That $x^2 + y^2 = z^2$ is only the beginning. One could spend a lifetime answering questions spawned from this single equation.

Letty's hand cramped as she scrawled a series of familiar theorems that had been proven through the centuries.

She would promise Amy that mathematics would never change—never lie to her or break her heart. Promise that a world existed where answers could always be had if one worked hard enough, no matter their sex or the status of their birth.

The fire softly sputtered in the grate as Letty worked, lost once again in the only place where everything made sense.

NOTHING MADE SENSE.

Grey paced the empty halls of Athena's Retreat and scowled. For the first time since Violet had left, his morning meal had not been punctuated with percussive booms or the shuddering of ceiling rafters.

He should be relishing the silence, not missing the mayhem.

The familiar scent of smoke damage filled the air, but no sheepish scientists mumbled their excuses for the "inadvertent" explosions or tried again to explain to him Sadi Carnot's work on the motive power of fire. Grey made his way to the common area on the second floor, where the rugs were still damp and yellowed smudges marred the walls. It would take numerous washings by the staff to remove the soot from the whitewash. Some stains were more easily erased than others.

No groups of women chattered excitedly about their work. No laughter or applause or moans of frustration bounced off the walls or rattled in corners. His footsteps echoed in the empty corridor as he passed deserted workrooms. No one popped their heads out of the doors and invited him in to celebrate an achievement unlocked, a discovery made, or simply to offer him a slice of dubious-smelling cake.

Out of habit, he increased his pace when he walked by Lady Potts's door. *Not* because he was nervous one of her charges might have been left behind and lay in wait in the darkness. That would be ridiculous.

No, Grey knew Athena's Retreat was empty. He'd failed Violet in her one request of him. He might have done it to keep these women safe from what could be a deadly threat, but that didn't shrink the weight of guilt he carried as he left the laboratories behind.

He'd avoided the ground floor, where Letty's workroom was located, but he felt her presence in every square inch of this building.

Or rather, her absence.

"My lord?" Winthram appeared in the doorway connecting Athena's Retreat with Beacon House. "Johnson says you've a visitor. Shall I tell them you are indisposed?"

The doorman was out of his usual uniform and was instead dressed in a simple dove grey overcoat, a bright gold cravat peeking out at the neck.

Grey ignored the news of the waiting visitor and regarded the young man instead.

"Are you ready?" he asked.

Winthram nodded. "Yes, my lord. Ready as I can be, I suppose."

Grey had arranged for Winthram to meet with James Tierney. Once employed by the Department, Tierney now operated a small bookkeeping firm. Much like Athena's Retreat, Tierney's firm was not what it seemed. He employed a small group of operatives who specialized in solving problems and making discreet inquiries on behalf of folks who needed help the most.

"We will miss you," Grey said. "Violet and Arthur may never forgive me for letting you go."

Winthram took off his hat and swept his unruly forelock into place, then settled the hat back on his head in a nervous gesture.

"Isn't certain they'll hire me, my lord."

They would. Winthram would make a fine agent, and it was past time for him to experience the thrill of being a hero.

The irony that the ladies of the club would cast Grey in the role of the villain was not lost on him.

Wishing Winthram luck, he made his way upstairs and stopped short in the doorway of his office at the sight of his visitor.

"What do you want?"

Nevin whipped around, mustache quivering. "Hallo. You startled me."

A leather folio sat on the edge of Grey's desk, Letty's name embossed in gold across the bottom. The package must have arrived from the stationer while he was with her.

With Margaret's help, he'd had Letty's presentation for the Rosewood copied out as a gift. Thick, creamy parchment covered with beautiful, *legible* script.

"Do you not have to prepare yourself for Friday?" Grey asked.

"It is Friday's presentation I wish to speak with you about. May I?" Nevin gestured to the settee.

Nevin resembled his mother. Like Lady Melton, he had round eyes, irises the color of strong, dark tea. When he'd been younger, he would plead with those eyes more than with words. Lady Melton and the ladies of Melton's household were helpless before such silent pleading.

It had even worked with Grey on more than one occasion, when Nevin asked for intercession between himself and whatever plans his father had made.

"Go ahead," Grey muttered sharply, dropping into the chair behind his desk.

Melton must not have spoken to his son yet, for Nevin's head went back at the harsh reply. He took his time settling on a cushion and rubbed his hands down his pant legs.

"Did you know Letty Fenley is almost completely self-taught?" Nevin said.

This was a surprise.

"Maria Agnesi, Émilie du Châtelet, Mary Somerville . . . they are well-known female mathematicians. Do you recognize any of these names?"

Grey shook his head. He didn't even know the names of any male mathematicians.

"They were from wealthy families or noble blood. They had tutors or boarding schools. Their families encouraged them. Letty has had none of this," Nevin said.

He stared at his knees for a long moment, then looked at Grey. "You can't let her go forward with her proof."

"Go forward with what?" Grey asked, keeping his voice neutral.

Nevin sighed. "I know Letty is entered in the Rosewood as Rupert Finchley-Buttonwood."

Grey supposed it was worthless to argue. If Nevin knew Letty well, he'd already have figured out what she was planning.

"What are you going to do about it?" Grey asked.

"She is under your protection, is she not?"

Grey's anger, having finally been leashed, now hurled itself against his constraints when Nevin used wording that implied that Letty was his mistress. "You once again besmirch Miss Fenley's name with your accusation."

Unnerved, Nevin stood. "I am not saying 'under your protection' as in . . . you know. I am saying you publicly sided with her at the Ackley ball." He sighed. "I am not besmirching her. I am trying to protect her as well. Grey, her proof is flawed. Even if she somehow manages to present, her proof is flawed."

This had never occurred to Grey, that Letty could be incorrect. "She says she has worked on it for years. Violet is certain. Madame Gault is certain."

Nevin shook his head. "I attended a reception for the finalists, and our abstracts were presented. She wasn't there, but I read hers, and it was based on the same work she was doing six years ago. It's flawed. She shouldn't be on the stage. She doesn't belong."

Grey tried to sort through the implications of Nevin's revelations, but his thoughts moved at a sluggish pace. He'd slept poorly since the club's closure, haunted by his last glimpse of Letty's face as his betrayal had become clear.

Nevin paused. "I say, Greycliff, are you well?" His look of supplication had been replaced with concern.

Or was it pity?

"Thank you. I am fine, cousin." Grey bit into the words, a delicious flood of ice making its way through his veins. Calling on the cold, Grey hardened his jaw and narrowed his stare. "I have never been better. As your father may have told you, I am considering new prospects."

"The directorship." Nevin nodded. "Father says you will be a worthy successor." He glanced at the floor, then back at Grey. "That is what you want? To be like Father?"

Grey bristled. Who was Nevin to question Grey's decisions?

On his desk sat a jar of mineral oil. At the bottom rested a lump of pure sodium, a gift from Milly and Willy. On the low shelf behind the desk sat three binders full of clippings, sketches, academic journals, and handwritten notes. Hanging from a coatrack was a top hat. The hatband was made of hundreds of tiny iridescent feathers from a peregrine, a prototype by Flavia Smythe-Harrows of her newest innovation. Men's hats to match women's bonnets. The hats would be sold in mated pairs.

It made no difference that he would be leaving these women behind. *Of course* he wanted to be like Melton. The rational arguments he'd carefully constructed played out in his head. Grey would use the office for the benefit of the people in his country without voice. His time in the North had driven home the realization that he and the rest of the aristocracy had benefited, and continued to benefit, from the labor and the life's blood of working men and women without an equal return. If he could wrestle the reins of the Department from the Funders, he might be able to take small steps to change this uneven relationship.

Rational and well constructed—and incomplete. Even as he stood among the detritus of those women's dreams, the siren song of Melton's offer played in his ears. Power. Control. Acceptance.

"I have business to attend to," Grey told his guest curtly. "As to whether or not Letty presents her work to the Rosewood judges? That is her decision. Whatever she chooses to do, it is no longer my concern."

If he said it enough times, he might begin to believe it.

18

*Miss Cordelia rushed into the turret chamber as the evil Sir Gold-
enhawk jumped out the window and escaped across the rooftops.
Like a broken toy, Count Blacksoul lay splayed and still on the hard
floor, hands around a bloodied wound. A vase of roses had fallen in
the fight, and the spill of red petals beneath him melted into the
crimson stains.*

*Cordelia dropped to her knees at the count's side and took his
hand in hers.*

"Don't leave me," she begged him.

*The count did not respond, his fingers limp and cold in hers.
Tears slid down Cordelia's cheeks. "Why did you hide your true nature from me?" she asked him. "You took such great pains to present
yourself as callous and cruel, when all along . . ."*

"Psst. Letty. It is time."

Letty slipped her copy of *The Perils of Miss Cordelia Braveheart and
the Castle of Doom* under her mattress to keep it from prying hands. Not
that this would make a difference. Rather than purchase a copy of his

own, Sam had bribed their younger sister Laura to sneak him Letty's book. In revenge, Letty kept placing his bookmark in the wrong pages, so he kept having to start over again. At this rate, he would never find out if Cordelia got a happy ending.

Setting her top hat on her head, Letty picked up a leather folio from her bed. It had come two days ago, wrapped in plain paper and without a note, but she knew who had done this for her. Holding the folio to her face, she fancied she could smell bergamot and lemon verbena beneath the pungency of polished leather.

Even her anger at Grey's betrayal hadn't been great enough for her to toss the gift aside. Of course, that was purely for aesthetic reasons. It had nothing to do with her stupid, sinful hope that Grey might, like Count Blacksoul, find a way to redeem himself.

Sam's face fell when she opened the door. "What have you done to your hair?"

Originally, Letty had planned to put her hair into a braid and pin it down. After Grey's betrayal, she'd stood in front of the mirror and thought about how he'd run his hands through her hair, over and over. Yesterday, snatching a pair of shears, she'd destroyed what he'd admired.

Halfway through, she'd slowed her movements and shaped her hair with deliberation. Shaping a new woman.

"Mam is going to kill you." Her brother whistled a long, low note. "So is Da. You look like a six-year-old boy dressed in his father's clothes."

Letty adjusted her hat and preceded Sam down the stairs. "If you and Lucy cover for me, they won't know where I've been. I'll figure something out to explain. At least I look like a boy. Is anyone else around?"

"No. We are free and clear, unless you want to give up and . . . Wait for me, Lett—ugh. Why do you never wait for me?"

It took twenty minutes for them to come clear enough of Clerkenwell to spy a hackney. The entire time, Sam gave Letty pointers out of the side of his mouth.

"Pick up your chin. Push your chest out and shoulders back. Don't move aside when someone walks past—hold your ground. They should move for you."

It irritated Letty that she had to disguise herself. The men's clothing hung as heavy on her as if it were woven of steel. If these past weeks had taught her anything, it was that shielding yourself from pain and humiliation meant also carrying a barrier between yourself and happiness and friendship. The layers of undershirt, shirt, waistcoat, and jacket were weighing her down.

What else could she do? How else to protect herself as she snuck past the battlements erected to keep her small and silent?

"Walk as though you've the most precious jewels in the world hanging between your legs," he advised.

When Letty tried to follow that advice, Sam shook his head in disbelief. "If you walk like that, you'll crush them. When I say 'precious jewels,' it's a metaphor. They aren't *rocks*. More like priceless sacs of future prime ministers. Why are you making that face?"

"This is ridiculous," she snapped. "Men can't be having these thoughts when walking down the street."

Sam scoffed. "'Course we do. Why do you think men make such a grand mess of things most of the time? Watch this."

Two older women were approaching them on the narrow wooden walkway outside a row of shops. Sam pulled out his timepiece and glared at it as the women came abreast of him. He raised his head, sniffed, then scowled back at the watch.

The women stepped off the walkway and into the dirty street to let Sam pass them by. Without a word, they climbed back onto the walkway once he'd passed, continuing their conversation as though nothing had happened.

Letty hurried to catch up with her brother. "They let you through."

Sam nodded. "That's the trick to fooling everyone. Act as though you deserve the world, and the world treats you accordingly."

Letty mulled this secret as they hailed a hack. She took off her top hat and brushed off the brim. "That would never work for women, would it?" she asked.

"Dunno. Never seen any women who acted that way. The Queen might, I suppose." Sam seemed unconcerned about whether a woman could push aside perambulating strangers with the same efficacy as a man. Instead, he told her about Flavia's wish to create a line of bonnets and hats for exclusive sale at Fenley's Fripperies.

"They have to be the most hideous creations I have ever encountered." Sam shook his head. "Mrs. Hutchins nearly fainted dead when she opened the hatbox and saw what she thought was a vulture staring at her. Do you know, she sent a list of every single species of grouse there is in the British Isles? The woman is mad, I tell you."

"Flavia is not mad. She's simply trying to find her place." Letty plucked at her starched cravat. She must have tied it too tight, and she was struggling to breathe.

When they reached Bluestone Hall, Sam leaned his head out of the hack and whistled. Pulling his head back in, he took hold of Letty's hand. "Ware, Letty. There's a crowd of those Guardians with their signs, facing off against your science ladies. Things could get sticky."

"Oh, Sam. I told the ladies to stay away."

Furious with Grey's decision to close the club, Margaret, Mala, and Althea had mended fences with Lady Potts and met at her town house to discuss alternatives. Letters of protest had been written to Arthur, as well as to Violet. Letty had not joined their port-fueled meetings, too nervous about the presentation—and too brokenhearted over Grey—to be social.

Margaret had sent a note of encouragement the night before. The members of Athena's Retreat may not have a club to call their own, she'd written, but their sisterhood was undiminished, as evidenced by their plan to fill the hall at the Rosewood to the rafters and show their support.

The dull murmur of a crowd lapped against the side of the hack. Beads of sweat broke out on Letty's upper lip.

"Stay here," Sam said, then leaped from the hackney. A moment or two later, he heaved himself back in.

"Driver says the Guardians don't want women in the audience of the Rosewood. They should be home cleaning or mending or whatever nonsense they've come up with."

"How did *they* find out?" Letty asked. She pulled off her gloves and wiped her damp hands on her trousers.

The last time the Guardians staged a demonstration, a man had almost died.

Sam squeezed her hand. "Let's turn around. Mam and Da will never even know you've left the house. You don't have to go through with this."

Letty shook her head. "Listen to me, Sam. After this is over, I am leaving."

"What?" Her brother turned his body to face her, knees akimbo in the cramped space. "Leaving the club?"

"Go back to the private sphere and get out of the public square!"

"Abandon your convictions, not your children!"

"What kind of hat is that?"

Armitage and his band of angry men were holding their banners and shouting their slogans. The ladies of Athena's Retreat would be shouted down and humiliated. And if something went wrong, if the crowd's anger tipped over into violence, Letty would never forgive herself.

"I'm going north to be with Violet."

Before Sam could object further, Letty spoke rapidly. "If anyone finds out a woman competed in the Rosewood, there will be a scandal. Fenley's Fantastic Fripperies won't survive. It will be a hundred times worse than what happened six years ago."

"Da and I can fix it. We can outsell and outlast anything," Sam assured her.

Letty set the top hat carefully on her head, her fingers going to the exposed skin at the back of her neck. "Just be ready to cut and run the instant I come back outside. I'm not staying to listen to the other presentations, so if you don't see me within the hour, leave without me."

Sam rolled his eyes. "You read too many novels. Nothing will happen. Now you've made a mess of your cravat."

Her brother retied the knot at her throat and fussed with the folds until he was satisfied.

They slipped from the hack, and while Sam paid the driver, Letty kept her head down. A quick glimpse at the crowd showed there were as many women as there were men. Confident and smug, Victor Armitage stood in the center of the Guardians. Lady Potts wore one of Flavia's hats, a honey buzzard bobbing in an ocean of ribbons and roses.

Unwilling to risk discovery, Letty scurried to the side door. A burly man loomed in front of her, blocking her path. When his arm swung, she cringed, opening her mouth to scream.

"Good luck, then," the man said, gripping Letty's shoulder with the force of iron pincers. Don't worry 'bout those women coming in and disrupting you. We'll take care of 'em."

What should she do? Protest that "those women" belonged, not just in the audience, but at the lectern presenting their work? What would be the outcome of speaking up if Letty revealed herself now but lost the chance to make history?

Relying on instinct, Letty nodded brusquely and growled, "Carry on." The man let go, sending her lurching to the side. Recovering, she made it to the entrance and followed the directions of a bent-backed assistant.

The stage upon which they would present their work was bedecked with two enormous urns filled with hothouse flowers, a blue-curtained backdrop, and a polished oak lectern. With a wary eye, she wagered it was exactly as tall as she. Before the stage, in front of the rows of seats, a table had been constructed for the Rosewood judges. This, too, was decorated with flowers, interspersed with jugs of water and stacks of parchment and inkstands. This was for show, of course. The true judging would happen over the next month or two as the men worked the various theorems and proofs to find any flaws.

Behind the stage were three large rooms reserved for the convenience of the Rosewood participants. Peeking through a crack in the door of the first room, she spied Nevin talking with a portly bear of a man. From what she could hear, they were discussing the virtues of a hair oil that could be found at Fenley's Fripperies.

"The neroli oil give the mustache a shine like no other," Nevin was saying.

"Indeed," the other man agreed. "It is expensive, but they use the finest ingredients, picked and prepared by a small community of blind virgins."

Letty rolled her eyes. Where had Sam concocted such nonsense? Blind virgins? More like canny crones in Liverpool. Still, it made her laugh to know men were as susceptible to silly advertising as women.

Exploring farther on, she came to a tiny room right off the back of the stage. Inside, thick velvet curtains were piled in heaps and hanging from lines strung across the room, and crates full of ropes and pulleys stood against the wall. A rickety table sat to one side, loaded with jugs of water and half a dozen inkwells. This must be a storage room, where the refreshments for the judges' table were kept. Confident none of the participants would come so far backstage, Letty set her folio down and took off her hat. Removing her gloves, she ran her fingers through her shorn locks, marveling at the texture.

Letty's skin itched, and the waistcoat and jacket constricted her. Walking with impunity down the street, not having to struggle with hairpins and corsets—none of that made up for the fact that she was in hiding when she'd done nothing wrong. Tugging at her cravat, Letty forced her breathing to slow and closed her eyes, picturing the myriad colors of green she'd seen in Richmond.

All the reasons she'd had for going on stage disguised as a man felt hollow in this moment. Letty had seen recognition for her work as a redemption as well. Neither of those goals would be met by delivering a presentation under a false name while misrepresenting herself.

She'd boxed herself into a corner, however.

Unless Letty were to abandon her work, she would have to go on living with the bitterness of a lie always upon her tongue.

GREY SLEPT POORLY again the previous night.

Eight hours of uninterrupted sleep.

A strict diet.

Limited social interactions.

So many rules broken since Letty Fenley came into his life.

Now, as he crept through the warren of corridors and curtains backstage at the Rosewood presentation, Grey could add deceiving the public to his list.

The scent of vanilla and oranges stopped him in his tracks, and he pivoted toward a slice of light cutting through the shadows.

Pushing open the door to a tiny storeroom, he beheld his quarry and asked her a vital question.

"What have you done to your hair?"

Rather than appearing surprised at his appearance, Letty scowled and crossed her arms. "If you've come to talk me out of this, you are wasting your breath."

She'd cut her hair almost to her ears. A rumpled cravat covered the teardrop-shaped cup at the base of her throat, and an ill-fitting jacket puffed out at the waist like a boy's who'd gotten into a schoolyard tussle.

"I never once entertained the notion I could convince you of anything," Grey snapped in return.

Taken aback by his rebuttal, Letty dropped her arms to her sides. "What are you doing here, then?"

Excellent question.

Unable to formulate a concise answer, Grey shrugged. "I came to see what I could do to help."

Tugging at the shoulders of her jacket, Letty appeared uncomfortable in the poorly tailored clothing. "Shouldn't you be preparing for your new position?"

When he said nothing, she crossed her arms. "There's trouble out front. Somehow, the Guardians got wind of the club members' plan to attend. Why don't you go outside and keep them safe?"

Grey tightened his grip on a cloth-wrapped bundle beneath his arm. "Grantham and your brother are out there. One of Grantham is worth ten of Armitage's men, in size at least."

The size of the crowd outside had taken him aback. There must have been fifty or sixty women queuing to purchase tickets.

On the fringes were the Guardians, again with their signs and banners. Their shouted slogans had taken lodging in his skull, and he sought the relief of silence. When he'd caught sight of the slender man ducking into the side entrance, something in the way he'd tilted his head had attracted Grey's notice and he'd followed the youth into the heart of the building.

Grey would know her anywhere. Whether she wore rags or trousers or covered herself in a suit of armor, the way she moved was as familiar to him as the back of his own hand.

More so. She was bright as the promise of dawn, giving off her own light, slicing her way through a world seeking to trip her up at every corner.

"Do you think to expose me?" she asked.

Despite an attempt to style it in the current mode by sweeping it across her forehead, much like her, her hair refused to be tamed. Before, she'd suborned it in heavy braids, but now free, it stood in uneven tufts, light as dandelion fluff, curling in a wayward manner.

"You've exposed yourself well enough. You're practically bald."

While Letty tried to smooth her hair, he closed the door behind him. As luck would have it, the key stood in the lock, and he turned it, then approached a wobbly stage prop table at her side, setting his bundle next to the leather folio. The gold-leaf embossing on the folio's cover glinted in the light.

"Thank you for that," she said grudgingly.

"May I?" he asked.

Letty hesitated, confused. Removing his gloves, he combed his fingers through what was left of her hair, still soft and—he leaned in—still smelling of cake.

The hurt in her eyes made him wince, but he worked on, then stepped away from her and stared at the result.

"You could pass for a young man," he said.

She nodded, slapping her gloves against her bare hand in a decent impression of a youngblood bored with his surrounds.

"Or, you could be yourself."

The gloves fell from her fingers, but Letty didn't bother to pick them up. "Why are you even here?" she mumbled, crossing her arms. "You've shuttered the club. Haven't you done enough damage?"

All night, he'd wrestled in the sheets, unable to shut down his brain.

His skin had been hot to the touch, and the sky outside bruised green and grey—the London fog threatening a return. He'd thrown open a window, glad for the cool air despite the dank. For once, there were no noises next door. It smelled of coal and dirt—not a trace of saltpeter or burnt cheese at all.

And no scent of cake in his hallways.

Empty.

Silent.

Unwilling to wait until a reasonable hour, he'd gone over to the club and knocked on Margaret Gault's door, enduring the disappointment in her words and the anger in her gaze as he asked for her help.

Now, he untied the twine holding the bundle together and revealed a dress, similar in color to the ball gown Letty had worn at the Ackleys'. Margaret had assured him the dress would fit Letty well enough. Shaking it out, he laid it on the table, along with underclothes.

Letty walked backward, bumping against the hanging curtains until she hit the wall and nearly disappeared in the velvet folds.

"You do not need the club to do your work," Grey said. "It happens here." He flipped away her hair from her forehead. "And in here." His palm slipped from her face to her breastbone. He pulled her closer, and she didn't resist.

Holding Letty's trembling body, Grey bent his forehead to touch hers. "This isn't about Athena's Retreat. This is about the reclamation of your place in the world and the men who will learn to listen to you. It is your choice alone as to whether you present under your own name, but it will always be your work. And I do care about your work. I will always be in awe of you. You don't need to wear a dress to take the stage as Letty Fenley. I simply thought . . ."

He broke off as Letty carefully unknotted the cravat at her throat. With a soft *shush*, it came undone and slipped to the floor next to her gloves.

After a moment, he found his voice again. "I thought I would bring it in the event you . . ."

In the distance, the crowd still shouted, but the noise barely registered over the beat of Grey's heart as Letty's fingers drifted down the graceful curve of her bare neck to the sides of her jacket.

Without a word, she shimmied out of the jacket and dropped it to the floor. Grey glanced once more to the door and assured himself it was locked. When he returned his gaze to her, Letty's hands were on her waistcoat buttons, but her mouth was bent in a frown.

"What if I lose?" Her voice shook, and she stared at him. Fear, longing, a plea for reassurance, a demand for touch—he read that and more as her eyes traveled his face.

He knew he should leave and let her ready herself for the stage, but the pull between them was too strong.

"May I?" He gestured to her waistcoat, but they both knew what he was asking.

"Yes," she whispered, holding her arms out to the side as though waiting for a valet.

With a heady deliberation, he unbuttoned her waistcoat and proceeded next to unfasten her starched white shirt.

"What if my proof is incorrect and I am a laughingstock?"

The clothes were too big. Grey yanked yards of linen from her trousers and pulled the shirt over her head. A length of cotton was wrapped around her ribs, hiding her small breasts. It was the work of seconds to unwrap them. He kissed her furled pink nipples and ran his tongue along the red marks where the bandages had dug into her skin.

"What if it is?" he whispered to the underside of her breast while his fingers unbuttoned her trousers.

Grey dropped to his knees and removed her shoes and socks, then pulled the pants from her shapely calves. When she was utterly naked, he sat back on his heels and took in the vision of Letty bared before him. The curls at the juncture of her thighs were wet with anticipation, and a rosy flush rose from her chest to her cheeks.

"What if you were wrong and have to begin again? Science is the art of constant discovery. A wise woman told me that once." Grey wrapped his hand around her ankle and reveled in the coolness of her skin, the tenderness beneath his calloused hands. Her slight gasp as he slipped his hand up her calf to her thigh sent a bolt of desire straight to the base of his spine, and his cock shot hard.

Her fingers ran through his hair as he leaned forward and set his lips to her belly, nuzzling the salty skin. She made a noise of contentment low in her throat.

"I want to kiss you here, Letty," he said as he cupped her quim, pressing the heel of his hand against her.

"Oh?" she asked. "Yes?"

He left tiny kisses on her belly, like offerings, then parted the tuft of downy hair below and set his mouth to her.

"Oh," she said with comprehension. "Yessss." Hissing with pleasure, she pulled his hair taut with one hand when he suckled her.

As he teased her clit with the flat of her tongue, her legs trembled, and he wrapped his arms around her hips to hold her steady. She leaned back against the wall and clenched the corner of the curtain with her free hand, pulling it halfway off the hooks above.

"Shh," she hissed to herself as men's voices sounded in the distance. Grey increased the tempo of his ministrations, and she panted with unsteady breaths. He wanted to find a way inside her, to fuse himself to her, heart to heart, bone to bone.

Unexpected, her sudden climax jolted them both. Letty lost hold of the curtain and covered her mouth with her hands, muffling a scream, and Grey held her steady as she shuddered with pleasure. He kissed his way back up her belly. When he stood, Letty set her hands on either side of his face, her eyelids heavy with satisfaction.

"Come in me," she told him.

"Are you certain?" he asked, but even as he finished the words, he was reaching to unfasten the placket of his trousers.

Come in me.

In a dream state, he lifted her and set her back against the wall, pulling her legs around his waist. The scent of her made him dizzy, and he kissed her long and hard, while she wrapped her palm around the length of him and fitted him to her.

"So perfect," he crooned when the head of his cock slipped inside her. Blood pounded against his veins, louder than the shush of her breath. He reached to the side and pulled one of the curtains around them both, protecting her back from the wall.

Words came from somewhere deep within him, praise for how sweet and wet she felt around his cock, admiration for the way she tilted her hips so he could push himself up, inch by inch, into the center of her. When he could go no farther, he stood for a moment, buried deep within her but still wanting more.

Come in me.

Into her body, into her blood. Grey wanted to imprint himself on every inch of her, so that his touch and pleasure would be forever synonymous.

"More," she whispered, and with elegant deliberation, she took hold of his arse and ground herself against him.

Good God.

Grey pulled halfway out, then thrust himself back in again, nearly coming when his name twisted in her throat. Again, and again, he drove himself deep inside her, slippery with her pleasure, searching for communion. The slick slap of damp skin sounded overloud in the cocoon of velvet, and Letty tightened her grip.

Time narrowed to the seconds between when he left her then found his way back, until a dark tension heralded his release.

An urge as dark and primal as any he'd ever had swept over him. To stay inside her until the end. That way, she could never leave him.

Before he could give in to the temptation, Letty pulled him even closer and whispered in his ear.

With those three words, everything changed.

19

YOU HAVE TWENTY minutes to read your presentation, sir. If you need water, there is . . ."

Two men had come to a halt outside the storeroom door. Letty froze, terror putting a premature end to the residual waves of pleasure coursing through her body. Grey still held her against the wall, although she was surprised he hadn't dropped her when she made her ill-timed declaration. Her stomach was wet and sticky with his seed, and the reality of where they were and what they had done came down on her like an anvil.

"Did you . . . ?" she hissed.

"It's locked," he assured her. Slowly, he lowered her to the floor.

Grey said nothing about her confession, and Letty couldn't find a way to loosen her tongue, either. He searched her face, his eyes once again opaque.

Stupid heart. Stupid, *stupid* heart.

I love you.

Why had she told him, knowing he couldn't love her in return?

The fierce intimacy of their encounter dissolved. He dipped his handkerchief in the water from one of the jugs, and she set to cleaning herself as best she could while he tucked in his shirt.

Something elemental had fed her during their lovemaking—hot and bright, forged in the conflagration of their bodies moving in wordless tandem. If Grey hadn't pulled out, she wouldn't have reminded him, letting caution fall far behind in the race to culmination, never thinking of anything beyond the safety of his arms.

They weren't safe, though.

And whatever beauty they might have wrought between them was imaginable only to her.

In this, as in everything that had come before, she was alone.

Naked and cold, Letty faced the table. Two choices lay before her. She knew Grey was watching her decide.

If she walked onto the stage without the armor of a suit and top hat, exposing herself in a dress, she would lose everything. The judges might let her speak, but they wouldn't hear her. It would be a stunt. A joke.

Or, would it be taking a stand? A public acknowledgment of where she'd come from and how difficult the journey.

She wished she could overcome her mortification and ask Grey for his perspective.

In the end, though, as he'd said, the choice rested with her.

With trembling fingers, Letty pulled on the drawers and chemise. Grey tied the corset's strings without comment. She kept her back to him while she finished. Only when she'd cinched the waist of the dress as best she could with a sash did she face him once again.

"You are . . ." He paused and swallowed.

She couldn't help it, then. Her bottom lip quivered, and tears burned her eyes.

Not now!

Grey shook his head and set his thumb to the corner of her eye, catching a tear.

"You are the most remarkable person, man or woman, I have ever known," he told her. "You honored me beyond words today. I cannot wait to watch you take your rightful place on the stage."

With a formal bow, Grey presented her with his arm.

Slipping out the door and through a corridor of screens and curtains, they made their way to an alcove with a view of the stage. The assistant she'd seen before darted back and forth on the other side of the stage, most likely searching for the mysterious Mr. Finchley-Buttonwood.

Nevin stood before the audience, a slight frown on his face. Behind him, a large slate board held an initial equation.

"To the distinguished judges of the Rosewood committee and my peers . . . ," he said.

A muffled shout could be heard from outside the auditorium. Rows upon rows of wooden seats stood half-empty. The few ladies who had managed to slip inside sat quietly with their hands folded, nodding in anticipation.

"Good thing Victor Armitage stopped most of the ladies from entering," Letty whispered. "Surely, Nevin would otherwise be overwhelmed by the high spirits of women such as these. Who knows what heights of depravity they might indulge in after listening to eight hours of advanced mathematics?"

Grey stared at her blankly, and she shook her head. "Never mind."

Nevin cleared his throat and spoke despite the interruption. "I offer proof of Fermat's last theorem when n equals five."

At his words, the floor beneath her shuddered and Letty lost her balance, falling against Grey's hard chest.

How could this be?

How could this be?

"That is *my* defense," she hissed.

Grey frowned, peering at her. "What do you mean?"

Had the lovemaking shaken something loose in her brain and she'd made a mistake?

"How—"

"Shush." Letty put a finger to his lips. "I must listen."

A black hole opened in her gut as Nevin spoke.

"I shall define a set of auxiliary primes theta . . ."

"Letty?" Grey whispered, tugging at her arm.

Letty turned to him. "Did *you* do this?"

Setting his hands on her shoulders, Grey held her stare. "Did you hear me? You are next. The assistant is searching for you."

She stared at the folio in her hands. "You took my work to have it copied. Did you show it to him?"

Still holding her, Grey's head tilted, as though she were no longer speaking English.

"Was it not enough you took the club, took my body, and took my heart? You took my *work* . . ."

Grey's skin was flushed, but his eyes seemed vacant and lost. He set one hand to his forehead, seeming confused. "He said your proof was incorrect, and he was worried you would embarrass yourself. That you were untrained and therefore . . . I don't know how long he was in my office with your folio. If I'd thought . . . I'd never imagined he would . . ."

He'd not yet retied his cravat after their lovemaking, and he rubbed a hand over the open V.

"Hot in here," he muttered. "Hard to breathe."

Nevin continued to speak. It was difficult to follow while her world was going up in flames, but the instant he deviated from her work and suggested an approach back in line with his own direction, Letty understood.

She'd made a mistake.

It hadn't been a fatal flaw. The judges might have pointed it out and she'd have had to reexamine the last set of equations. Nevin had already anticipated the dilemma and used his own work to overcome the problem and take the credit.

Funny how six years ago, she'd thought her life could not get worse. Could she ever have anticipated that the author of her destruction would appropriate her work in front of the best mathematicians in London?

Or that she would tell Grey she loved him and watch him react— not even with horror, but with ambivalence?

"That is *your* work?" Grey stared at Nevin, then back at her. His face darkened, and he cursed under his breath as he walked toward the stage.

"What are you doing?" Letty hissed, grabbing his arm and pulling him back. "What are you going to do—charge out there and accuse him?" she asked.

By God, he truly was hot. She could feel his body heat through his shirt and jacket. Letty put a hand to his forehead.

"Come away from there," she said. "Come and drink something. You are burning up."

Grey's eyes flashed with lightning, an angry echo of the brilliance that had shone when Milly and Willy had taught him the trick of fire. He jerked his arm from her, weaving unsteadily on his feet.

"No. This is what happens when I let myself feel. It is making me sick."

She should back away at the venom in his words, but her worry overrode anything else. "Please, Grey. Let me take you home."

"Do not." He stared through her, back to the past. "Do not worry for me. Do not care for me. Do not love me, Letty. Do not love me, because I cannot let myself love you in return."

All Letty could do was concentrate on the patch of exposed skin at his throat.

"I see," she said

And she did.

Nevin came to a sudden halt and bit his lower lip. An echo of the Guardians' arguments outside reached the stage. The Rosewood judges sat in the front row and muttered to one another.

"Pray, continue, Mr. Hughes," one of them said.

"No. Tell them to open the doors." Grey spoke loud enough for Nevin to hear him.

"Oh, no, Grey . . ."

Nevin squinted to the side where they stood and turned bluish white, sweat suddenly beading on his forehead.

"Tell them the truth about Letty's work," Grey continued. "Tell them she is brave and brilliant and deserves to be standing in your place."

"Ahem." Nevin stared at the sliver of chalk in his hand, then gazed out at the seats where his mother and father sat.

The noise of the crowd outside grew ever louder as someone pounded on the door.

Letty clasped her hands and pressed them against her stomach, reminding herself of how to breathe as Grey pushed her forward to the edge of the curtain.

"I would like . . ." Nevin cleared his throat and finally met her eyes. "In all good conscience, I cannot continue this presentation. While part of this proof is of my own devising"—Nevin darted a glance backstage and turned practically translucent at the expression on Grey's face—"the bulk of this work is the product of the mathematician known as Rupert Finchley-Buttonwood."

The judges spoke over one another in consternation, and Nevin bowed his head, shoulders heaving, as he struggled for air.

Grey reached over and squeezed Letty's hand, his eyes glazed and unfocused. Letty didn't care. She needed the touch to center her as she gazed out at the stoic expression on the Earl Melton's face and the arguments between the judges.

"Except it isn't Finchley-Buttonwood's work, either," Nevin announced.

"Whatever is going on, Mr. Hughes?" One of the judges stood, his white silk sash slipping off his shoulder as he scanned the slate board behind Nevin and then looked out into the audience.

Letty took a deep breath and let go of Grey's hand.

The laws of the universe were not created by the cries of desire, the storms in a man's eyes, shared laughter, or awkward embraces. The laws of the universe would continue to hold whether Grey loved her or not. The laws of the universe treated them equally. At least Letty hoped so, trusting gravity to keep her from flying away as she opened her mouth to speak.

"What's going on is that you would never have allowed me to enter the Rosewood if you knew I was a woman."

THE INSTANT LETTY stepped onto the stage and made her declaration, Grey wanted to call her back. The dress was slightly too big and her cap too small, leaving the nape of her neck bare. Exposed.

Some in the audience were clapping, others shouting in derision. The judges were arguing among themselves. Letty looked tiny and so alone.

"Stop," Nevin said as the noise grew louder. "Stop. Stop!"

The room quieted as he shouted the command, and every pair of eyes turned to him.

"Just . . . listen to her proof. Judge the work," he said. One shoulder came up in a shaky shrug, his bravado now seemingly tapped. "Simply judge the work."

Having made her way to the slate board, Letty now faced Nevin. The judges exchanged glances and took their seats, the audience's reaction cooling to occasional murmurs.

Nevin's eyes darted to his father, to the slate board, and then to Letty before he held out the piece of chalk.

When Letty nodded, he walked off on the opposite side of the stage from where Grey stood. She turned and gazed out at the crowd before facing the slate board and raising her hand.

"Let p be an odd prime. If there exists an auxiliary prime . . ."

Her voice was high and reedy, and some in the audience leaned forward to hear. One of the judges talked over her and told her to speak up. Grey wanted to run out and pummel the bastard, but Letty didn't waver. She took a deep breath and drew an equation.

$$x^n + y^n = z^n$$

Grey couldn't tell if it was his blurred vision or Letty's terrible handwriting that made the equation almost unreadable.

"N is any positive integer not divisible by three such that if x raised to the power of p plus . . ."

Even if his head were not filled with tiny hammers, Grey would never have understood the words coming out of Letty's mouth. He swayed, catching himself at the last minute on the curtains, hands trembling, and he cursed himself for being ten times a fool.

The seizures were returning.

Fever, headache—these were not the usual warning signs. Had they'd changed with age? Instead of bending light and ringing in his ears, he felt aches and heat, confusion, and sheer terror.

I love you.

He'd told her he couldn't love. That day in the workroom he'd said as much, hadn't he? Nothing stronger than affection. No joy. No rage. No sorrow.

She'd done it anyway, pulled the emotions out of him, and look at him now. Barely able to stand on his two feet.

The expression on her face when he'd turned away had pierced his heart.

The pounding in his head had increased to an agonizing degree, and he exited the building, pushing through the crowd outside in a desperate search for his carriage. He had to get home before the seizure felled him. Somehow, he would wrest control of the disease and force it back into submission.

From the edge of the crowd, Grantham emerged, carrying Flavia Smythe-Harrows in his arms. Atop her head, a mangled swan flopped in crazy circles.

"Greycliff," Grantham called, but Grey ignored him.

Details ran together as Grey made for the edge of the crowd. Was that the lightning in his veins? Blood in his mouth?

Vaguely aware of Grantham at his side, he resisted his friend's gentle touch, but it was too late.

The ground rose to meet him as Grey's worst nightmare came true.

"HE'S NOT SUCH a big fellow. Carried him home in one hand, you know. Had the Smythe-Harrows chit in m'other. Nothing to it."

Grey's first thought was that he'd died.

Not because harps were playing or he felt particularly at peace, as one might expect in the afterlife. No, it was because Grey's version of hell would certainly include Grantham flirting over his prone, aching body.

If he wasn't dead, he was going to kill Grantham.

Grey let out a long groan.

"...wouldn't say I was a hero, but... Awake are you, Greycliff? Feeling better after a good night's sleep?"

Grey opened his eyes. Mrs. Sweet sat at his bedside, her mouth pinched in a frown of disapproval.

So she'd found out his secret as well.

By God, the whole of London must be talking about him. How Lord Greycliff took a fit in front of hundreds.

"Finally," said Grantham with a huge grin. "Thought you'd be napping for ages. Had to lift you into the carriage myself. Did it with one hand."

Mrs. Sweet rolled her eyes. "Can you wait outside, Lord Grantham?"

Grantham seemed to take no offense at Grey's housekeeper giving him orders.

"'Course, Mrs. Sweet." Grantham winked at her, then poked Grey in the chest with a thick finger. Grey winced and coughed, although Grantham hadn't poked him that hard.

"Do as Mrs. Sweet says," Grantham said, nodding at the housekeeper. Then he whispered in Grey's ear, "Not joking. Do everything she says, or she'll feed you her soup."

Straightening, he strolled from the room with a flippant wave and Grey regretted his irritation. Grantham was a good friend. He'd shown not a hint of disgust.

"How is it no one has killed him yet?" Grey asked, his throat raw and swollen. Had he cried out during his seizure? Obviously, he'd fallen. His entire frame was battered and bruised, joints aching.

"I've brewed a pot of willow bark tea," Mrs. Sweet said, setting a cool hand to his forehead.

The burning heat of yesterday had subsided, yet he still felt overwarm.

"One or two days of rest, tea, and a poultice of herbs and oils," she continued, "and you will be well enough to go back about your business."

His business? Grey stared at the blue damask canopy overhead.

"I suppose the warning signs will be the same the next time this occurs?" he asked dully, trying to make out the design in the material above him. Were they blue leaves with gold edging, or gold edging with blue leaves?

Mrs. Sweet took his wrist in one hand and pulled out a dented gold timepiece from her apron with the other. "Sometimes a bit different. You were foolish to ignore them."

"Foolish," he repeated. Terrified, more like, trying to will away the signals his body had been sending that something was wrong.

She set his arm on the bed and tucked her watch away. "Lucky for you this seems to be on the wane. You've a mild case, but there is a much worse type of influenza in St. Giles right now. If you can spare me, a group of women who practice medicine are going into the borough to dispense free care."

"Of course, you must do as you wish," he said automatically while his mind was occupied with closing Beacon House and moving back to his estates.

"Thank you, my lord. Now, you must rest." Mrs. Sweet set to folding a stack of cloths at his bedside.

Wait a moment.

Grey sat with alacrity, then put a hand to his head. He was dizzy. Dizziness was a sign of a fit. Hadn't Mrs. Sweet said he had a mild case, though? A mild case of epilepsy? That didn't sound right.

"Influenza doesn't cause seizures," he told her.

Pausing in the act of passing him a cup of tea, Mrs. Sweet nodded. "True, unless it is an extraordinarily high fever."

Grey took the tea and sniffed. Disgusting. He set it aside on his bedside table.

"But you said I was lucky this was on the wane. That there is another type of influenza in St. Giles."

"Yes." Mrs. Sweet forced the teacup into his hands.

"Do you mean . . . ? But I fell in the street." He spoke slowly, trying to make himself understood. "I had a seizure."

"I don't believe so." Mrs. Sweet's manner was infuriatingly matter-of-fact as she gestured to her mouth.

Obediently, Grey took a sip, then gagged. "Ugh. This is disgusting." He set it aside again. "What do you mean, 'I don't believe so'? Why else would I lose consciousness in the middle of the street?"

Mrs. Sweet's lips thinned in a manner that never boded well. "We are at odds here, my lord. You wish information, and I wish you to drink the tea for your fever."

"Fine, fine." By God, was he cursed to be forever surrounded by stubborn women? Grey gulped the contents of the cup.

"Blergh." He frantically rubbed the taste off his tongue with his sheet. "I've done it. Now will you speak to me?"

Staring pointedly at the sheet, she tightened her lips around a scold but held it in. "In the past three days, have you had headaches?" she said.

"Yes."

"Have you had pain in your joints and a general achiness in your body?"

"Yes, and yes."

"When Lord Grantham brought you home, you had a fever and sunken eyes, most likely because you have not been drinking enough small beer or water. You have a mild case of influenza."

"Influenza? Not a seizure?"

"Have you had seizures before?" she asked.

He paused and drew breath, then coughed out his answer. "All during my childhood."

"Well, if you stopped once you became an adult, they are most likely gone for good. I've never heard of them coming back for anyone who has outgrown them." She poured him a glass of water from a pitcher, then pulled his bedclothes straight and smiled.

"Seizures are unpleasant but not always debilitating. Some physicians subscribe to the outdated notion they are indicative of moral failings." Shaking her head, she patted his shoulder and picked up the teacup and saucer.

"Lucky for us we live in an age of science and reason. Why, the other day one of the club members told me soon we will be able to light our homes with gas. Imagine! No more candles and lamp oil. What will be next? Mechanical carriages?"

Laughing at the nonsensical idea, she left the room.

Grey slumped back on the mattress as facts swirled through his sluggish brain.

He had not had a seizure—he had influenza.

Pushing aside the bedcovers, he went to the bellpull on unsteady feet, then returned to bed and tucked the coverlet back under his chin.

Thompson, Grey's valet, poked his head in, and Grey asked him to summon Grantham if the earl hadn't already left.

Grantham would tell the truth. The same aggravating personality that made him a pain in one's arse also rendered him transparent when he attempted prevarication.

"All right, then?" Grantham asked as he came into Grey's room and sat in a chair by the bedside. When one of the legs squeaked, Grantham shot out of it as though his bottom were on fire.

"Is there a damned hedgehog in here?" he bellowed.

Sweet Jesu.

"No." Grey said a silent prayer for patience. "Sit," he ordered.

Grantham examined the underside of the chair first, then set himself gingerly back on the cushion.

"What happened to me yesterday?" Grey asked.

Grantham rolled his eyes up and to the side, crossing his legs and tapping his knee in thought. "I was busy having fun cracking heads and rescuing ladies when you came out of the building and listed sideways. I helped you to the carriage and brought you here. Mrs. Sweet scolded me, then tossed me out."

"The part in the middle, when I fainted in the street." Grey watched Grantham's face closely. "That was pathetic, was it not?"

Grantham's head moved back, his brows coming together. "What's pathetic about being sick? If I had to drink that muck Mrs. Sweet is always ladling out, I wouldn't tell her I was sick, either. She blamed me— can you imagine?—for not telling you to take to your bed sooner."

"No, I mean pathetic when I lost control and fainted in the street."

Grantham's fingers stilled, and a canny light sparked in his eye. "What are you saying, Grey? Are you somehow better than the rest of us mortals?"

His tone gentle now, Grantham lost his air of bemusement. "Can you not fall ill without bringing shame and ignominy on your house? You have an influenza. You fainted. That is all."

That was all.

"I had fits when I was a boy." Grey blurted out the confession, eyes never leaving Grantham's face. "I thought they'd returned."

Grantham tugged on his chin in thought. "Don't think so. You'd know better than I, of course, but we had a gamekeeper who had fits now and again. Didn't look the same." He scratched his head. "Tell me first if it happens again. I can put a cushion under you."

Grantham spoke as though it made no difference. As though it were perfectly acceptable to go through life with such a disorder. A horrible, terrible epiphany waited on the horizon to clobber him over the head, but Grey pushed it away.

First, he would write a letter to Violet. Next, he would . . .

Grey yawned and settled his head back on the pillow.

Next, he would . . .

The world slowly receded, and Grey, for the first time in a very long time, relinquished control and allowed sleep to take over.

20

THE NEXT DAY, Grey felt much better. By midmorning, he'd bullied his valet into dressing him and made his way to Violet's blue parlor. Once there, he had the fire built as high as it could go and ordered a tea tray brimming with whatever sweets Cook could sneak past Mrs. Sweet's keen eye.

After the servants closed the door behind them, he pulled out his copy of *The Perils of Miss Cordelia Braveheart*. Chuckling to himself at the scenarios Miss Cordelia seemed to find herself in and cringing at the ridiculous hoops the count had to jump through to have her, Grey found himself wanting to turn to someone and make a comment.

Not someone.

Letty.

Grey crept through the pages, searching for hints of her. The way she might smile at something Miss Cordelia said to the count, or the absurdity of a hidden treasure in a bird's nest. Obstacle after obstacle presented itself, yet Cordelia and her hero still managed to find their way back to one another.

Was it rubbish? Did the search for true love exist only between the pages of a book? Or was something more elemental conveyed amid the falling off cliffs and swooning on rooftops.

As he read, Grey was reminded how one small act of love can forever change the path of another person and how many small acts of love, taken together, can wield tremendous power.

Reading the story of a love—great or small—might even inspire a person to take a risk and search out a love of their own.

He fell asleep at the thought and awoke to the sound of a footman clearing his throat.

"The Earl Melton to see you, my lord. Mrs. Sweet says you are not to have visitors, but the earl insisted I announce his visit."

Before the footman could finish the sentence, Melton was coming through the door. Grey gestured to the armchair by the fire. The chair was a favorite of Grantham's, and one of the arms was at a slight angle, because the earl insisted on slouching to one side, but it was the most comfortable seat in the room.

Melton's eyes darted from the cooling pot of Mrs. Sweet's evil potion to the lap blanket to Grey's head. Grey lifted a hand and smoothed back any curls that might have been standing on end but said nothing to his godfather's scrutiny.

Were they once again on opposite shores? If they were, there was no meeting in the middle. Not this time.

"To say I am disappointed in Nevin is not even close to the level of dismay I felt when I realized what he had done. To that woman. To our family name. To himself, most of all."

How the admission must pain the earl. Grey had discovered with his and Melton's strained rapport that seeing the worst in someone you love can leave you disoriented alongside the hurt.

"If you wish to exact some form of punishment on Miss Fenley's behalf..."

Grey cut Melton off with a raised palm. "I am not entitled to speak for her. She does that well enough on her own."

The earl winced and shifted his gaze to the fireplace.

"However, I may call on Nevin soon," Grey said. "I thought we might go for a ride."

Grey nodded when Melton's brows raised in question. He'd decided sometime this morning while getting dressed. He'd made a mistake by cutting himself off from his cousin. Nevin still had time to undo some of the damage he had wrought.

What had Violet told Grey all those years ago?

Everyone deserves a second chance.

Nevin hadn't just cheated Letty. He'd cheated himself of the respect he'd been wanting for so long. Having learned his own lesson in humility at the Rosewood, Grey hoped to assist Nevin in his journey to become a better man.

This was one step in Grey's budding plan to make up to Letty all he'd taken from her. He couldn't undo the past, but he could help to ensure that one less man in the world would hurt another woman in the same way again.

A small step, but much like most small acts of love, it had the potential to inspire more.

"Well." Melton's shoulders settled against the chair's back, and he stared for a moment at the sagging right arm. "He would like that." In the next moment, however, worry clouded Melton's gaze. "This business with the Rosewood, however, will give Armitage more fodder for his challenge."

"Armitage will not be the next director," Grey said.

His godfather smiled, anxiety dissipating at the steel in Grey's voice. "Yes, of course, my boy. You would never let anyone stand in your way."

"That is true, isn't it?" Grey shook his head. "I was willing to sacrifice the passions and dreams—the very lives of these women—for a blind desire to wield control."

Melton frowned. "Come now. You are speaking of a handful of women, most of whom have the means to do their experimentation somewhere else. Compare that to the hundreds of thousands of people whom you will help as director."

Could Grey ever explain the wonders of sapphic chemists and bird hats, hedgehog reproductive rates or the truly hideous aspects of South American spiders? Or were these secret delights irrelevant to the decision he'd made even before the Rosewood?

"Armitage will not be the next director, but there could emerge another contender. Let us not pretend I am the only man in England who could run the directorship. Others have the same experience and temperament. Will they have any compassion? Judgment? Conscience?"

Emerald eyes glittered in the firelight. "What are you saying, Greycliff? No man can be trusted to be director?"

It wasn't easy, giving up on a dream.

Change is uncomfortable. It takes effort and commitment, and there will invariably be frustration.

"No man should be trusted," Grey replied. "The Department has no check on its power. Between its secrecy and the benefits apportioned out to a select few—men like Sir Gerald, who would turn it over to a snake like Armitage—we can no longer let it stand. I will accept the directorship only to dismantle it."

There was such a thing as too much power. Too much control. Why, look at the myriad ways Grey had structured his life to hold on to control.

All the cages he'd built and willingly entered.

All the rules.

All the sacrifices.

The time for standing to the side and determining the direction of other people's lives was over. Now the question awaited him:

What if he didn't take himself out of the fray?

What if he launched himself into it?

"WOULD MADAME GAULT consent to go walking with me?" Sam asked.

Letty pulled her hand from the warm waters of a canal and watched as a solitary wave traveled on. She knew that the speed of the wave depended on the size of the wave and the depth of the water, but she was particularly fascinated by the fact that two solitary waves would never merge. Unlike a regular wave, a smaller wave would be overtaken by a larger one.

"I've excellent prospects," he said.

Letty resisted the tug of the outside world and turned the canal into a river, then two rivers each, with a wave of different heights and speeds. If she compared the one—

"Unless Lord Greycliff is courting her?"

Letty wrenched herself from the riverbank and landed back in her room, half her clothing draped across the bed and an open trunk at her feet that she'd been packing for her trip to Yorkshire.

She'd written to Violet two days ago and accepted a position at the academy.

It had been three days since the Rosewood. On Sam's insistence, Letty had stayed away from the club and the reporters outside. Absent since the previous year's attempt at respectability, they'd returned in force to write stories about the women who would bring down the British Empire.

With math.

Sam set a plate of ginger biscuits on her bedside table, the scent as comforting as it was enticing. Having come home from the emporium for supper, he still wore the shop's distinctive uniform: a wine-colored jacket with black velvet collar, black waistcoat, and black trousers for the men and a similarly colored dress with a high collar for the women. The uniforms had been Sam's idea and, to his frustration and Da's great delight, other shops had followed suit.

"Is Lord Greycliff courting Madame Gault?" he asked again.

"No. He isn't courting anyone," she told him with certainty.

Letty knew Grey wasn't courting anyone because he wasn't capable of such romantic nonsense. He would decide upon an aristocratic bride by virtue of her pedigree or likelihood to breed well and announce their nuptials in the pages of the broadsheets under columns reserved for shipping news or prices of grain.

At night, he would take his beautiful body to his wife's bed, hiding himself away from her while engaging in perfunctory copulations, then return, unaffected, to his daily life.

Unloved.

Unloving.

"Then I am going to ask her. She likes me, I think. Does she like me, do you think?"

Should she bring her collection of novels with her up north? Letty sighed. Despite all, despite Nevin and Grey and her heart feeling like a massive bruise in her chest, the stories beckoned to her.

There could be healing found in the celebration of love, even if it belonged to fictional characters.

Love is love, after all.

"Letty. Letty? Letty." Sam tugged on the ribbons of her cap.

"Are you trying to drive me mad?" Letty dropped her copy of *The Perils of Miss Cordelia Braveheart* on her bed and readjusted the head covering. Her mam had cried to see Letty's hair shorn and had insisted she wear caps two sizes too big for her head to cover the disaster. "You can't ask Margaret to go out walking with you, for goodness' sake. She's almost ten years older than you."

Sam patted his hair. "I enjoy the company of mature women," he assured her.

"She likes to talk about compression versus tension in cantilever bridges as opposed to—"

"Yes, yes," her brother interrupted, falling onto her bed and pushing aside a stack of shawls. "I know about compression. Don't we sell hundreds of ladies' undergarments a year?"

Letty slapped his arm. "Why the sudden notion she would be interested in you?"

Holding the plate of ginger biscuits out to her, Sam widened his eyes, in an obvious attempt to appear innocent. "Why else would she and the other two ladies from the club come to call on us three times in the past two days? It couldn't be to visit *you*. You told them you were sick and to go away."

True. Letty was sick to her stomach with remorse. The freedom she'd experienced on the stage of the Rosewood had dissipated in the cold light of her new reality.

She had defended her proof in its original form without including Nevin's corrections. There had been a joyful, sustained applause from the few women in the audience and a more tepid acceptance from the men, but the judges had seen her flaws right away.

One or two of them had been somewhat kind, while a few others had been devastating in their criticisms. Somehow, she'd kept the fortitude to remain and listen to the rest of the presentations from the seats reserved for the participants. Nevin had not been among them.

There had been moments of brilliance, but most theories presented were careful and conservative. No risks. No experimentation.

Sam was waiting for her afterward and had ushered her through the vestiges of the Guardians without incident.

There had been no sign of Grey.

Had it been her declaration of love or the fever that sent him rushing from the building? Either way, Letty had heard nothing from him and couldn't bring herself to communicate with him, either.

The next day, there had been articles written about her in the broadsheets. Many of them chose to gloat over her mistakes, but some of them had been laudatory. Astonished, even, that a woman's mind could hold such complex thoughts without making her a madwoman.

Still, whatever hope she'd had of a return to a normal life in society was gone now. The whispers would be louder, the stares even more pointed.

Letty prepared herself to retreat to her old ways, to sink into her head by the riverbank and contemplate solitary waves. To remain a spinster, seeing her family rarely as the girls grew up and as Sam grew older and took over the emporium.

And if it wasn't easy to leave behind her newfound friends? To live without the stimulation and camaraderie of the Retreat? To forget a certain lord, handsome and aloof—a mass of contradictions?

Letty had never chosen easy.

She'd chosen to bear the burdens of past mistakes, afraid to set them down and prove she wasn't penitent enough. The more she considered this, the more she feared she'd been living a punishment she didn't deserve.

Grey had found his way into her heart by teaching her not just about pleasure, but also about the myriad ways in which the past weighed one down.

A month ago, Letty would never have imagined the imperious Lord Greycliff was once an outcast in his own home. A month ago, she would have scoffed if someone had insisted a viscount's life could be as narrow and limited as a shopgirl's. With his honesty, he'd reminded her that for many, the struggle to be free of their burdens is invisible to the eye.

Letty thumbed through the book's pages. The dull cloth cover gave no hint as to the many trials and tribulations the brave Miss Cordelia was about to face.

"Aren't you at least going to say goodbye to them?" Sam asked.

Letty set down the book and picked at a loose thread on one of the shawls. "I will write to them."

Sam whistled a low, mournful tune.

Let them see you shine.

The woman Letty had seen in Grey's eyes in the carriage and at the ball, that woman had been brave.

Letty had liked being that woman.

Despite her sickening fear, she'd been brave enough to don a ball gown and stand up for herself in front of the ton. She'd made friends. Letty had been brave enough to make love in a carriage and to revel in the power of her sexuality. She'd stepped out onto a stage and defended her proof in a borrowed gown, with her detractors banging at the door.

A brave woman would get out of the house and back into the world. Even if it were only to apologize to her friends.

"Why are you sighing?" Sam asked as he brushed biscuit crumbs from his jacket. While she'd been woolgathering, he'd eaten them all.

"Get your topper, Sam. I need fresh air."

Sam flashed her his toothiest of smiles. "Excellent. I have a hackney waiting outside." For all his blather, Letty knew he'd irritated her precisely so she'd leave her packing aside.

"I love you, Sammy," she said.

"All right, then." Sam rolled his eyes as they went downstairs. "No need to do it so brown." He helped her on with a light pelisse and messed about with the ribbon at the crown of her bonnet. "Are we off to your club to see Madame Gault?"

Letty shook her head at the hope in his voice. "I am off to the club to clean out my workroom and say goodbye to my friends. You are off to buy those bonnets from Flavia."

"What?" Sam blanched. "We'll never sell those. They'll hang about the shop giving everyone an apoplexy."

"It doesn't matter." Letty waited while Sam told the housemaid where they were going. "There are things in life more important than money, Sam."

He hoisted her into the hack with a snort of disbelief. "They are horrible. Why would we do it?"

"Because Flavia was brave to take this step." Letty leaned out of the hackney's window and gazed at the clear blue sky. "Bravery should always be rewarded."

LETTY'S WORKROOM FELT empty. It wasn't simply because all evidence of recent gatherings, such as port bottles and jam-smeared plates, had been cleared away. Something about the listing of her decrepit old chairs and the bareness of her worktable spoke to the end of an era.

Even if Grey reversed his decision and reopened Athena's Retreat, the tenuous nature of its existence had communicated itself to the walls and floorboards of the place.

An eerie silence echoed in the hallways where these past weeks it had reverberated with thumps and screeches, moans and curses.

Lady Potts knew some exceedingly fine curses.

Although Letty had been bracing for her apology, her friends were not at the club. Relieved, she turned to the distraction of packing.

There wasn't much. Filling one of the crates Sam had brought were most of her books, a chipped mug filled with sticks of graphite, and a cloth bag full of chalk for her slate. She pulled a stack of broadsheets from another crate and wrapped her dishes, thinking about jam tarts and friendship.

Having left the door slightly ajar, she heard voices from the hallway carrying into her workroom as the ladies passed by.

"He said I could not have a room in the basement of the club for my ants because wet earth would rot the building support struts. Instead, he's going to convince his cook to give up the root cellar behind the carriage house."

"How exciting, Lily." That was Flavia's voice.

He? Why, they couldn't be speaking of Lord Greycliff, could they? Told Lily Mazuirka she could use the root cellar for her ant studies? How could he?

"Not as exciting as Mr. Fenley's offer to buy your hats, Flavia. Won't your mother be surprised."

Letty poked her head out of the doorway. Lily was leaning her head in toward Flavia's as they made their way toward the back of the building, whispering and giggling with one another.

How could he promise Lily a place for her experiments when the club was to be permanently closed? Did he think to toy with the poor woman?

Do not care for me.

It would be easy for Letty to slink home without confronting Grey one last time.

Do not love me, Letty.

He'd rejected her love.

Hadn't he?

Heedless of her dusty skirts, Letty didn't even stop to put her cap back on. Through the warren of hallways, doors, and stairs, she made her way to Beacon House. Corralling the big footman, Johnson, Letty demanded to know Greycliff's whereabouts.

"He isn't expecting you yet, Miss Fenley. He won't like as you interrupt them too soon," Johnson protested.

"Isn't expecting me yet?" she echoed. "Interrupt whom?"

Johnson shook his head. "Oh, no, miss. He'll have my hide do I say anything. Why, even Mrs. Sweet doesn't know about what they've gone and hauled to the attic and—wait, wait, come back."

Too late.

Letty picked up her skirts and set off past Violet's workrooms and the family parlor, up to where the servants kept their quarters. Having never visited this floor, Letty paused at the top of the landing to get her bearings. The booming voice of the Earl Grantham told her which way to go next.

"Repeat this to me once more, Grey. How am I supposed to be the villain? I am tall, blond, and majestically handsome; doesn't that make me the hero?"

Grey's reply was muffled, and Letty tiptoed toward a partly opened door.

"That's an impressive curse. Too bad I *have* met my mother. What? Twirl my mustache? I don't have a mustache. Do I get to punch you or not?"

Setting her back to the wall, Letty edged closer to the doorway.

". . . fight me. Then I collapse, and she will run to my side. I shall awaken, get to my knees, and grovel."

Goodness.

Grey had read to the end of *The Perils of Miss Cordelia Braveheart*.

Grantham was not convinced. "Is this to do with Arthur? He went and got himself shot to impress Vi, now you must pretend to be stabbed.

What in the hell will I do if I ever have the misfortune of falling in love? Jump off a bridge?"

"I've been stupid," Grey said. "I made the wrong choices, and I need to show her I've learned. Even if she never wants anything to do with me again, I have to show her I understand."

Unable to stay outside, she poked her head through the doorway. Grey stood by the turret's mullioned window with his back to her. A long black case sat at his feet.

"You could simply tell her," Grantham said. He wore a huge-brimmed, black felt hat. One side was affixed with an enormous gold pin from which a red plume feather stuck out at an odd angle, like a French swordsman from the previous century.

"I think she'd prefer to see me on my knees," Grey said.

Grantham settled the hat more firmly on his head, then caught sight of Letty.

"Avast, you cur!" he shouted, and held up his fists.

Grey slapped a hand over his eyes. "No, you muttonhead. It isn't a pirate romance. Haven't you read the book?"

"I am halfway through," Grantham said. "Never read such nonsense in my life. Everyone knows if you leap from a horse to the back of an alligator going down an Amazonian river, you should . . . That isn't the point. The point is standing in the doorway."

Grey turned around. He must have found a trunk where the castoffs of his ancestors were stored. Clad in a loose linen shirt with billowing sleeves and tight, black, satin breeches encasing his muscled legs, he'd affixed a red velvet cape to his neck. Just like Count Blacksoul.

"Did you want me to stab you now?" asked Grantham. He advanced on Grey. "I shall fight you and steal the swooning miss . . ." He turned to Letty. "You may swoon at any time, Miss Fenley. And I—"

"Shut up, Grantham," said Grey, his eyes never leaving Letty's face.

"We haven't even tipped over the roses," Grantham objected.

"Go away, please, my Lord Grantham," Letty said.

Grantham issued a noisy sigh and ripped the hat from his head. "I went through all this trouble . . ."

However, as he passed Letty, the earl leaned over and whispered in her ear, "Go easy on him, Miss Fenley. He's a right mess."

Grey remained silent until Grantham had stomped down the stairs, then tugged at the collar of the cape. "It was influenza."

Letty blinked. "I beg your pardon?"

Grey elaborated. "At the Rosewood. I had influenza, and when I left the building, I fainted."

Pieces fell into place. His fever. His fear.

"You must have thought your seizures had returned."

Grey's shoulders dropped. "This whole time, I've . . ." He glanced over at the roses.

Letty shook her head. "You don't need to spread them on the ground."

"I've gone through the trouble of dressing up," he argued, "and procuring myself a villain."

Letty ventured farther into the room and admired the roses. A draft from the open window carried their scent through the tiny chamber. Beside the table holding the roses, a couch sat against one wall, draped in a blush-colored satin coverlet. At Grey's feet, two fencing épées glinted in the light.

"Is one of those for me?" she asked.

"Grantham was going to be the evil Sir Goldenhawk, and we were going to reenact the last chapter from *The Perils of Miss Cordelia Braveheart*," he explained. "I wanted to find a way to show you I understand now why these books are important to you. What was it you said? 'Mistakes can be mended, grudges can be reconciled, and happy endings can come to each of us.'"

Letty had never heard of anything so romantic, not even in Mrs. Foster's novels.

Still. Was she ready to forgive him?

For this was what he'd hoped for, obviously.

Forgiveness.

Eyeing Letty as though she might lunge for the swords, Grey met her in the center of the room and tentatively reached for her hand. Letty did not pull away, but neither did she move toward him. It should have pleased her that Grey was nervous. Instead, she felt a hint of trepidation herself.

"I couldn't believe it took that idiot count until the end of the book to realize he didn't need to hide," Grey said. He kept his gaze on their hands while he spoke. "All along, his disfigurement kept him captive in walls thicker and stronger than any castle."

Letty had read the book so many times. How had she never seen the similarities?

"You aren't disfigured," she said. "You don't hide away from the world."

Pressing her hand against his heart, Grey leaned down so their foreheads touched.

He closed his eyes as he spoke, as though to see inside his head for the right words. "So many of my decisions were determined by a condition I no longer have. I turned my back on joy and laughter and put my energies into controlling everything around me. All for nothing. Do you know what is worse?"

Letty closed the last of the distance between them, resting her head against his chest, listening to the beating of his newly wakened heart as he spoke in a voice filled with wonder and with sorrow.

"Worse, I've tried to impose this prison on everyone else around me. Madame Gault must have thought I was torturing her with fish and cold greens."

Grey rested his chin on Letty's head and sniffed her hair.

Why was he forever doing that?

"I could have been a mentor to Nevin," he continued. "Instead of holding him at arm's length, I could have given him the confidence to hold his own with Melton."

He sighed. "I could have unbent and asked for help with the club, rather than trying to control everything myself. Grantham spoke the truth, you see. Melton is retiring as head of the Department, and I will take his place."

Letty nodded. "And you closed the club because he asked it of you?"

"No," Grey answered quickly. "No. I'm fairly confident Victor Armitage set that fire to rattle me and take credit for my actions. I didn't close the club to satisfy Melton. I did it because I simply couldn't bear the thought of anything happening to you."

Letty knew he spoke the truth. The tension she'd been holding for days melted away, and she resettled herself into her skin.

"I'm closing the Department."

Letty took a step back in surprise. "How on earth . . . ?"

"I will take the directorship only long enough to dismiss the Funders and transfer our operatives to other positions in the government."

Grey tugged her into another embrace. "The truth is, I wanted the directorship more than I cared about my promise to Violet. I thought I knew better than her, than any of you, what the club needed. What the country needed. I've always believed that the greater my remove from the people I cared about, the better the decisions I made."

Remembering how she felt beneath the weight of her disguise, Letty understood. "You think you have the upper hand, but soon that hand is tight about your throat."

"Looking back over my life, there were so many opportunities I squandered. Acquaintances that could have become friends, friendships that could have gone deeper."

Setting his hand beneath her chin, he tilted her head and spoke slowly. "The only person I hurt worse than myself was you, Letty."

A frisson of desire shimmied through her. No matter how betrayed she'd felt, this physical craving lurked behind their every interaction.

It wasn't so strong, however, that Letty could not put it aside and give him her complete attention. Beneath his words, Letty heard genuine remorse. She'd wanted a peek behind his wall of perfectly sculpted ice. Here it was.

He was still unalterably beautiful.

"I'm not going to knock over the vase of roses," Grey informed her, although he sounded disappointed, "but I am going to grovel for you."

True to his word, he went onto one knee. The breath left her lungs as she beheld the sight of this man—of all men—humbling himself before her.

"I don't ever again want to live as a prisoner of my past. I"—Grey swallowed—"I care for you, very much. I . . ."

He squeezed her hands and closed his eyes, bracing himself. After a moment, one eyelid popped open. "This is going to take some getting used to."

"Grey, you don't have to—"

"I love you, Letty." The words came sliding out, and he appeared surprised, then pleased. "That wasn't bad. I'll say it again."

Tears burned at the sight of Grey's luminous smile. Here he was, the man Letty had glimpsed in Milly's lab, the man who'd tickled little Fermat's stomach and fenced with Winthram. She'd feared him lost forever.

"I love you, Letty Fenley. I am sorry I haven't said it before. I'm even more sorry I couldn't say it back to you at the Rosewood."

Letty tugged at his hands as a rebel tear escaped. "Stand up. It's disconcerting to peer down the top of such a large head. Like looking at a pumpkin wearing a wig."

"Right." Grey stood with a fluid grace, keeping hold of her hands. "How strange it must be for you, staring at us giants. You're like a grumpy Thumbelina."

"You are incorrigible," she complained.

Grey kissed her then. He kissed her as though she mattered to him, as though she'd lodged herself as deeply into his heart as he had into hers.

"Marry me, Letty?" he asked when they came up for air. "Marry me, and help me relearn how to live outside my walls?"

How tempting. Who would have thought that day when they'd argued outside the candlemaker's that Letty's heart would be breaking over this egotistical, aggravating young lord?

Letty shook her head. "I leave at the end of the week and stay with Violet for a spell."

Grey's eyes held a hint of storms at her answer. "You cannot leave at the end of the week. I have proposed *marriage* to you."

What if she did marry him and neither of them were strong enough to keep the past at bay? What if society never accepted her and, by extension, shunned him? What if he came to believe she wasn't worth it?

"I cannot marry you," Letty said. Stupid man. His new epiphany had done nothing to change the world around them. "I am still me, and you are still you."

"What does that mean?"

"It means I am the daughter of a shopkeeper with a damaged reputation, who has just made a spectacle of herself in front of the greatest mathematicians in England, and you are a viscount who has closed my club, and your godfather hates me, and I—unnnnf."

Goodness, Grey was an accomplished kisser! Letty's objections dribbled out of her head as she reveled in the warmth of his mouth and the comfort of his arms. He bit gently on her lower lip and tugged; a peppery sensation coursed through her veins and settled between her thighs. Longing to feel his skin beneath her fingertips once again, Letty tugged at her gloves. Why was she still wearing them? For that matter, why were they still clothed? Here they were in a room alone, with a perfectly serviceable couch in the corner.

Whispering in her ear, he left a tiny kiss on her earlobe, like a dangling pearl. "I am not closing the club. Athena's Retreat is open, as of this morning. I have delivered a message to Armitage that if he so much as steps a toe within a mile of here, I will use the last of my influence to open an investigation into his dealings with the Funders."

Somewhat contorted in the act of taking off her gloves while trying to untie his blasted cape, Letty searched his face. There were no lies in his clear gaze.

Grey brushed his knuckles against her cheek. "I would never close the doors forever on that girl who needs Athena's Retreat so desperately. More importantly, your reputation is not an obstacle to me."

"It is an obstacle to everyone else," she argued.

"I am so weary of worrying about everyone else." He brushed the corner of her mouth with his thumb. "Aren't you?"

How irritating. Not content with his own act of bravery, Grey now must go and expect one of her, as well? Mulberry-colored curtains waved in a breeze as the faintest of noises from the street below wafted through the window. The entirety of London was out there, a mass of people who would continue to disapprove of them both.

It would be difficult, but not as difficult as living her life as though what people said about her were the truth.

"I suppose," she granted. "I suppose if you are going to break free of your past, I should as well."

Could she do this? Leave off her armor for good? Move through the world anticipating kindness and not rejection?

For the first time since she entered the room, Letty opened herself to the possibility that this was real. Her throat tightened with nerves.

"What about Lord Melton?" she asked.

Grey, too, sensed a shift in mood. He placed his hand over his heart in a solemn gesture. "I love my godfather." After a short pause, he chuckled. "I don't know I'll ever be at ease saying that word."

The smile fell from his face as he continued. "Although he has promised to acknowledge you in public"—at her gasp of surprise, he nodded—"there are still going to be differences in how we believe people should be treated. Some of our differences can be reconciled, and some cannot, but he has no say in who I love. You have changed my life for the better, and I cannot imagine living it without you at my side."

"Oh," she whispered. What could one say when one's heart felt ready to burst?

"Now"—Grey untied his cape and let it drop to the floor—"I am not going to make love to you until you have agreed to my proposal. Will you marry me, Letty?"

What an irresistible offer.

As the sun shone through the hundreds of glass diamonds in the window and thousands of rainbows scattered across the floor, a wave of happiness lifted her into his arms.

"Yes, I will," she promised. "And we will live happily ever after."

Author's Note

LETTY FENLEY IS loosely based on Sophie Germain, who was born to a wealthy Parisian family in 1776. Although her parents were at first unsupportive, Sophie eventually persuaded them to allow her to study mathematics. Her studies were unorthodox, however, cobbled together from her family library and her correspondence with other mathematicians—correspondence in which Sophie often used a male alias. Her reception in the field of mathematics was mixed, with some men supporting her work and others thinking her unnatural. She is most famous for her work in number theory and her work on Fermat's last theorem, which has been immortalized as the Sophie Germain identity. Some would argue that her more important contribution to science, however, was her work on elasticity. In 1811, she entered a contest sponsored by the French Academy of Sciences to formulate a theory of elastic surfaces. However, because she did not have formal training in the calculus of variations, she made a number of mathematical errors. Germain reentered the contest twice more before she won. Please note for modern readers the term *number theory* is used in the text despite its first known use in 1864. In addition, the expression for the velocity of propagation of the wave in these pages is taken directly from John Scott-Russell's *Report on Waves: Made to the Meetings of the British Association for the Advancement of Sciences in 1842–43,* where k is the height of the crest of the wave above the plane of repose.

First stated in 1637, Fermat's last theorem was finally proven by Andrew Wiles, who was awarded the Wolfskehl Prize in 1997 for his work.

Acknowledgments

Thank you to my lovely husband for all his encouragement and to my amazing children for their constant support and love. Thank you to Mom and Doug for all your help and email marketing! Many thanks to my agent, Ann Leslie Tuttle, for sticking with me. Thank you to my delightful editor, Sarah Blumenstock, for being so positive and kind. So many thanks to Jessica Mangicaro for all her patience while answering my fifty bazillion questions about marketing during my debut. Thanks to Jessica Brock and all the folks at Berkley who work so hard to promote the books they love. Thanks to Rita Frangie for the beautiful covers and to all the extremely talented designers at Berkley for their mesmerizing graphics. Thank you to my copy editor, Elizabeth Johnson, for her diligence and patience. Believe me, all errors and questionable choices in this book are my fault alone.

Thanks to the Berkletes for talking me down off the ledge multiple times a day. I cannot wait to see each and every one of you in person!! Thank you to my Sprint Team for being there in the early-morning hours and the rest of the day as well. Big shout-out to the 2021 Debuts and Romancing the '20s—what an incredibly talented group of authors. I've loved watching everyone's journey and am so thrilled by your successes. Thank you to Maureen Everett (maureeneverettdesign .com) for teaching me how Instagram works and for all the phenomenal designs. Thank you to Anita Mumm for being the first person I trust to see my terrible first drafts. Thanks to Elizabeth Jasicki for the wonderful narration of *A Lady's Formula for Love* and *A Perfect Equation*.

Thanks to all the bookstagrammers out there who supported *A Lady's Formula for Love* and who take so much time to read and review books. I appreciate your dedication, your gorgeous aesthetic, and your recommendations—I've found so many new books. Thank you to every person who read *A Lady's Formula for Love* and took the time to leave a review. I don't care how mean it was; I am still so thrilled that people have bought or borrowed my book and read my words. Amazing. Thank you!

As always, thanks to the Park Ave Moms and the Highland Hotties for all the words of encouragement and funny text threads. These friendships are what fuel me when the world gets to be too much. Here's hoping that by the time this book is out, we will have been able to embrace each other once again. Special thanks to my running partner, Nicole V, for slowing your pace by at least two minutes per mile as I wheezed about this book, and then supplying me with the idea for the ending.

And to every girl who has been made to feel bad about themselves because they said *yes* or because they said *no*—you are beautiful, you are worthy, and nobody's words have more power over your body or your heart than your own. Don't just smash the patriarchy—grind them under your heel!!

Don't miss

A LOVE
BY DESIGN

coming spring 2023 from Jove!

Y OU WILL TAKE that *monstrosity* back to where you purchased it, or I will remove your spine with my bare hands."

"If you put your tiny hands anywhere near my perfectly fashioned body, I will crush you. What do you have against sweet little bunnies? Everyone loves bunnies."

George Willis, Earl Grantham, stood in the foyer of a large town house off Kingsbury Road and held a toy rabbit aloft, safe from the threatened predations of his onetime romantic rival, Arthur Kneland.

Two years ago, Grantham had proposed to his best friend, the Lady Violet Greycliff. Violet, a genius chemist and the founder of a secret society of women scientists, had chosen instead to marry Kneland, her former bodyguard. Grantham had opined—aloud and on multiple occasions—that her choice was a consequence of inhaling a few too many gases in her quest to prove Avogadro's law. Kneland had responded by dosing Grantham's tea with emetics.

The affection between the two men bordered on unseemly.

"Listen, Kneland," Grantham said with the patience of a saint, "I allowed Violet to marry you . . ."

Kneland—whose sense of humor matched his height—rudely interrupted. "Violet chose to marry me. You had nothing—"

"—despite your obvious *short*comings." Grantham continued. "If she saw fit to spend the rest of her days leg shackled to a dour little Scot, who was I to stop her? However, I will not begrudge my goddaughter the attention and belongings she so richly deserves."

Ever since the arrival of Violet and Arthur's little girl, Mirren Georgiana, Grantham had brought a baby gift whenever he came to visit. Kneland, being an aforementioned "dour little Scot," had objected to the increasing size and elaborateness of the gifts.

In fact, Kneland had called the steady stream of presents—culminating in this four-foot-tall stuffed rabbit made with costly angora wool, with sapphires for eyes, and clad in a custom-designed silk dress—"outrageous, exorbitant, and unreasonable."

Admittedly, tweaking the former counterassassin with increasingly preposterous trinkets did provide the *tiniest* bit of amusement. Who would begrudge him a sliver of light in an otherwise gloomy and miserable autumn?

"I will take that rabbit and shove it so far up your—"

Kneland, that's who.

A tiny flush high on the man's cheekbones stood out against his weathered white skin, eliciting the sole clue that he was enjoying himself as much as Grantham.

"If you keep holding that monstrosity above your head, it leaves your underbelly exposed to any sharp blade that happens to be in someone's hands," said Kneland through gritted teeth.

"Tiny hands that can't fit around a knife handle," Grantham observed. He sighed, tired of holding the damn thing up in the air, and set his other hand on his hip. "Well, where is Vi? Let's ask her if baby Georgie would like a bunny."

"My wife is not at home. She is fetching a guest from the train station," Kneland informed him. His brows met, and he craned his neck to peer around Grantham into the street. "I believe that's her carriage now."

Grantham looked at Arthur.

Arthur looked at Grantham.

Grantham looked at the rabbit.

A grin ghosted across Arthur's face . . .

And they were off.

"What on earth?" the housekeeper, Mrs. Sweet, said, entering the foyer just as the men tore past her.

"Good day, Mrs. Sweet. Don't you look radiant?" Grantham called as they ran by.

While Grantham had the superior muscular physique, Arthur was slippery like a weasel, and the men were well matched as they raced through the hallways of Beacon House. Turning the corner into the kitchen, they both headed toward a thick oak door, which led to what was once a series of outbuildings but had been transformed some seven years earlier into Athena's Retreat, the first social club for ladies in London.

Grantham took the opportunity to jab Arthur in the ribs with his elbow.

Hard.

While Arthur slowed, using precious breath to utter an *impressive* curse, Grantham flung open the door and slammed it back shut behind him.

Breathing heavily, he approached a fork in the hallway. Each corridor ended in a door. The door to the left led to the public rooms of Athena's Retreat. There a group of members attended lectures on the natural sciences, drank tea, and held discussions on topics such as the use of botanicals in household cleansers.

The door on the right led to the true Athena's Retreat. Behind the facade of the public rooms were workrooms and laboratories given over to women scientists from all over England. Women who were forced to keep their work secret from society due to myriad prejudices found a haven in this warren of strange sounds, nasty smells, and the low vibrations of brilliance.

The carriage house that served both Athena's Retreat and Beacon House was at the back of the public-facing rooms. However, there was a stairway outside the second floor of the hidden rooms that might get him there quicker if he—

Too late. The evil little Scot caught up to him and used his cursed assassin tricks to swipe Grantham's legs out from under him.

"Damn, but I love the sound of your giant arse hitting the floorboards," Kneland twittered as he flew through the door on the left.

Feck.

Grantham heaved himself up and resumed his journey at twice his original pace, all the while plotting his next baby gift.

Perhaps a live circus including pygmy monkeys?

Shouldn't Baby Georgie have her own boat?

Contemplating how he might haul a yacht down Knightsbridge Road, Grantham slammed open the door to the outside staircase and decided to leap from the second-floor landing onto a patch of brush in the kitchen garden rather than waste time taking the stairs.

In the seconds before his brain reminded him that any decision prompted by his manly bits never turned out well, he caught sight of Violet Kneland and her companion.

Maggie.

Instead of neatly dropping feet first into the shrubbery—for which Cook might scold him, but he'd soon charm her into forgetting—he fell headfirst in an ungainly heap atop an untrimmed hedge of dog roses.

Of course, she was now known as Madame Margaret Gault.

Try as he might, Grantham could never quite twist his tongue around the name.

Almost his whole life, he'd called her Maggie.

His Maggie.

While upside down he watched as she walked 'round the corner of the carriage house, the wind unfurling the hem of her simple bronze pelisse. A brown capelet hung about her shoulders, and a matching muff hid her hands. Catching sight of him, she paused, tilting her head so he caught a glimpse of lush auburn curls peeking out from beneath her tea-colored bonnet trimmed with bright red berries. Her fair skin showed no hint of the freckles that once plagued her every summer, and thick brown lashes shielded her hazel eyes.

Unusually tall for a woman, nevertheless, she moved with effortless grace, and not even the eye-watering clash of colors that adorned Violet next to her could detract from her beauty.

For she was a beauty, Margaret Gault. Once wild and graceless, she'd bloomed into a woman of elegant refinement.

A woman who was more than met the eye.

A woman who would rather feast on glass than give him the time of day.

"Good afternoon, Grantham." Violet greeted him with a huge smile, seemingly nonplussed by the fact that he'd just dove headfirst into her rosebushes. She wore a shocking yellow day dress beneath a burgundy velvet paletot, and atop her head sat a garish blue bonnet topped with a life-sized stuffed parrot.

Swallowing a barrelful of curses, Grantham tried wriggling out of the bushes, every single thorn piercing his flesh a hundredfold as Margaret watched without a word.

"*Ahem.*" He cleared his throat as he managed to get to his feet despite being trapped in the center of one of the bushes. Pulling a branch from his hair, a shower of wrinkled brown rose petals drifted down his shoulders. "You are especially . . . vibrant today, Violet. I brought this for Baby Georgie."

He thrust the torn, dirtied rabbit at Violet, who received it with a bemused air. One of the buttons had come off, and the lovely silk was stained green and brown.

"Madame Gault," he said, bowing to Margaret. "So lovely to see you again."

No matter how strongly Grantham willed it, Margaret did not speak to him in return. Instead, she bent her knee a scant inch in a desultory curtsy, her lush mouth twisted like the clasp of a coin purse, no doubt to hold inside all the names she was calling him in her head. He had a good idea what some of them were, considering that Margaret, Grantham, and Violet had been friends since they were eight years old.

He hadn't seen Margaret for thirteen years until their reunion—if one could call it that—a year and a half earlier in the small parlor of Athena's Retreat. He hadn't exactly met the moment back then, either—although to be fair, there'd been a hedgehog involved. The handful of times he encountered her before she'd returned to Paris, she'd avoided meeting his eyes with her own, as though he were an inconsequential shadow cast by their past.

Someone to be dismissed.

Someone who had broken her heart and whom she would never forgive.

"Look who is come back to live in England for good." Violet linked her arm with Margaret's and beamed up at her friend.

This was news. He'd thought Margaret would stay in Paris, where she had employment as one of the few women engineers in all of Europe.

Now she was come home.

Something leapt in his chest, and he tasted the bitter orange flavor of hope.

"Clean yourself up and come inside for tea," said Violet.

Margaret did not echo the invitation. Instead, she tightened her hold on a stylish carpet bag and accompanied Violet and Arthur into the building.

There are moments in life when the world shifts as though a door has opened somewhere out of sight. Whether you run toward that opened door or not depends on how fast you're stuck in place. Grantham considered for a moment how painful it would be to get himself unstuck.

Eyeing the tangle of branches in front of him, he inhaled the scent of rosehips and crushed greenery. Gritting his teeth, he made his way through the thorns toward the open door.

"HOW WONDERFUL YOU are back to stay, Margaret. Do you know, Grantham visits nearly every day when he is in London? It will be just like our summers at the Abbey—the three of us together again."

Margaret Gault smiled at her friend and avoided comment by sipping her tea. Violet sat next to her on a low settee, serving her guests small plates of rock-hard biscuits.

Arthur, Violet's taciturn husband, stood across the room, giving off the impression of a coil poised to spring. His nearly black eyes somehow remained on Violet at the same time they roved over the room.

This small blue parlor was a favorite of Violet's. The velvet curtains had faded over the years from violet to periwinkle, and a cheerful fire lent its warmth to the wan October sunlight revealing delicate etchings on the glass sinumbra lamps. Training her gaze on a charming print of a tiny cottage amid the gorse-covered hills of the Scottish Highlands, Margaret let Violet's chatter wash over her.

"... all the members of Athena's Retreat are over the moon at the news that you've returned for good," Violet was saying. "I know you will miss seeing Letty and Greycliff right away, but they have decided to remain in Herefordshire until the baby is born."

Last spring, Violet and Arthur went north to Yorkshire for half a year. Violet had suffered a miscarriage and needed time to heal, and as luck would have it, Margaret needed to be in London to work on a project for her father-in-law's engineering firm. She'd stayed in rooms at Athena's Retreat and served as the club's temporary secretary.

Her time at the Retreat served as an awakening of sorts. Sitting with club members from various scientific disciplines and learning about their work had inspired new ideas of her own. Margaret had made friends with like-minded—and sometimes not-so-like-minded— women who had both relied upon her and challenged her.

She'd become especially fond of Letty Fenley, an extraordinarily talented mathematician who had fallen in love with Violet's first husband's son, Lord William Greycliff. Watching her fierce and prickly little friend bring the reserved viscount to his knees had been delightful if somewhat bittersweet.

Little wonder that upon returning to Paris afterward, Margaret's perfectly ordered life lost its previous appeal. For the first time since her husband's death seven years earlier, she'd felt lonely.

Loneliness alone would not have precipitated moving back to England but for her father-in-law's sudden announcement. In the absence of a son to carry on the work of the family firm, he would be closing Henri Gault and Son.

Once more, because of one man's unilateral decision, Margaret's life was upended. For a few days, she'd railed against the perfidy of men who, in their shortsightedness, could not imagine a woman taking the reins of such a prestigious firm.

This time, however, she was not a lovesick seventeen-year-old with no other prospects in sight.

This time, she was a grown woman with a *plan*.

Never again would a man have power over how she lived her life or achieved her goals. There would be an engineering firm bearing the Gault name—Margaret Gault. Nothing would stop her from achieving her dreams.

Within hours of her decision, Margaret wrote to Violet, asking to again stay at Athena's Retreat. Tonight, she would unpack her belongings and settle in. In two days, Margaret had a meeting with a prospective client. She would reunite with her friends Althea and Mala for afternoons of tarts and port-soaked wisdom, and she would find a set of rooms for her new offices.

Margaret had planned for everything.

"I didn't say 'pony,'" said a baritone voice. "I said 'ponies.' Plural. A herd of them. Don't you think Baby Georgie—"

"Her name is Mirren," Arthur growled.

"... would like a herd of ponies?"

Everything except for *him*.

Seated diagonally across from Margaret, somehow taking up most of the space in the room, was the Earl Grantham.

George Willis.

Georgie.

Shocking how the painfully thin boy who'd been a collection of elbows and feet that had never stopped tapping and twitching had grown into this giant of a man, golden maned and powerfully built. He slouched with leonine insolence in an enormous chair, which appeared delicate beneath his large frame. When he gestured, the reach of his muscular arms strained the costly wool of his topcoat at its seams.

Grantham's face was a study in contrasts: full lips so perfectly shaped they appeared feminine were set in a squared jaw, the elegant line of his nose ending abruptly at a small white scar and continuing thereafter at an angle. With his sky blue eyes and golden curls, he could be a picture of angelic perfection if there weren't a hint of wickedness in the set of his dark brows.

Distracted by his beauty and his perpetual good cheer, one almost missed the pale lines at the corners of his eyes and mouth, deeper than one might expect in a man of two and thirty, even though he'd spent a half-dozen years in the wilds of North America.

In the handful of times Margaret had been in Grantham's presence since their reunion, she'd seen only the tiniest glimpses of the man who'd forged those lines. A flash of something hard and desperate beneath his usual cheer had her wondering in the dark of night how his life had been.

What had hurt him.

Whom he'd hurt in return.

By the time Violet came back from up north, Margaret had developed a preternatural sense for when he was nearby. She only looked at him from the corners of her eyes, stepping around the edge of his voice and turning sideways in the wake his presence left, like when a child walking along a cliff encounters a wind strong enough to push her off her feet and send her falling.

When she'd left for Paris, she'd thought herself inured to his presence. Safe from any falls.

She'd been wrong.

He addressed Violet now.

"The last time I visited Grange Abbey, two of your sisters tried to trap me into marriage and your mother made certain at every meal I was seated directly in front of where she used to set the Christmas pudding. D'you remember the year we decided to improve on the size of the pudding's flames?"

Even Arthur's face cracked into a grin when Grantham told the story of how the three of them managed to burn a hole through the massive dining table that had previously withstood the depredations of nearly two hundred years of Grange offspring until Violet came along.

"My theory was sound," Violet insisted. "The problem was in the execution."

"The problem," Grantham said, "was the two of you scientific geniuses relying on a henchman who thought a cupful of brandy was a piddling amount of fuel if we were to make the Christmas pudding a true spectacle."

"It wasn't brandy," Violet explained to Arthur. "I'd been researching accelerants and came up with a formula that I was quite sure would create the highest flames with the smallest measure of liquid."

Arthur let his piercing gaze rest on Margaret. "Did you perhaps inject a note of sanity into their madness, Madame Gault?" he asked.

"I am afraid not, Mr. Kneland," she confessed. "After estimating the height and intensity of the flames according to Violet's formula, I designed the optimal platform atop which we set the pudding. I should have used less flammable construction materials, for once the pudding was lit—"

"And my father's eyebrows were singed—" said Violet

"And your sister Poppy wet herself from screaming." Grantham chuckled.

"And my other sister Lily bruised her forehead from ducking under the table—"

"And your other sister Iris wet herself from laughing," Margaret reminded her.

"The flames from the pudding consumed the platform, then most of the tablecloth and a good deal of the table beneath it," Violet finished.

"It really was a terrific fire for all that it demolished the pudding,"

Margaret said wistfully. Violet and Grantham sighed in agreement, and Arthur frowned.

"No disrespect, Madame Gault," he said, a note of fear in his voice, "but for how long, exactly, will you be staying at Athena's Retreat?"

Margaret laughed in appreciation as Violet scolded him.

"Margaret is the most sensible woman I know. She'd never let Grantham and I talk her into anything so dangerous now."

For this first time since she arrived, Margaret let her gaze meet Grantham's.

"You have nothing to fear, Mr. Kneland," she said. "I learned the hard way to never again agree to Lord Grantham's proposals."

Photo by Asa Shutts

ELIZABETH EVERETT lives in Upstate New York with her family. She likes going for long walks or (very) short runs to nearby sites that figure prominently in the history of civil rights and women's suffrage. The Secret Scientists of London series is inspired by her admiration for rule breakers and belief in the power of love to change the world.

CONNECT ONLINE

ElizabethEverettAuthor.com

ElizabethEverettAuthorBooks

ElizabethEverettAuthor

Ready to find
your next great read?

Let us help.

Visit prh.com/nextread

Penguin
Random
House